nickelodeon

THE LOUD HOUSE

3 IN 1 #3

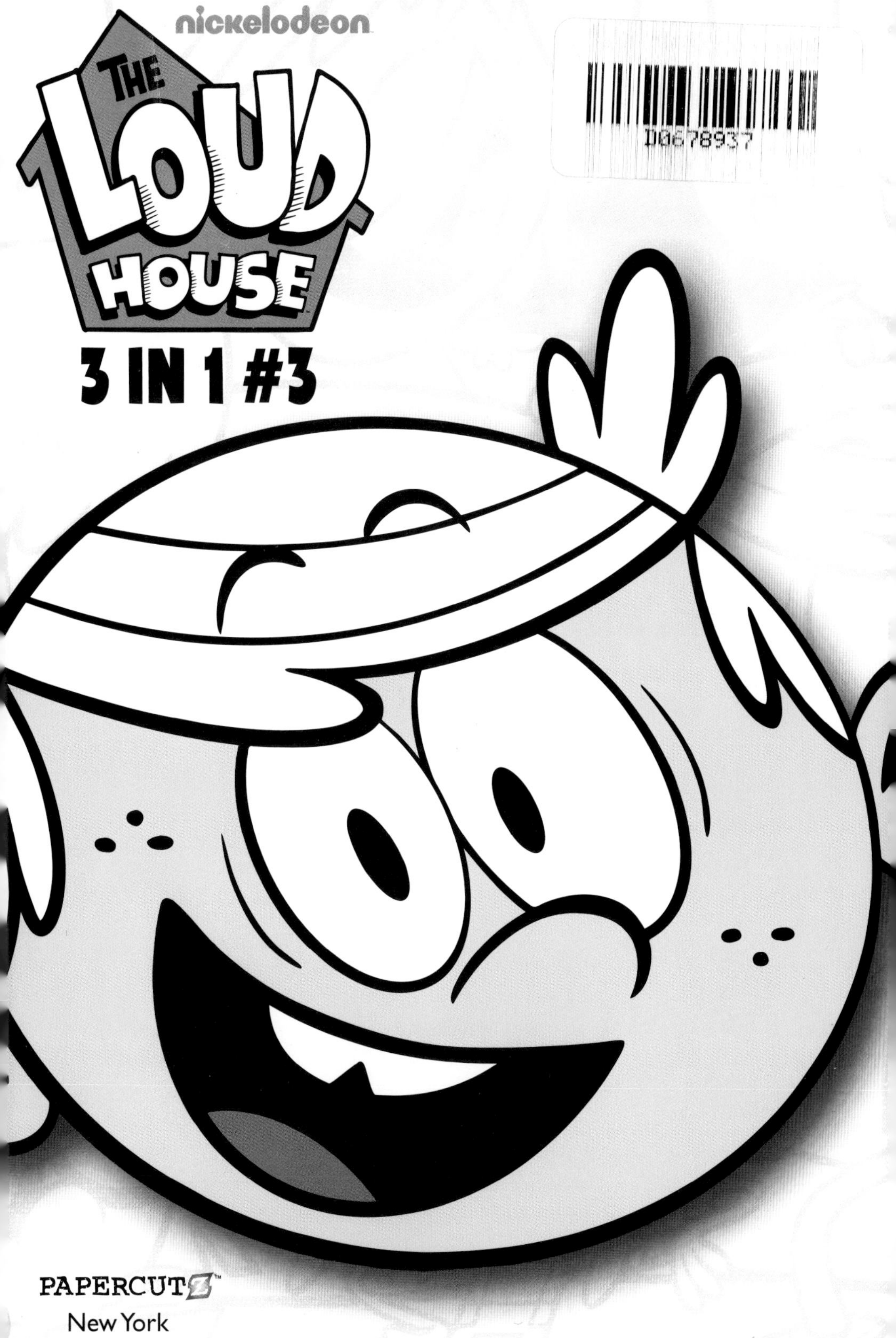

PAPERCUTZ
New York

nickelodeon GRAPHIC NOVELS AVAILABLE FROM PAPERCUTZ

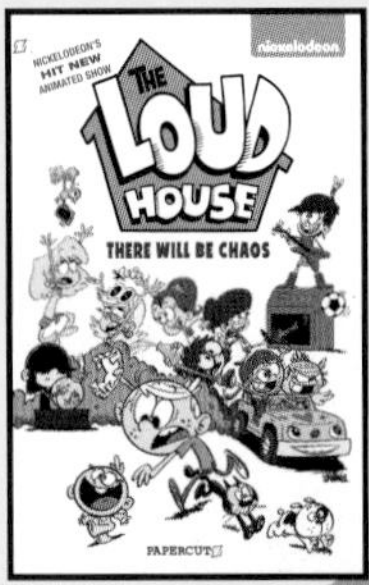
THE LOUD HOUSE
THERE WILL BE CHAOS

THE LOUD HOUSE
#1
"There Will Be Chaos"

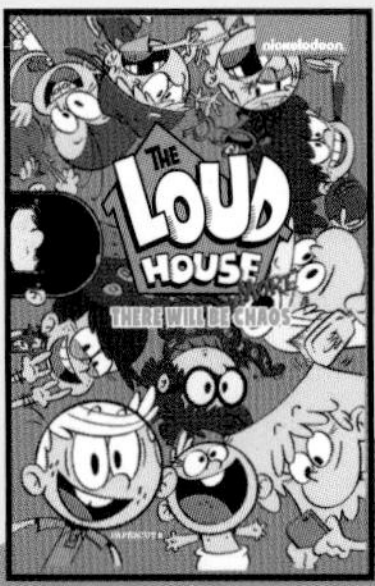
THE LOUD HOUSE

THE LOUD HOUSE
#2
"There Will Be More Chaos"

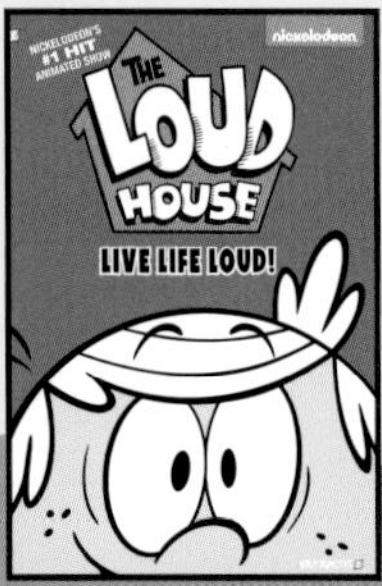
THE LOUD HOUSE
LIVE LIFE LOUD!

THE LOUD HOUSE
#3
"Live Life Loud!"

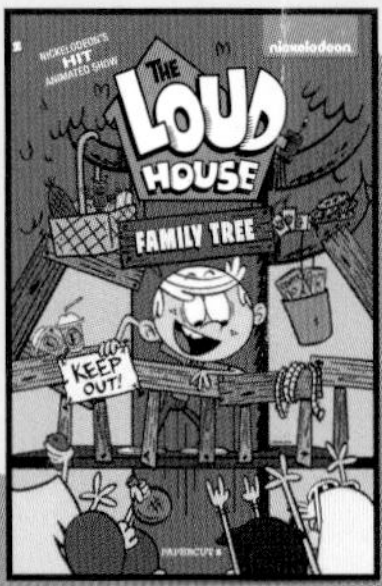
THE LOUD HOUSE
FAMILY TREE
KEEP OUT!

THE LOUD HOUSE
#4
"Family Tree"

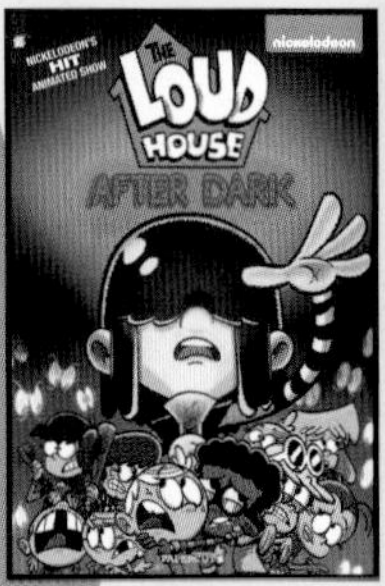
THE LOUD HOUSE
AFTER DARK

THE LOUD HOUSE
#5
"After Dark"

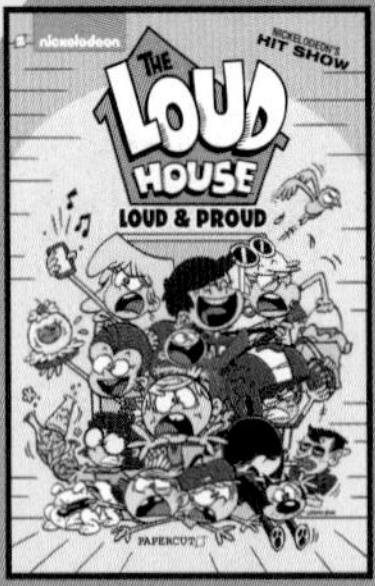
THE LOUD HOUSE
LOUD & PROUD

THE LOUD HOUSE
#6
"Loud and Proud"

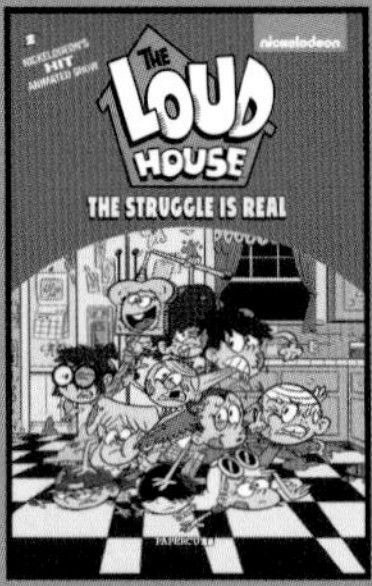
THE LOUD HOUSE
THE STRUGGLE IS REAL

THE LOUD HOUSE
#7
"The Struggle is Real"

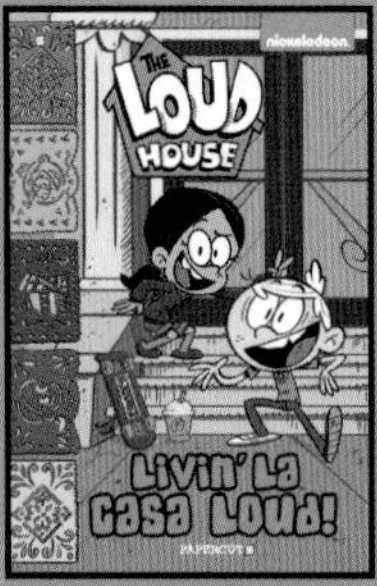
THE LOUD HOUSE
Livin' La Casa Loud!

THE LOUD HOUSE
#8
"Livin' La Casa Loud"

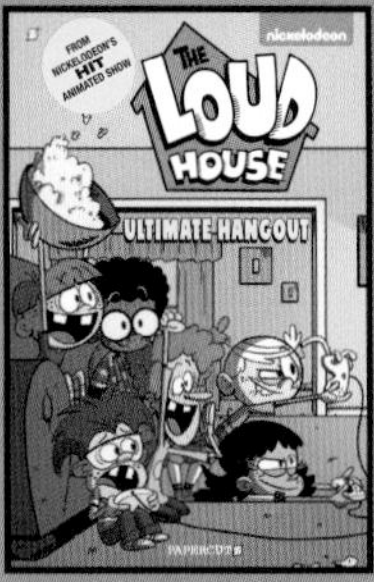
THE LOUD HOUSE
ULTIMATE HANGOUT

THE LOUD HOUSE
#9
"Ultimate Hangout"

COMING SOON

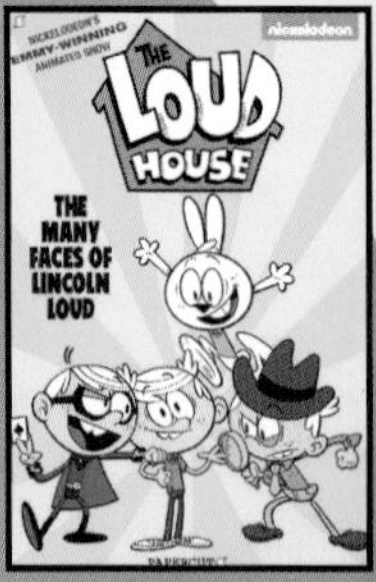
THE LOUD HOUSE
THE MANY FACES OF LINCOLN LOUD

THE LOUD HOUSE
#10
"The Many Faces of Lincoln Loud"

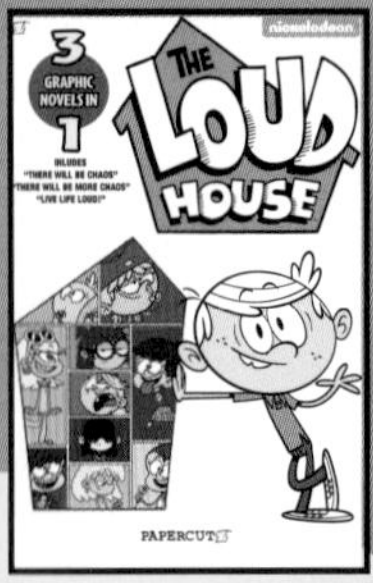
3 GRAPHIC NOVELS IN 1
THE LOUD HOUSE

THE LOUD HOUSE
3 IN 1
#1

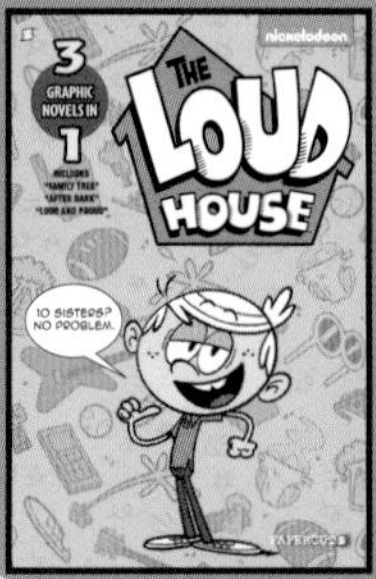
3 GRAPHIC NOVELS IN 1
THE LOUD HOUSE
10 SISTERS? NO PROBLEM.

THE LOUD HOUSE
3 IN 1
#2

COMING SOON

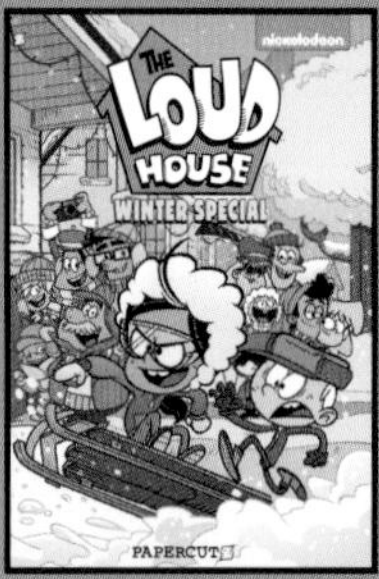
THE LOUD HOUSE
WINTER SPECIAL

THE LOUD HOUSE
WINTER SPECIAL

COMING SOON

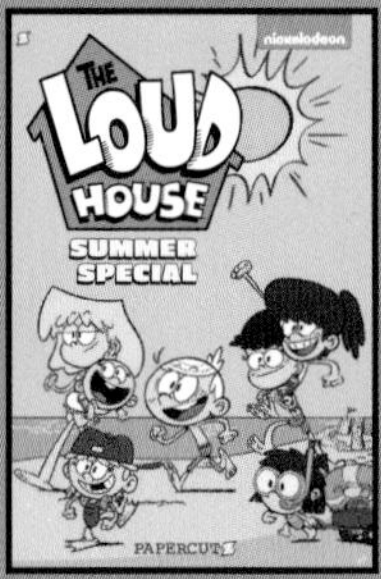
THE LOUD HOUSE
SUMMER SPECIAL

THE LOUD HOUSE
SUMMER SPECIAL

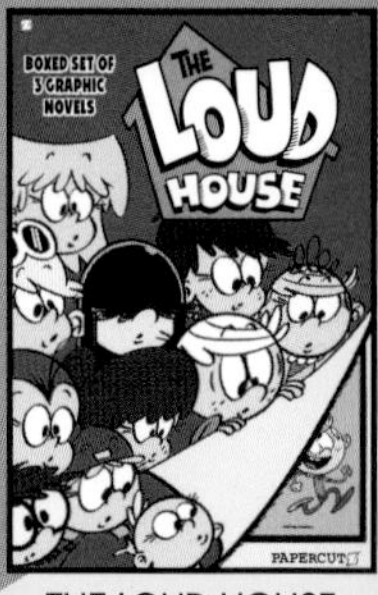
BOXED SET OF 3 GRAPHIC NOVELS
THE LOUD HOUSE

THE LOUD HOUSE
BOXED SET
$23.99

The Loud House graphic novels are available for $7.99 each in paperback, $12.99 each in hardcover. THE LOUD HOUSE 3 IN 1 graphic novels are available for $14.99 each in paperback only.
Available from booksellers everywhere. You can also order online from Papercutz.com, or call 1-800-886-1223, Monday through Friday, 9-5 EST. MC, Visa, and AmEx accepted. To order by mail, please add $5.00 for postage and handling for the first book ordered, $1.00 for each additional book and make check payable to NBM Publishing. Send to: Papercutz, 160 Broadway, Suite 700, East Wing, New York, NY 10038.

Nickelodeon graphic novels are also available digitally wherever e-books are sold.

nickelodeon THE LOUD HOUSE 3 IN 1 #3

JAMES SALERNO — Sr. Art Director/Nickelodeon
JAYJAY JACKSON — Design/Production
JEFF WHITMAN — Editor
ERIC STORMS — Editorial Intern
JOAN HILTY — Comics Editor/Nickelodeon
DAWN GUZZO, PRINCESS BIZARES, CARLO PADILLA, SAMMIE CROWLEY, SEAN GANTKA, DANA CLUVERIUS, MOLLIE FRELICH, and ANGELA ENTZMINGER — Special Thanks
JIM SALICRUP
Editor-in-Chief

ISBN: 978-1-5458-0560-2

Papercutz books may be purchased for business or promotional use. For information on bulk purchases please contact Macmillan Corporate and Premium Sales Department at (800) 221-7945 x5442.

Printed in Canada
July 2020

Distributed by Macmillan
First Printing

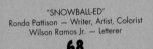

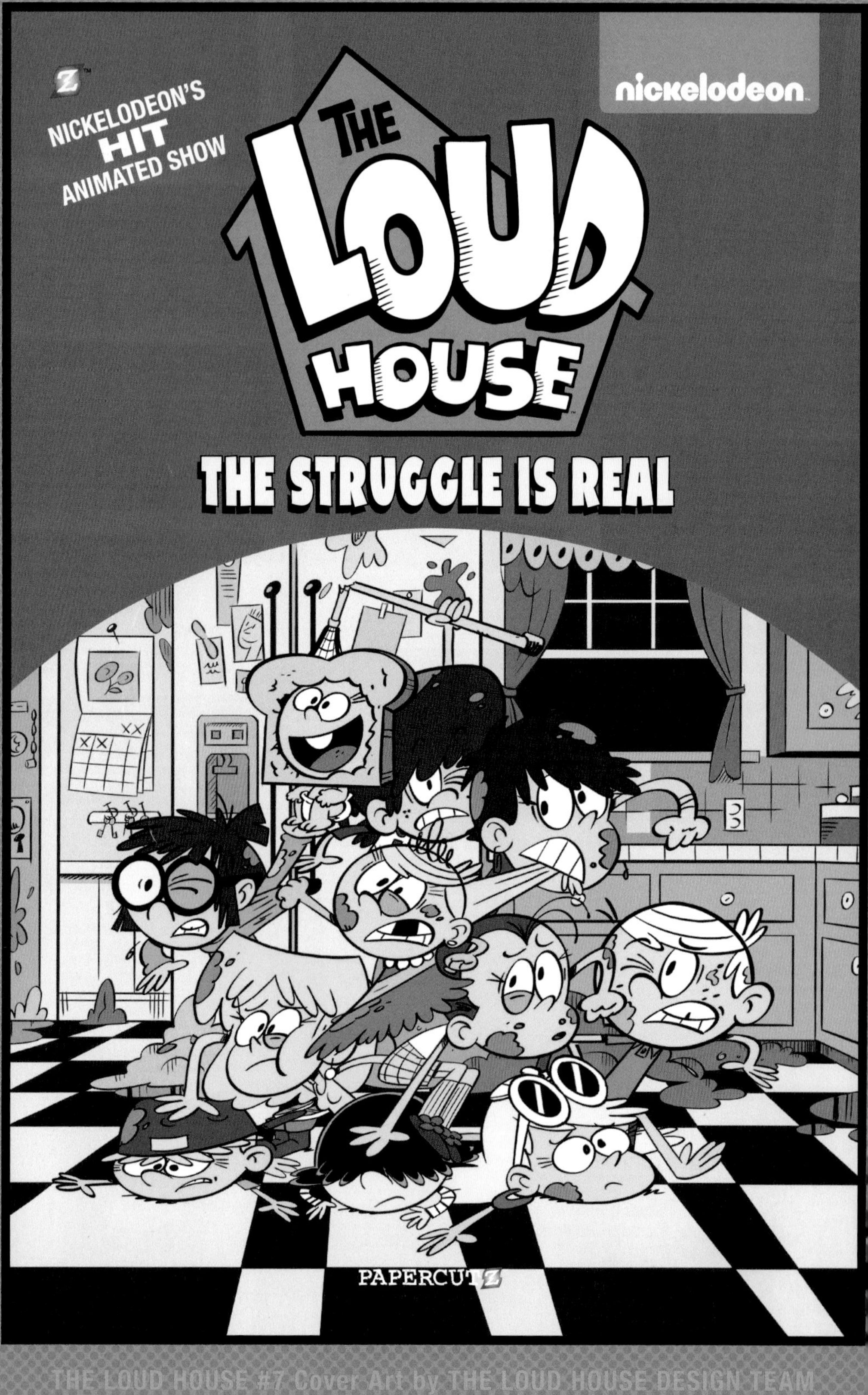

THE LOUD HOUSE #7 Cover Art by THE LOUD HOUSE DESIGN TEAM

"BUSINESS CENTS"

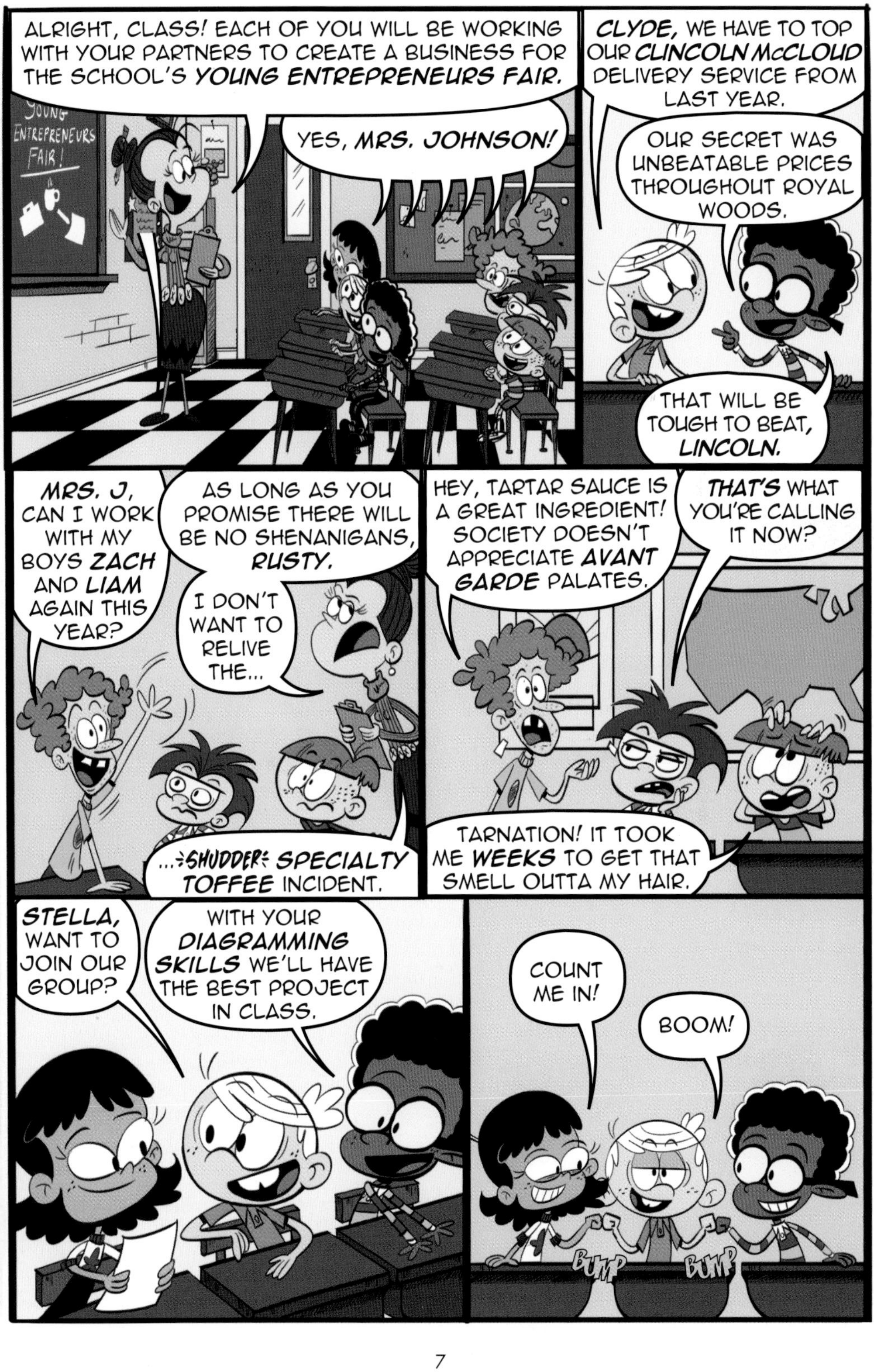
ALRIGHT, CLASS! EACH OF YOU WILL BE WORKING WITH YOUR PARTNERS TO CREATE A BUSINESS FOR THE SCHOOL'S YOUNG ENTREPRENEURS FAIR.
YOUNG ENTREPRENEURS FAIR!
YES, MRS. JOHNSON!
CLYDE, WE HAVE TO TOP OUR CLINCOLN McCLOUD DELIVERY SERVICE FROM LAST YEAR.
OUR SECRET WAS UNBEATABLE PRICES THROUGHOUT ROYAL WOODS.
THAT WILL BE TOUGH TO BEAT, LINCOLN.
MRS. J, CAN I WORK WITH MY BOYS ZACH AND LIAM AGAIN THIS YEAR?
AS LONG AS YOU PROMISE THERE WILL BE NO SHENANIGANS, RUSTY.
I DON'T WANT TO RELIVE THE...
...SHUDDER SPECIALTY TOFFEE INCIDENT.
HEY, TARTAR SAUCE IS A GREAT INGREDIENT! SOCIETY DOESN'T APPRECIATE AVANT GARDE PALATES.
THAT'S WHAT YOU'RE CALLING IT NOW?
TARNATION! IT TOOK ME WEEKS TO GET THAT SMELL OUTTA MY HAIR.
STELLA, WANT TO JOIN OUR GROUP?
WITH YOUR DIAGRAMMING SKILLS WE'LL HAVE THE BEST PROJECT IN CLASS.
COUNT ME IN!
BOOM!
BUMP
BUMP

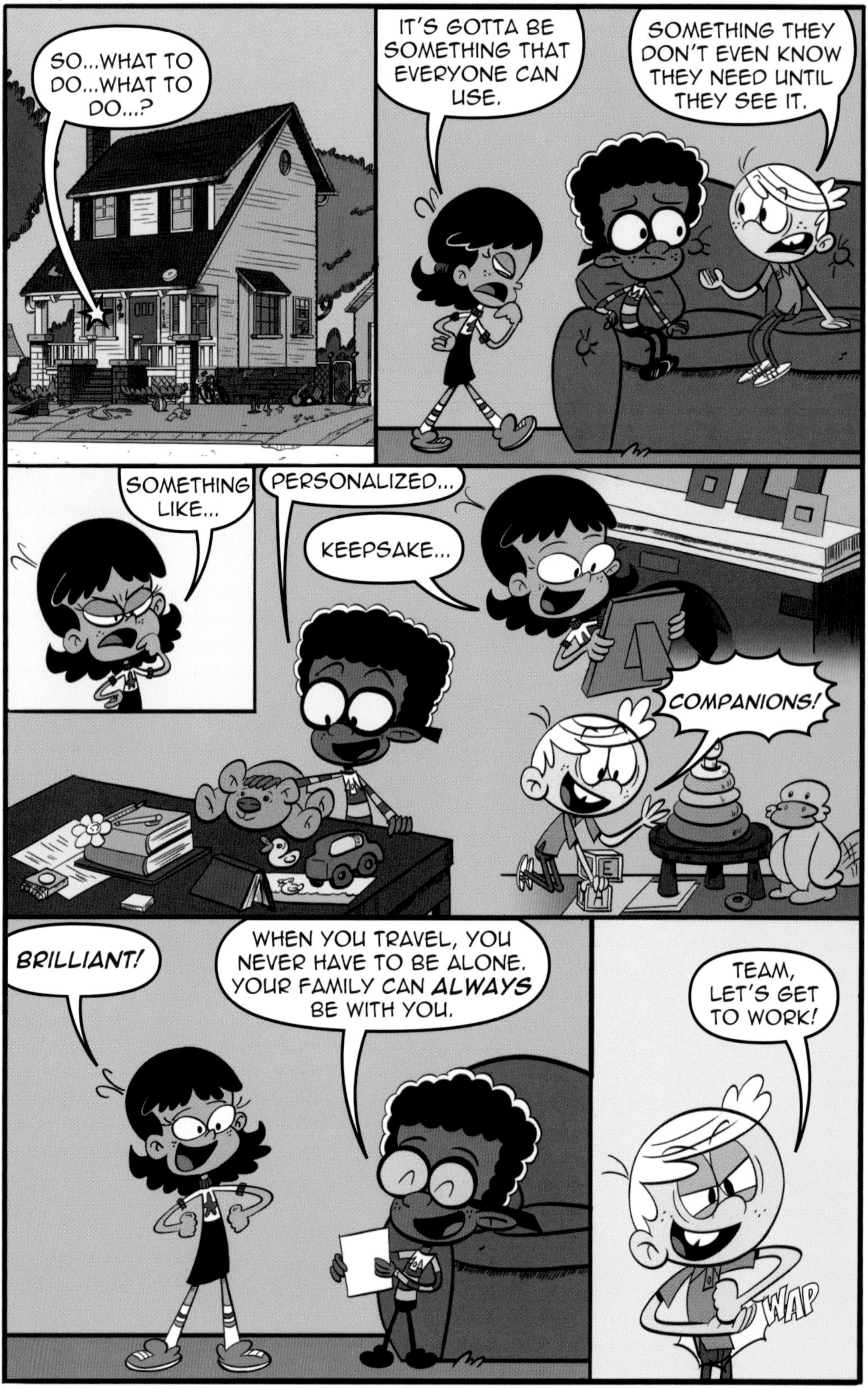
SO...WHAT TO DO...WHAT TO DO...?
IT'S GOTTA BE SOMETHING THAT EVERYONE CAN USE.
SOMETHING THEY DON'T EVEN KNOW THEY NEED UNTIL THEY SEE IT.
SOMETHING LIKE...
PERSONALIZED...
KEEPSAKE...
COMPANIONS!
BRILLIANT!
WHEN YOU TRAVEL, YOU NEVER HAVE TO BE ALONE. YOUR FAMILY CAN *ALWAYS* BE WITH YOU.
TEAM, LET'S GET TO WORK!
WAP

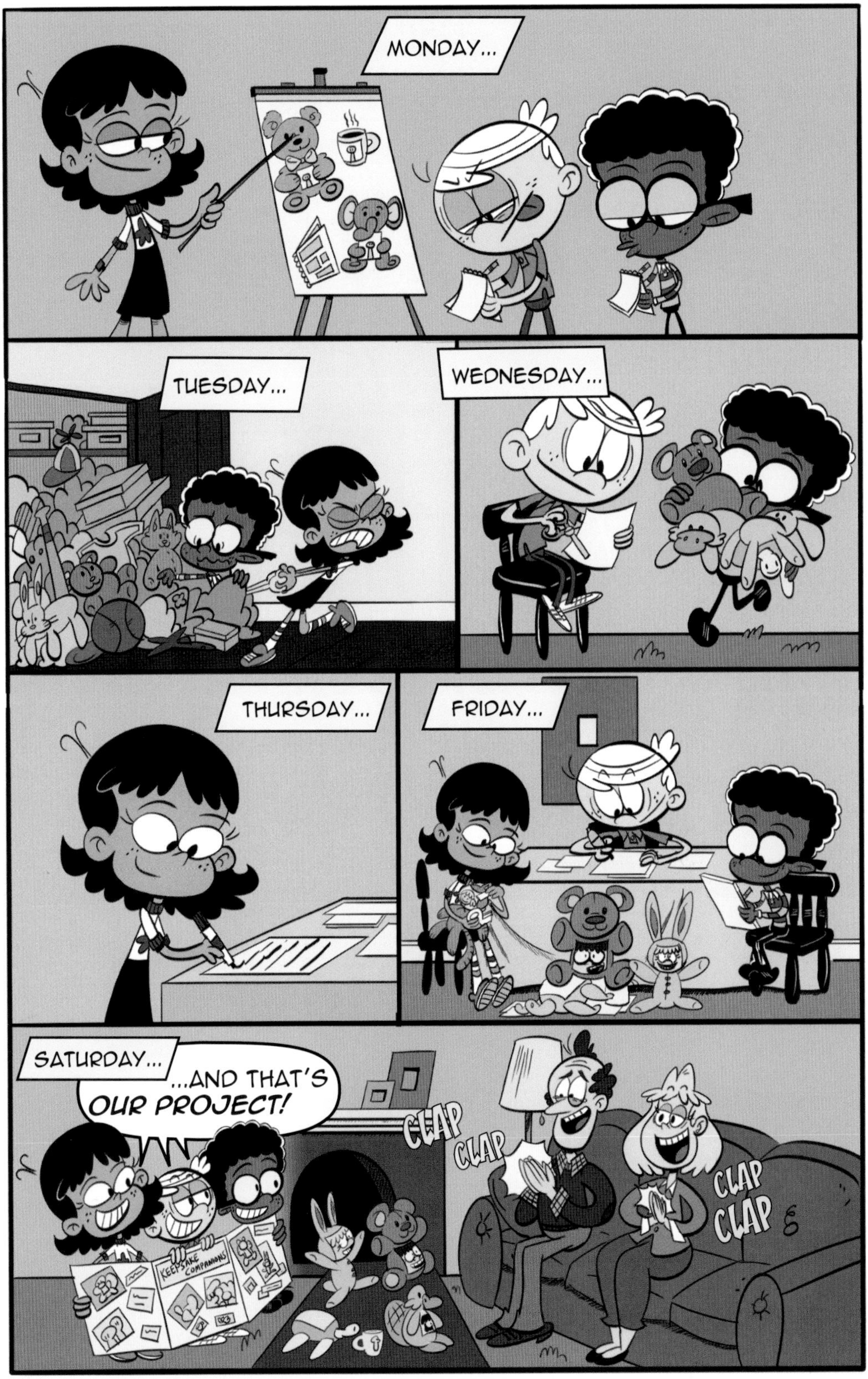
MONDAY...
TUESDAY...
WEDNESDAY...
THURSDAY...
FRIDAY...
SATURDAY...
...AND THAT'S OUR PROJECT!
CLAP
CLAP
CLAP
CLAP
KEEPSAKE COMPANIONS

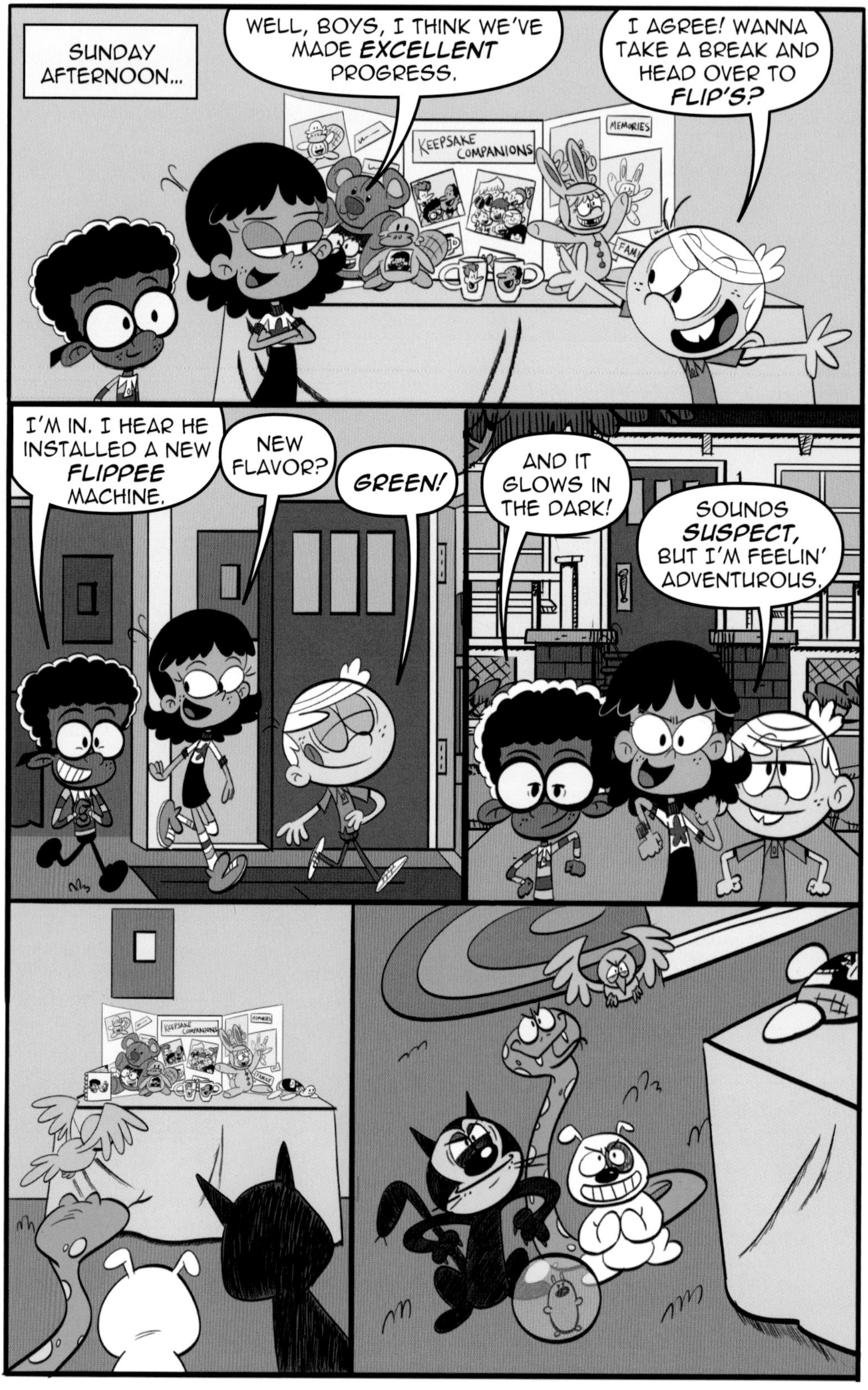
SUNDAY AFTERNOON...
WELL, BOYS, I THINK WE'VE MADE EXCELLENT PROGRESS.
I AGREE! WANNA TAKE A BREAK AND HEAD OVER TO FLIP'S?
KEEPSAKE COMPANIONS
MEMORIES
I'M IN. I HEAR HE INSTALLED A NEW FLIPPEE MACHINE.
NEW FLAVOR?
GREEN!
AND IT GLOWS IN THE DARK!
SOUNDS SUSPECT, BUT I'M FEELIN' ADVENTUROUS.

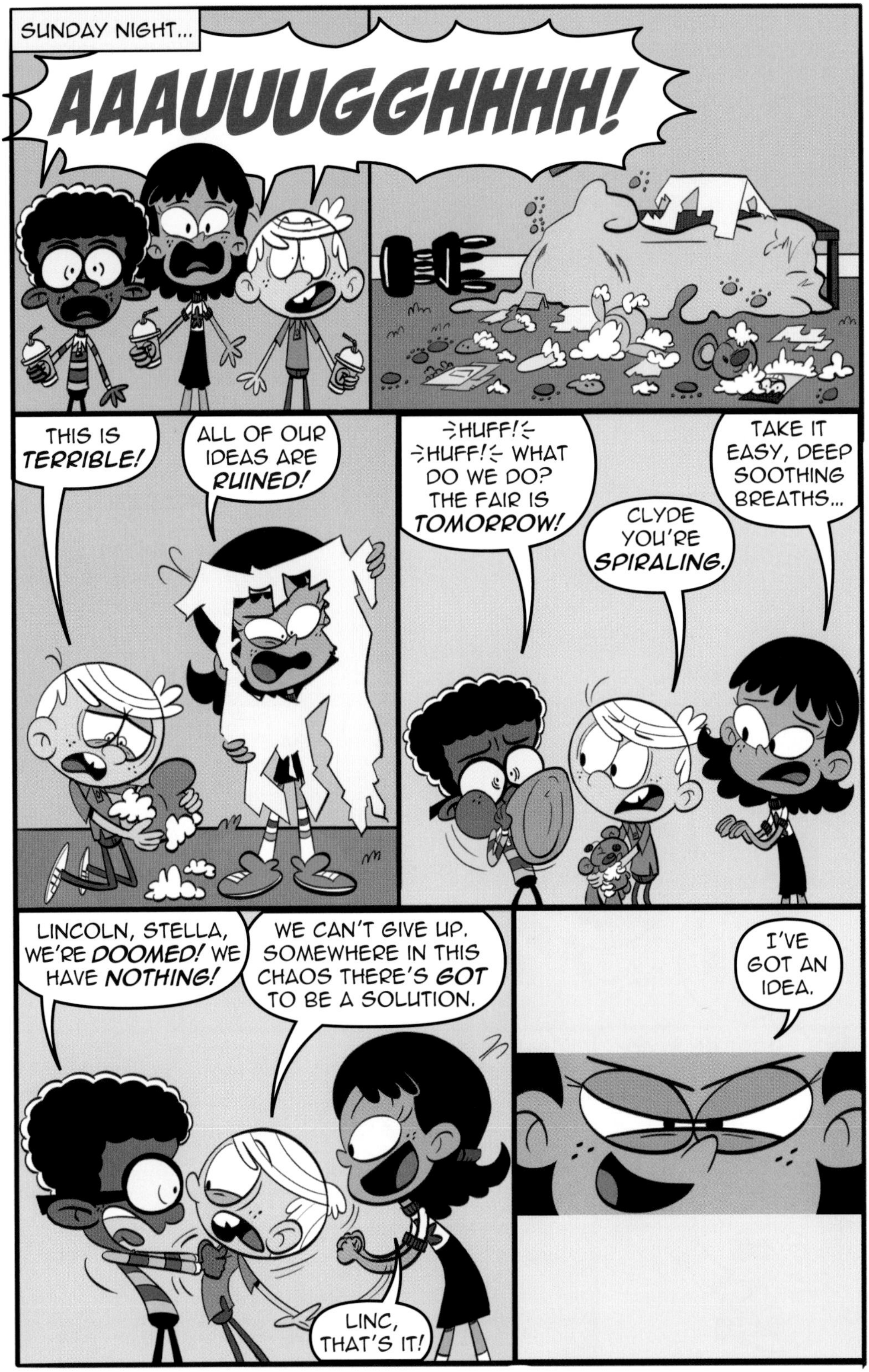
SUNDAY NIGHT...
AAAUUUGGHHHH!
THIS IS TERRIBLE!
ALL OF OUR IDEAS ARE RUINED!
HUFF! HUFF! WHAT DO WE DO? THE FAIR IS TOMORROW!
CLYDE YOU'RE SPIRALING.
TAKE IT EASY, DEEP SOOTHING BREATHS...
LINCOLN, STELLA, WE'RE DOOMED! WE HAVE NOTHING!
WE CAN'T GIVE UP. SOMEWHERE IN THIS CHAOS THERE'S GOT TO BE A SOLUTION.
LINC, THAT'S IT!
I'VE GOT AN IDEA.

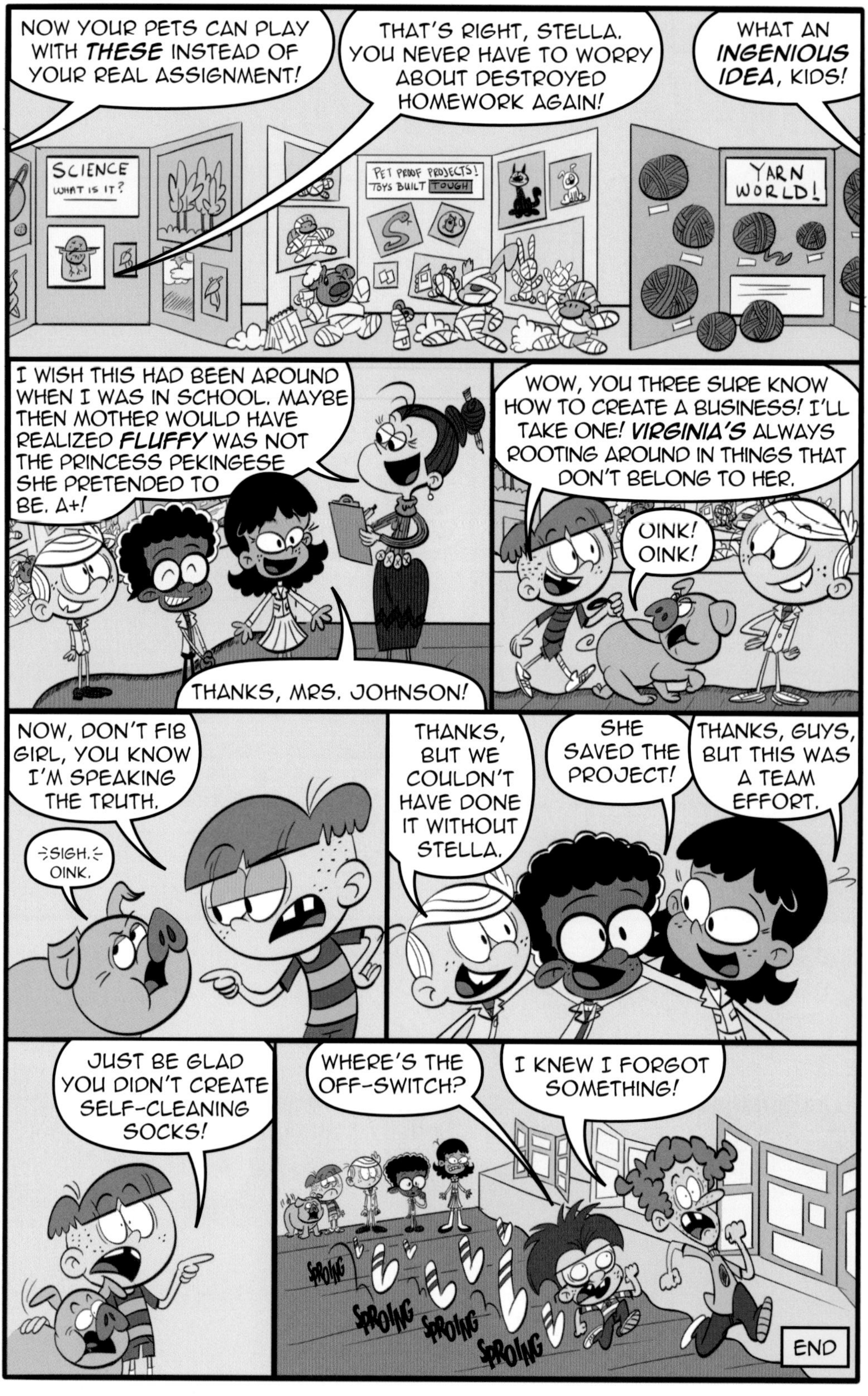
NOW YOUR PETS CAN PLAY WITH THESE INSTEAD OF YOUR REAL ASSIGNMENT!
THAT'S RIGHT, STELLA. YOU NEVER HAVE TO WORRY ABOUT DESTROYED HOMEWORK AGAIN!
WHAT AN INGENIOUS IDEA, KIDS!
SCIENCE WHAT IS IT?
PET PROOF PROJECTS! TOYS BUILT TOUGH
YARN WORLD!
I WISH THIS HAD BEEN AROUND WHEN I WAS IN SCHOOL. MAYBE THEN MOTHER WOULD HAVE REALIZED FLUFFY WAS NOT THE PRINCESS PEKINGESE SHE PRETENDED TO BE. A+!
THANKS, MRS. JOHNSON!
WOW, YOU THREE SURE KNOW HOW TO CREATE A BUSINESS! I'LL TAKE ONE! VIRGINIA'S ALWAYS ROOTING AROUND IN THINGS THAT DON'T BELONG TO HER.
OINK! OINK!
NOW, DON'T FIB GIRL, YOU KNOW I'M SPEAKING THE TRUTH.
SIGH. OINK.
THANKS, BUT WE COULDN'T HAVE DONE IT WITHOUT STELLA.
SHE SAVED THE PROJECT!
THANKS, GUYS, BUT THIS WAS A TEAM EFFORT.
JUST BE GLAD YOU DIDN'T CREATE SELF-CLEANING SOCKS!
WHERE'S THE OFF-SWITCH?
I KNEW I FORGOT SOMETHING!
SPROING
SPROING
SPROING
SPROING
END

"PREP TALK"

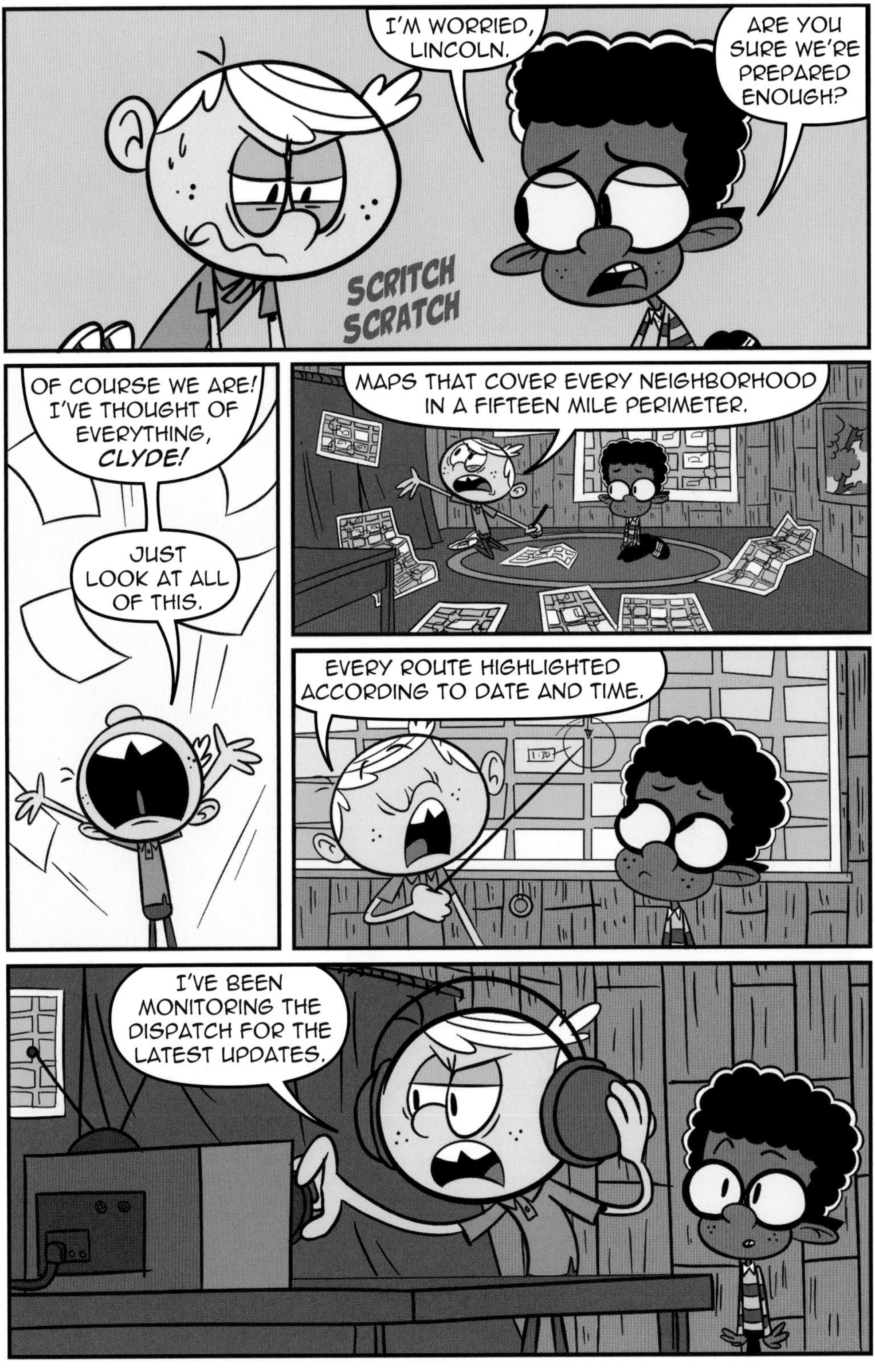

I'M WORRIED, LINCOLN.
ARE YOU SURE WE'RE PREPARED ENOUGH?
SCRITCH SCRATCH
OF COURSE WE ARE! I'VE THOUGHT OF EVERYTHING, *CLYDE!*
JUST LOOK AT ALL OF THIS.
MAPS THAT COVER EVERY NEIGHBORHOOD IN A FIFTEEN MILE PERIMETER.
EVERY ROUTE HIGHLIGHTED ACCORDING TO DATE AND TIME.
I'VE BEEN MONITORING THE DISPATCH FOR THE LATEST UPDATES.

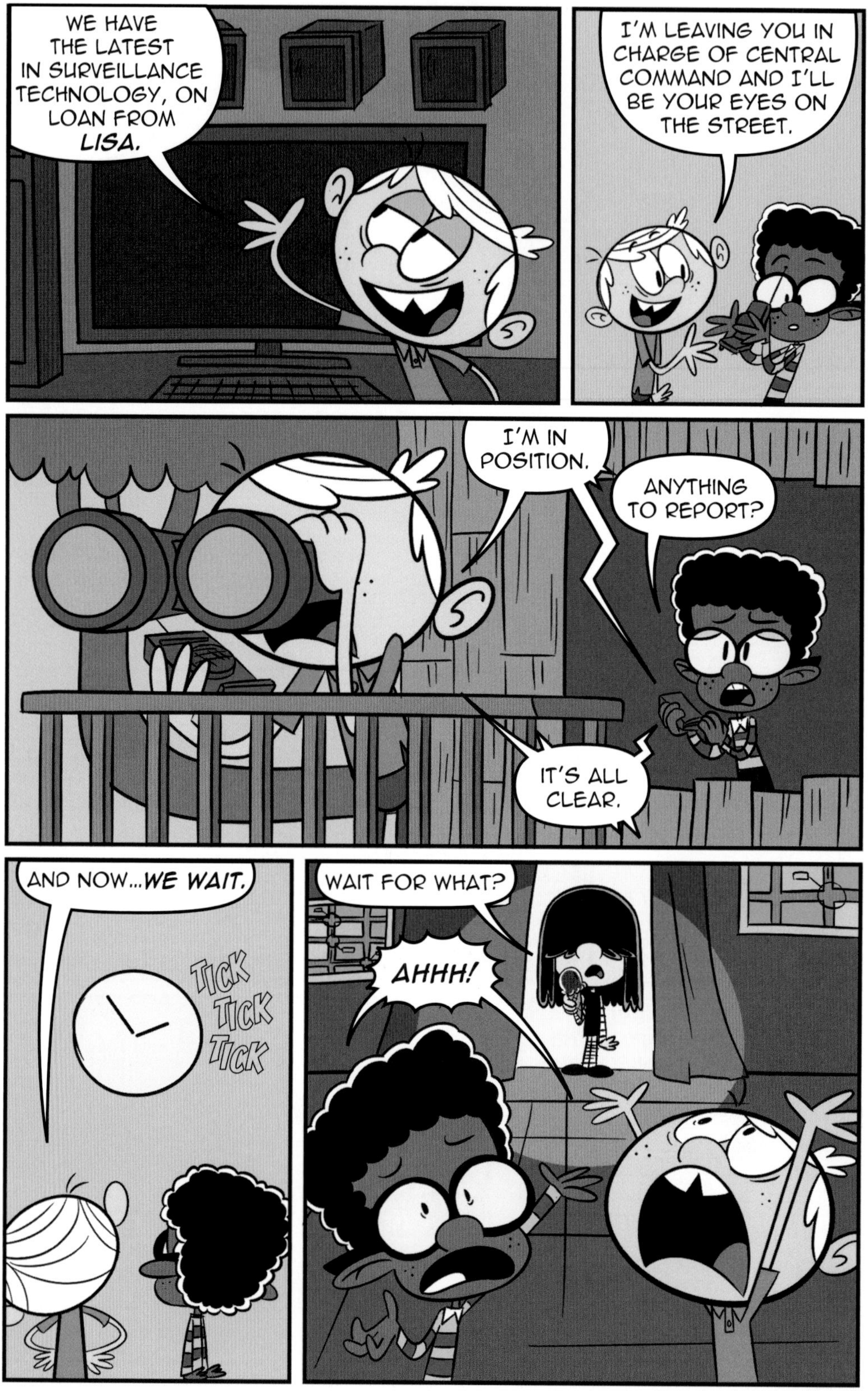
WE HAVE THE LATEST IN SURVEILLANCE TECHNOLOGY, ON LOAN FROM *LISA.*
I'M LEAVING YOU IN CHARGE OF CENTRAL COMMAND AND I'LL BE YOUR EYES ON THE STREET.
I'M IN POSITION.
ANYTHING TO REPORT?
IT'S ALL CLEAR.
AND NOW... **WE WAIT.**
TICK
TICK
TICK
WAIT FOR WHAT?
AHHH!

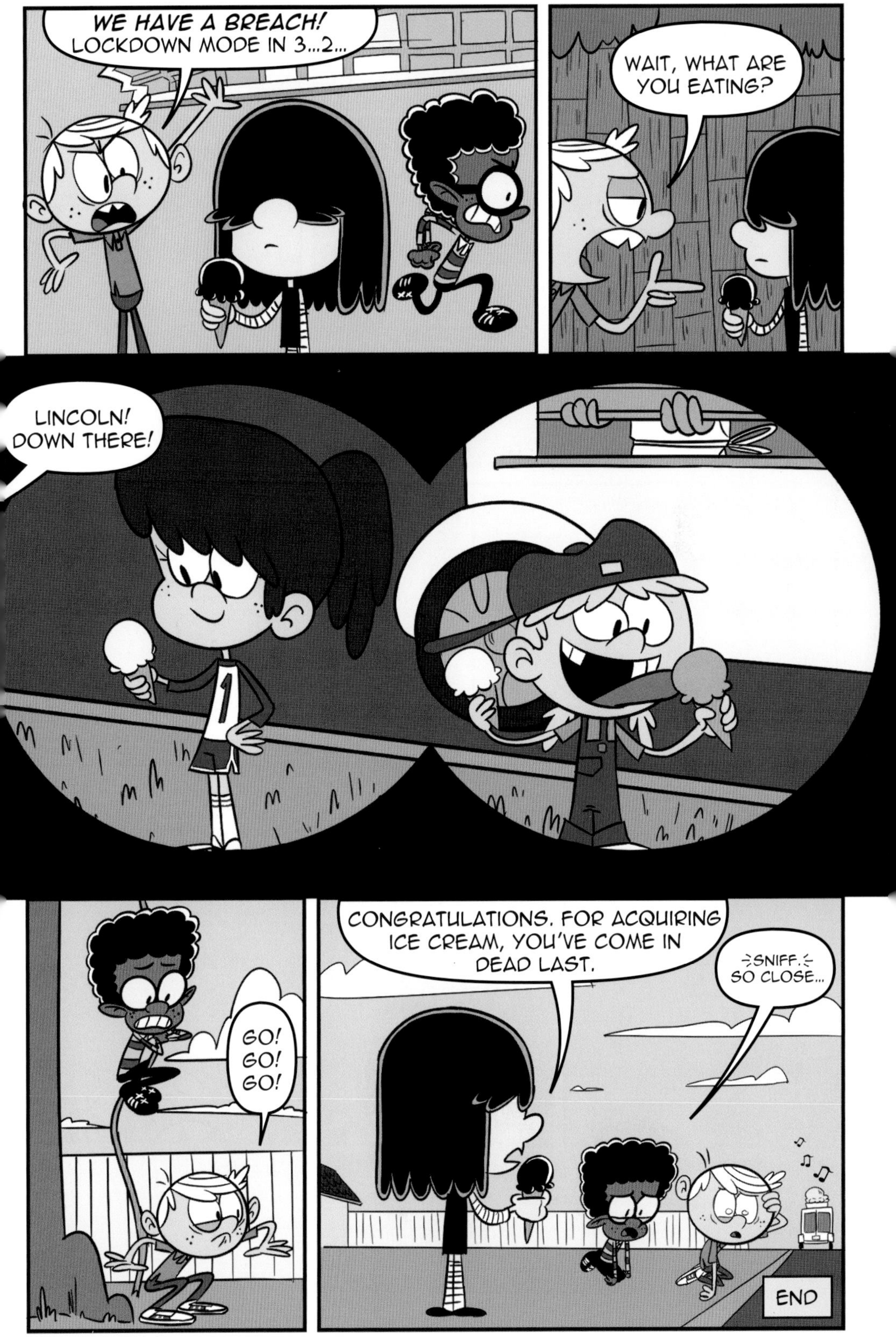
WE HAVE A BREACH! LOCKDOWN MODE IN 3...2...
WAIT, WHAT ARE YOU EATING?
LINCOLN! DOWN THERE!
GO! GO! GO!
CONGRATULATIONS. FOR ACQUIRING ICE CREAM, YOU'VE COME IN DEAD LAST.
SNIFF. SO CLOSE...
END

"UNDER REMOTE CONTROL"

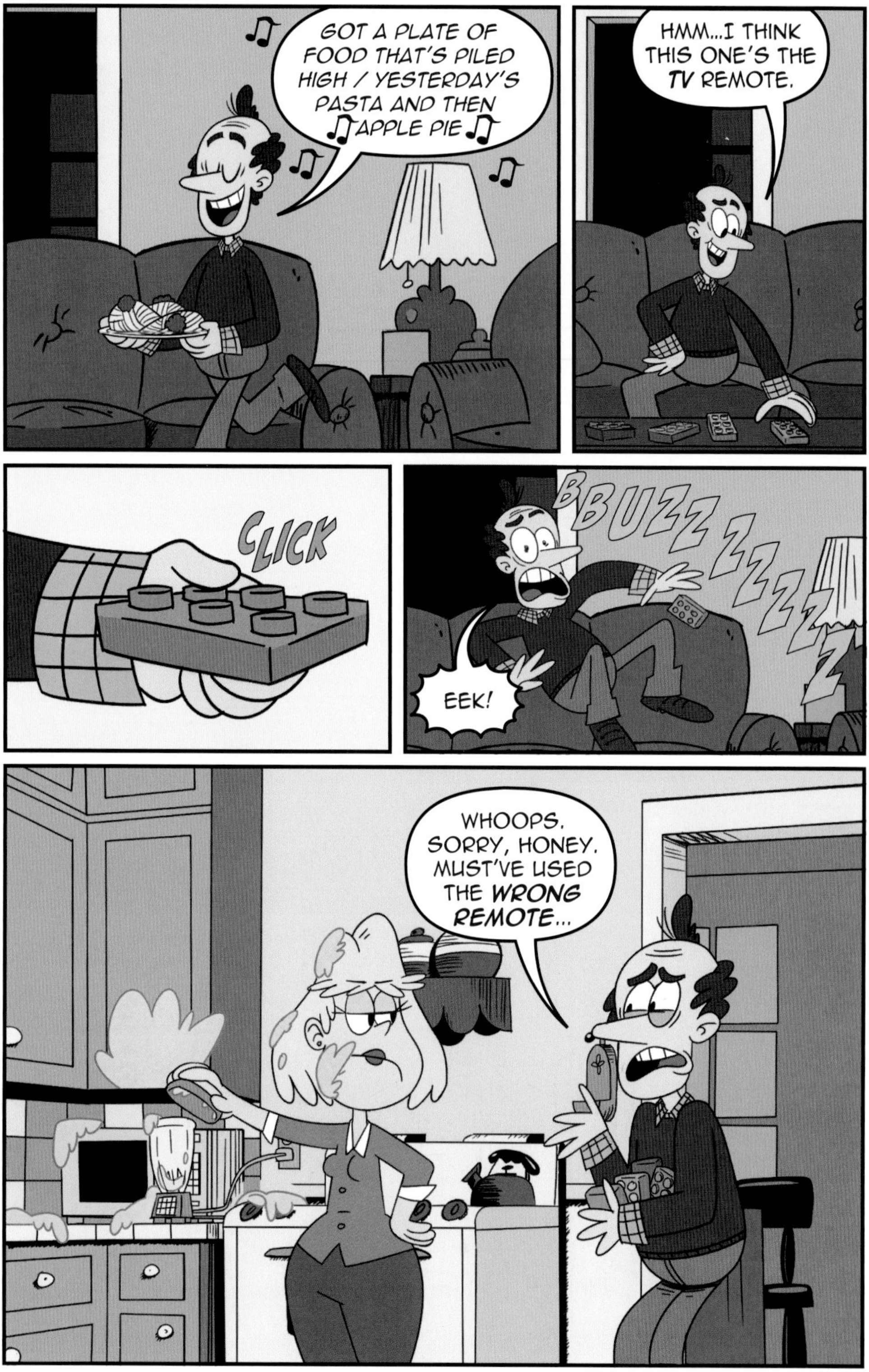
GOT A PLATE OF FOOD THAT'S PILED HIGH / YESTERDAY'S PASTA AND THEN ♫APPLE PIE♫
HMM...I THINK THIS ONE'S THE TV REMOTE.
CLICK
BBUZZZZZZZZ
EEK!
WHOOPS. SORRY, HONEY. MUST'VE USED THE WRONG REMOTE...

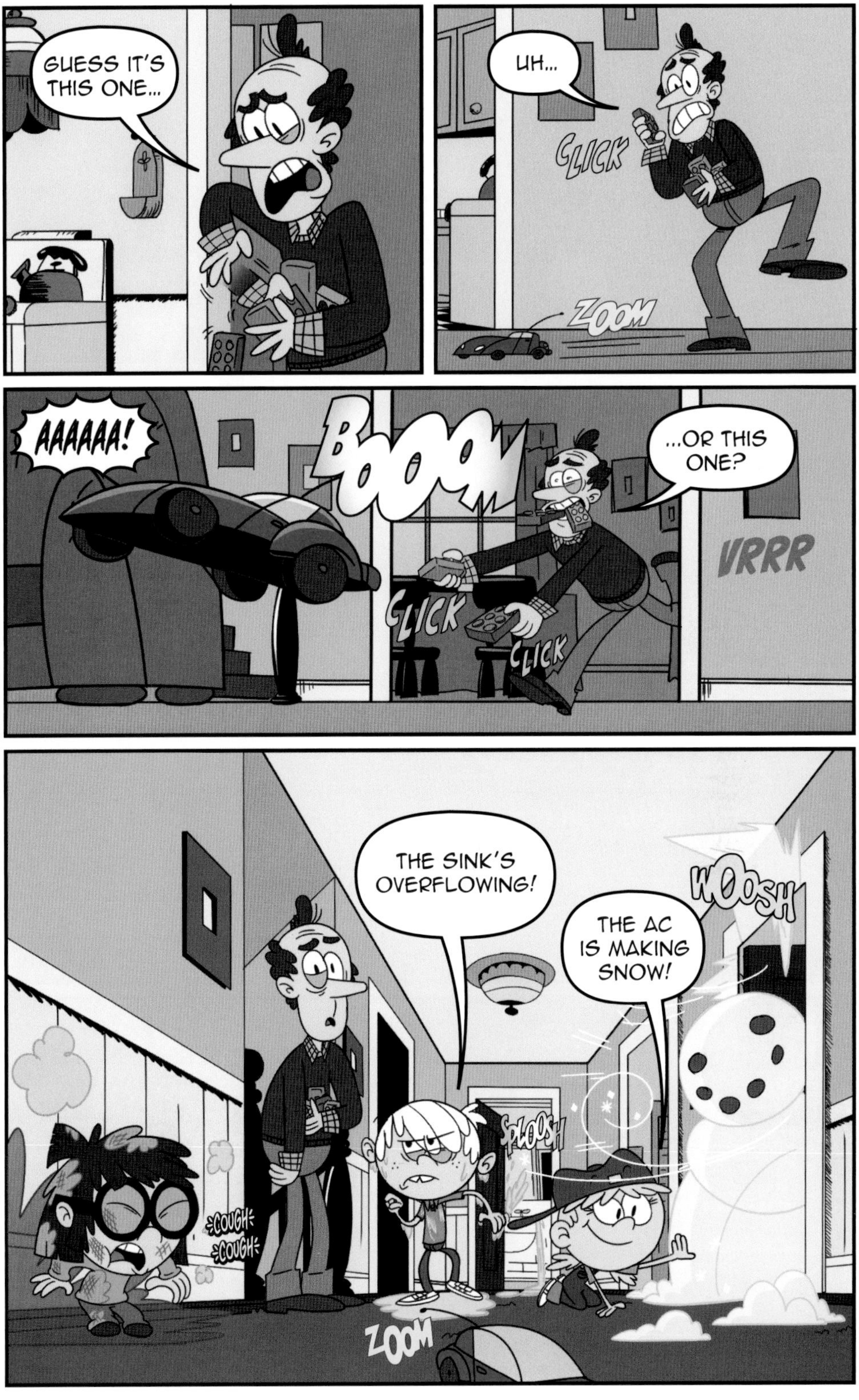
GUESS IT'S THIS ONE...
UH...
CLICK
ZOOM
AAAAAA!
BOOOM
...OR THIS ONE?
VRRR
CLICK
CLICK
THE SINK'S OVERFLOWING!
WOOSH
THE AC IS MAKING SNOW!
SPLOOSH
COUGH
COUGH
ZOOM

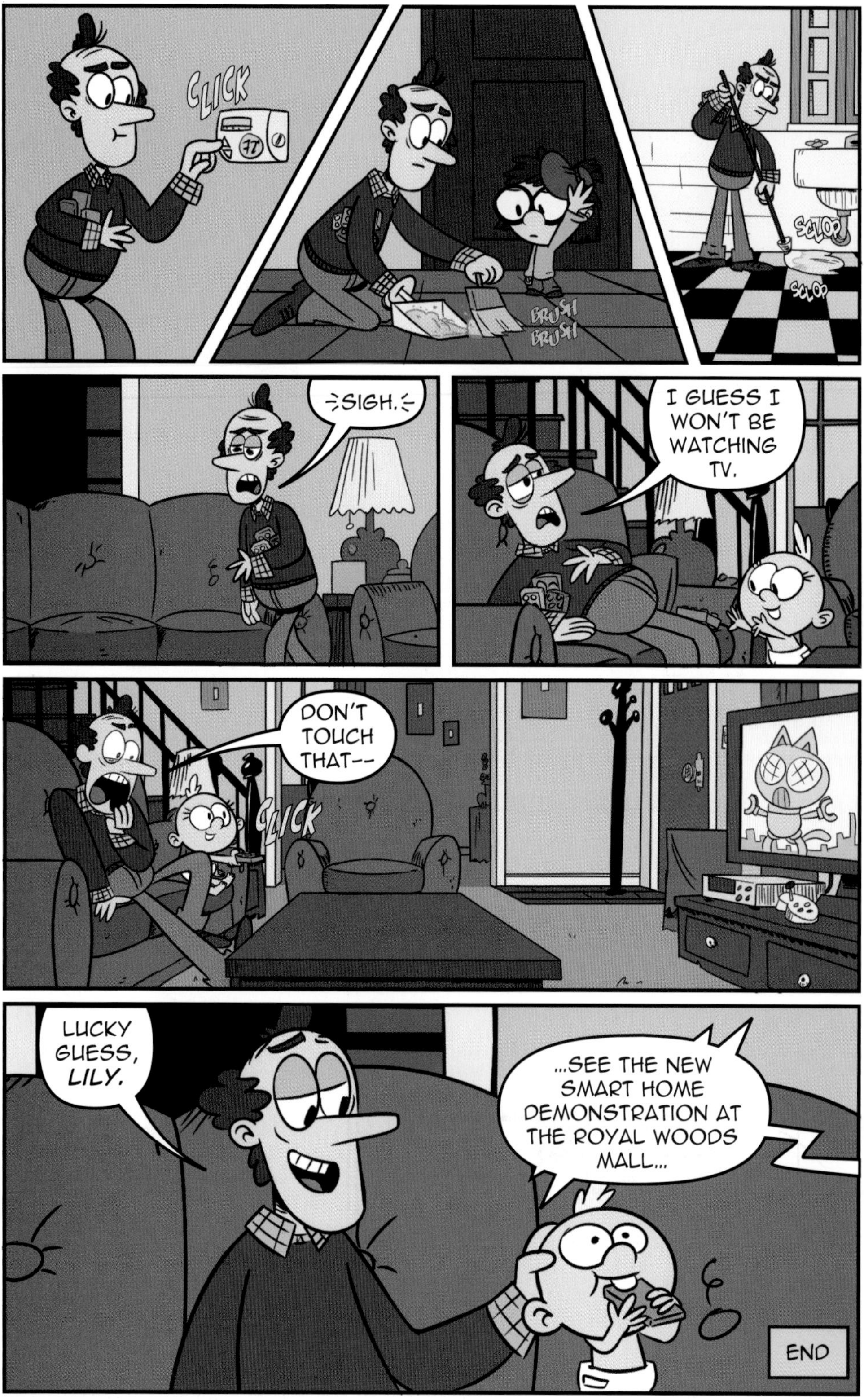
CLICK
BRUSH
BRUSH
SCLOP
SCLOP
-SIGH.-
I GUESS I WON'T BE WATCHING TV.
DON'T TOUCH THAT--
CLICK
LUCKY GUESS, LILY.
...SEE THE NEW SMART HOME DEMONSTRATION AT THE ROYAL WOODS MALL...
END

"GAME OVER"

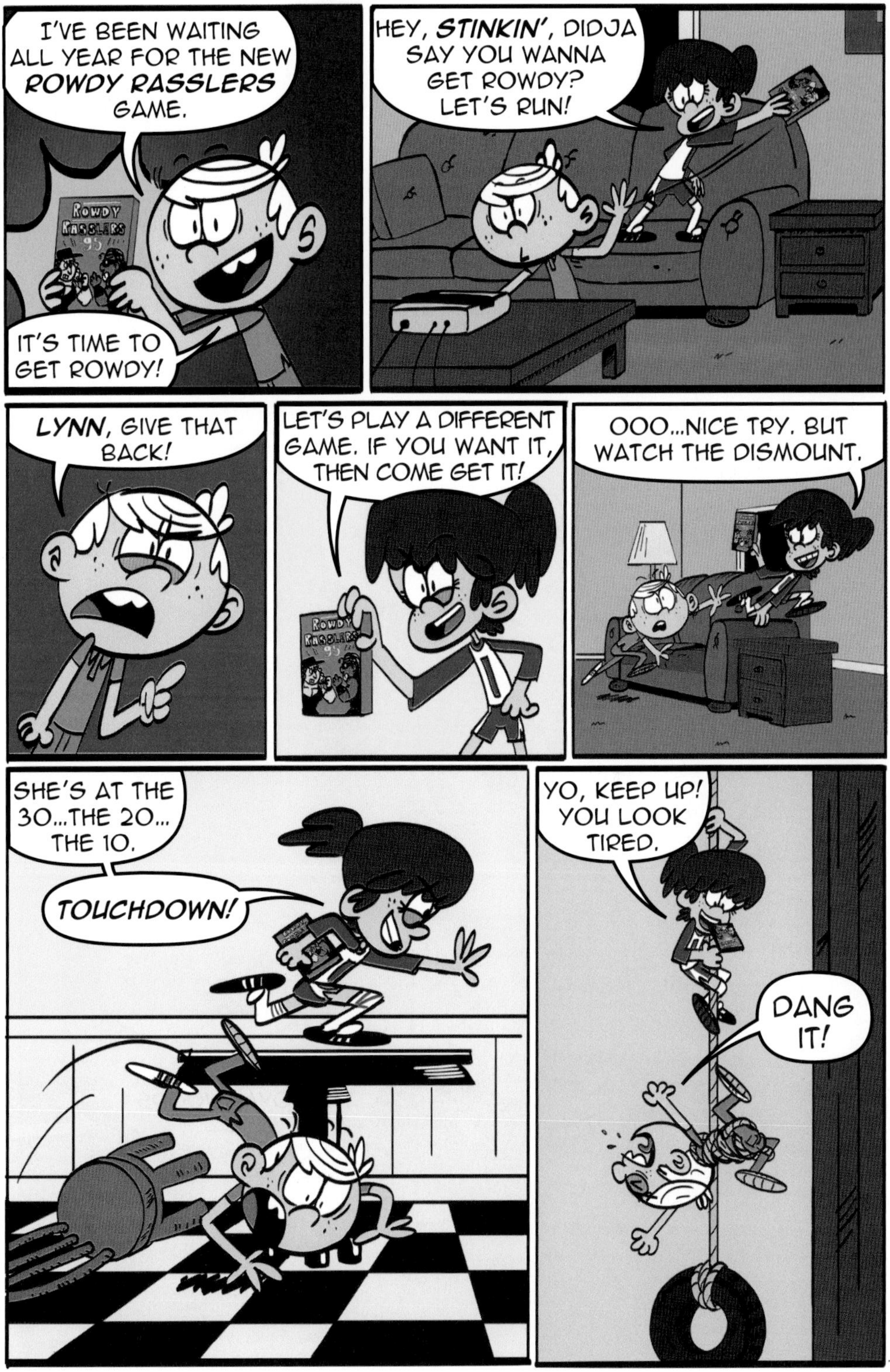
I'VE BEEN WAITING ALL YEAR FOR THE NEW *ROWDY RASSLERS* GAME.
ROWDY RASSLERS 95
IT'S TIME TO GET ROWDY!
HEY, *STINKIN'*, DIDJA SAY YOU WANNA GET ROWDY? LET'S RUN!
LYNN, GIVE THAT BACK!
LET'S PLAY A DIFFERENT GAME. IF YOU WANT IT, THEN COME GET IT!
ROWDY RASSLERS 95
OOO...NICE TRY. BUT WATCH THE DISMOUNT.
SHE'S AT THE 30...THE 20... THE 10.
TOUCHDOWN!
YO, KEEP UP! YOU LOOK TIRED.
DANG IT!

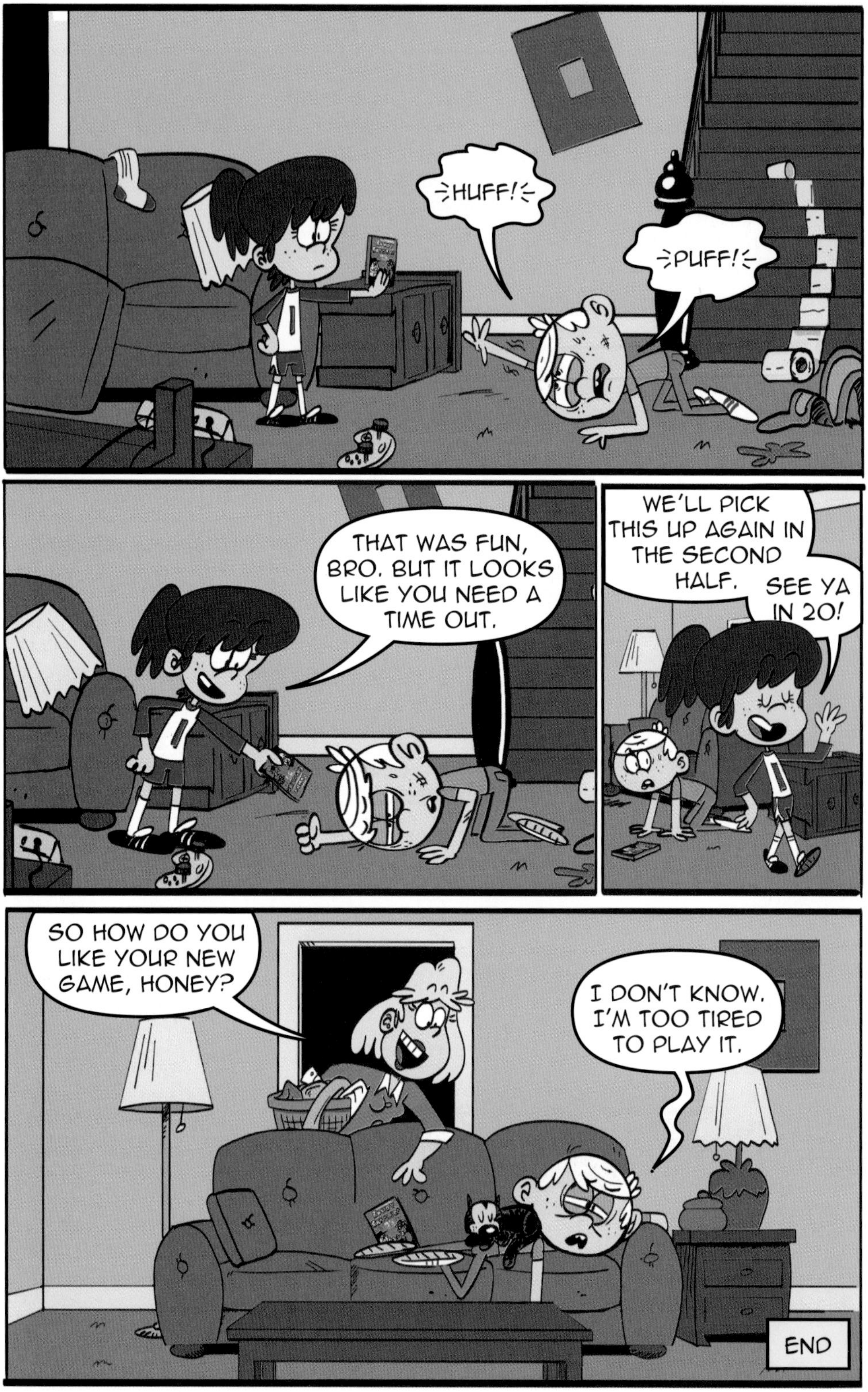
HUFF!
PUFF!
THAT WAS FUN, BRO. BUT IT LOOKS LIKE YOU NEED A TIME OUT.
WE'LL PICK THIS UP AGAIN IN THE SECOND HALF.
SEE YA IN 20!
SO HOW DO YOU LIKE YOUR NEW GAME, HONEY?
I DON'T KNOW. I'M TOO TIRED TO PLAY IT.
END

"FLIPPING THE SCRIPT"

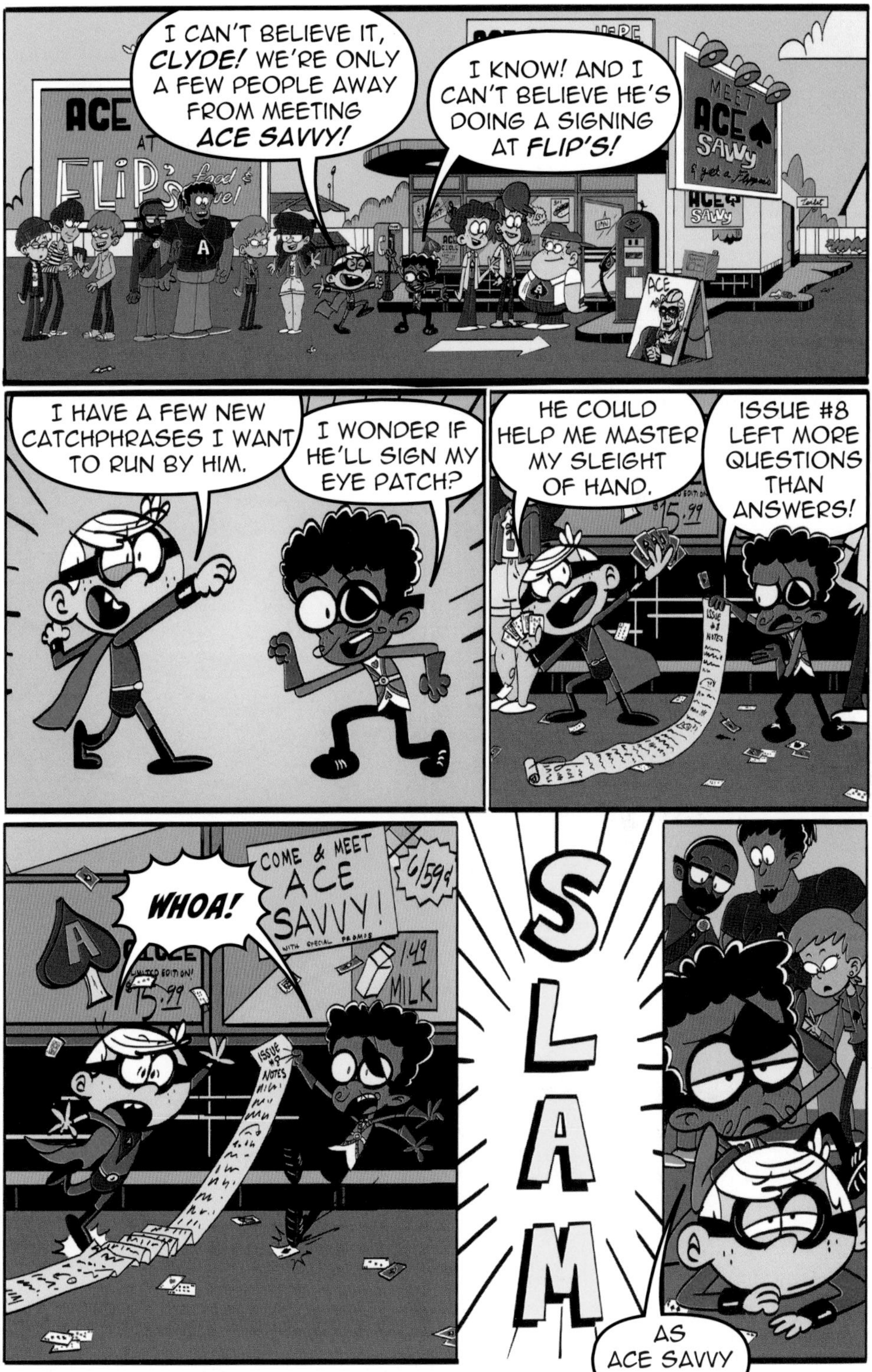
I CAN'T BELIEVE IT, CLYDE! WE'RE ONLY A FEW PEOPLE AWAY FROM MEETING ACE SAVVY!
I KNOW! AND I CAN'T BELIEVE HE'S DOING A SIGNING AT FLIP'S!
ACE AT FLIP'S food & fuel!
MEET ACE SAVVY
I HAVE A FEW NEW CATCHPHRASES I WANT TO RUN BY HIM.
I WONDER IF HE'LL SIGN MY EYE PATCH?
HE COULD HELP ME MASTER MY SLEIGHT OF HAND.
ISSUE #8 LEFT MORE QUESTIONS THAN ANSWERS!
ISSUE #8 NOTES
WHOA!
COME & MEET ACE SAVVY! WITH SPECIAL PROMOS
6/59¢
1.49 MILK
15.99
SLAM
AS ACE SAVVY SAYS--

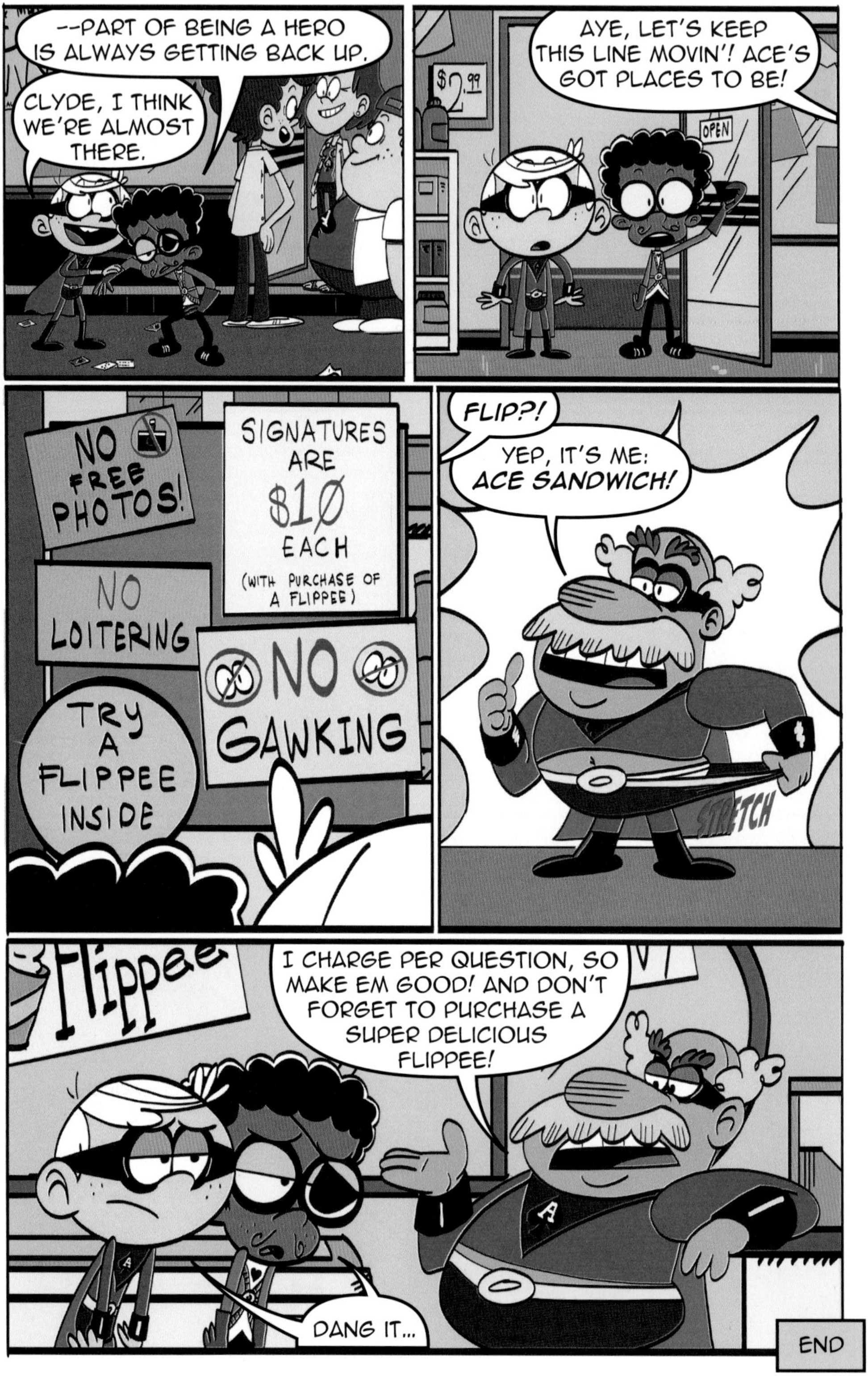
--PART OF BEING A HERO IS ALWAYS GETTING BACK UP.
CLYDE, I THINK WE'RE ALMOST THERE.
AYE, LET'S KEEP THIS LINE MOVIN'! ACE'S GOT PLACES TO BE!
$2.99
OPEN
NO FREE PHOTOS!
SIGNATURES ARE $10 EACH (WITH PURCHASE OF A FLIPPEE)
NO LOITERING
NO GAWKING
TRY A FLIPPEE INSIDE
FLIP?!
YEP, IT'S ME: ACE SANDWICH!
STRETCH
Flippee
I CHARGE PER QUESTION, SO MAKE EM GOOD! AND DON'T FORGET TO PURCHASE A SUPER DELICIOUS FLIPPEE!
DANG IT...
END

"I'M WITH THE BAND"

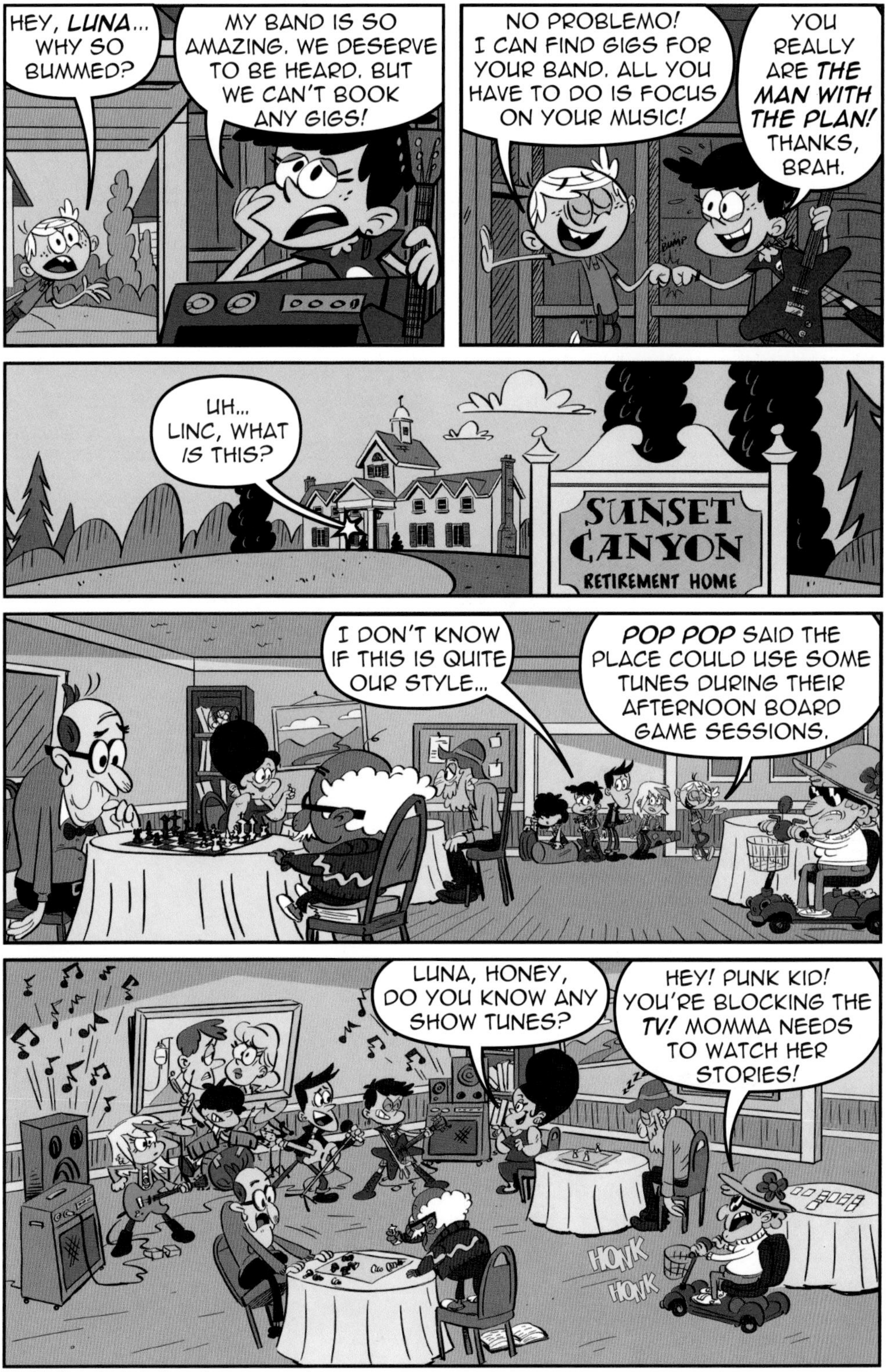
HEY, LUNA... WHY SO BUMMED?
MY BAND IS SO AMAZING. WE DESERVE TO BE HEARD. BUT WE CAN'T BOOK ANY GIGS!
NO PROBLEMO! I CAN FIND GIGS FOR YOUR BAND. ALL YOU HAVE TO DO IS FOCUS ON YOUR MUSIC!
YOU REALLY ARE THE MAN WITH THE PLAN! THANKS, BRAH.
BUMP
UH... LINC, WHAT IS THIS?
SUNSET CANYON
RETIREMENT HOME
I DON'T KNOW IF THIS IS QUITE OUR STYLE...
POP POP SAID THE PLACE COULD USE SOME TUNES DURING THEIR AFTERNOON BOARD GAME SESSIONS.
LUNA, HONEY, DO YOU KNOW ANY SHOW TUNES?
HEY! PUNK KID! YOU'RE BLOCKING THE TV! MOMMA NEEDS TO WATCH HER STORIES!
HONK
HONK

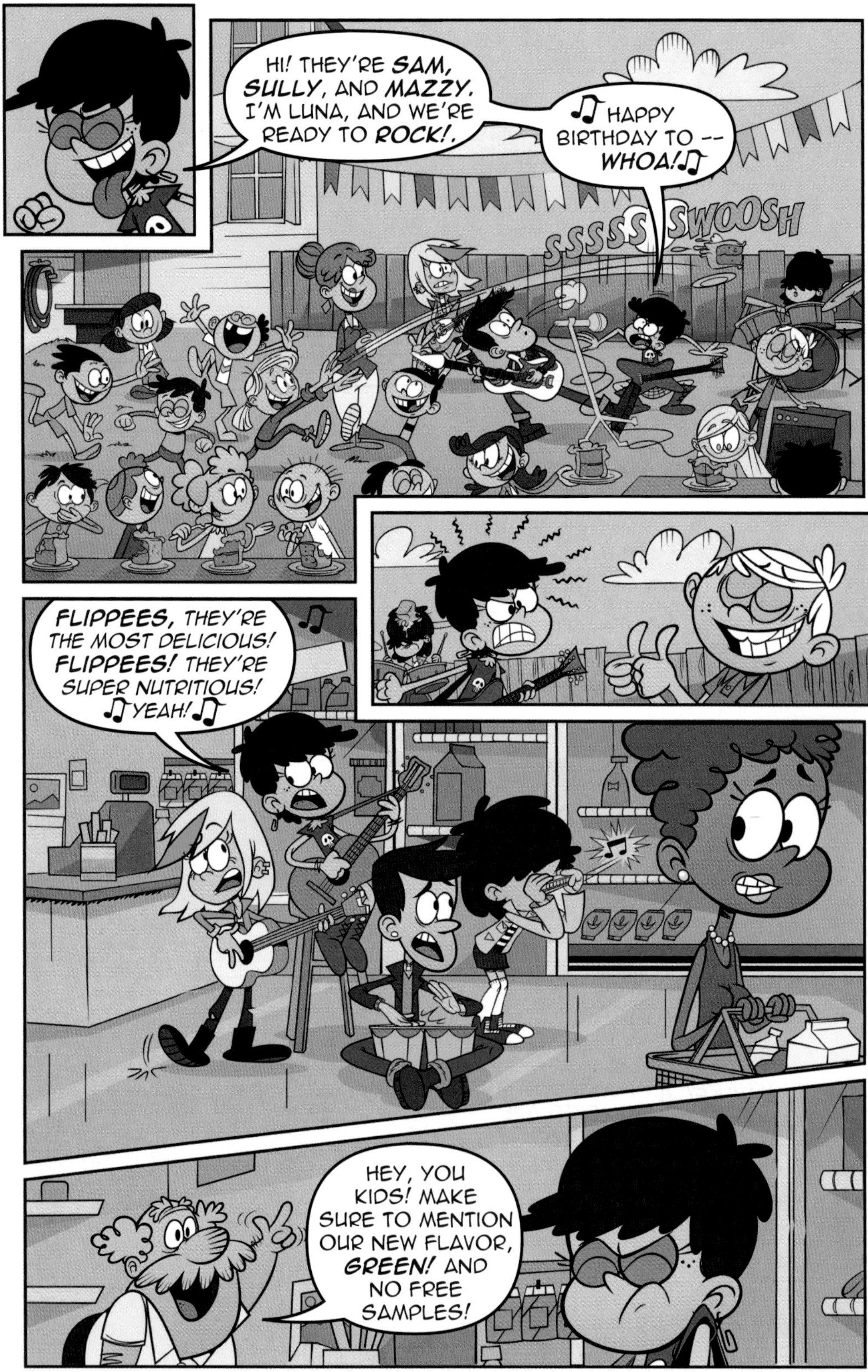
HI! THEY'RE SAM, SULLY, AND MAZZY. I'M LUNA, AND WE'RE READY TO ROCK!.
♫ HAPPY BIRTHDAY TO -- WHOA!♫
SSSSS SWOOSH
FLIPPEES, THEY'RE THE MOST DELICIOUS! FLIPPEES! THEY'RE SUPER NUTRITIOUS! ♫YEAH!♫
HEY, YOU KIDS! MAKE SURE TO MENTION OUR NEW FLAVOR, GREEN! AND NO FREE SAMPLES!

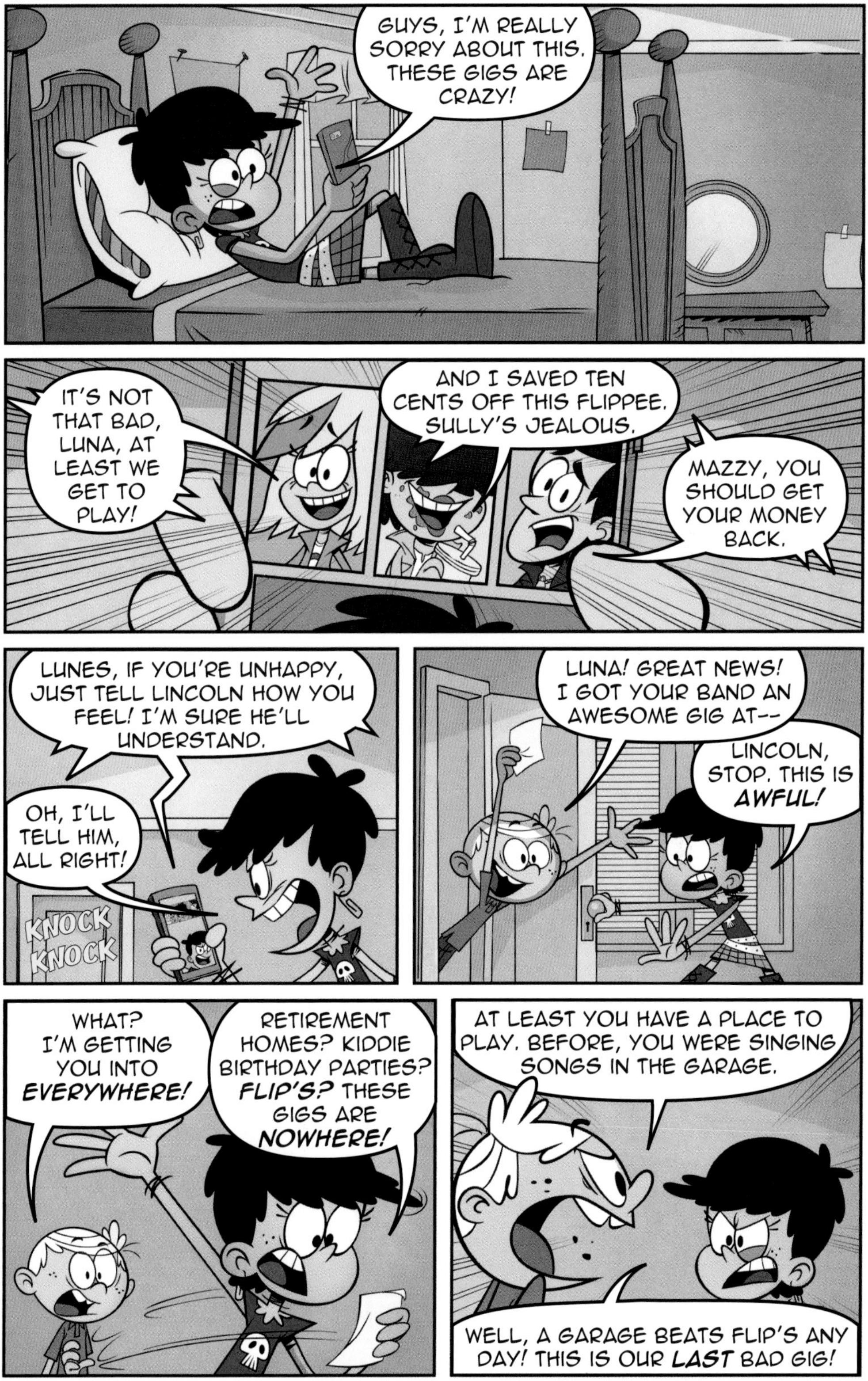
GUYS, I'M REALLY SORRY ABOUT THIS. THESE GIGS ARE CRAZY!
IT'S NOT THAT BAD, LUNA, AT LEAST WE GET TO PLAY!
AND I SAVED TEN CENTS OFF THIS FLIPPEE. SULLY'S JEALOUS.
MAZZY, YOU SHOULD GET YOUR MONEY BACK.
LUNES, IF YOU'RE UNHAPPY, JUST TELL LINCOLN HOW YOU FEEL! I'M SURE HE'LL UNDERSTAND.
OH, I'LL TELL HIM, ALL RIGHT!
KNOCK KNOCK
LUNA! GREAT NEWS! I GOT YOUR BAND AN AWESOME GIG AT--
LINCOLN, STOP. THIS IS *AWFUL!*
WHAT? I'M GETTING YOU INTO *EVERYWHERE!*
RETIREMENT HOMES? KIDDIE BIRTHDAY PARTIES? *FLIP'S?* THESE GIGS ARE *NOWHERE!*
AT LEAST YOU HAVE A PLACE TO PLAY. BEFORE, YOU WERE SINGING SONGS IN THE GARAGE.
WELL, A GARAGE BEATS FLIP'S ANY DAY! THIS IS OUR *LAST* BAD GIG!

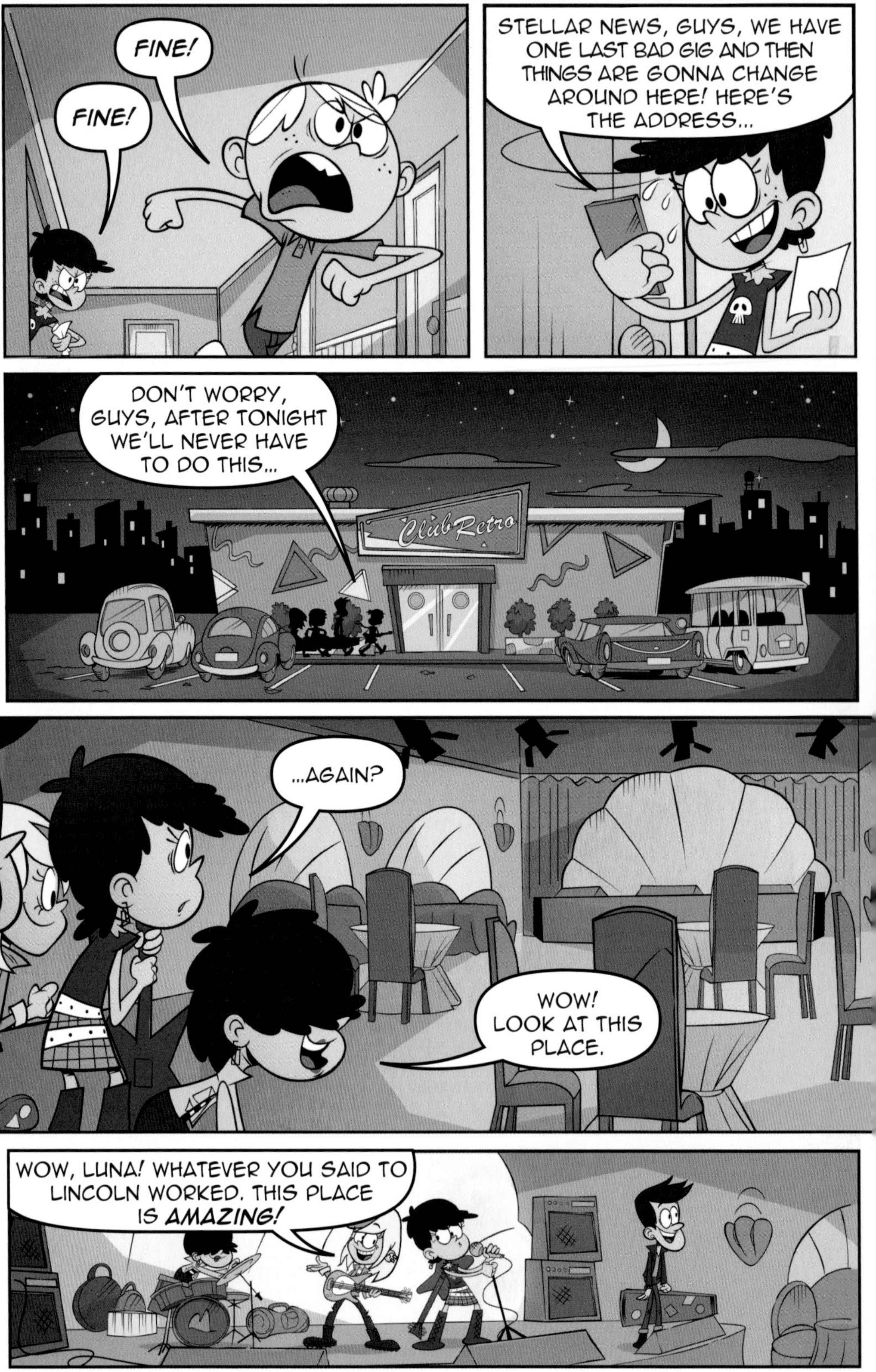

FINE!
FINE!
STELLAR NEWS, GUYS, WE HAVE ONE LAST BAD GIG AND THEN THINGS ARE GONNA CHANGE AROUND HERE! HERE'S THE ADDRESS...
DON'T WORRY, GUYS, AFTER TONIGHT WE'LL NEVER HAVE TO DO THIS...
Club Retro
...AGAIN?
WOW! LOOK AT THIS PLACE.
WOW, LUNA! WHATEVER YOU SAID TO LINCOLN WORKED. THIS PLACE IS ***AMAZING!***

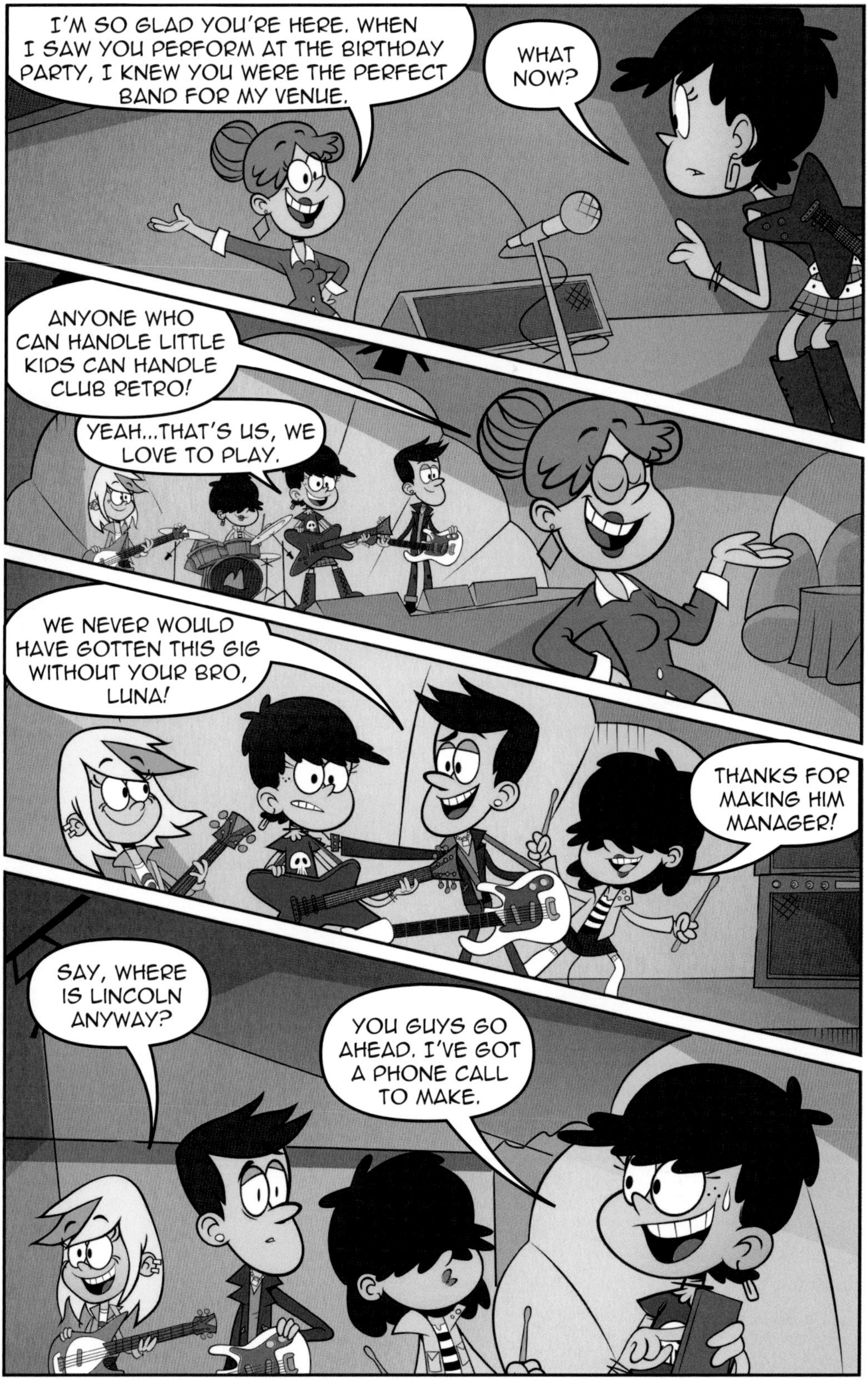

I'M SO GLAD YOU'RE HERE. WHEN I SAW YOU PERFORM AT THE BIRTHDAY PARTY, I KNEW YOU WERE THE PERFECT BAND FOR MY VENUE.
WHAT NOW?
ANYONE WHO CAN HANDLE LITTLE KIDS CAN HANDLE CLUB RETRO!
YEAH...THAT'S US, WE LOVE TO PLAY.
WE NEVER WOULD HAVE GOTTEN THIS GIG WITHOUT YOUR BRO, LUNA!
THANKS FOR MAKING HIM MANAGER!
SAY, WHERE IS LINCOLN ANYWAY?
YOU GUYS GO AHEAD. I'VE GOT A PHONE CALL TO MAKE.

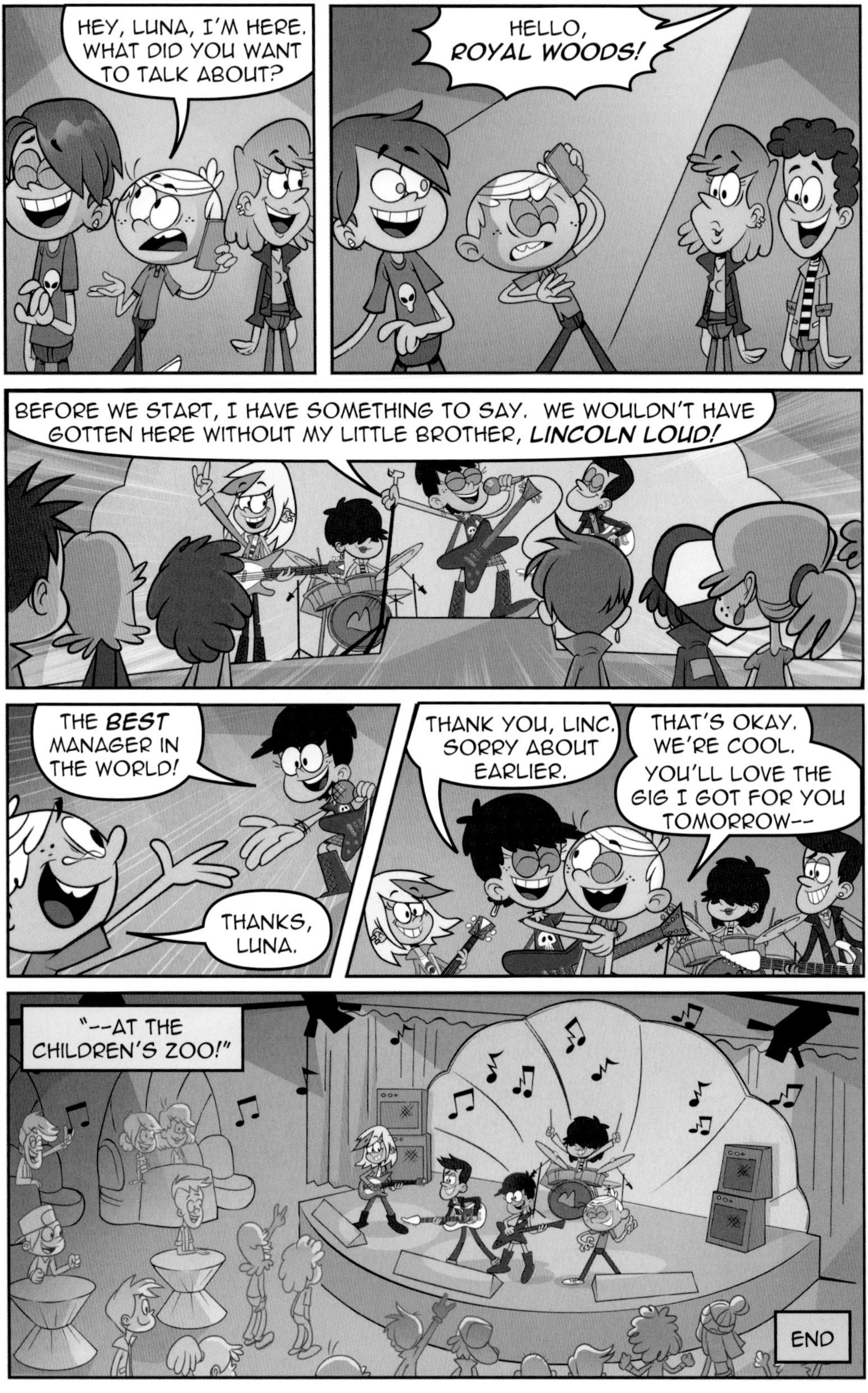
HEY, LUNA, I'M HERE. WHAT DID YOU WANT TO TALK ABOUT?
HELLO, **ROYAL WOODS!**
BEFORE WE START, I HAVE SOMETHING TO SAY. WE WOULDN'T HAVE GOTTEN HERE WITHOUT MY LITTLE BROTHER, **LINCOLN LOUD!**
THE **BEST** MANAGER IN THE WORLD!
THANKS, LUNA.
THANK YOU, LINC. SORRY ABOUT EARLIER.
THAT'S OKAY. WE'RE COOL. YOU'LL LOVE THE GIG I GOT FOR YOU TOMORROW--
"--AT THE CHILDREN'S ZOO!"
END

"FACE VALUE"

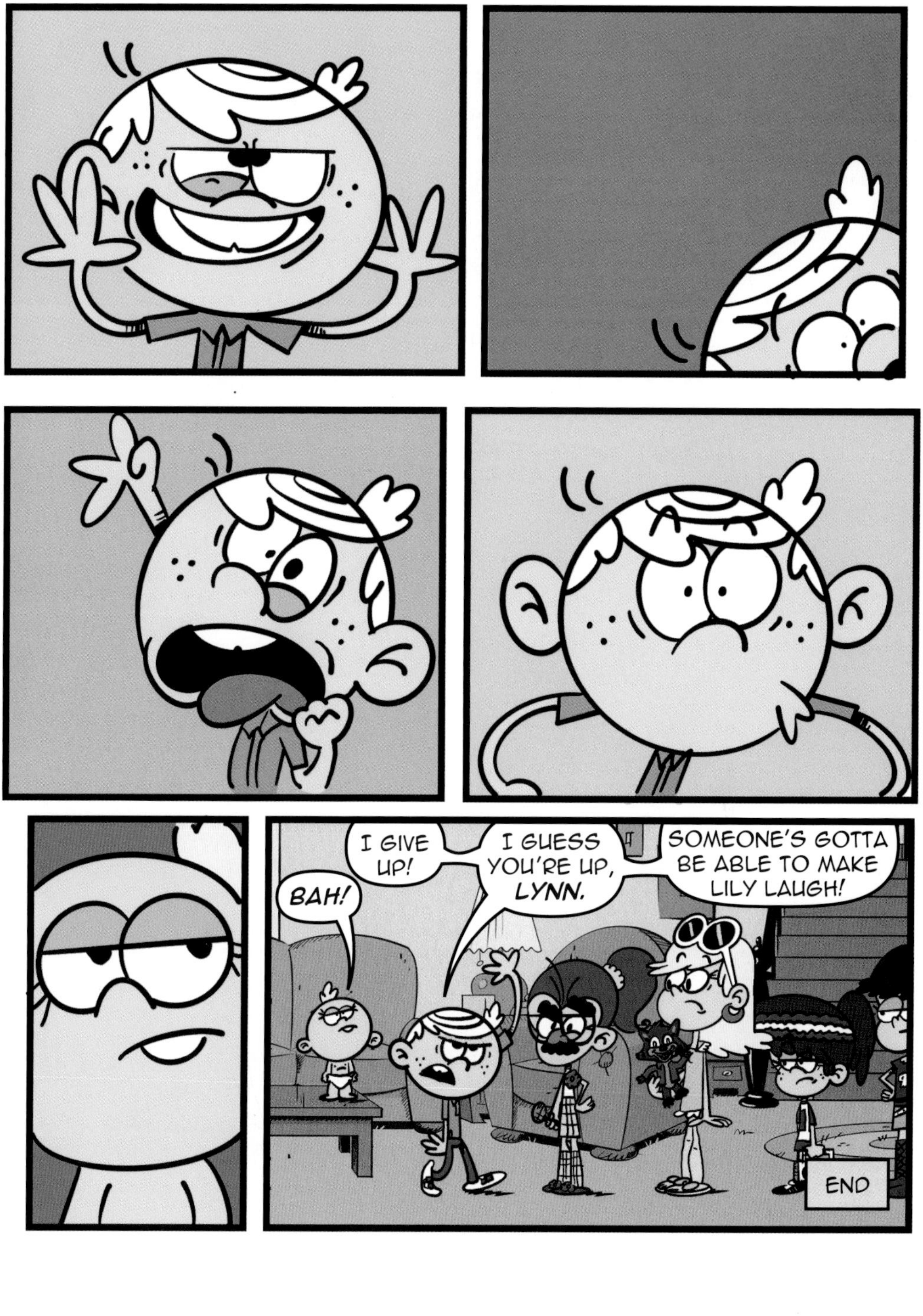
BAH!
I GIVE UP!
I GUESS YOU'RE UP, LYNN.
SOMEONE'S GOTTA BE ABLE TO MAKE LILY LAUGH!
END

"IMPROMPTOOT CONCERT"

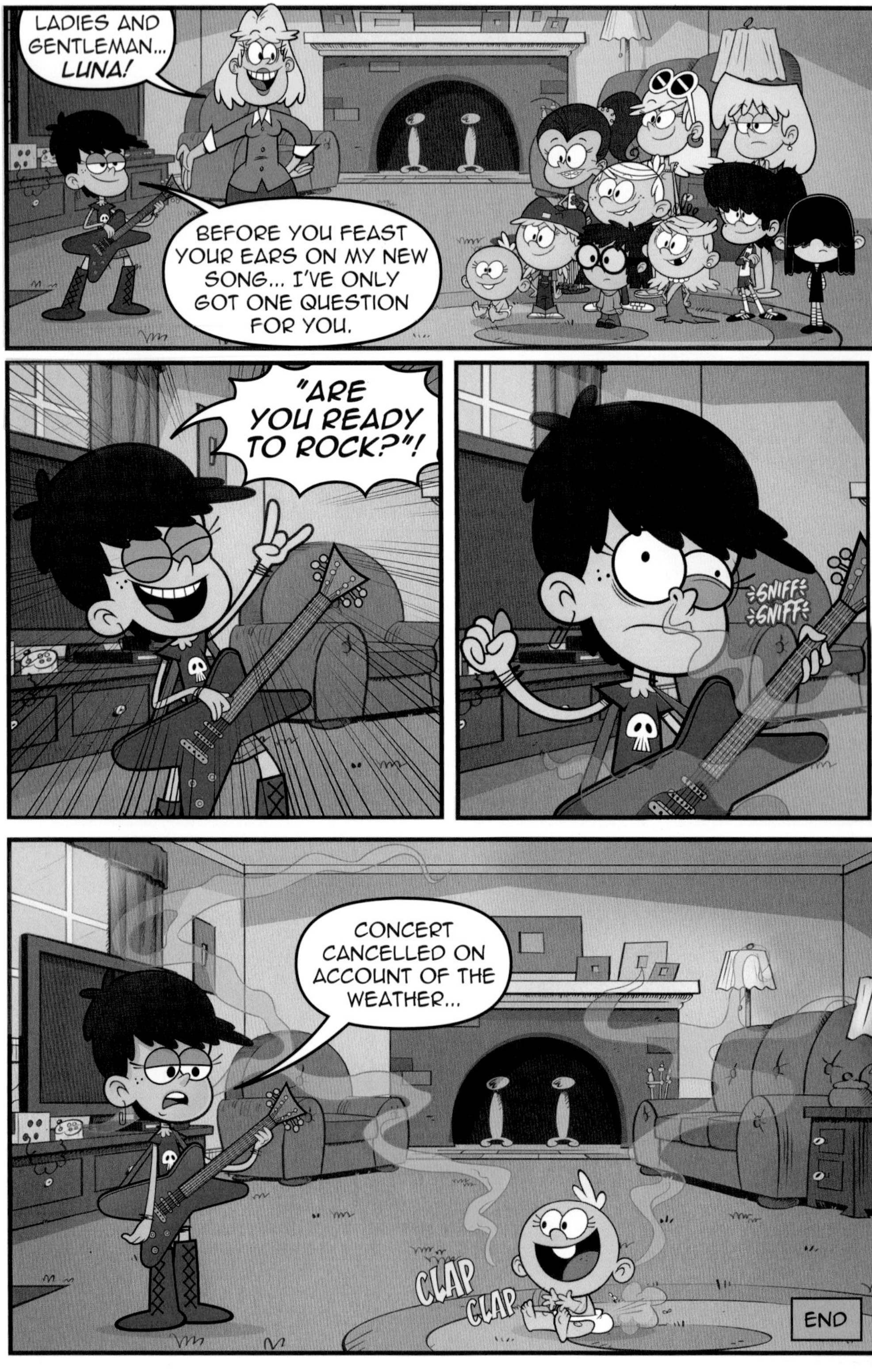
LADIES AND GENTLEMAN... LUNA!
BEFORE YOU FEAST YOUR EARS ON MY NEW SONG... I'VE ONLY GOT ONE QUESTION FOR YOU.
"ARE YOU READY TO ROCK?"!
SNIFF SNIFF
CONCERT CANCELLED ON ACCOUNT OF THE WEATHER...
CLAP CLAP
END

"CRUMBINAL JUSTICE"

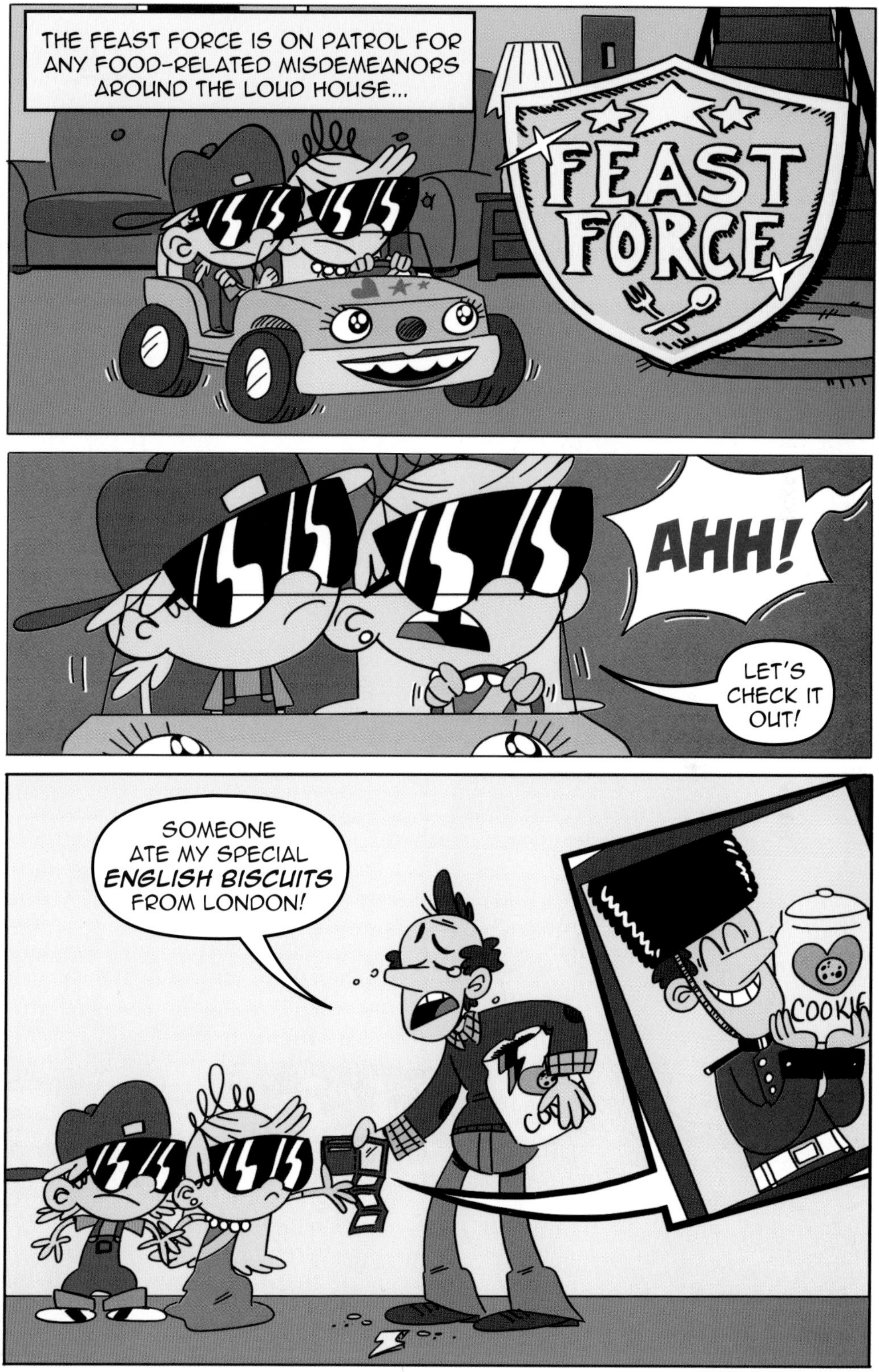
THE FEAST FORCE IS ON PATROL FOR ANY FOOD-RELATED MISDEMEANORS AROUND THE LOUD HOUSE...
FEAST FORCE
AHH!
LET'S CHECK IT OUT!
SOMEONE ATE MY SPECIAL ENGLISH BISCUITS FROM LONDON!
COOKIE

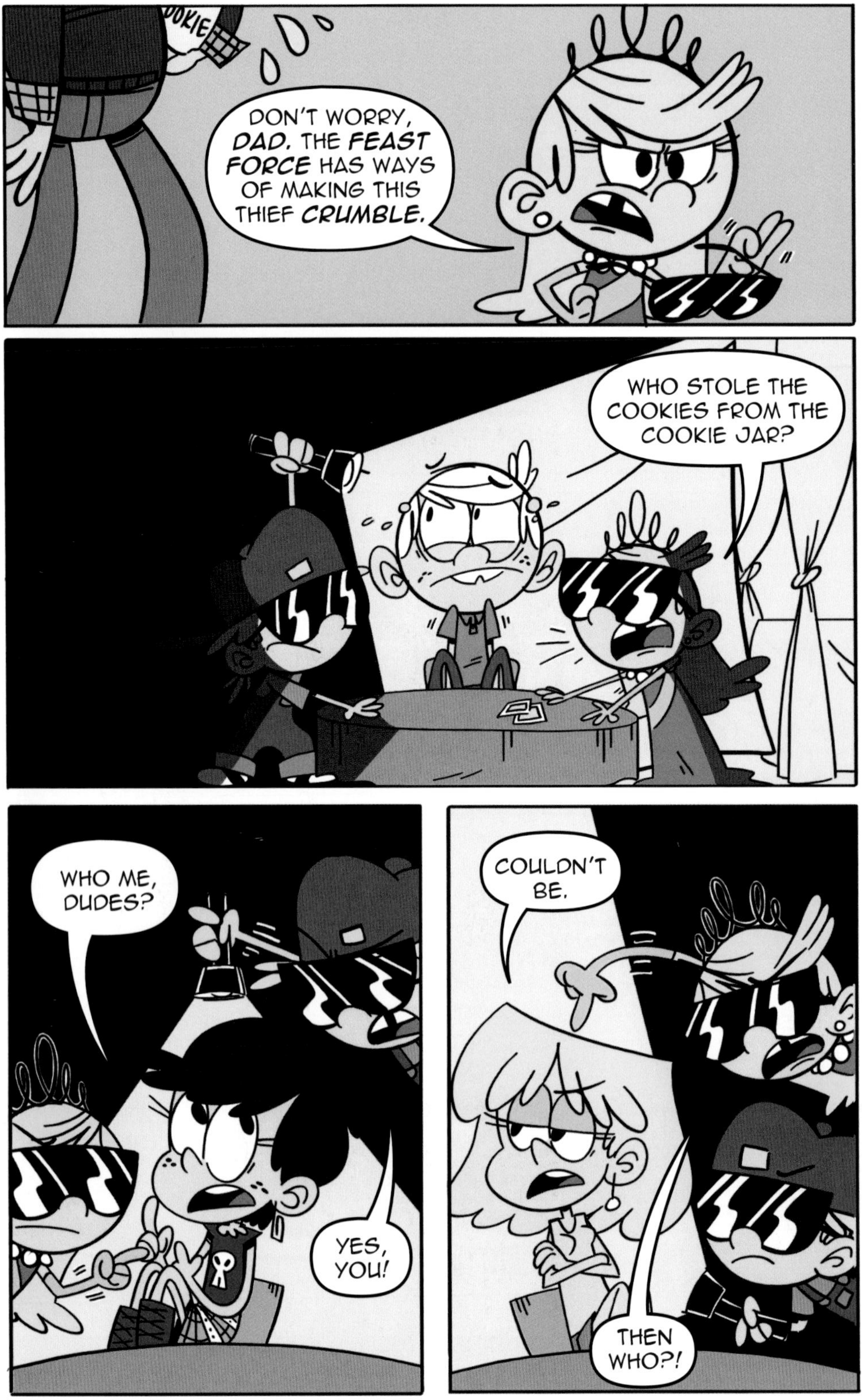
OOKIE
DON'T WORRY, DAD. THE FEAST FORCE HAS WAYS OF MAKING THIS THIEF CRUMBLE.
WHO STOLE THE COOKIES FROM THE COOKIE JAR?
WHO ME, DUDES?
YES, YOU!
COULDN'T BE.
THEN WHO?!

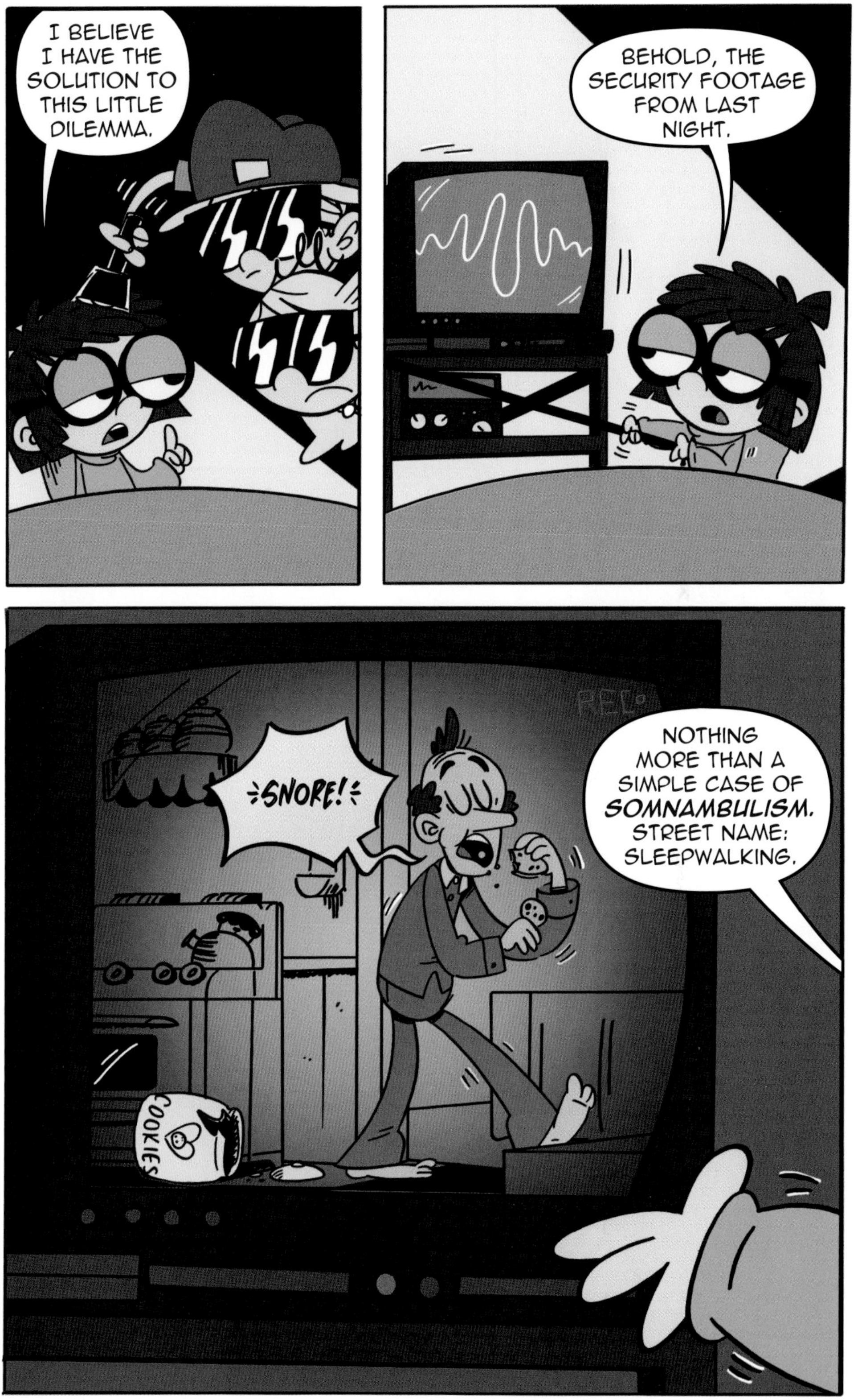
I BELIEVE I HAVE THE SOLUTION TO THIS LITTLE DILEMMA.
BEHOLD, THE SECURITY FOOTAGE FROM LAST NIGHT.
REC
SNORE!
NOTHING MORE THAN A SIMPLE CASE OF SOMNAMBULISM. STREET NAME: SLEEPWALKING.
COOKIES

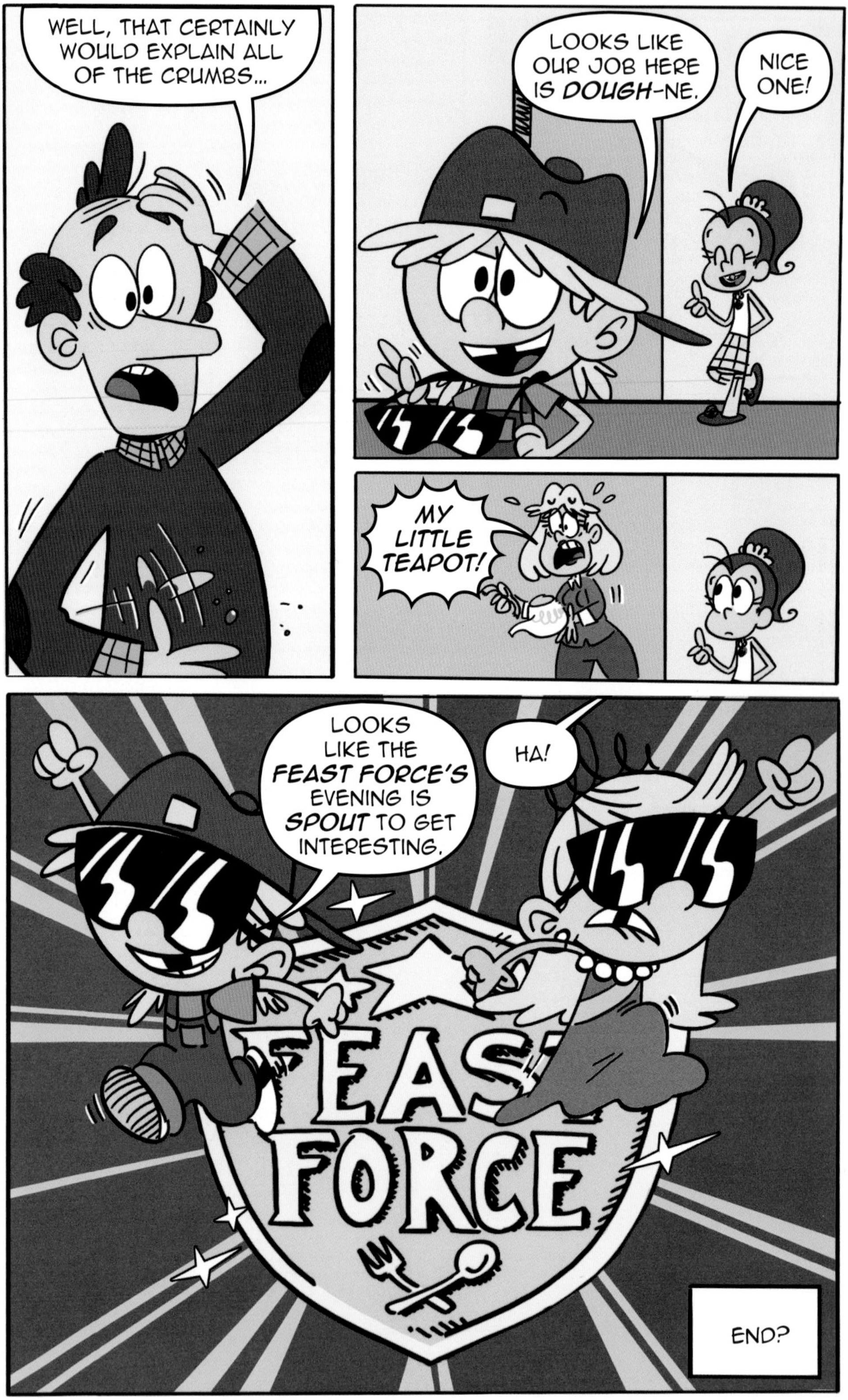
WELL, THAT CERTAINLY WOULD EXPLAIN ALL OF THE CRUMBS...
LOOKS LIKE OUR JOB HERE IS DOUGH-NE.
NICE ONE!
MY LITTLE TEAPOT!
LOOKS LIKE THE FEAST FORCE'S EVENING IS SPOUT TO GET INTERESTING.
HA!
FEAST FORCE
END?

"LOW ACHIEVEMENT"

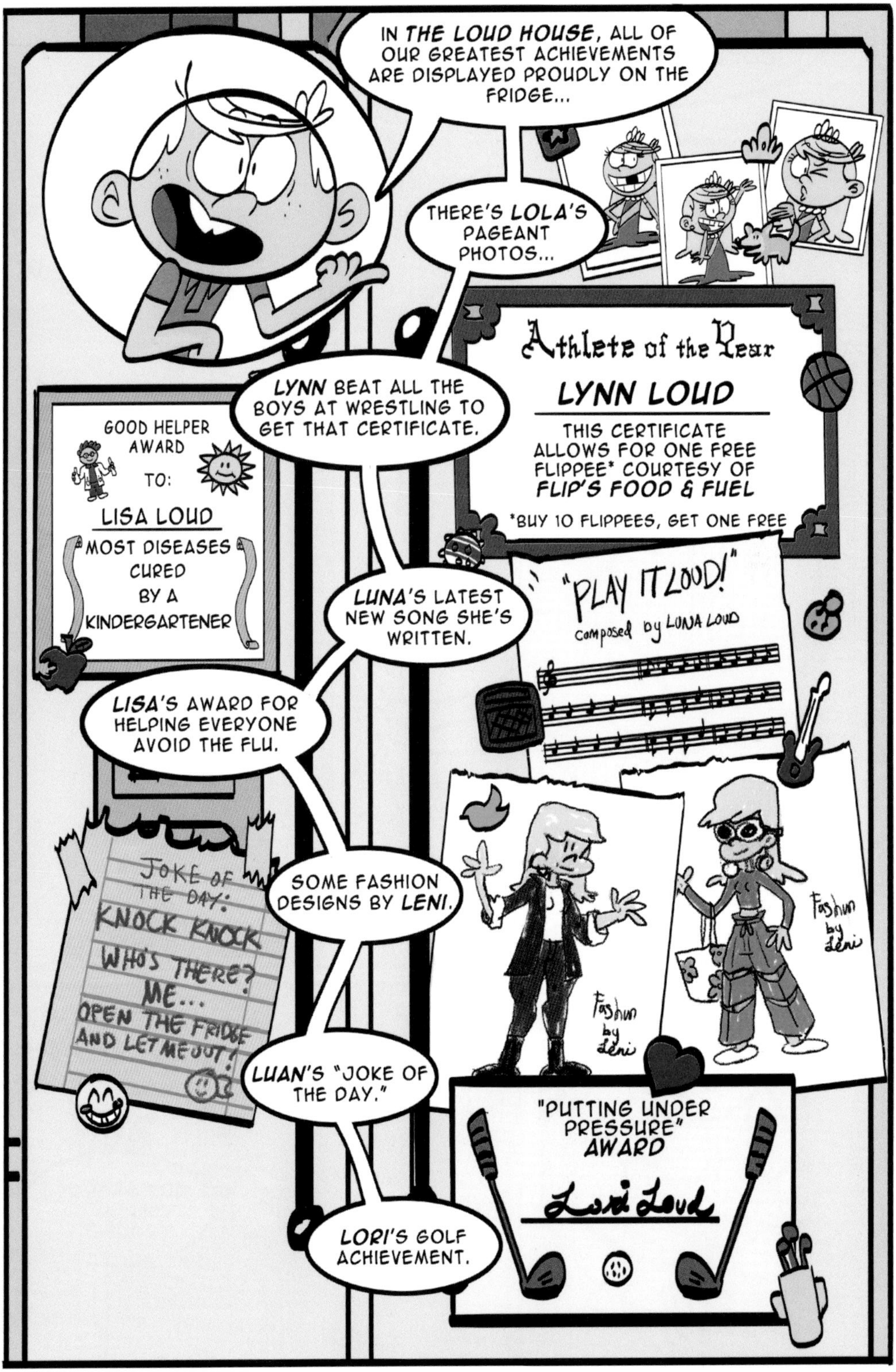

IN THE LOUD HOUSE, ALL OF OUR GREATEST ACHIEVEMENTS ARE DISPLAYED PROUDLY ON THE FRIDGE...
THERE'S LOLA'S PAGEANT PHOTOS...
Athlete of the Year
LYNN LOUD
THIS CERTIFICATE ALLOWS FOR ONE FREE FLIPPEE* COURTESY OF FLIP'S FOOD & FUEL
*BUY 10 FLIPPEES, GET ONE FREE
LYNN BEAT ALL THE BOYS AT WRESTLING TO GET THAT CERTIFICATE.
GOOD HELPER AWARD
TO:
LISA LOUD
MOST DISEASES CURED BY A KINDERGARTENER
"PLAY IT LOUD!"
composed by LUNA LOUD
LUNA'S LATEST NEW SONG SHE'S WRITTEN.
LISA'S AWARD FOR HELPING EVERYONE AVOID THE FLU.
JOKE OF THE DAY:
KNOCK KNOCK
WHO'S THERE?
ME...
OPEN THE FRIDGE AND LET ME OUT!
SOME FASHION DESIGNS BY LENI.
Fashun by Leni
Fashun by Leni
LUAN'S "JOKE OF THE DAY."
"PUTTING UNDER PRESSURE" AWARD
Lori Loud
LORI'S GOLF ACHIEVEMENT.

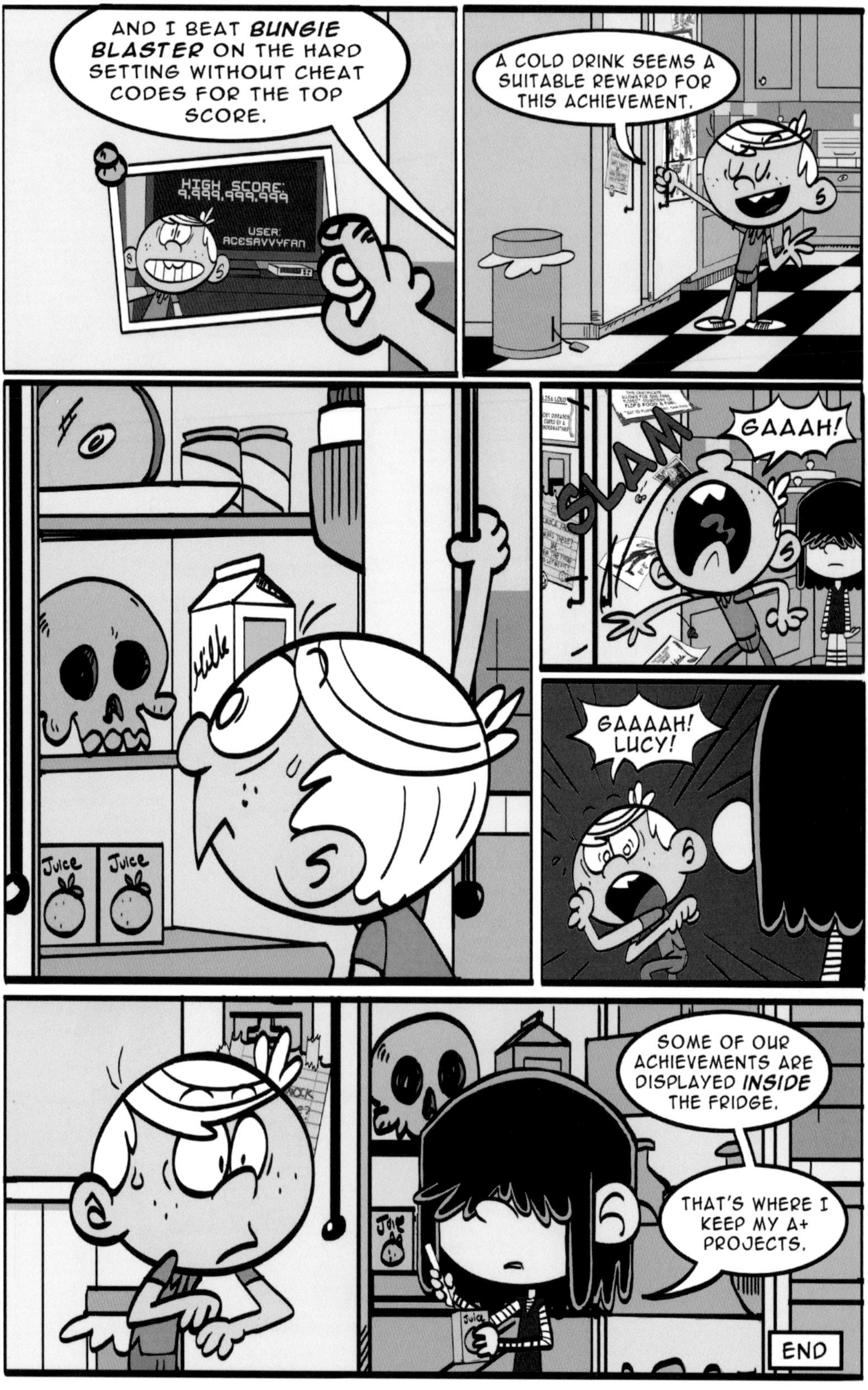
AND I BEAT *BUNGIE BLASTER* ON THE HARD SETTING WITHOUT CHEAT CODES FOR THE TOP SCORE.
HIGH SCORE: 9,999,999,999
USER: ACESAVVYFAN
A COLD DRINK SEEMS A SUITABLE REWARD FOR THIS ACHIEVEMENT.
Milk
Juice
Juice
SLAM
GAAAH!
GAAAAH! LUCY!
SOME OF OUR ACHIEVEMENTS ARE DISPLAYED *INSIDE* THE FRIDGE.
THAT'S WHERE I KEEP MY A+ PROJECTS.
END

"THE LOUD HOUSE GAMES!"

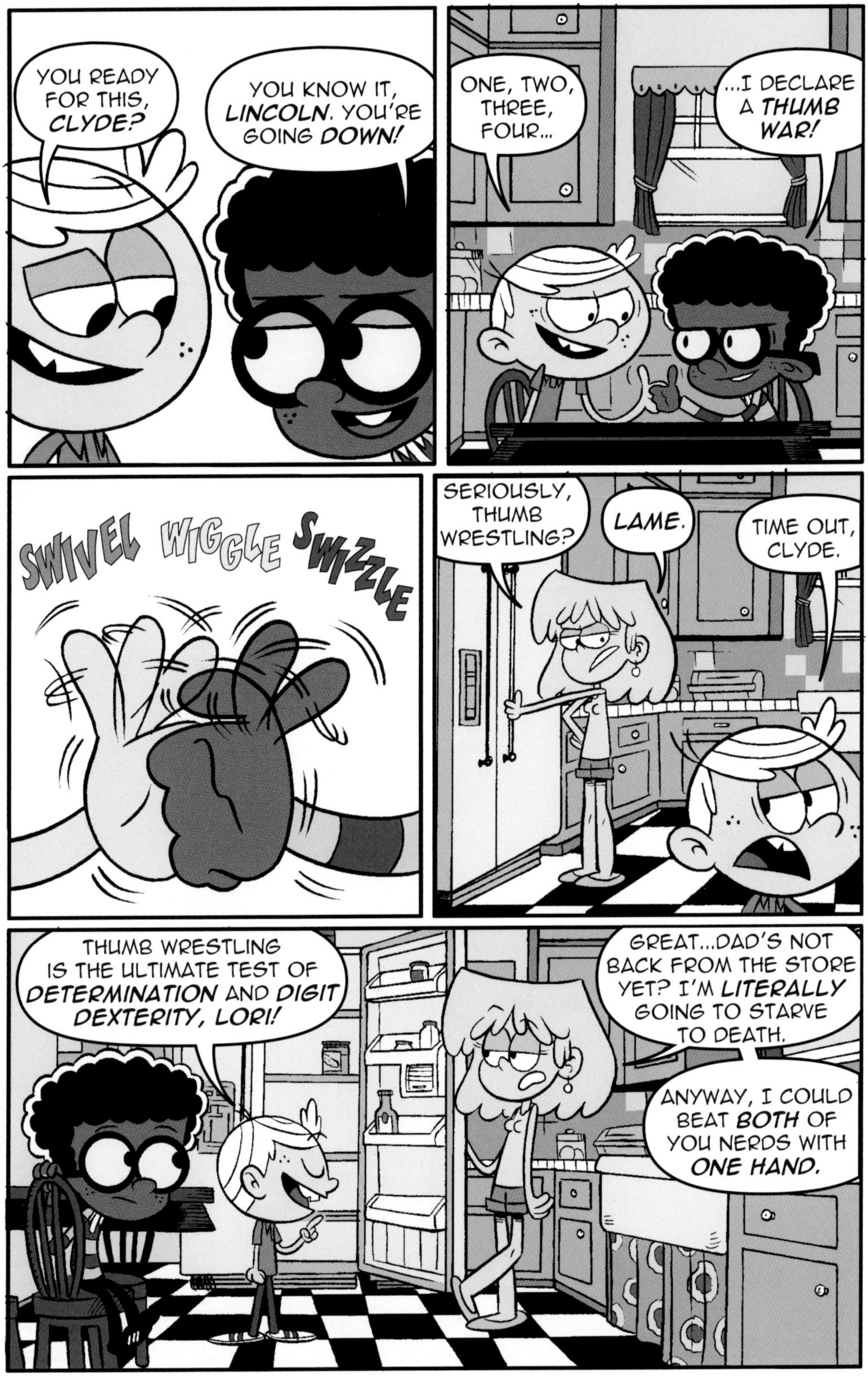

YOU READY FOR THIS, *CLYDE?*
YOU KNOW IT, *LINCOLN*. YOU'RE GOING *DOWN!*
ONE, TWO, THREE, FOUR...
...I DECLARE A *THUMB WAR!*
SWIVEL
WIGGLE
SWIZZLE
SERIOUSLY, THUMB WRESTLING?
LAME.
TIME OUT, CLYDE.
THUMB WRESTLING IS THE ULTIMATE TEST OF *DETERMINATION* AND *DIGIT DEXTERITY, LORI!*
GREAT...DAD'S NOT BACK FROM THE STORE YET? I'M *LITERALLY* GOING TO STARVE TO DEATH.
ANYWAY, I COULD BEAT *BOTH* OF YOU NERDS WITH *ONE HAND.*

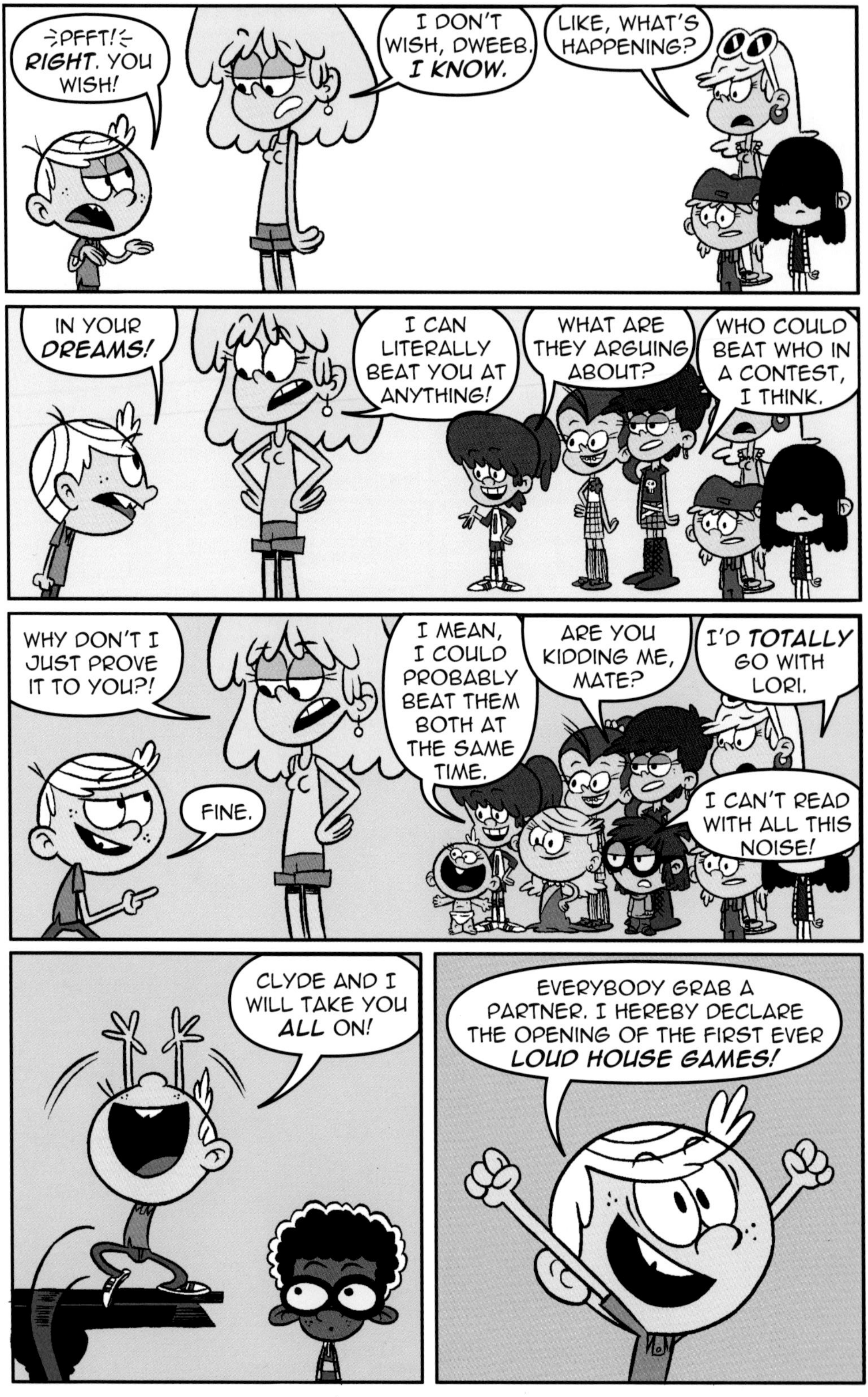

PFFT! RIGHT. YOU WISH!
I DON'T WISH, DWEEB. I KNOW.
LIKE, WHAT'S HAPPENING?
IN YOUR DREAMS!
I CAN LITERALLY BEAT YOU AT ANYTHING!
WHAT ARE THEY ARGUING ABOUT?
WHO COULD BEAT WHO IN A CONTEST, I THINK.
WHY DON'T I JUST PROVE IT TO YOU?!
FINE.
I MEAN, I COULD PROBABLY BEAT THEM BOTH AT THE SAME TIME.
ARE YOU KIDDING ME, MATE?
I'D TOTALLY GO WITH LORI.
I CAN'T READ WITH ALL THIS NOISE!
CLYDE AND I WILL TAKE YOU ALL ON!
EVERYBODY GRAB A PARTNER. I HEREBY DECLARE THE OPENING OF THE FIRST EVER LOUD HOUSE GAMES!

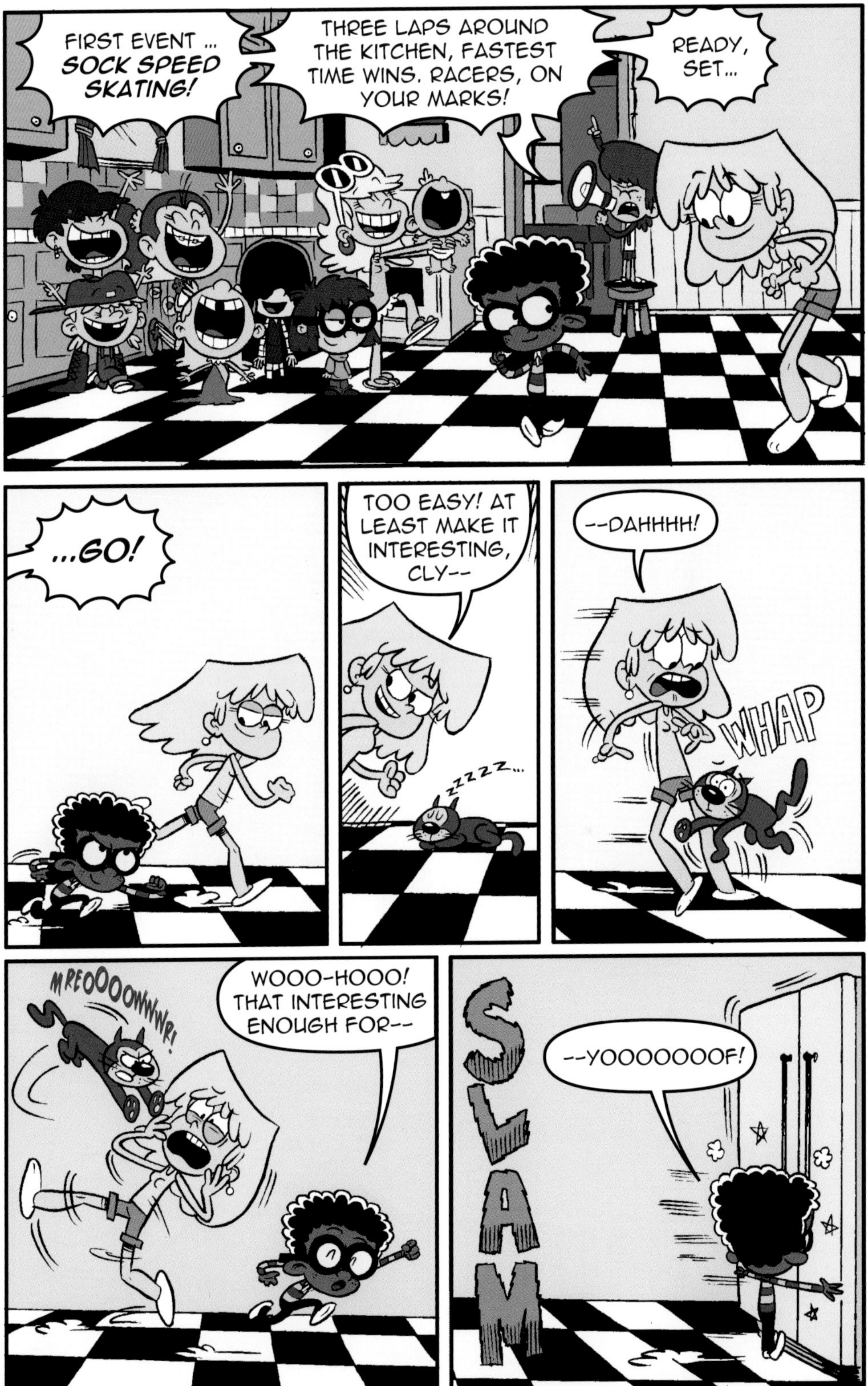
FIRST EVENT ... SOCK SPEED SKATING!
THREE LAPS AROUND THE KITCHEN, FASTEST TIME WINS. RACERS, ON YOUR MARKS!
READY, SET...
...GO!
TOO EASY! AT LEAST MAKE IT INTERESTING, CLY--
ZZZZZ...
--DAHHHH!
WHAP
MREOOOOWWWR!
WOOO-HOOO! THAT INTERESTING ENOUGH FOR--
SLAM
--YOOOOOOOF!

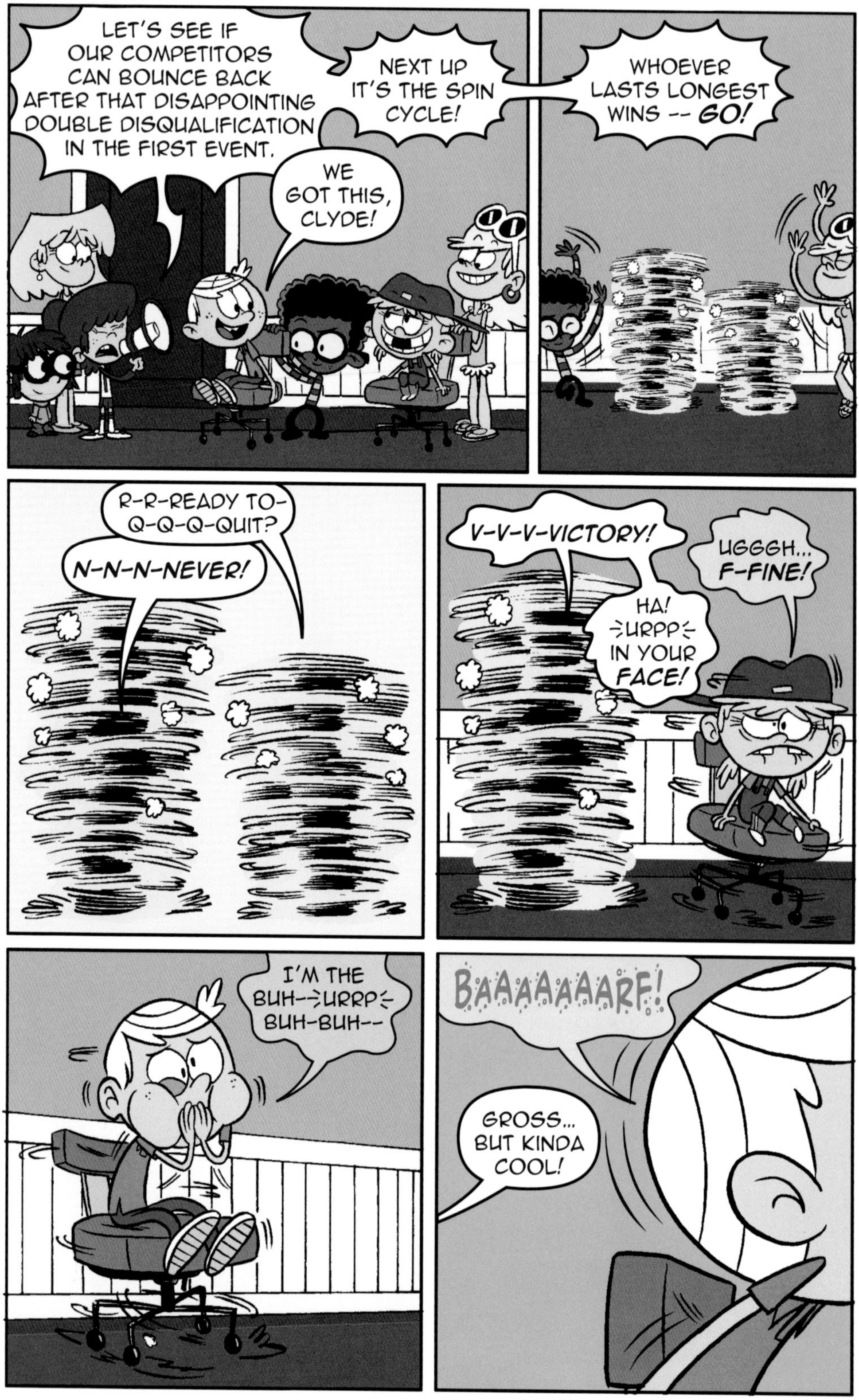
LET'S SEE IF OUR COMPETITORS CAN BOUNCE BACK AFTER THAT DISAPPOINTING DOUBLE DISQUALIFICATION IN THE FIRST EVENT.
NEXT UP IT'S THE SPIN CYCLE!
WE GOT THIS, CLYDE!
WHOEVER LASTS LONGEST WINS -- GO!
R-R-READY TO-Q-Q-Q-QUIT?
N-N-N-NEVER!
V-V-V-VICTORY!
HA! URPP IN YOUR FACE!
UGGGH... F-FINE!
I'M THE BUH--URRP BUH-BUH--
BAAAAAAARF!
GROSS... BUT KINDA COOL!

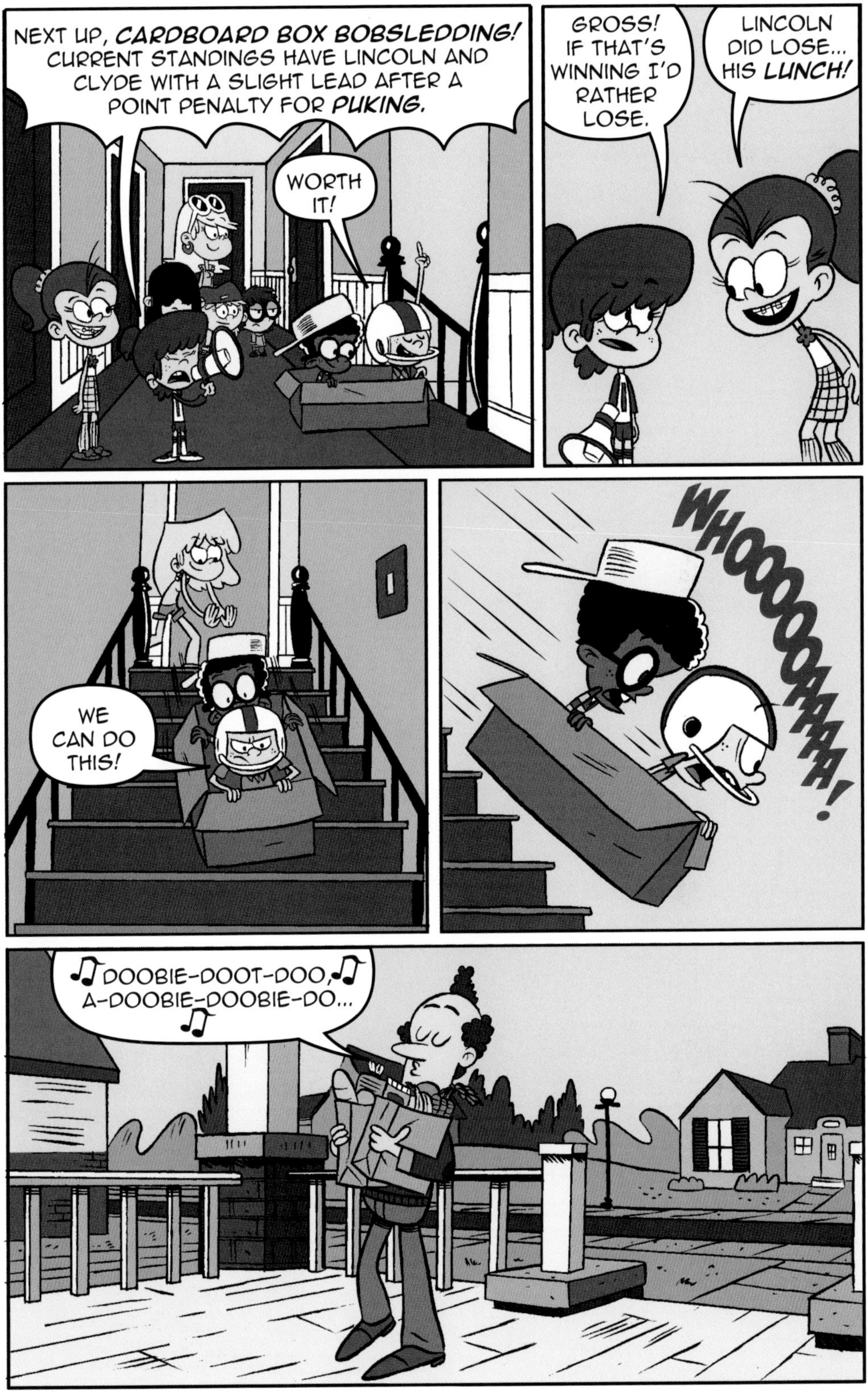
NEXT UP, CARDBOARD BOX BOBSLEDDING! CURRENT STANDINGS HAVE LINCOLN AND CLYDE WITH A SLIGHT LEAD AFTER A POINT PENALTY FOR PUKING.
WORTH IT!
GROSS! IF THAT'S WINNING I'D RATHER LOSE.
LINCOLN DID LOSE... HIS LUNCH!
WE CAN DO THIS!
WHOOOOOAAAA!
♫DOOBIE-DOOT-DOO,♫ A-DOOBIE-DOOBIE-DO... ♫

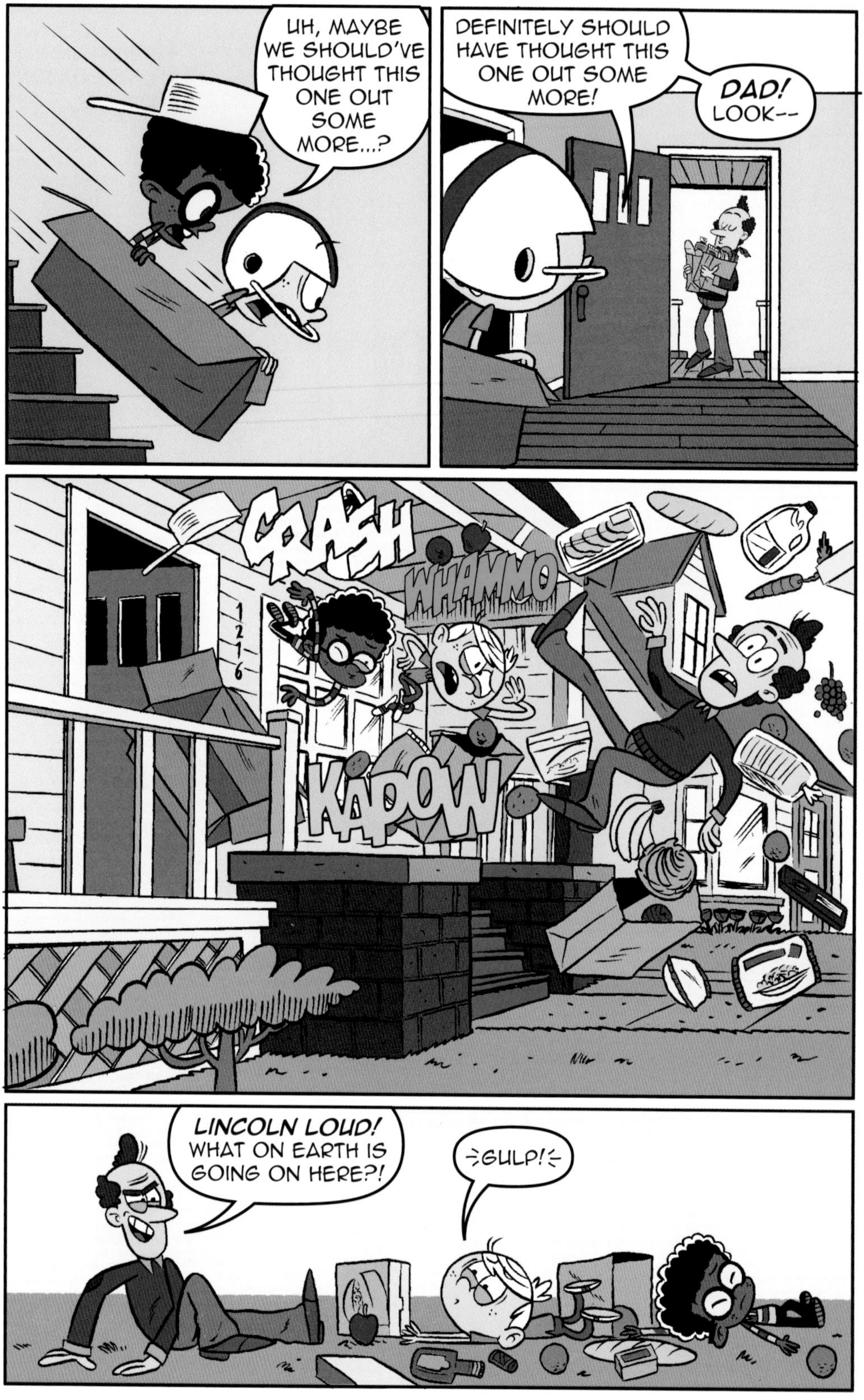
UH, MAYBE WE SHOULD'VE THOUGHT THIS ONE OUT SOME MORE...?
DEFINITELY SHOULD HAVE THOUGHT THIS ONE OUT SOME MORE!
DAD! LOOK--
CRASH
WHAMMO
1216
KAPOW
LINCOLN LOUD! WHAT ON EARTH IS GOING ON HERE?!
GULP!

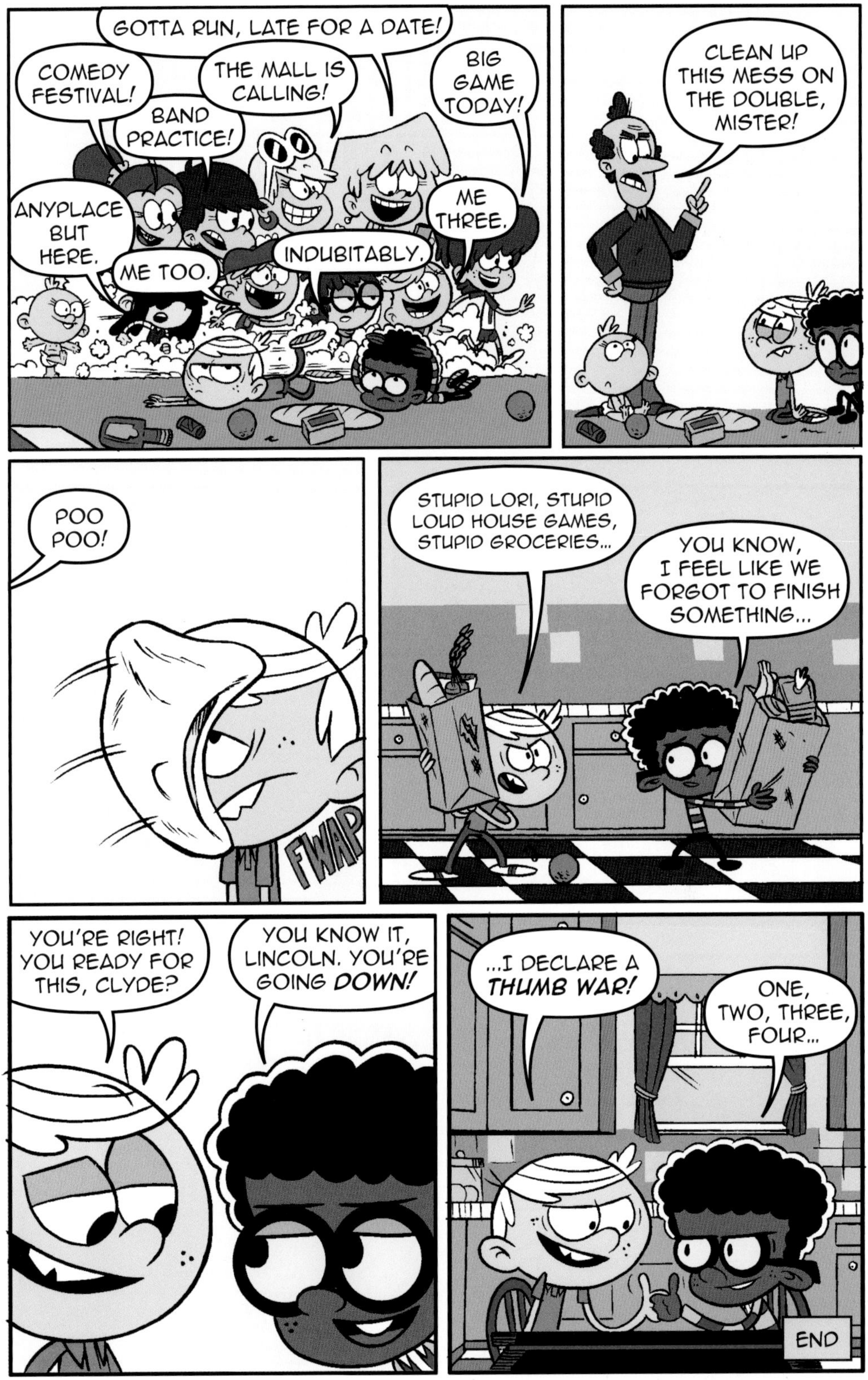
GOTTA RUN, LATE FOR A DATE!
COMEDY FESTIVAL!
THE MALL IS CALLING!
BIG GAME TODAY!
BAND PRACTICE!
ANYPLACE BUT HERE.
ME THREE.
ME TOO.
INDUBITABLY.
CLEAN UP THIS MESS ON THE DOUBLE, MISTER!
POO POO!
FWAP
STUPID LORI, STUPID LOUD HOUSE GAMES, STUPID GROCERIES...
YOU KNOW, I FEEL LIKE WE FORGOT TO FINISH SOMETHING...
YOU'RE RIGHT! YOU READY FOR THIS, CLYDE?
YOU KNOW IT, LINCOLN. YOU'RE GOING *DOWN!*
...I DECLARE A *THUMB WAR!*
ONE, TWO, THREE, FOUR...
END

"FIND OF THE CENTURY"

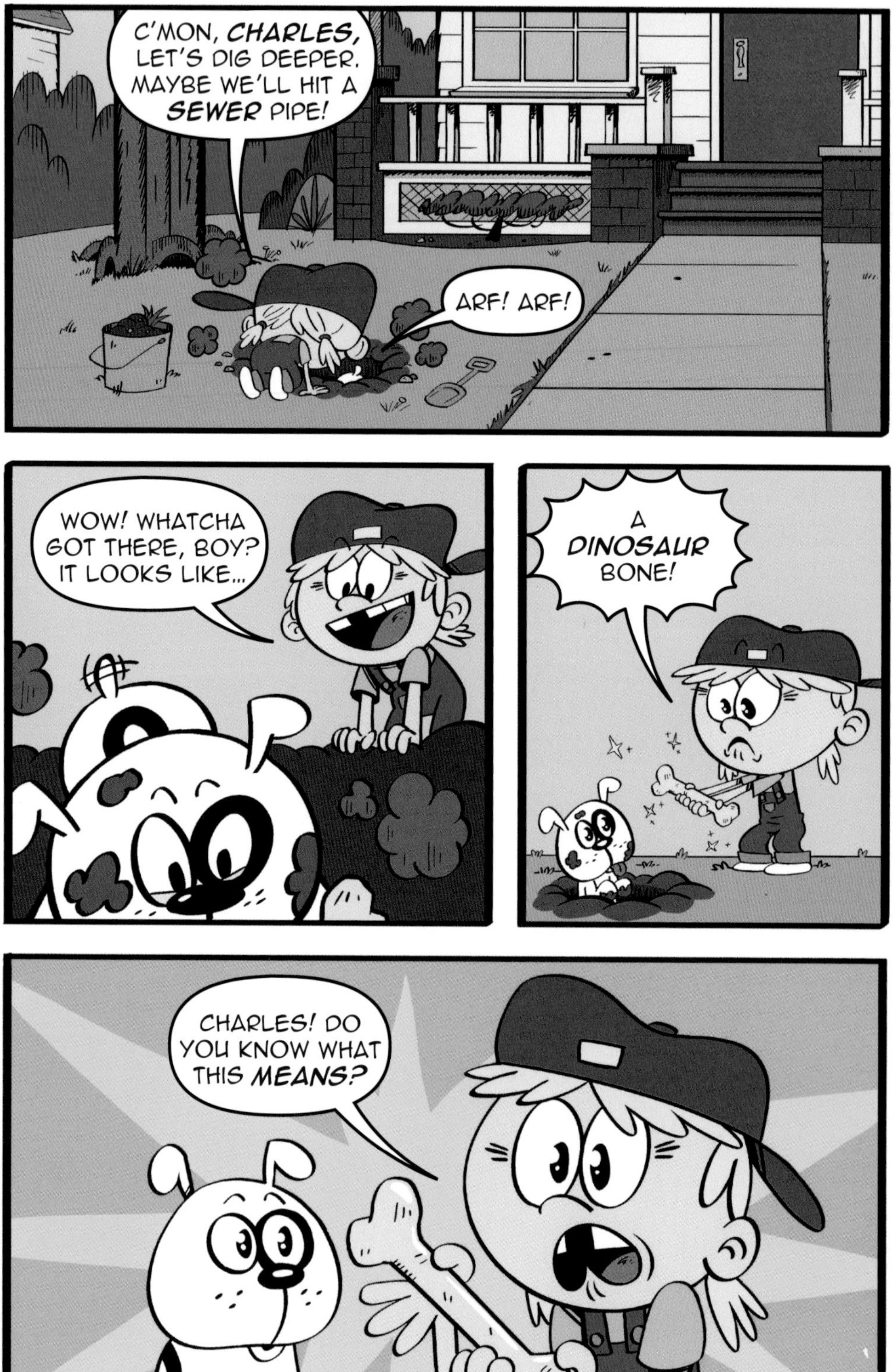

C'MON, CHARLES, LET'S DIG DEEPER. MAYBE WE'LL HIT A SEWER PIPE!
ARF! ARF!
WOW! WHATCHA GOT THERE, BOY? IT LOOKS LIKE...
A DINOSAUR BONE!
CHARLES! DO YOU KNOW WHAT THIS MEANS?

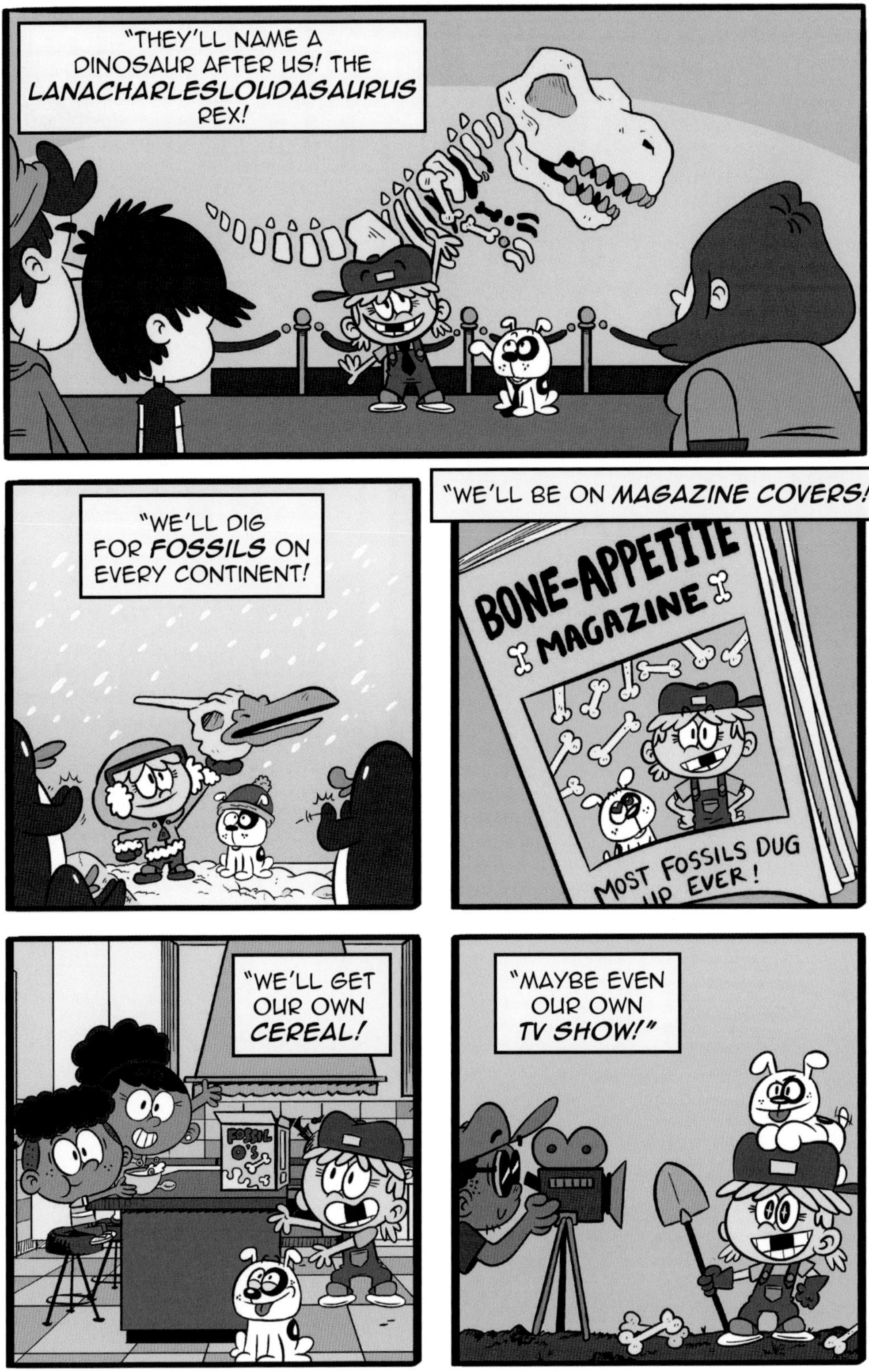
"THEY'LL NAME A DINOSAUR AFTER US! THE *LANACHARLESLOUDASAURUS* REX!
"WE'LL DIG FOR *FOSSILS* ON EVERY CONTINENT!
"WE'LL BE ON *MAGAZINE COVERS!*
BONE-APPETITE MAGAZINE
MOST FOSSILS DUG UP EVER!
"WE'LL GET OUR OWN *CEREAL!*
FOSSIL O'S
"MAYBE EVEN OUR OWN *TV SHOW!*"

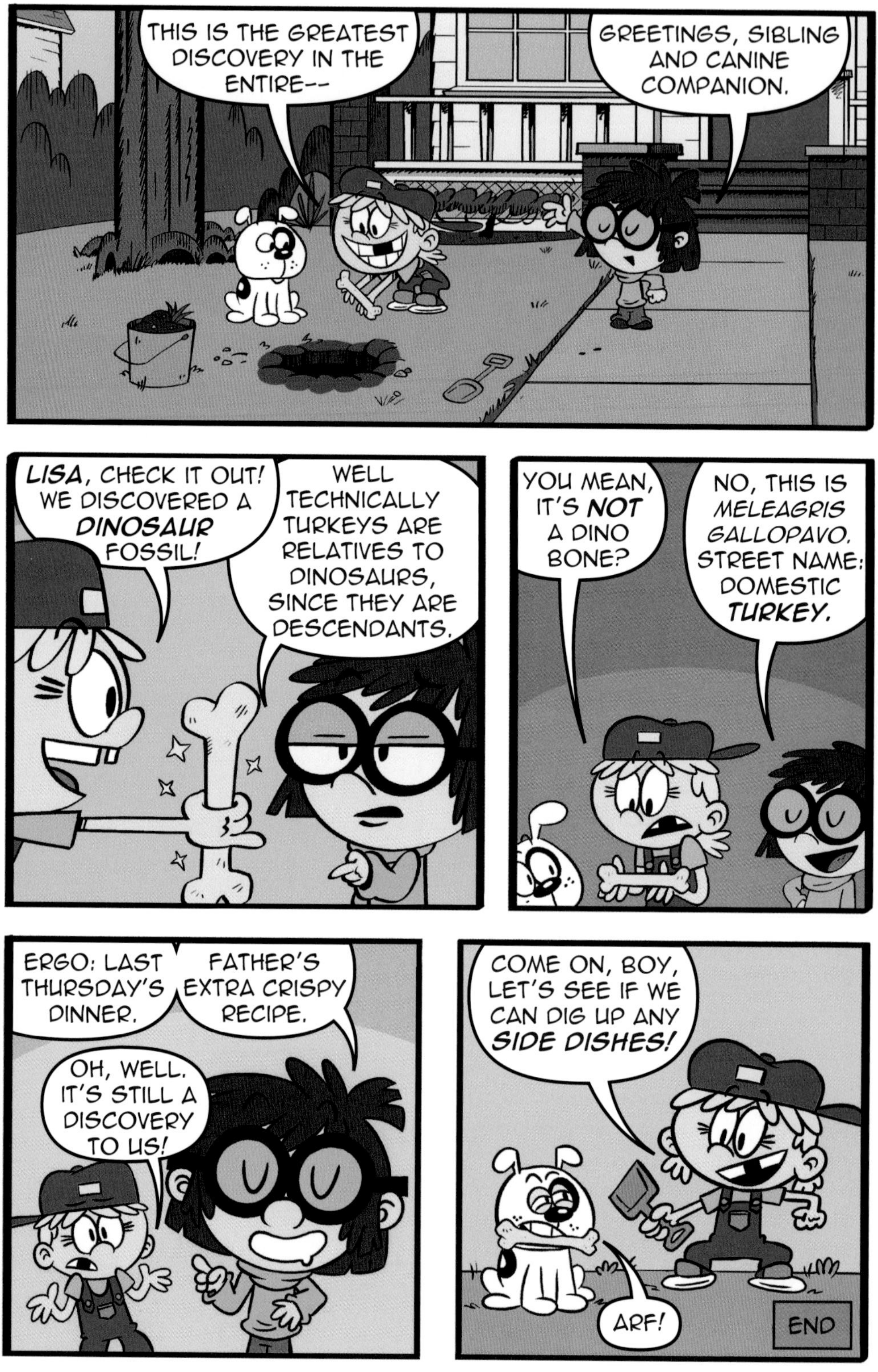

THIS IS THE GREATEST DISCOVERY IN THE ENTIRE--
GREETINGS, SIBLING AND CANINE COMPANION.
LISA, CHECK IT OUT! WE DISCOVERED A DINOSAUR FOSSIL!
WELL TECHNICALLY TURKEYS ARE RELATIVES TO DINOSAURS, SINCE THEY ARE DESCENDANTS.
YOU MEAN, IT'S NOT A DINO BONE?
NO, THIS IS MELEAGRIS GALLOPAVO. STREET NAME: DOMESTIC TURKEY.
ERGO: LAST THURSDAY'S DINNER.
FATHER'S EXTRA CRISPY RECIPE.
OH, WELL. IT'S STILL A DISCOVERY TO US!
COME ON, BOY, LET'S SEE IF WE CAN DIG UP ANY SIDE DISHES!
ARF!
END

"A MONSTER PLAN"

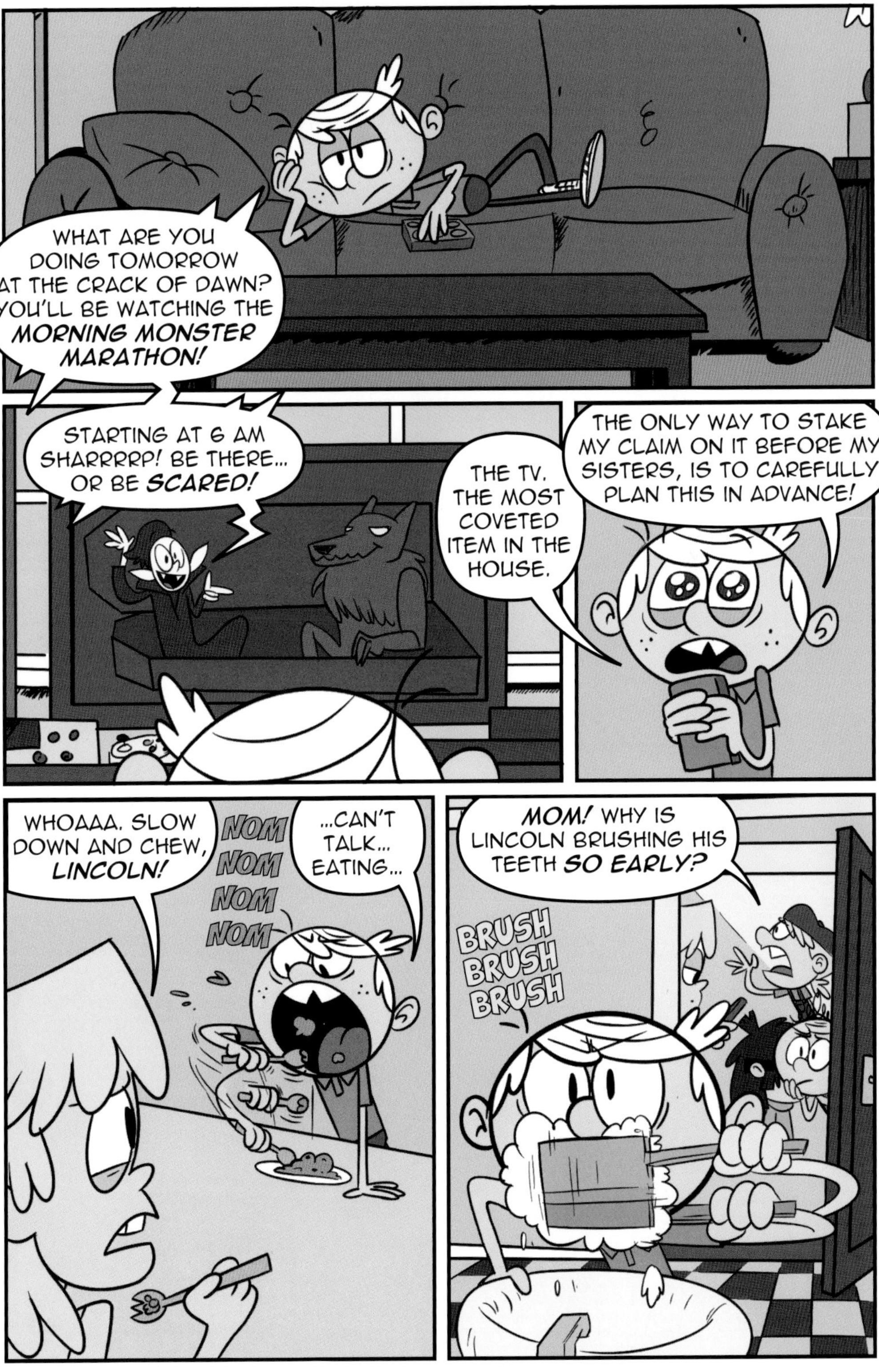
WHAT ARE YOU DOING TOMORROW AT THE CRACK OF DAWN? YOU'LL BE WATCHING THE *MORNING MONSTER MARATHON!*
STARTING AT 6 AM SHARRRRP! BE THERE... OR BE *SCARED!*
THE TV. THE MOST COVETED ITEM IN THE HOUSE.
THE ONLY WAY TO STAKE MY CLAIM ON IT BEFORE MY SISTERS, IS TO CAREFULLY PLAN THIS IN ADVANCE!
WHOAAA. SLOW DOWN AND CHEW, **LINCOLN!**
NOM NOM NOM NOM
...CAN'T TALK... EATING...
MOM! WHY IS LINCOLN BRUSHING HIS TEETH *SO EARLY?*
BRUSH BRUSH BRUSH

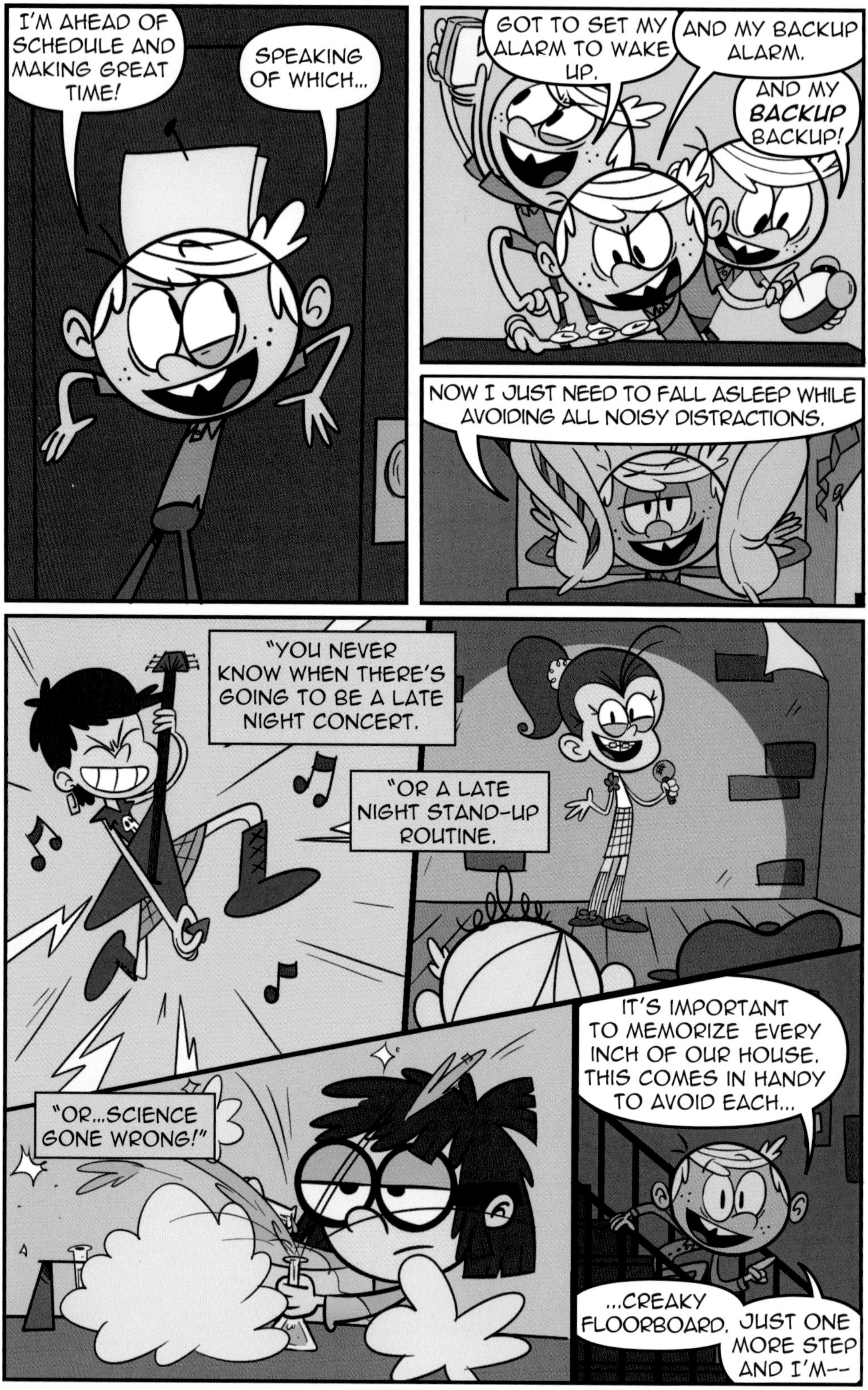
I'M AHEAD OF SCHEDULE AND MAKING GREAT TIME!
SPEAKING OF WHICH...
GOT TO SET MY ALARM TO WAKE UP.
AND MY BACKUP ALARM.
AND MY **BACKUP** BACKUP!
NOW I JUST NEED TO FALL ASLEEP WHILE AVOIDING ALL NOISY DISTRACTIONS.
"YOU NEVER KNOW WHEN THERE'S GOING TO BE A LATE NIGHT CONCERT.
"OR A LATE NIGHT STAND-UP ROUTINE.
"OR...SCIENCE GONE WRONG!"
IT'S IMPORTANT TO MEMORIZE EVERY INCH OF OUR HOUSE. THIS COMES IN HANDY TO AVOID EACH...
...CREAKY FLOORBOARD.
JUST ONE MORE STEP AND I'M--

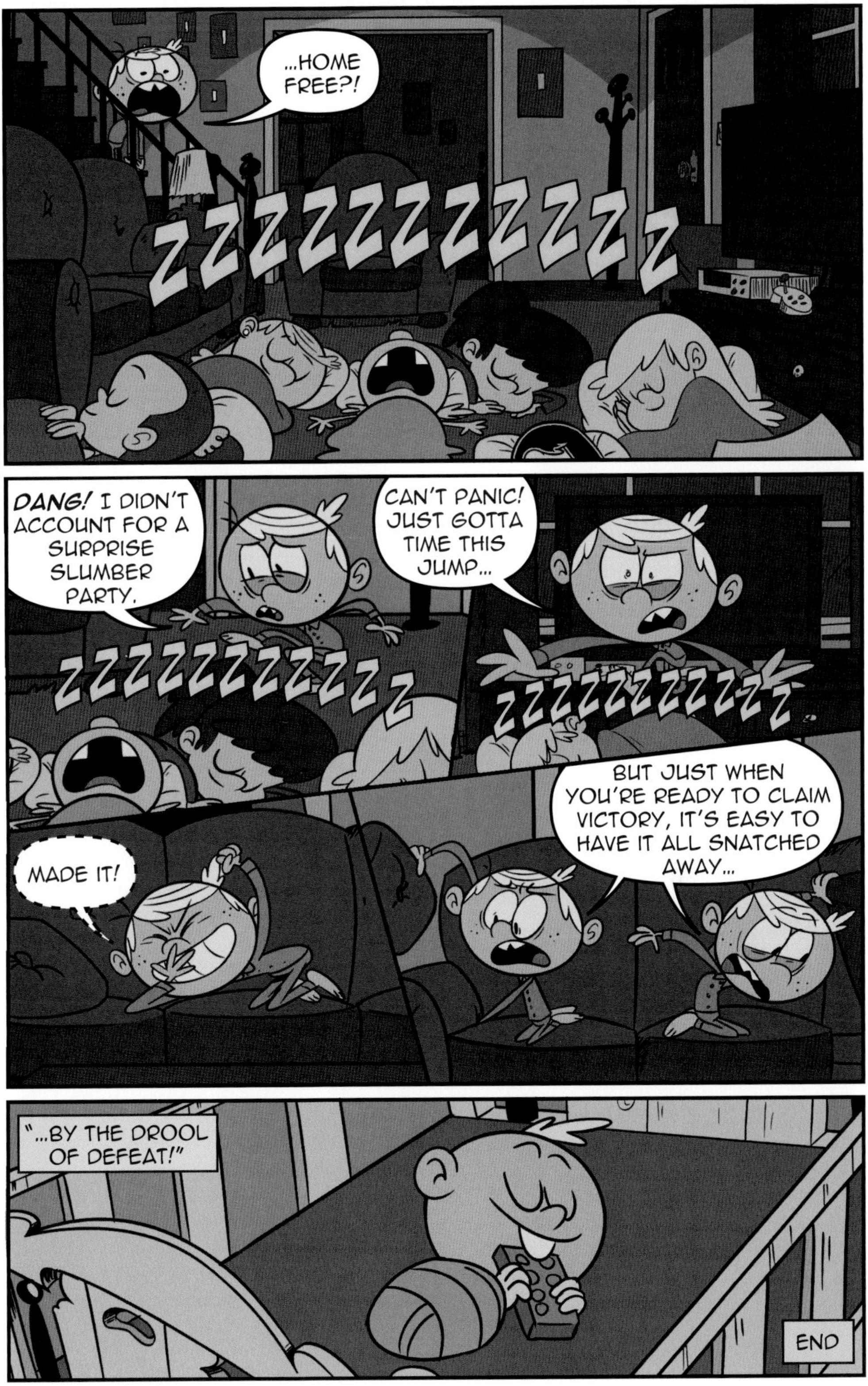
...HOME FREE?!
ZZZZZZZZZZZZ
DANG! I DIDN'T ACCOUNT FOR A SURPRISE SLUMBER PARTY.
ZZZZZZZZZZZ
CAN'T PANIC! JUST GOTTA TIME THIS JUMP...
ZZZZZZZZZZZZZ
MADE IT!
BUT JUST WHEN YOU'RE READY TO CLAIM VICTORY, IT'S EASY TO HAVE IT ALL SNATCHED AWAY...
"...BY THE DROOL OF DEFEAT!"
END

"Out of Tune"

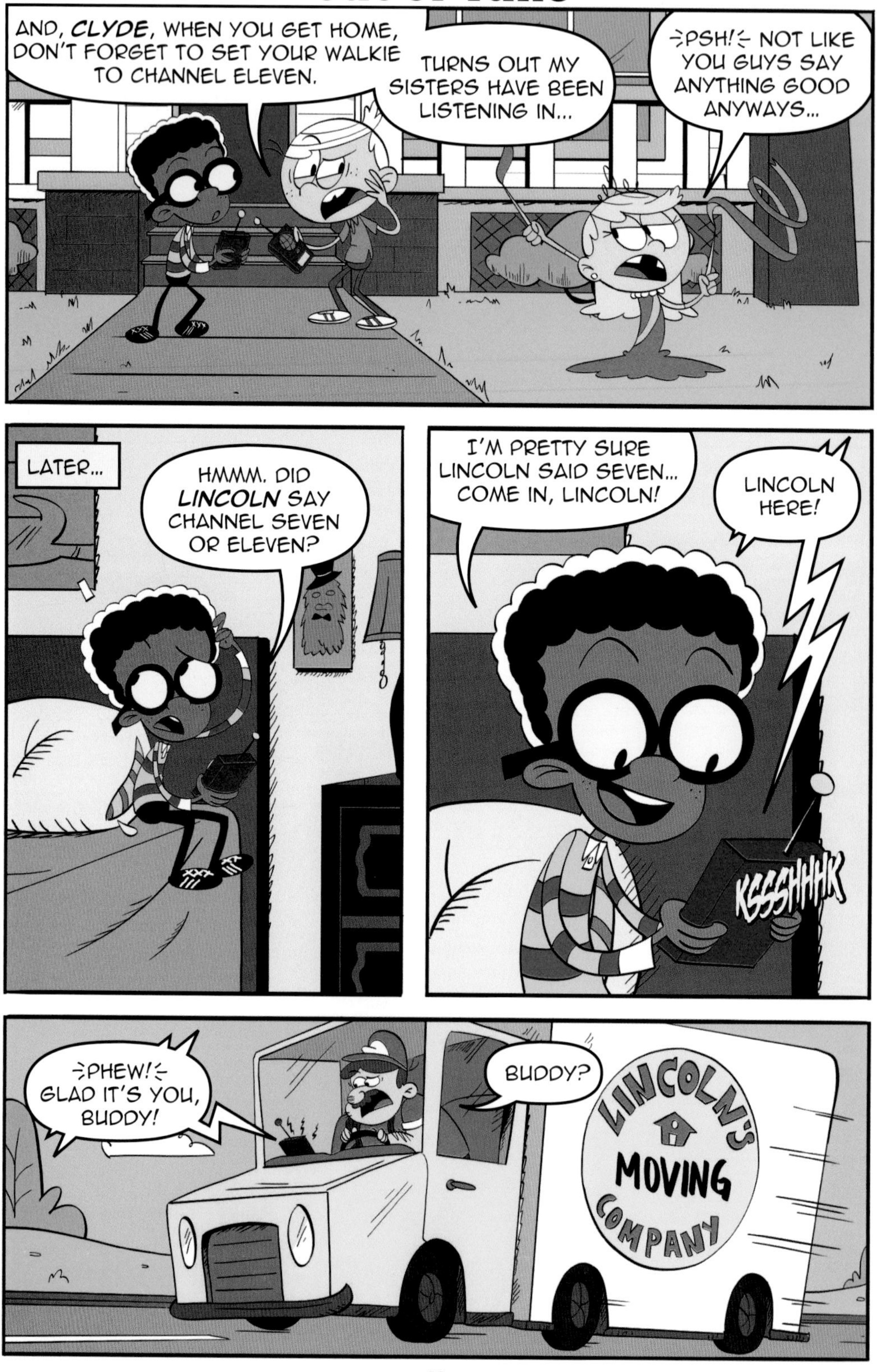

AND, CLYDE, WHEN YOU GET HOME, DON'T FORGET TO SET YOUR WALKIE TO CHANNEL ELEVEN.
TURNS OUT MY SISTERS HAVE BEEN LISTENING IN...
PSH! NOT LIKE YOU GUYS SAY ANYTHING GOOD ANYWAYS...
LATER...
HMMM. DID LINCOLN SAY CHANNEL SEVEN OR ELEVEN?
I'M PRETTY SURE LINCOLN SAID SEVEN... COME IN, LINCOLN!
LINCOLN HERE!
KSSSHHHK
PHEW! GLAD IT'S YOU, BUDDY!
BUDDY?
LINCOLN'S MOVING COMPANY

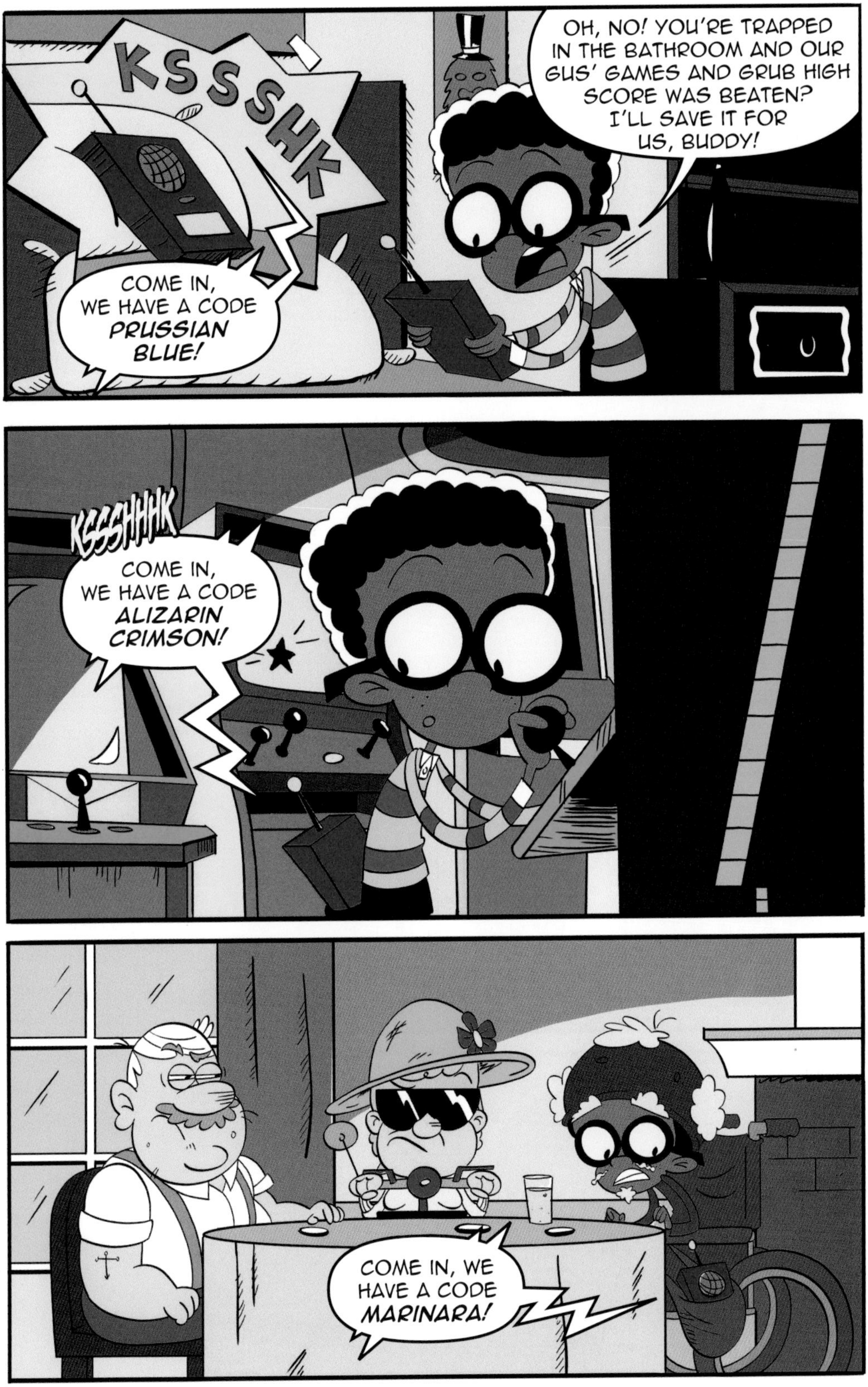
KSSSHK
COME IN, WE HAVE A CODE PRUSSIAN BLUE!
OH, NO! YOU'RE TRAPPED IN THE BATHROOM AND OUR GUS' GAMES AND GRUB HIGH SCORE WAS BEATEN? I'LL SAVE IT FOR US, BUDDY!
KSSSHHHK
COME IN, WE HAVE A CODE ALIZARIN CRIMSON!
COME IN, WE HAVE A CODE MARINARA!

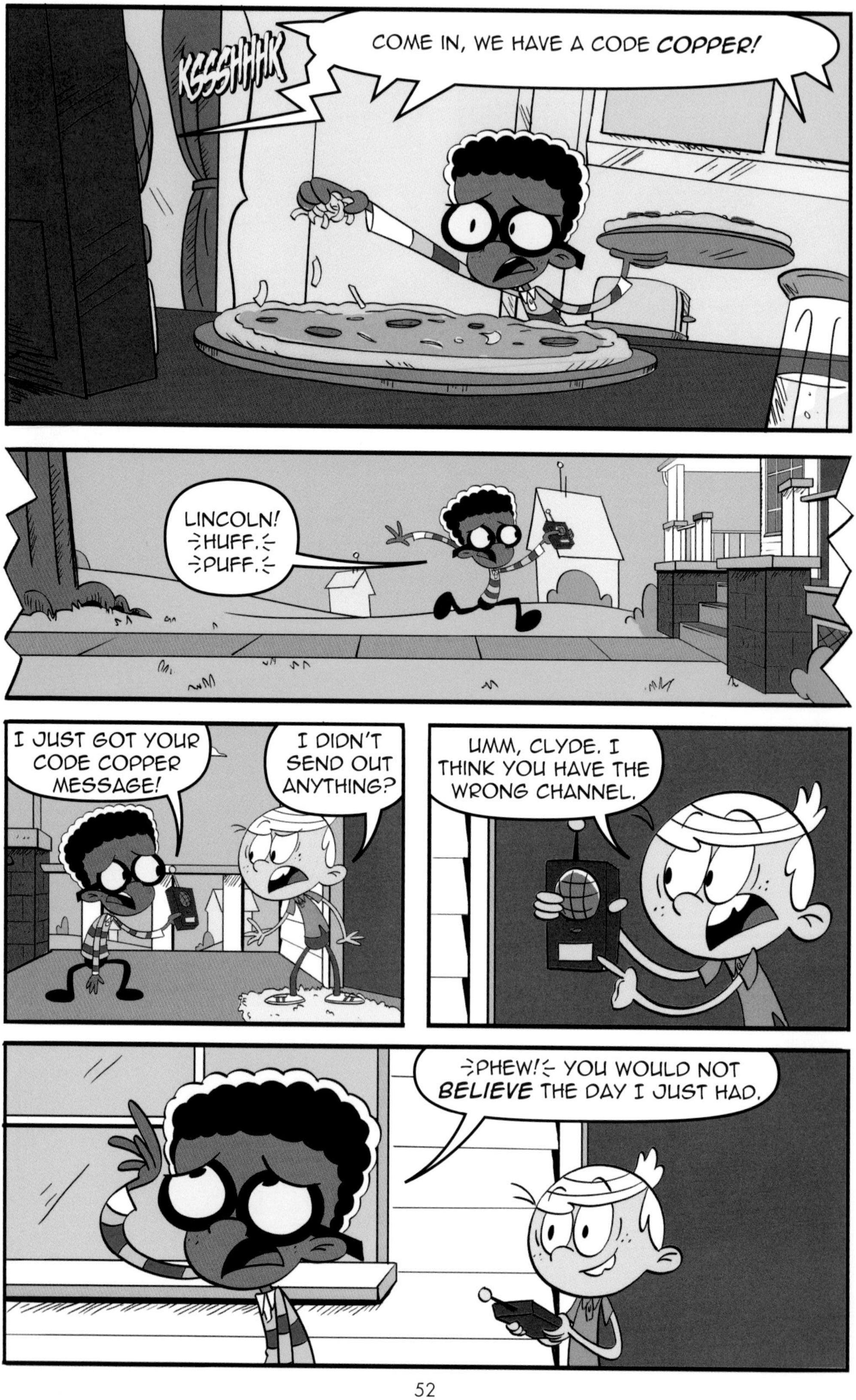
KSSSHHHK
COME IN, WE HAVE A CODE COPPER!
LINCOLN! HUFF. PUFF.
I JUST GOT YOUR CODE COPPER MESSAGE!
I DIDN'T SEND OUT ANYTHING?
UMM, CLYDE. I THINK YOU HAVE THE WRONG CHANNEL.
PHEW! YOU WOULD NOT BELIEVE THE DAY I JUST HAD.

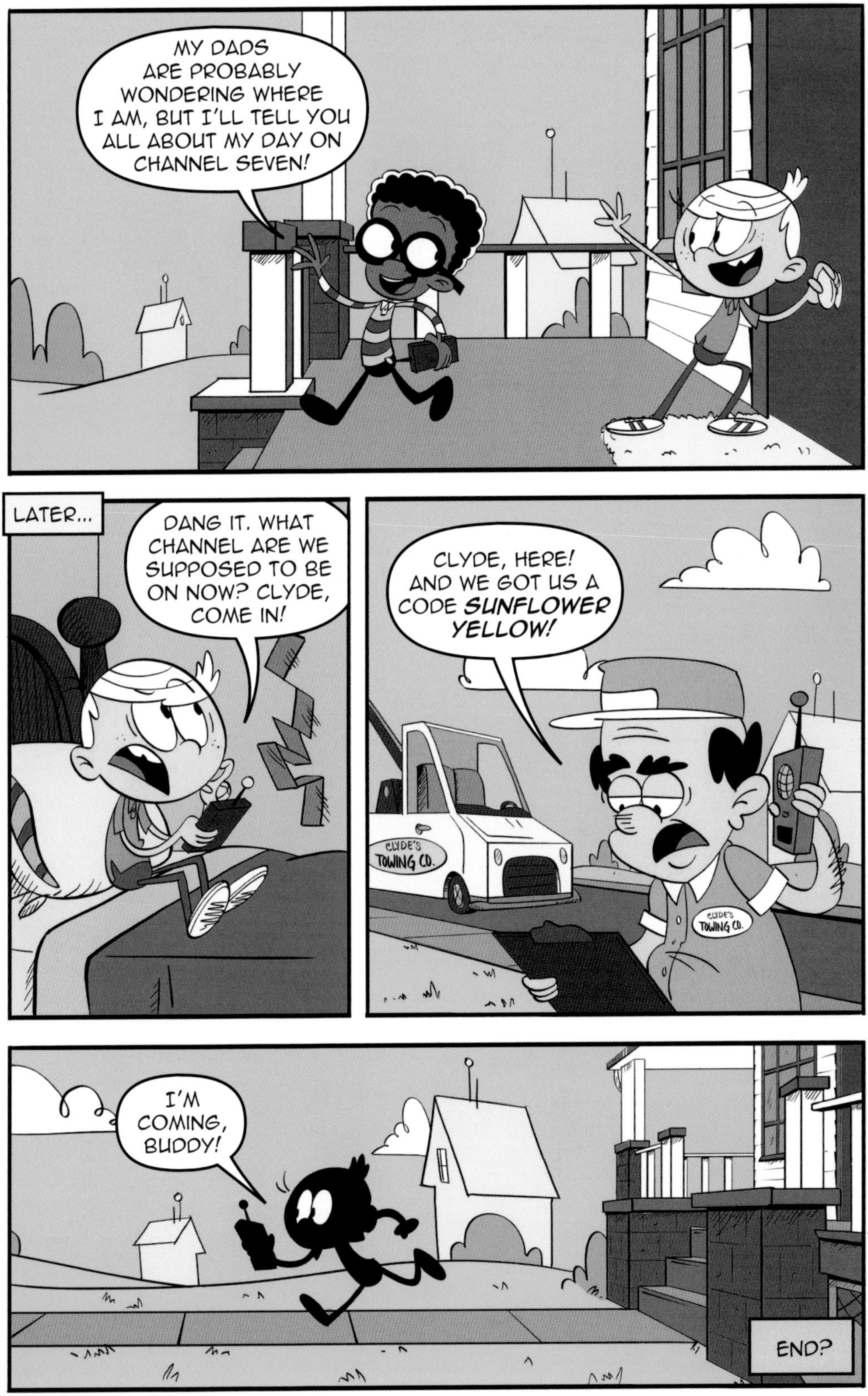
MY DADS ARE PROBABLY WONDERING WHERE I AM, BUT I'LL TELL YOU ALL ABOUT MY DAY ON CHANNEL SEVEN!
LATER...
DANG IT. WHAT CHANNEL ARE WE SUPPOSED TO BE ON NOW? CLYDE, COME IN!
CLYDE, HERE! AND WE GOT US A CODE SUNFLOWER YELLOW!
CLYDE'S TOWING CO.
CLYDE'S TOWING CO.
I'M COMING, BUDDY!
END?

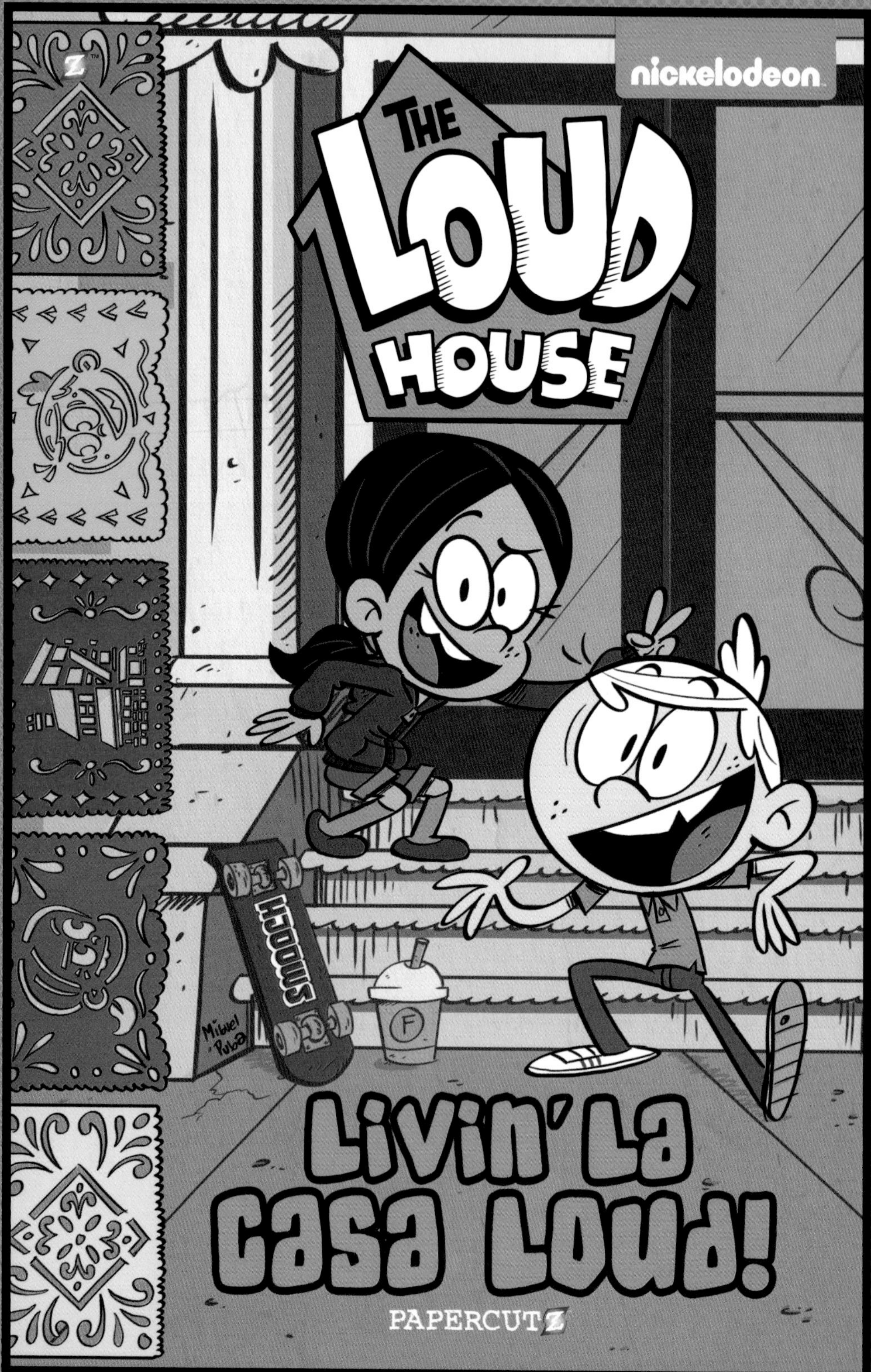
nickelodeon
THE LOUD HOUSE
SNOOPY
Miguel Puga
Livin' La Casa Loud!
PAPERCUTZ

THE LOUD HOUSE #8 Cover Art by Miguel Puga

"LITTLE BIG TOP"

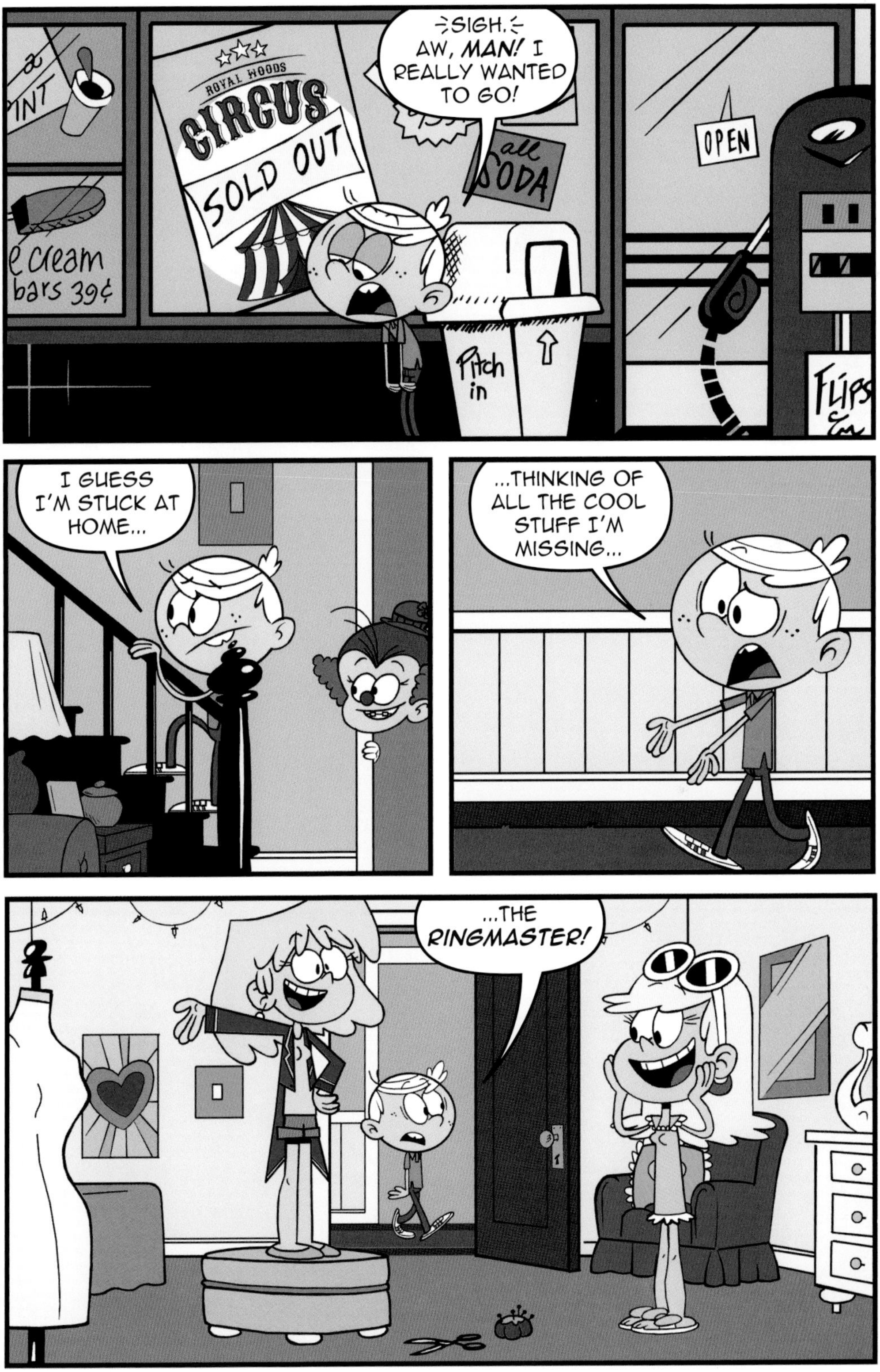
ROYAL WOODS
CIRCUS
SOLD OUT
ice cream bars 39¢
all SODA
OPEN
Pitch in
SIGH.
AW, MAN! I REALLY WANTED TO GO!
I GUESS I'M STUCK AT HOME...
...THINKING OF ALL THE COOL STUFF I'M MISSING...
...THE RINGMASTER!

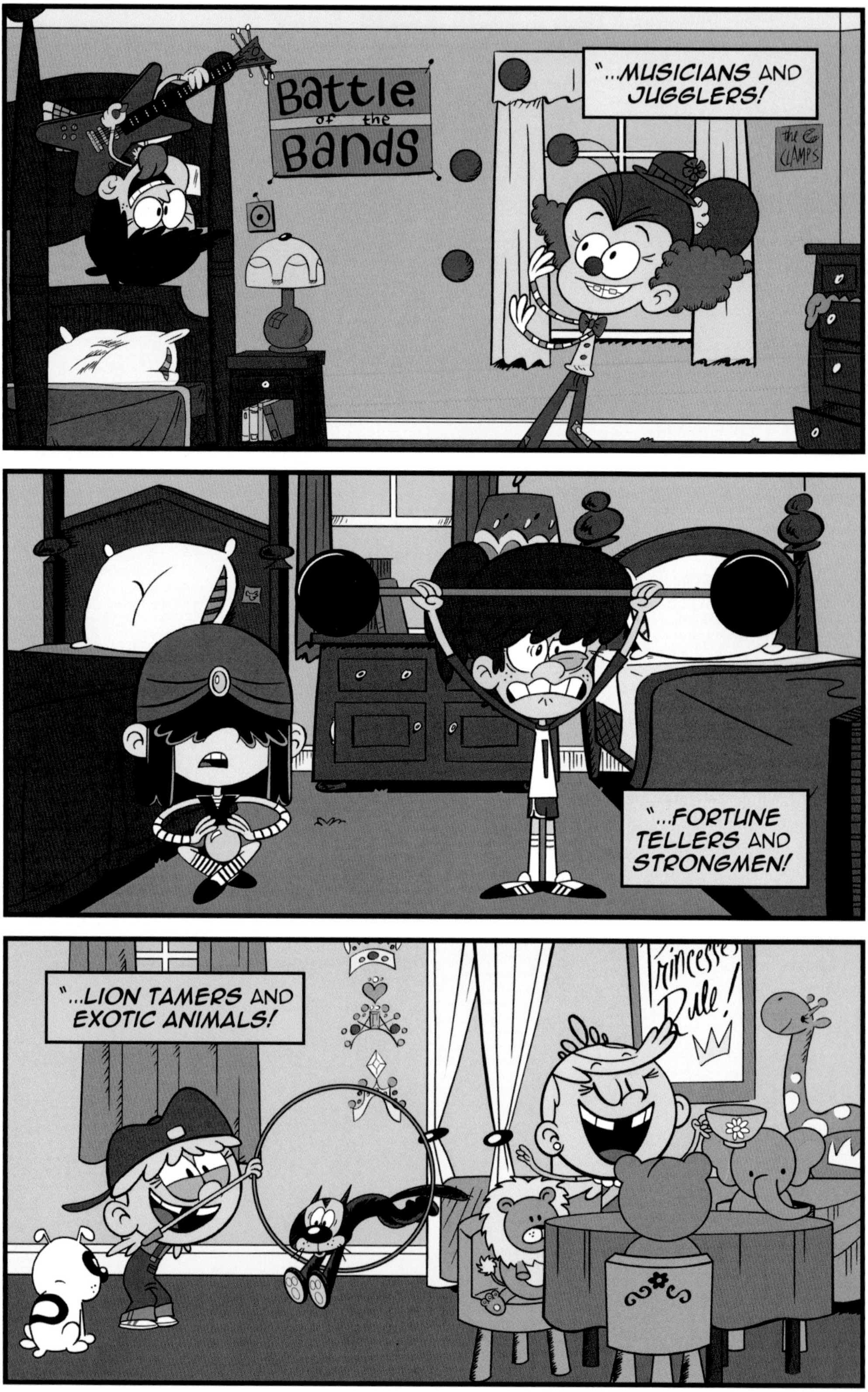
Battle of the Bands
"...MUSICIANS AND JUGGLERS!
the Clamps
"...FORTUNE TELLERS AND STRONGMEN!
"...LION TAMERS AND EXOTIC ANIMALS!

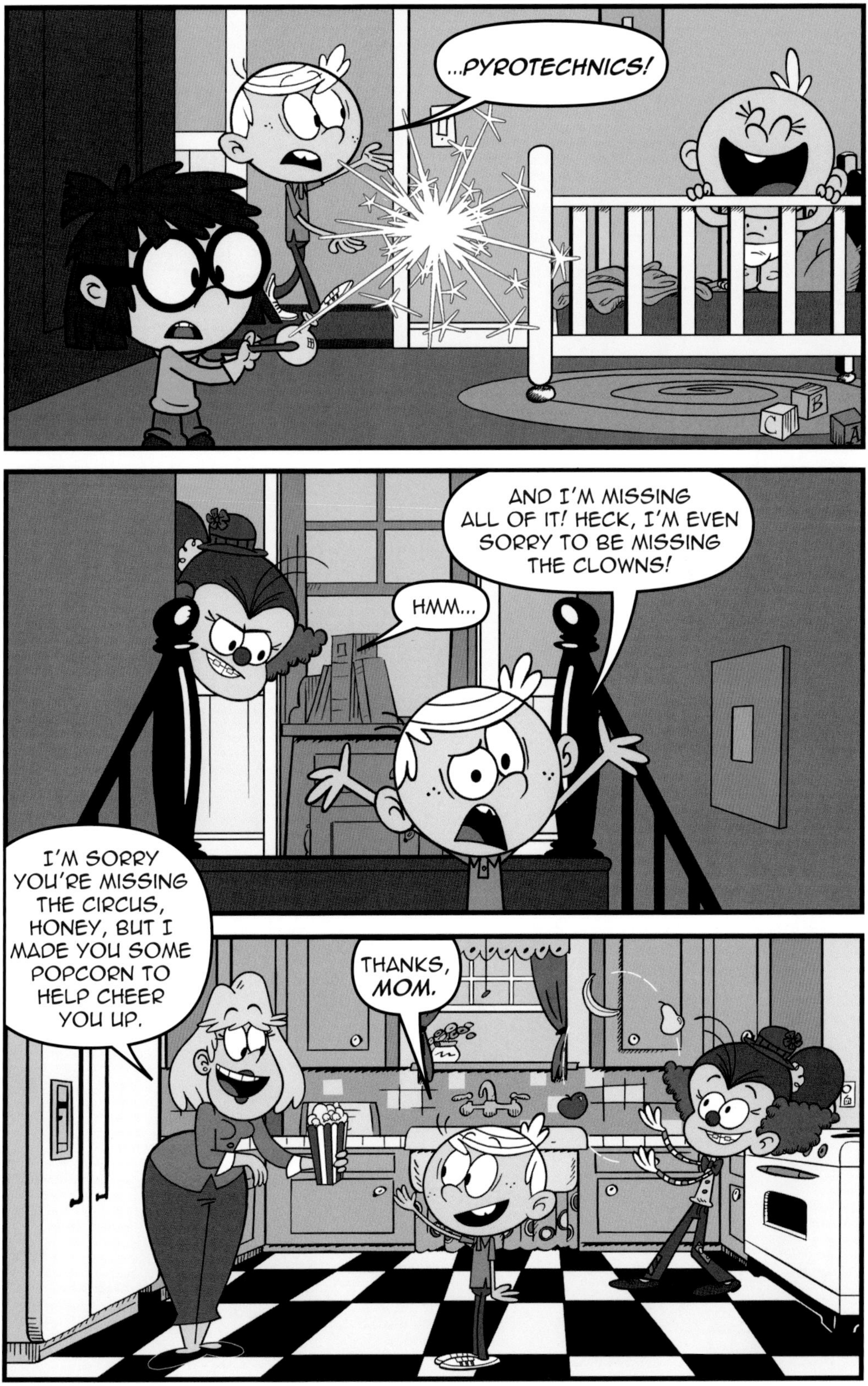
...PYROTECHNICS!
HMM...
AND I'M MISSING ALL OF IT! HECK, I'M EVEN SORRY TO BE MISSING THE CLOWNS!
I'M SORRY YOU'RE MISSING THE CIRCUS, HONEY, BUT I MADE YOU SOME POPCORN TO HELP CHEER YOU UP.
THANKS, MOM.

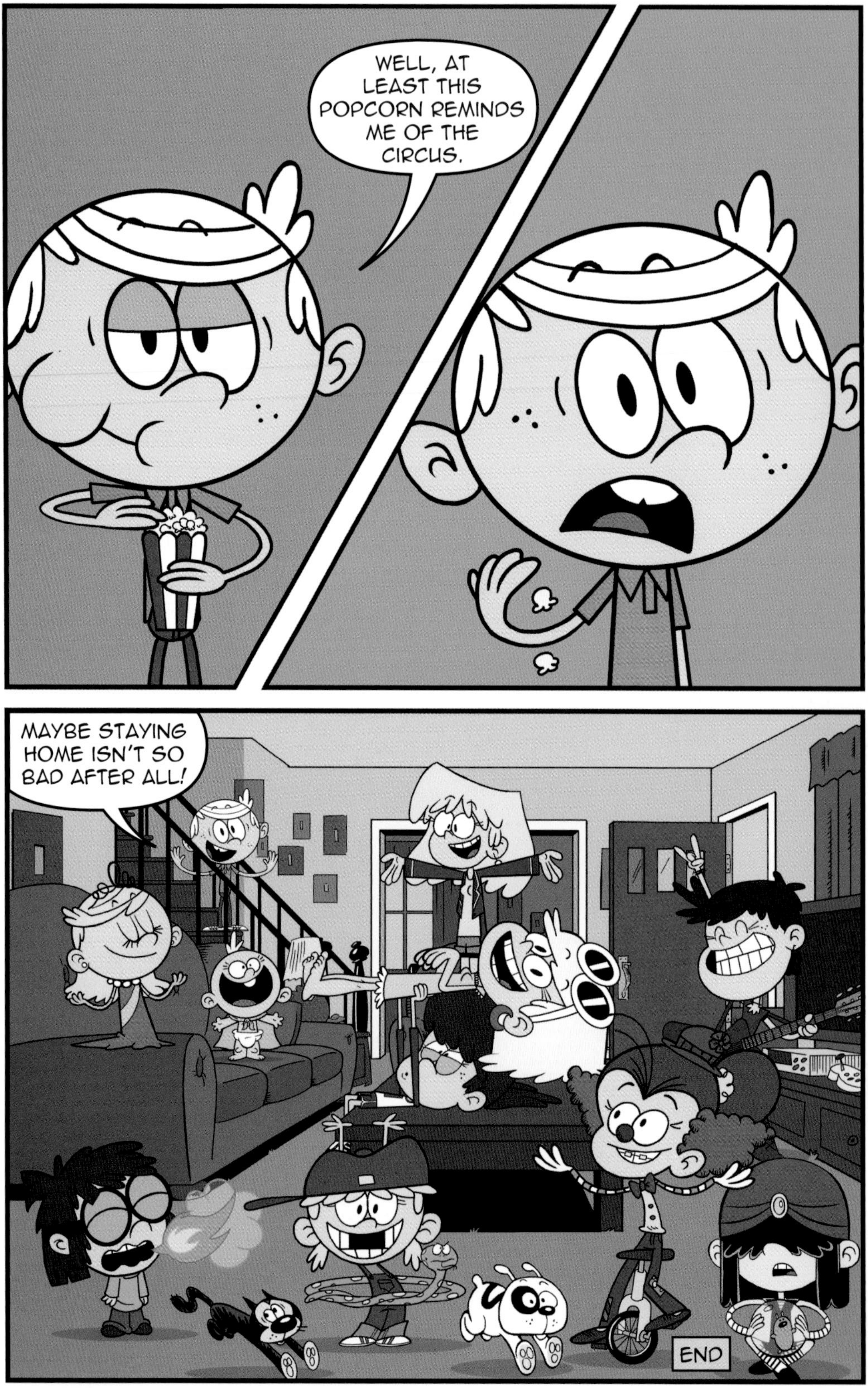
WELL, AT LEAST THIS POPCORN REMINDS ME OF THE CIRCUS.
MAYBE STAYING HOME ISN'T SO BAD AFTER ALL!
END

"HIDE AND SNEAK"

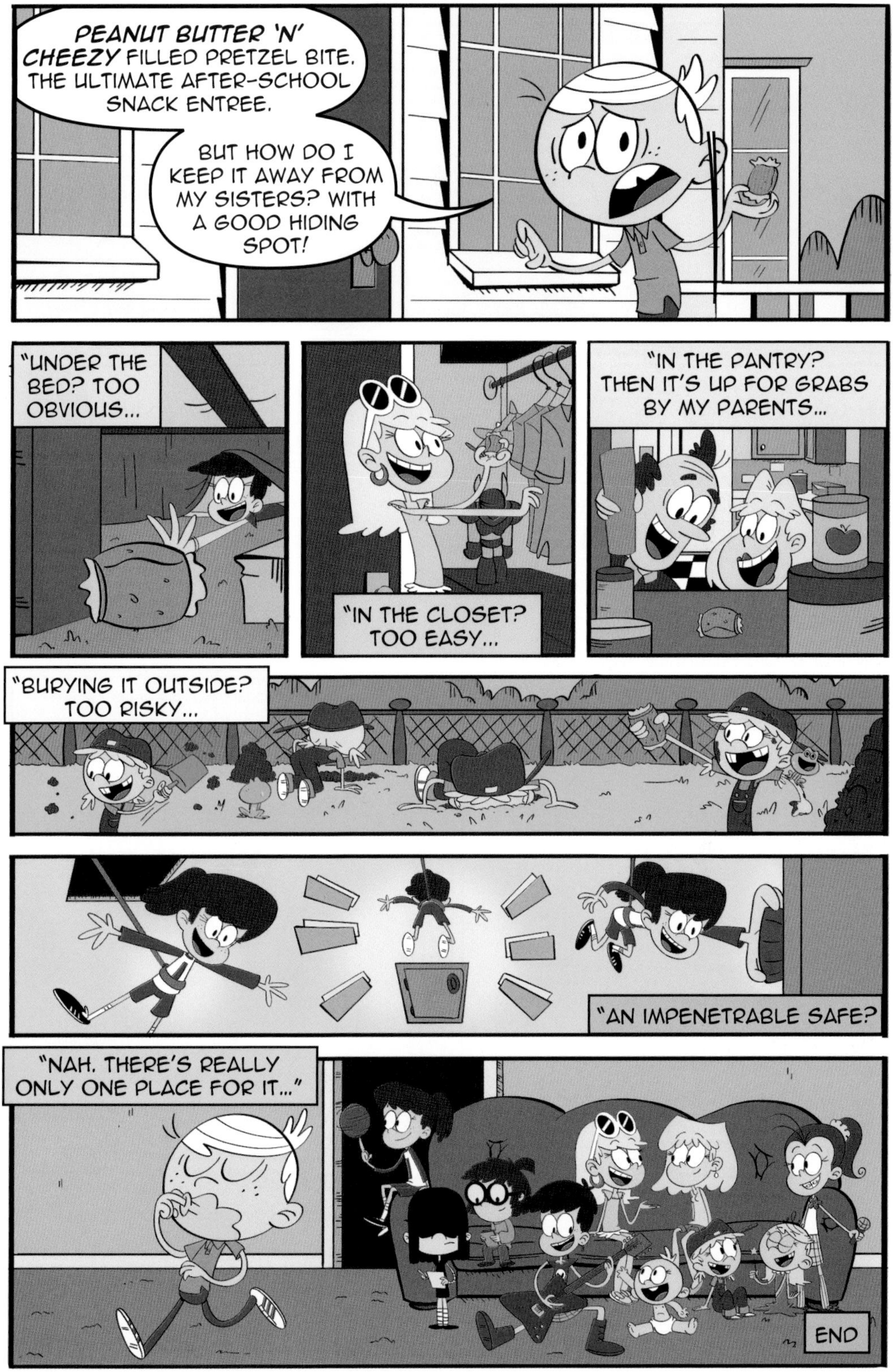
PEANUT BUTTER 'N' CHEEZY FILLED PRETZEL BITE. THE ULTIMATE AFTER-SCHOOL SNACK ENTREE.
BUT HOW DO I KEEP IT AWAY FROM MY SISTERS? WITH A GOOD HIDING SPOT!
"UNDER THE BED? TOO OBVIOUS...
"IN THE CLOSET? TOO EASY...
"IN THE PANTRY? THEN IT'S UP FOR GRABS BY MY PARENTS...
"BURYING IT OUTSIDE? TOO RISKY...
"AN IMPENETRABLE SAFE?
"NAH. THERE'S REALLY ONLY ONE PLACE FOR IT..."
END

"FASHION VICTIM"

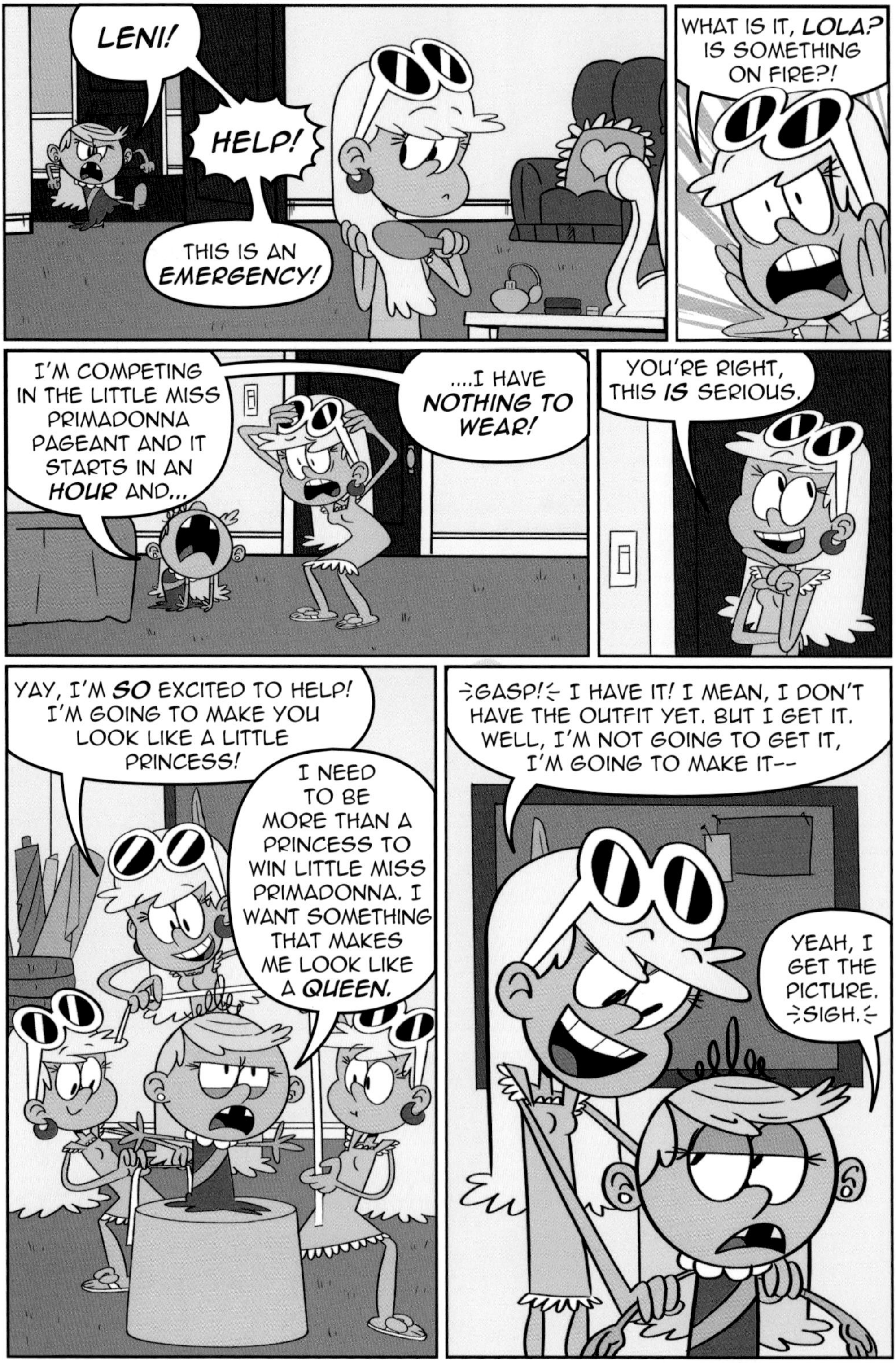
LENI!
HELP!
THIS IS AN EMERGENCY!
WHAT IS IT, LOLA? IS SOMETHING ON FIRE?!
I'M COMPETING IN THE LITTLE MISS PRIMADONNA PAGEANT AND IT STARTS IN AN HOUR AND...
....I HAVE NOTHING TO WEAR!
YOU'RE RIGHT, THIS IS SERIOUS.
YAY, I'M SO EXCITED TO HELP! I'M GOING TO MAKE YOU LOOK LIKE A LITTLE PRINCESS!
I NEED TO BE MORE THAN A PRINCESS TO WIN LITTLE MISS PRIMADONNA. I WANT SOMETHING THAT MAKES ME LOOK LIKE A QUEEN.
GASP! I HAVE IT! I MEAN, I DON'T HAVE THE OUTFIT YET. BUT I GET IT. WELL, I'M NOT GOING TO GET IT, I'M GOING TO MAKE IT--
YEAH, I GET THE PICTURE. SIGH.

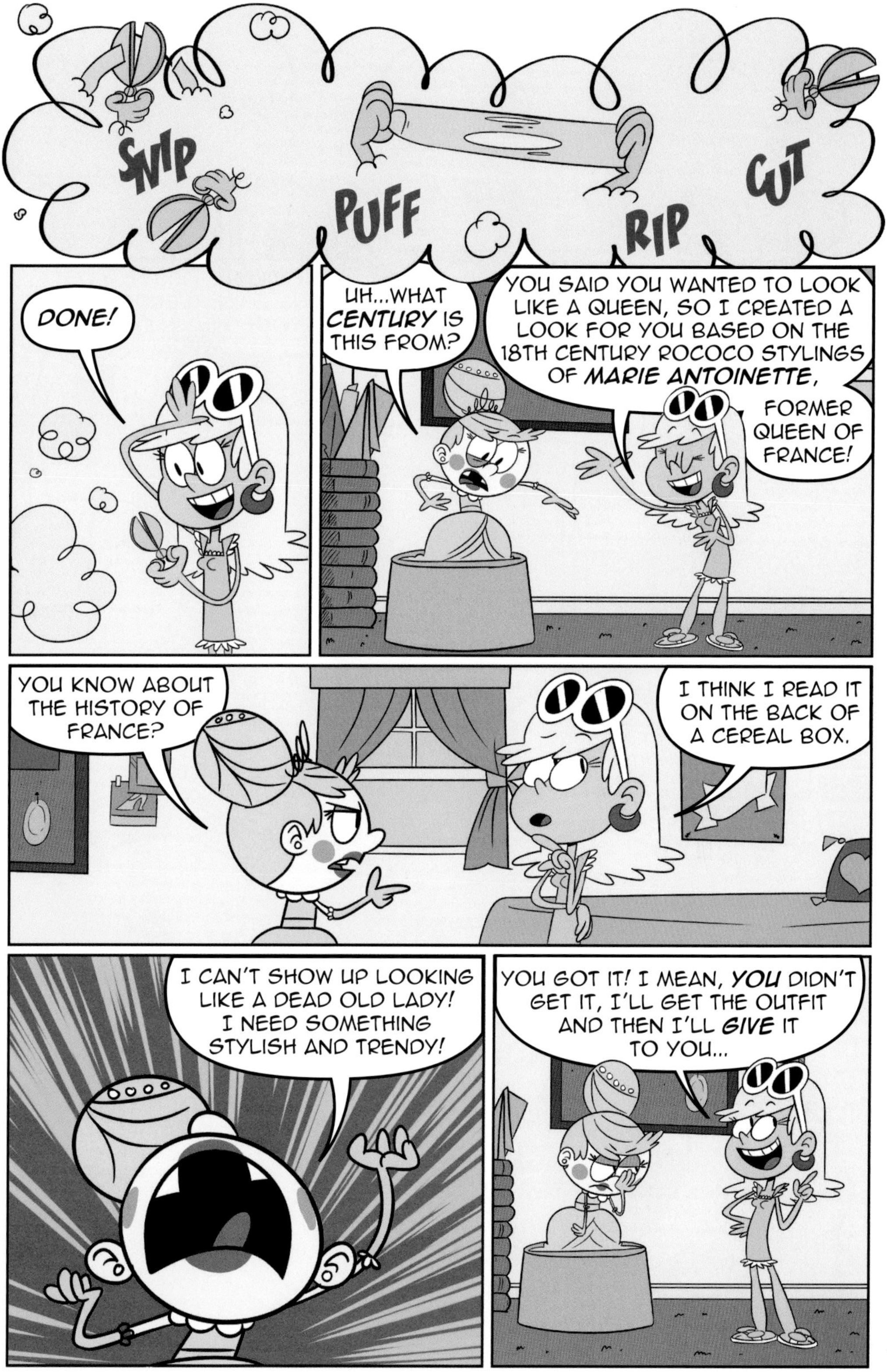

SNIP
PUFF
RIP
CUT
DONE!
UH...WHAT CENTURY IS THIS FROM?
YOU SAID YOU WANTED TO LOOK LIKE A QUEEN, SO I CREATED A LOOK FOR YOU BASED ON THE 18TH CENTURY ROCOCO STYLINGS OF MARIE ANTOINETTE,
FORMER QUEEN OF FRANCE!
YOU KNOW ABOUT THE HISTORY OF FRANCE?
I THINK I READ IT ON THE BACK OF A CEREAL BOX.
I CAN'T SHOW UP LOOKING LIKE A DEAD OLD LADY! I NEED SOMETHING STYLISH AND TRENDY!
YOU GOT IT! I MEAN, YOU DIDN'T GET IT, I'LL GET THE OUTFIT AND THEN I'LL GIVE IT TO YOU...

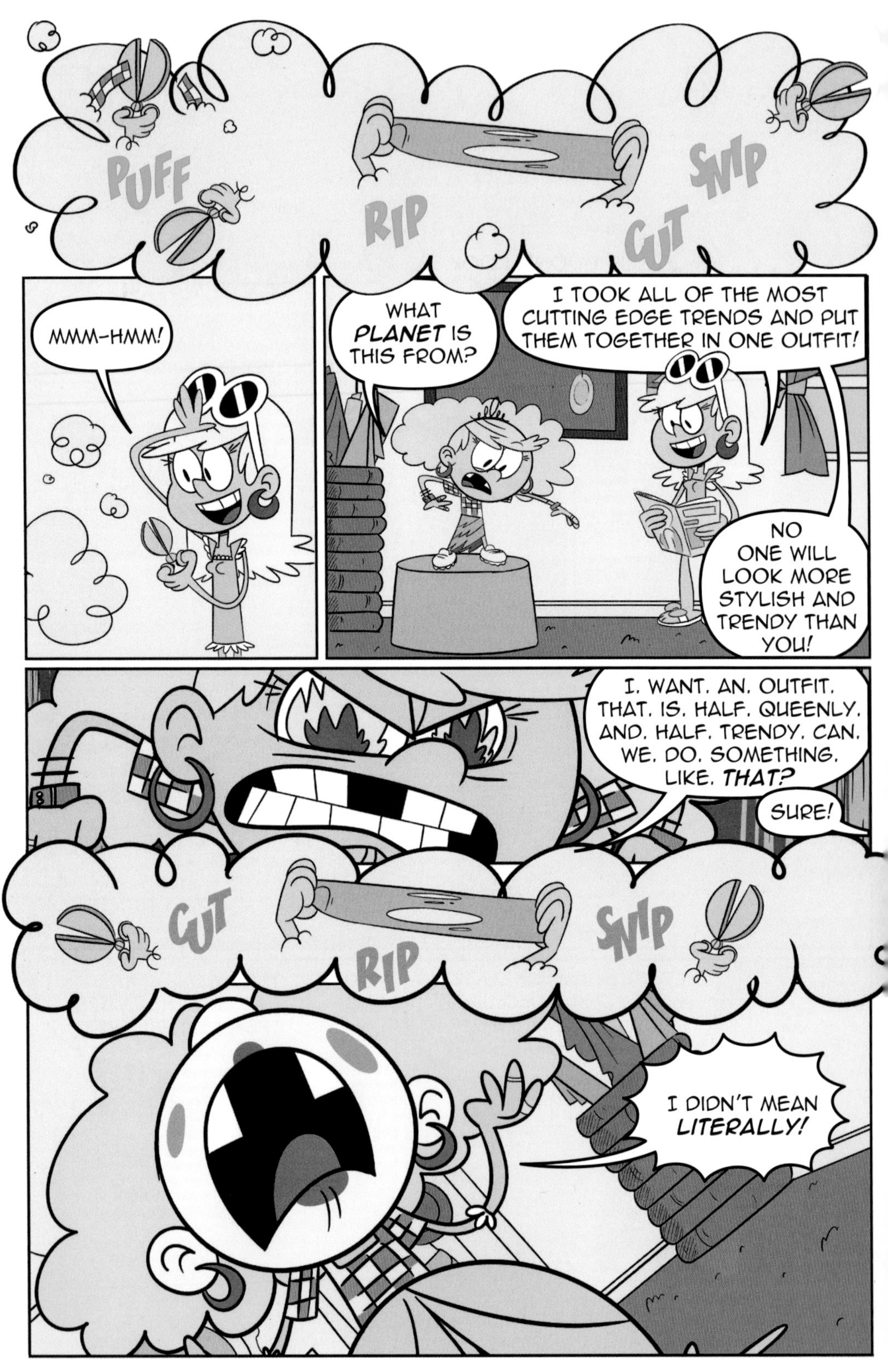
PUFF
RIP
CUT
SNIP
MMM-HMM!
WHAT *PLANET* IS THIS FROM?
I TOOK ALL OF THE MOST CUTTING EDGE TRENDS AND PUT THEM TOGETHER IN ONE OUTFIT!
NO ONE WILL LOOK MORE STYLISH AND TRENDY THAN YOU!
I. WANT. AN. OUTFIT. THAT. IS. HALF. QUEENLY. AND. HALF. TRENDY. CAN. WE. DO. SOMETHING. LIKE. *THAT?*
SURE!
CUT
RIP
SNIP
I DIDN'T MEAN *LITERALLY!*

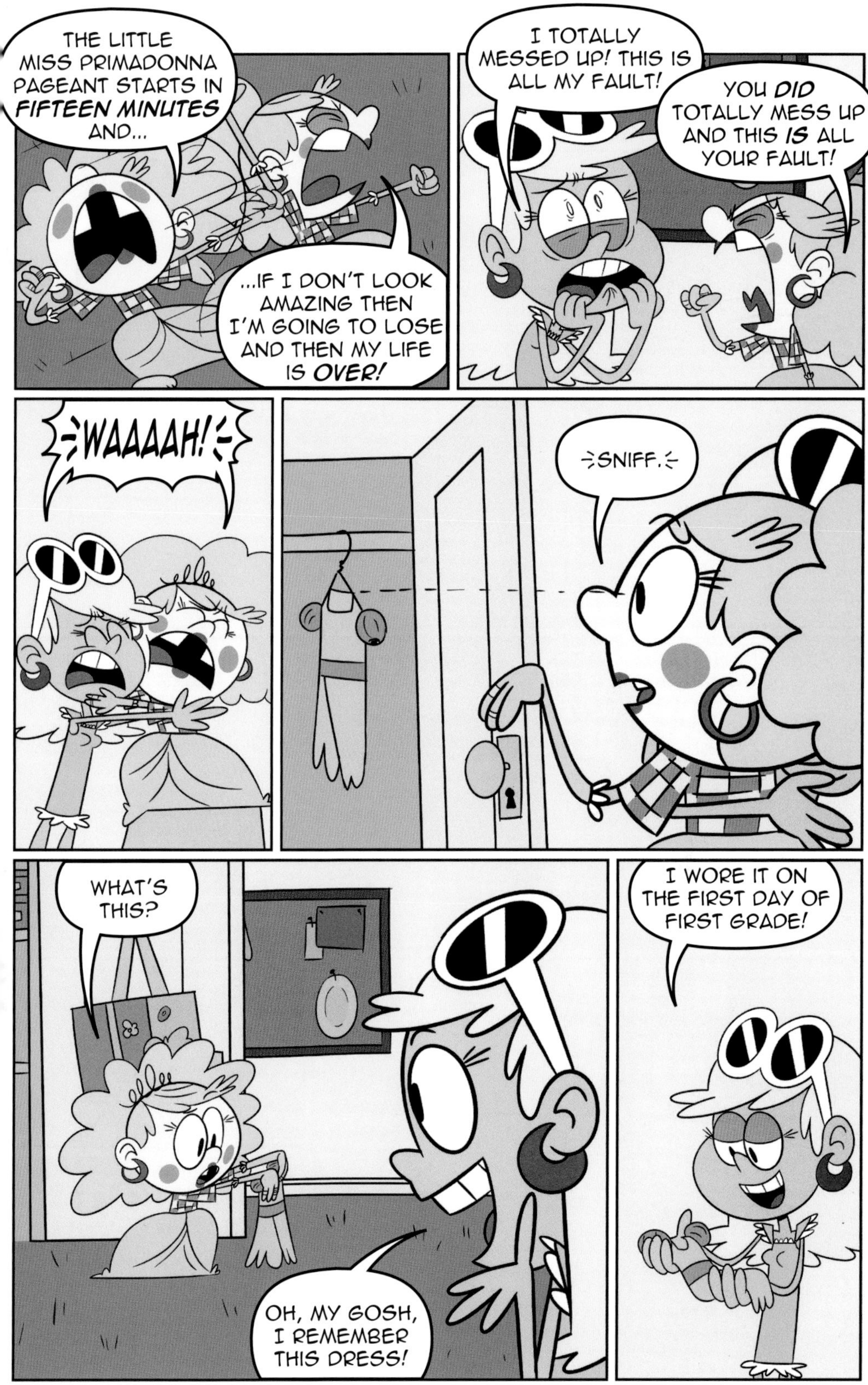
THE LITTLE MISS PRIMADONNA PAGEANT STARTS IN FIFTEEN MINUTES AND...
...IF I DON'T LOOK AMAZING THEN I'M GOING TO LOSE AND THEN MY LIFE IS OVER!
I TOTALLY MESSED UP! THIS IS ALL MY FAULT!
YOU DID TOTALLY MESS UP AND THIS IS ALL YOUR FAULT!
WAAAAH!
SNIFF.
WHAT'S THIS?
OH, MY GOSH, I REMEMBER THIS DRESS!
I WORE IT ON THE FIRST DAY OF FIRST GRADE!

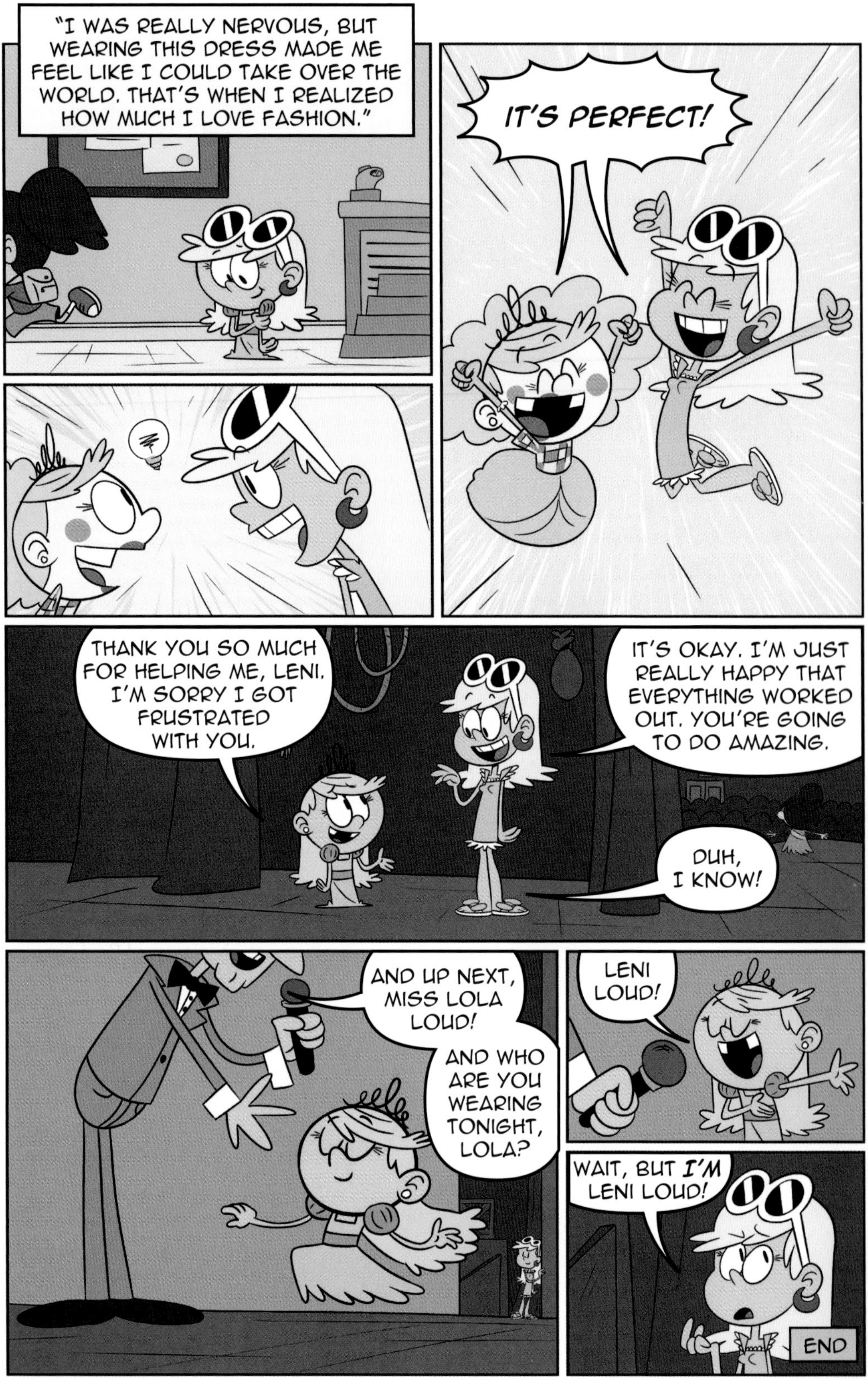
"I WAS REALLY NERVOUS, BUT WEARING THIS DRESS MADE ME FEEL LIKE I COULD TAKE OVER THE WORLD. THAT'S WHEN I REALIZED HOW MUCH I LOVE FASHION."
IT'S PERFECT!
THANK YOU SO MUCH FOR HELPING ME, LENI. I'M SORRY I GOT FRUSTRATED WITH YOU.
IT'S OKAY. I'M JUST REALLY HAPPY THAT EVERYTHING WORKED OUT. YOU'RE GOING TO DO AMAZING.
DUH, I KNOW!
AND UP NEXT, MISS LOLA LOUD!
AND WHO ARE YOU WEARING TONIGHT, LOLA?
LENI LOUD!
WAIT, BUT *I'M* LENI LOUD!
END

"FEEDING FRENZY!"

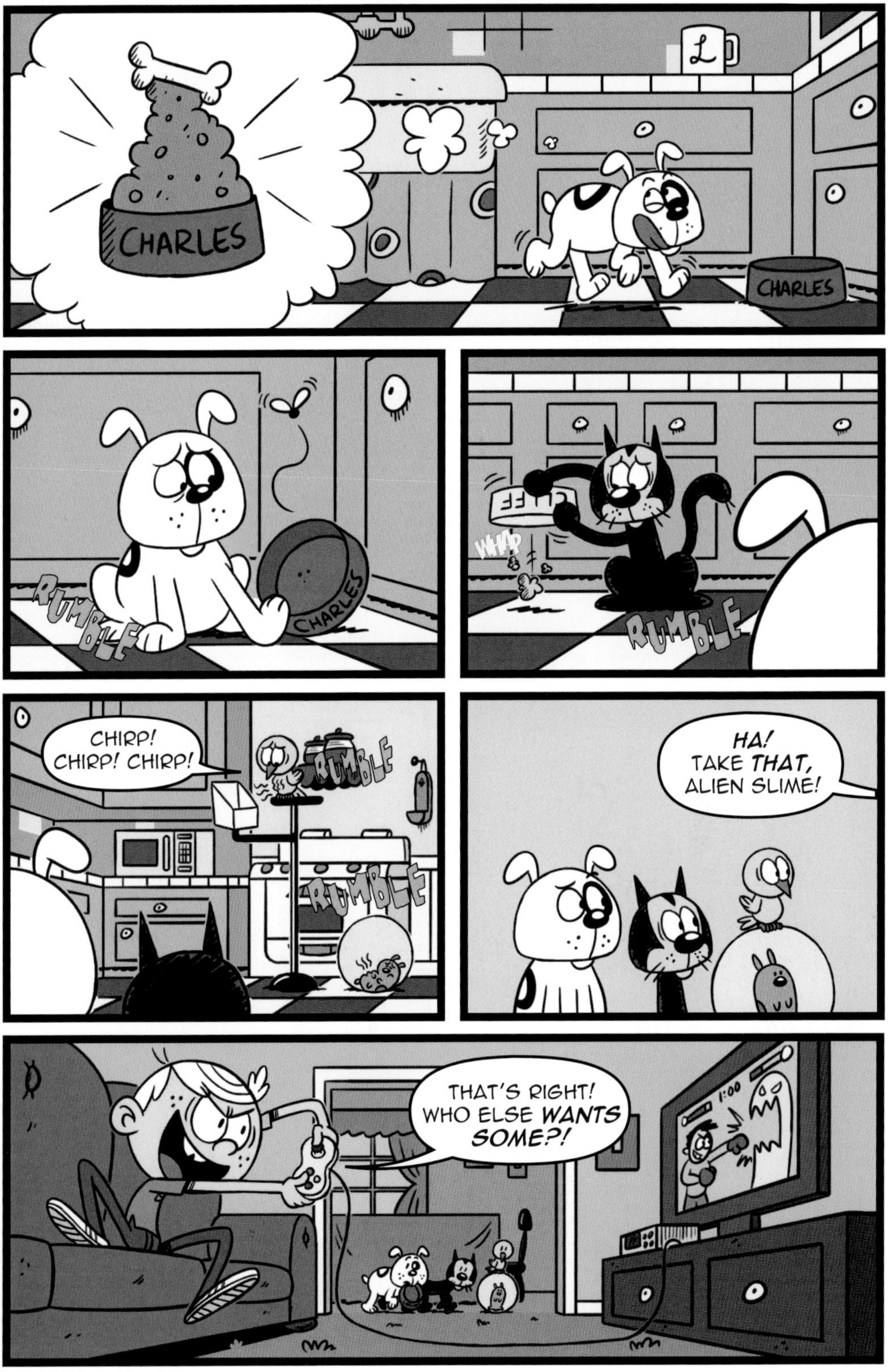
CHARLES
CHARLES
RUMBLE
CHARLES
WHAP
RUMBLE
CHIRP! CHIRP! CHIRP!
RUMBLE
RUMBLE
HA! TAKE THAT, ALIEN SLIME!
THAT'S RIGHT! WHO ELSE WANTS SOME?!
1:00

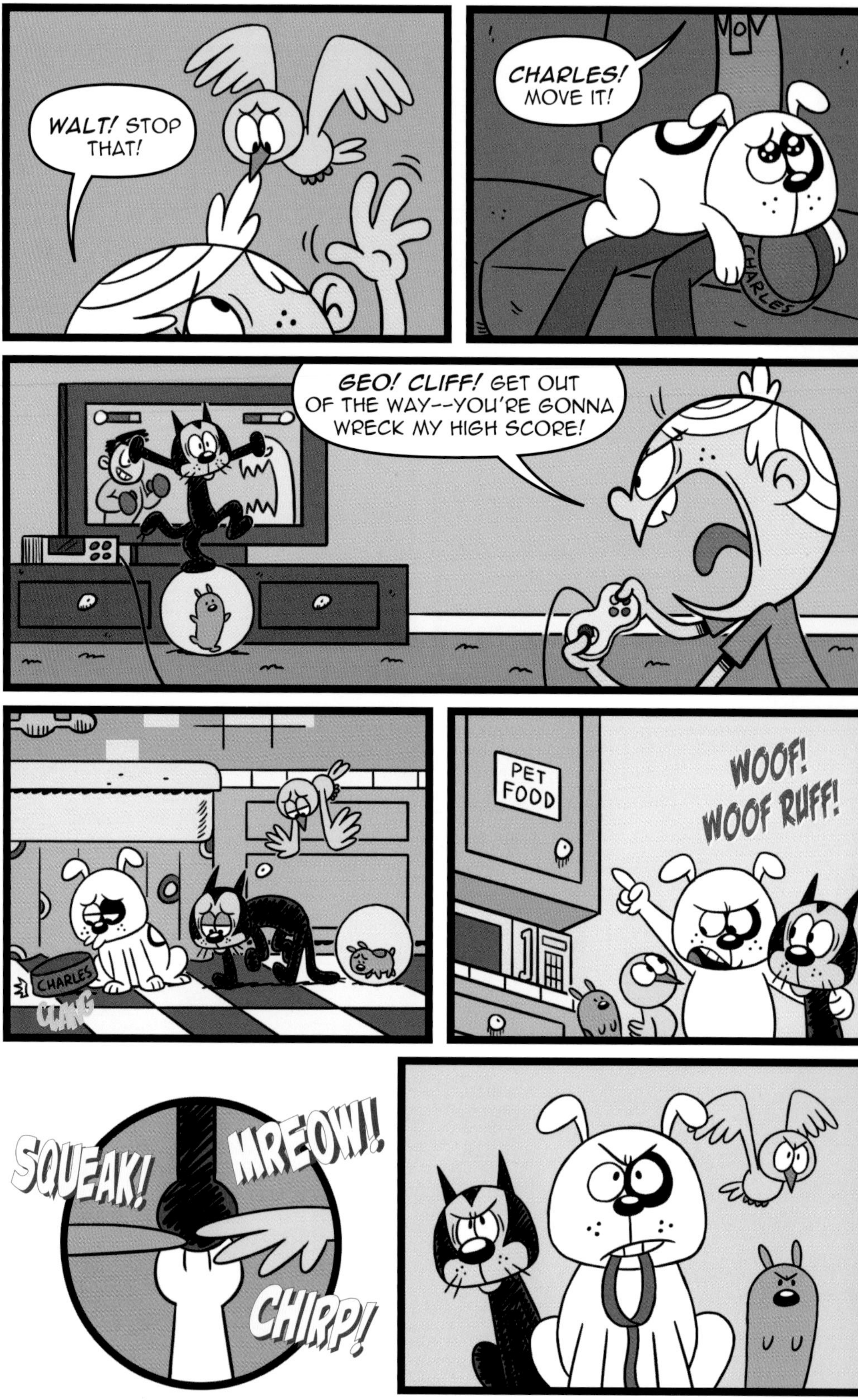
WALT! STOP THAT!
CHARLES! MOVE IT!
CHARLES
GEO! CLIFF! GET OUT OF THE WAY--YOU'RE GONNA WRECK MY HIGH SCORE!
CHARLES
CLANG
PET FOOD
WOOF! WOOF RUFF!
SQUEAK!
MREOW!!
CHIRP!

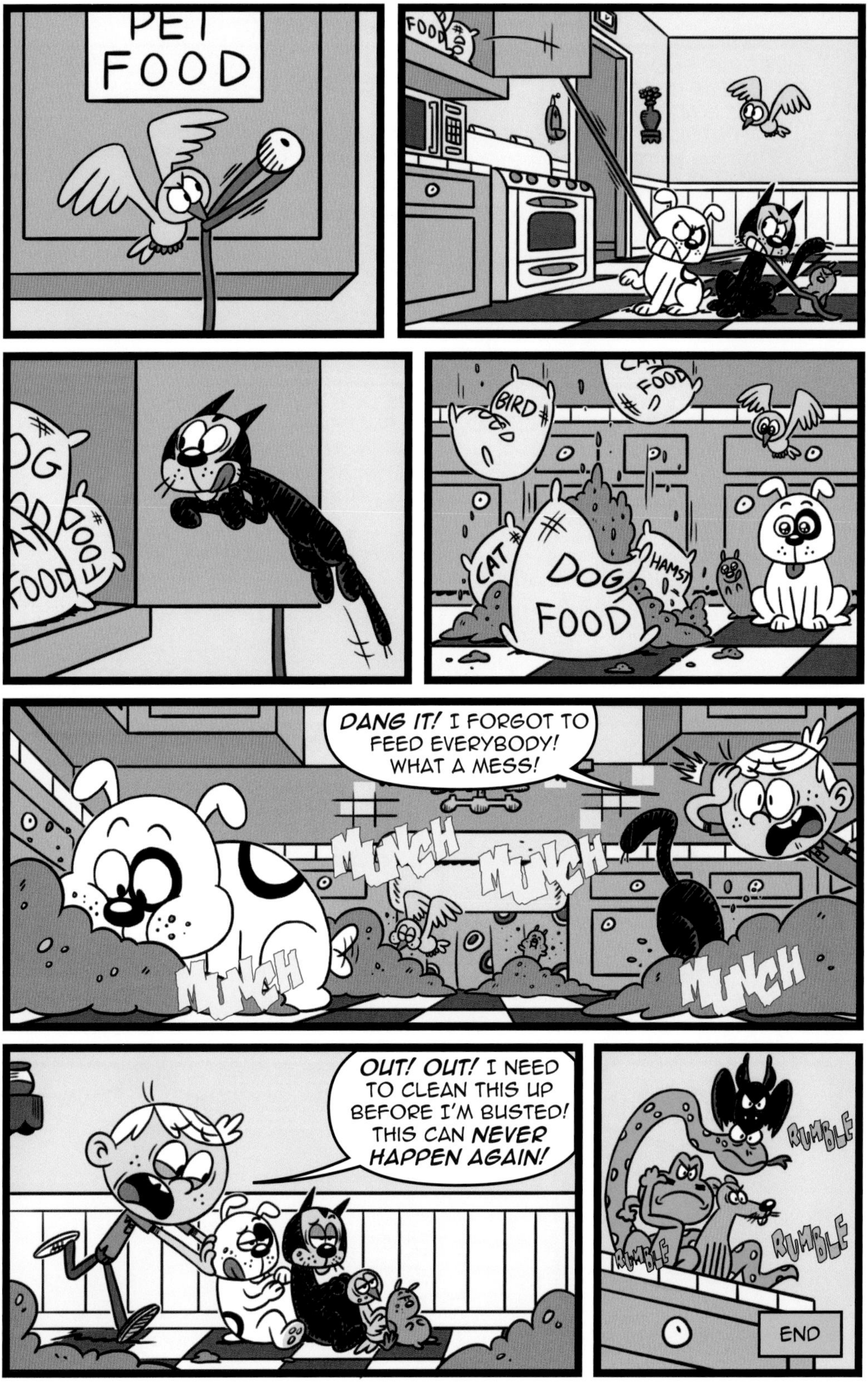
PET FOOD
FOOD
DOG FOOD
CAT FOOD
DOG FOOD
BIRD
CAT FOOD
CAT
DOG FOOD
HAMST
DANG IT! I FORGOT TO FEED EVERYBODY! WHAT A MESS!
MUNCH
MUNCH
MUNCH
MUNCH
OUT! OUT! I NEED TO CLEAN THIS UP BEFORE I'M BUSTED! THIS CAN NEVER HAPPEN AGAIN!
RUMBLE
RUMBLE
RUMBLE
END

"SNOWBALL-ED"

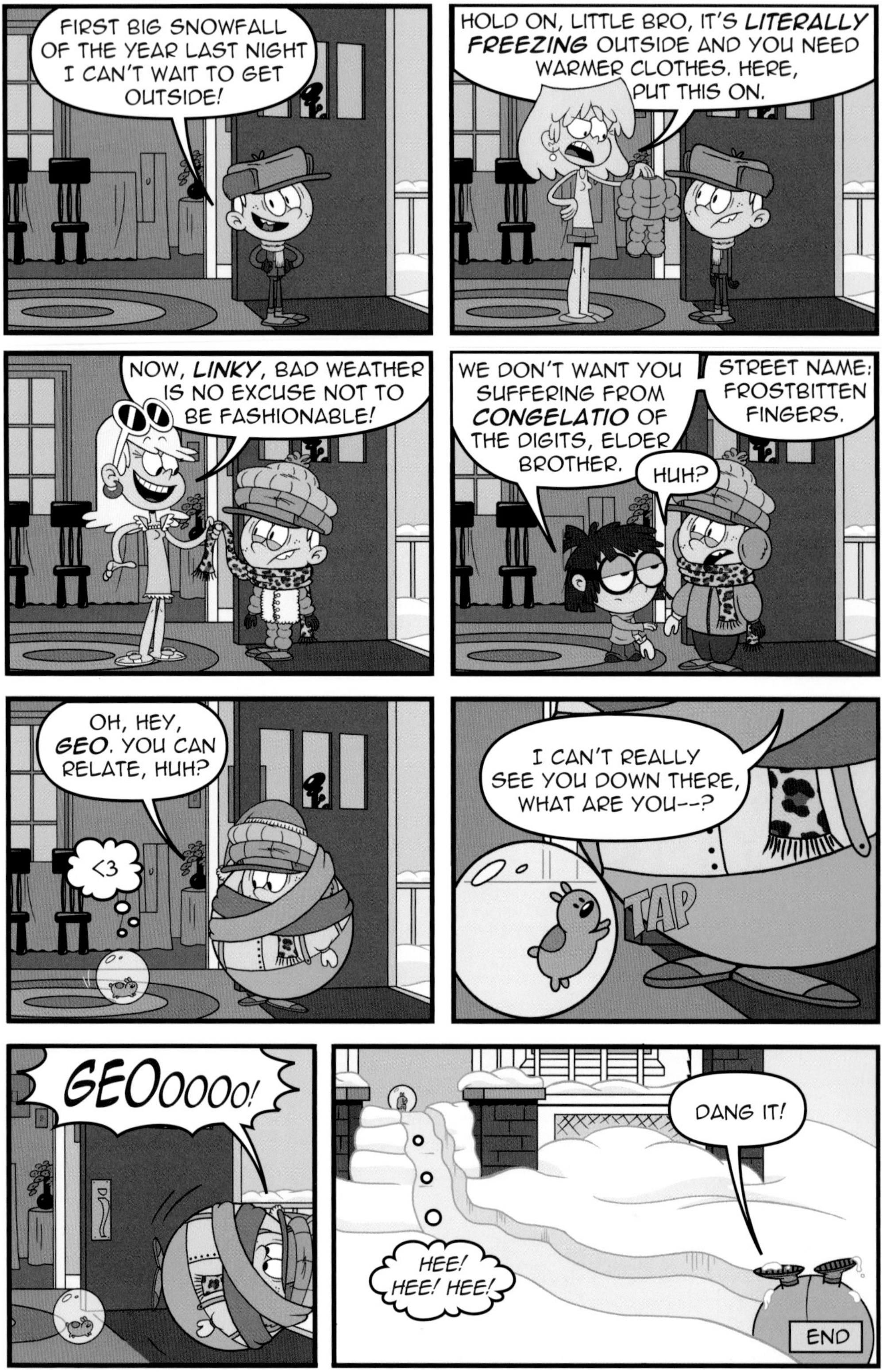

FIRST BIG SNOWFALL OF THE YEAR LAST NIGHT I CAN'T WAIT TO GET OUTSIDE!
HOLD ON, LITTLE BRO, IT'S *LITERALLY FREEZING* OUTSIDE AND YOU NEED WARMER CLOTHES. HERE, PUT THIS ON.
NOW, *LINKY*, BAD WEATHER IS NO EXCUSE NOT TO BE FASHIONABLE!
WE DON'T WANT YOU SUFFERING FROM *CONGELATIO* OF THE DIGITS, ELDER BROTHER.
STREET NAME: FROSTBITTEN FINGERS.
HUH?
OH, HEY, *GEO*. YOU CAN RELATE, HUH?
<3
I CAN'T REALLY SEE YOU DOWN THERE, WHAT ARE YOU--?
TAP
GEOOOOO!
DANG IT!
HEE! HEE! HEE!
END

"SUPER HANGOUT TIME ACTIVATE!"

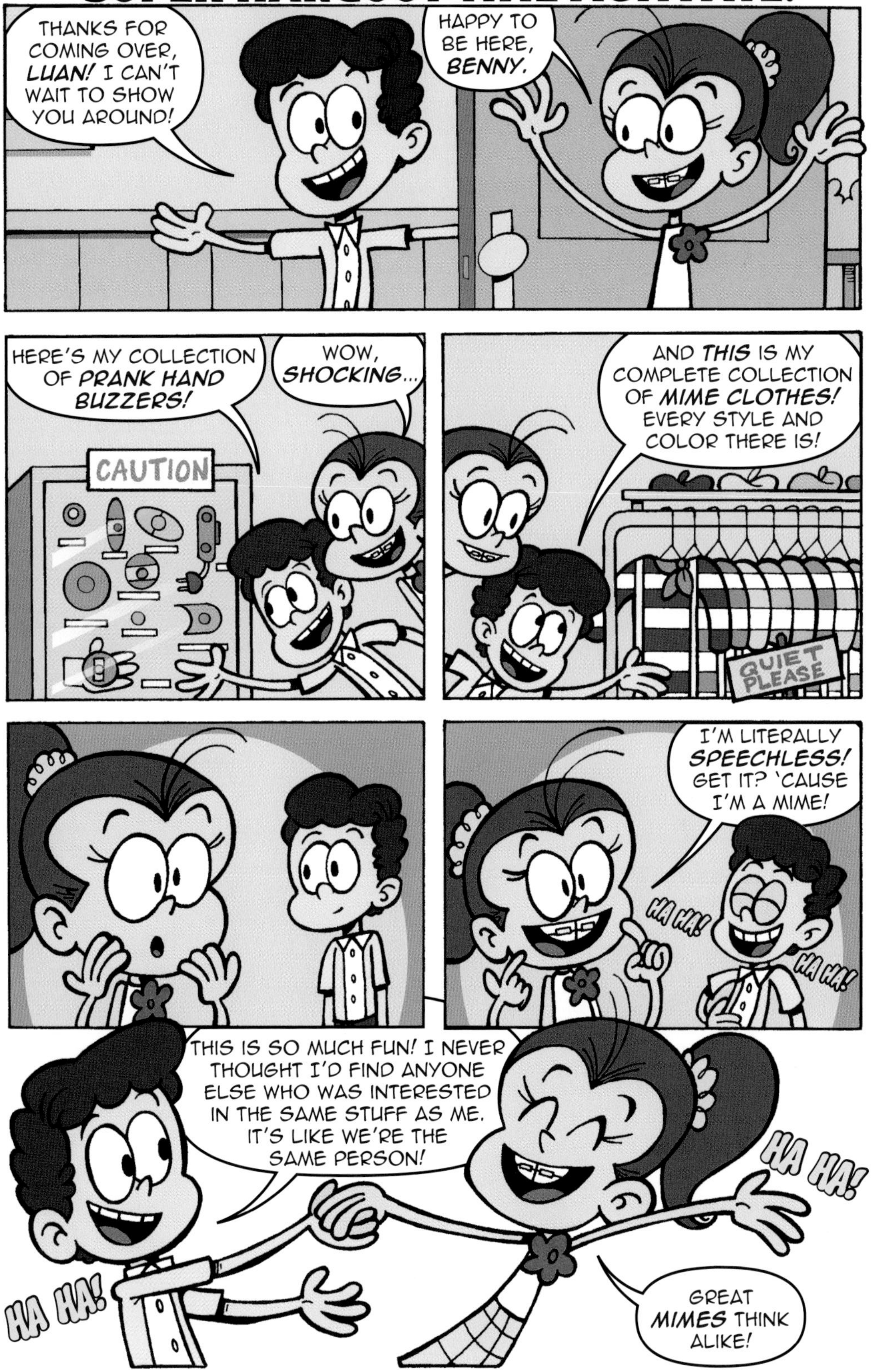
THANKS FOR COMING OVER, LUAN! I CAN'T WAIT TO SHOW YOU AROUND!
HAPPY TO BE HERE, BENNY.
HERE'S MY COLLECTION OF PRANK HAND BUZZERS!
CAUTION
WOW, SHOCKING...
AND THIS IS MY COMPLETE COLLECTION OF MIME CLOTHES! EVERY STYLE AND COLOR THERE IS!
QUIET PLEASE
I'M LITERALLY SPEECHLESS! GET IT? 'CAUSE I'M A MIME!
HA HA!
HA HA!
THIS IS SO MUCH FUN! I NEVER THOUGHT I'D FIND ANYONE ELSE WHO WAS INTERESTED IN THE SAME STUFF AS ME. IT'S LIKE WE'RE THE SAME PERSON!
HA HA!
HA HA!
GREAT MIMES THINK ALIKE!

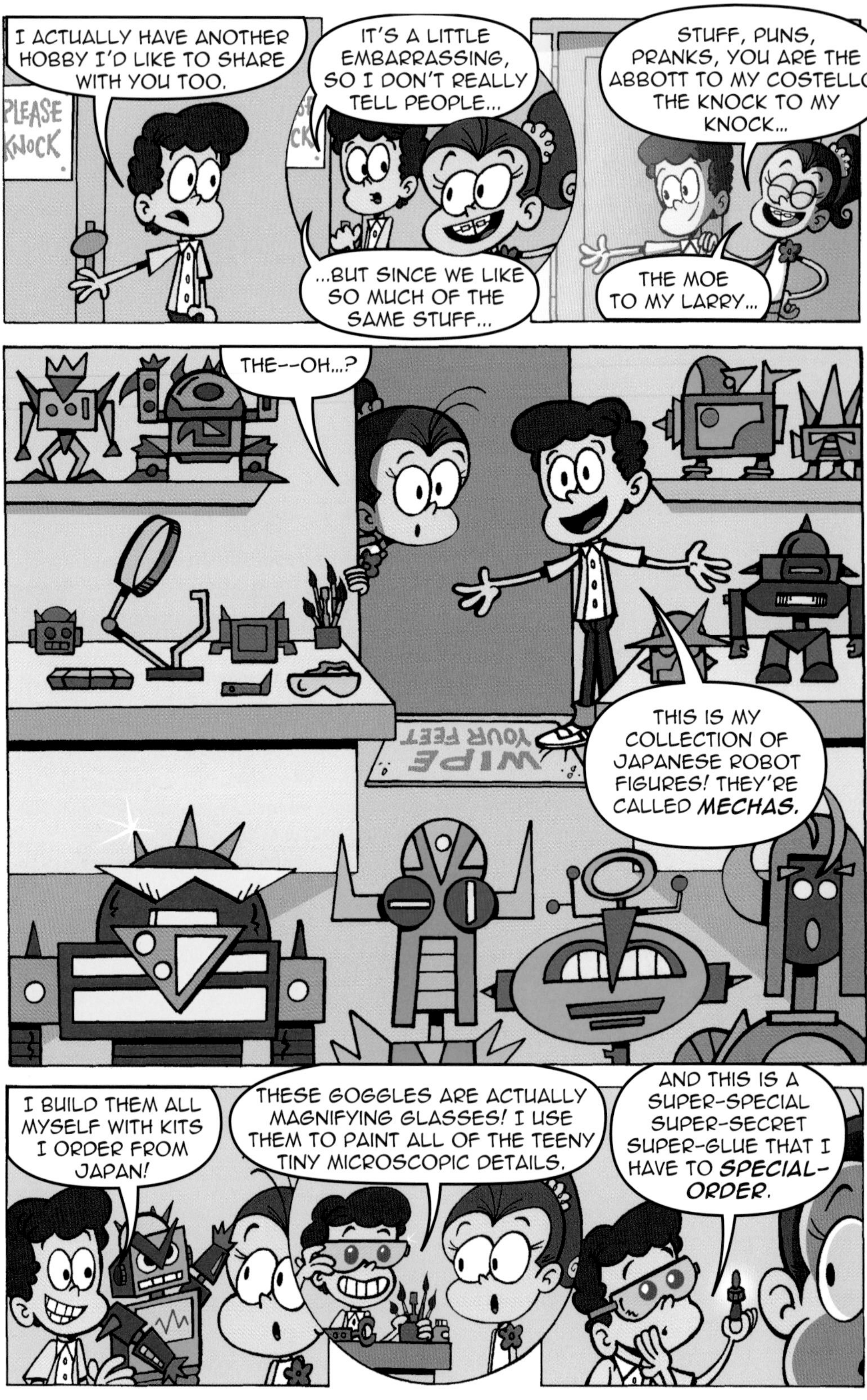
I ACTUALLY HAVE ANOTHER HOBBY I'D LIKE TO SHARE WITH YOU TOO.
PLEASE KNOCK
IT'S A LITTLE EMBARRASSING, SO I DON'T REALLY TELL PEOPLE...
...BUT SINCE WE LIKE SO MUCH OF THE SAME STUFF...
STUFF, PUNS, PRANKS, YOU ARE THE ABBOTT TO MY COSTELLO, THE KNOCK TO MY KNOCK...
THE MOE TO MY LARRY...
THE--OH...?
WIPE YOUR FEET
THIS IS MY COLLECTION OF JAPANESE ROBOT FIGURES! THEY'RE CALLED ***MECHAS.***
I BUILD THEM ALL MYSELF WITH KITS I ORDER FROM JAPAN!
THESE GOGGLES ARE ACTUALLY MAGNIFYING GLASSES! I USE THEM TO PAINT ALL OF THE TEENY TINY MICROSCOPIC DETAILS.
AND THIS IS A SUPER-SPECIAL SUPER-SECRET SUPER-GLUE THAT I HAVE TO ***SPECIAL-ORDER***.

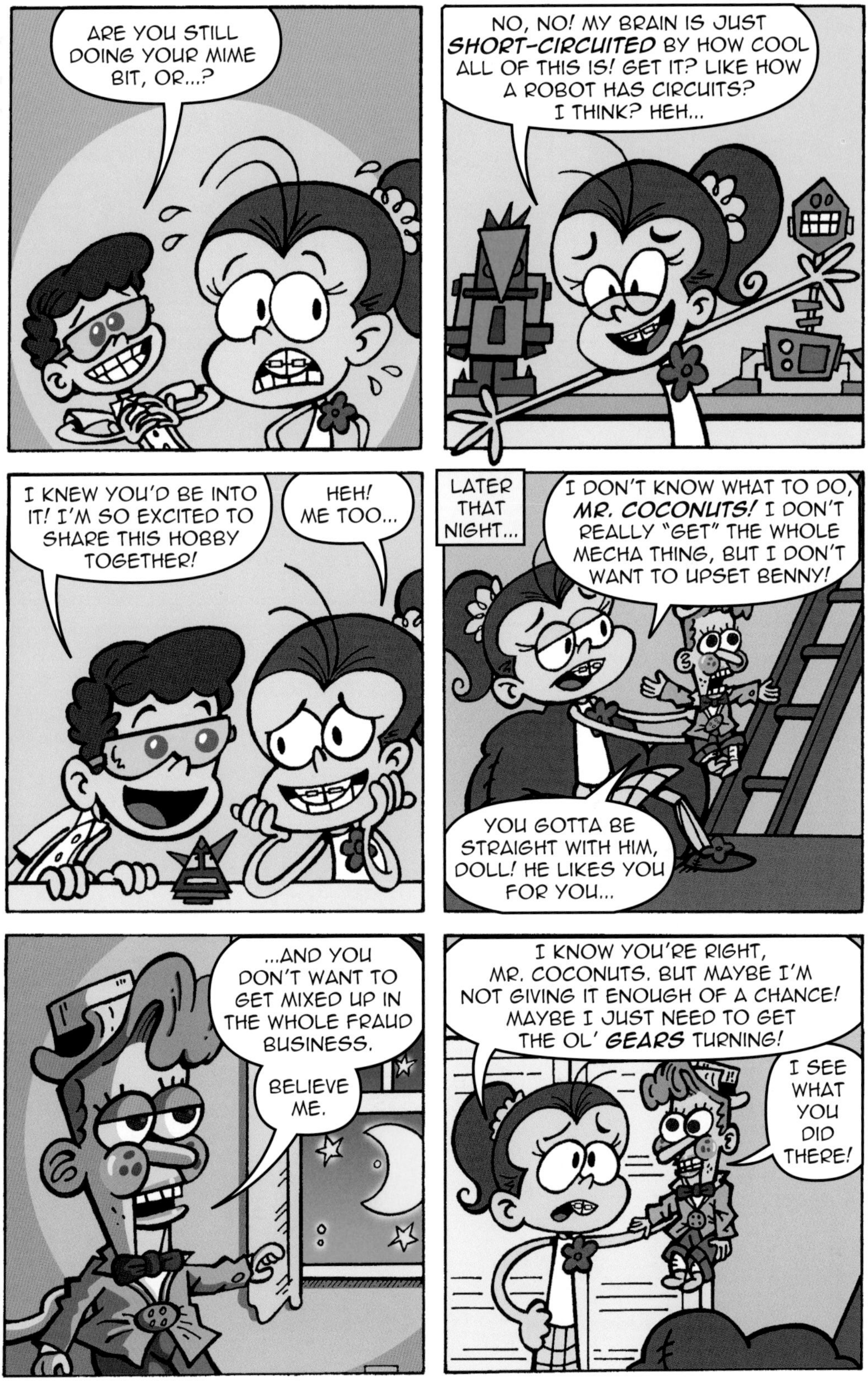
ARE YOU STILL DOING YOUR MIME BIT, OR...?
NO, NO! MY BRAIN IS JUST SHORT-CIRCUITED BY HOW COOL ALL OF THIS IS! GET IT? LIKE HOW A ROBOT HAS CIRCUITS? I THINK? HEH...
I KNEW YOU'D BE INTO IT! I'M SO EXCITED TO SHARE THIS HOBBY TOGETHER!
HEH! ME TOO...
LATER THAT NIGHT...
I DON'T KNOW WHAT TO DO, MR. COCONUTS! I DON'T REALLY "GET" THE WHOLE MECHA THING, BUT I DON'T WANT TO UPSET BENNY!
YOU GOTTA BE STRAIGHT WITH HIM, DOLL! HE LIKES YOU FOR YOU...
...AND YOU DON'T WANT TO GET MIXED UP IN THE WHOLE FRAUD BUSINESS.
BELIEVE ME.
I KNOW YOU'RE RIGHT, MR. COCONUTS. BUT MAYBE I'M NOT GIVING IT ENOUGH OF A CHANCE! MAYBE I JUST NEED TO GET THE OL' GEARS TURNING!
I SEE WHAT YOU DID THERE!

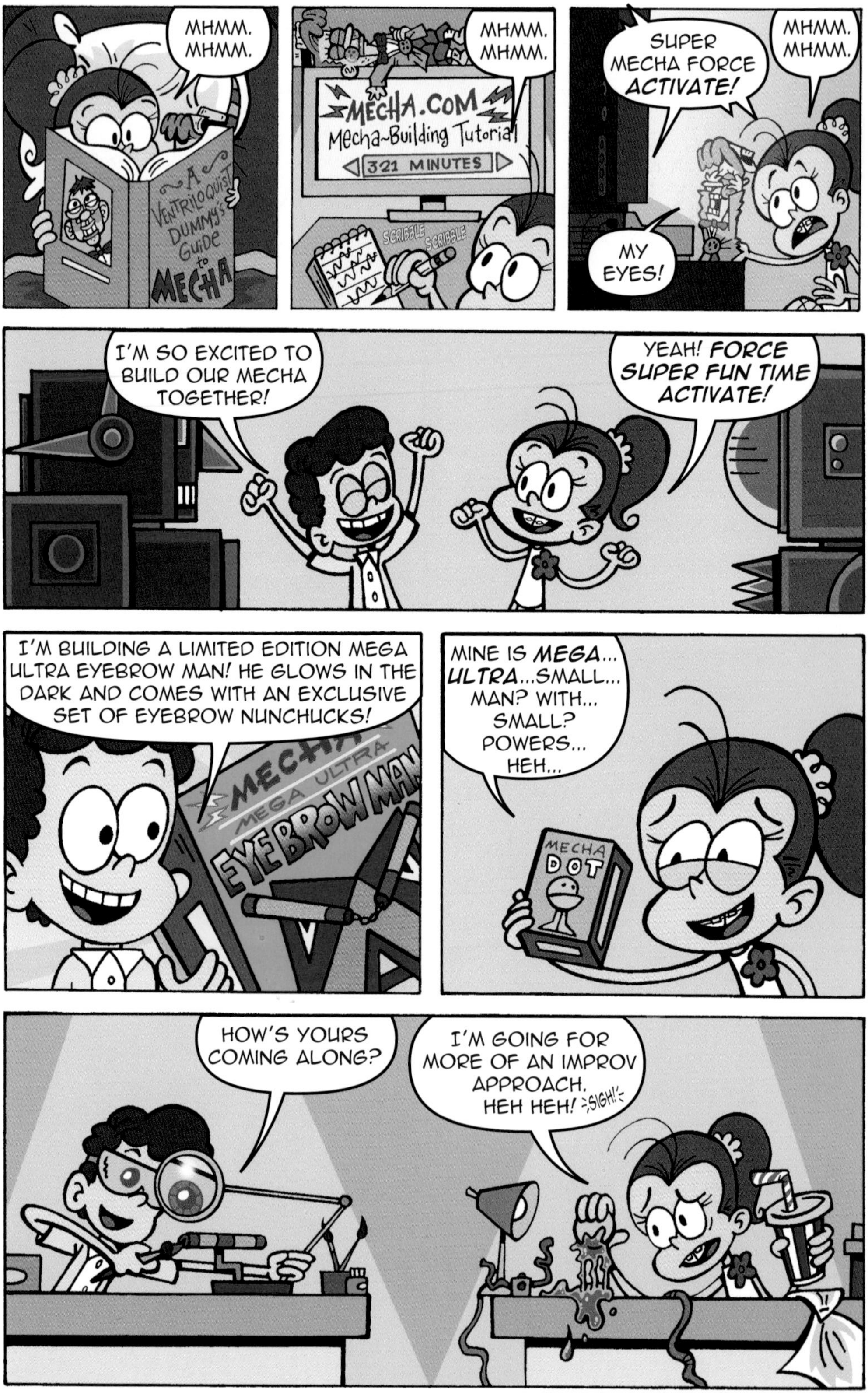
MHMM. MHMM.
A VENTRILOQUIST DUMMY'S GUIDE to MECHA
MHMM. MHMM.
MECHA.COM
Mecha~Building Tutorial
321 MINUTES
SCRIBBLE SCRIBBLE
SUPER MECHA FORCE ACTIVATE!
MHMM. MHMM.
MY EYES!
I'M SO EXCITED TO BUILD OUR MECHA TOGETHER!
YEAH! FORCE SUPER FUN TIME ACTIVATE!
I'M BUILDING A LIMITED EDITION MEGA ULTRA EYEBROW MAN! HE GLOWS IN THE DARK AND COMES WITH AN EXCLUSIVE SET OF EYEBROW NUNCHUCKS!
MECHA MEGA ULTRA EYEBROW MAN
MINE IS MEGA... ULTRA...SMALL... MAN? WITH... SMALL? POWERS... HEH...
MECHA DOT
HOW'S YOURS COMING ALONG?
I'M GOING FOR MORE OF AN IMPROV APPROACH. HEH HEH! SIGH!

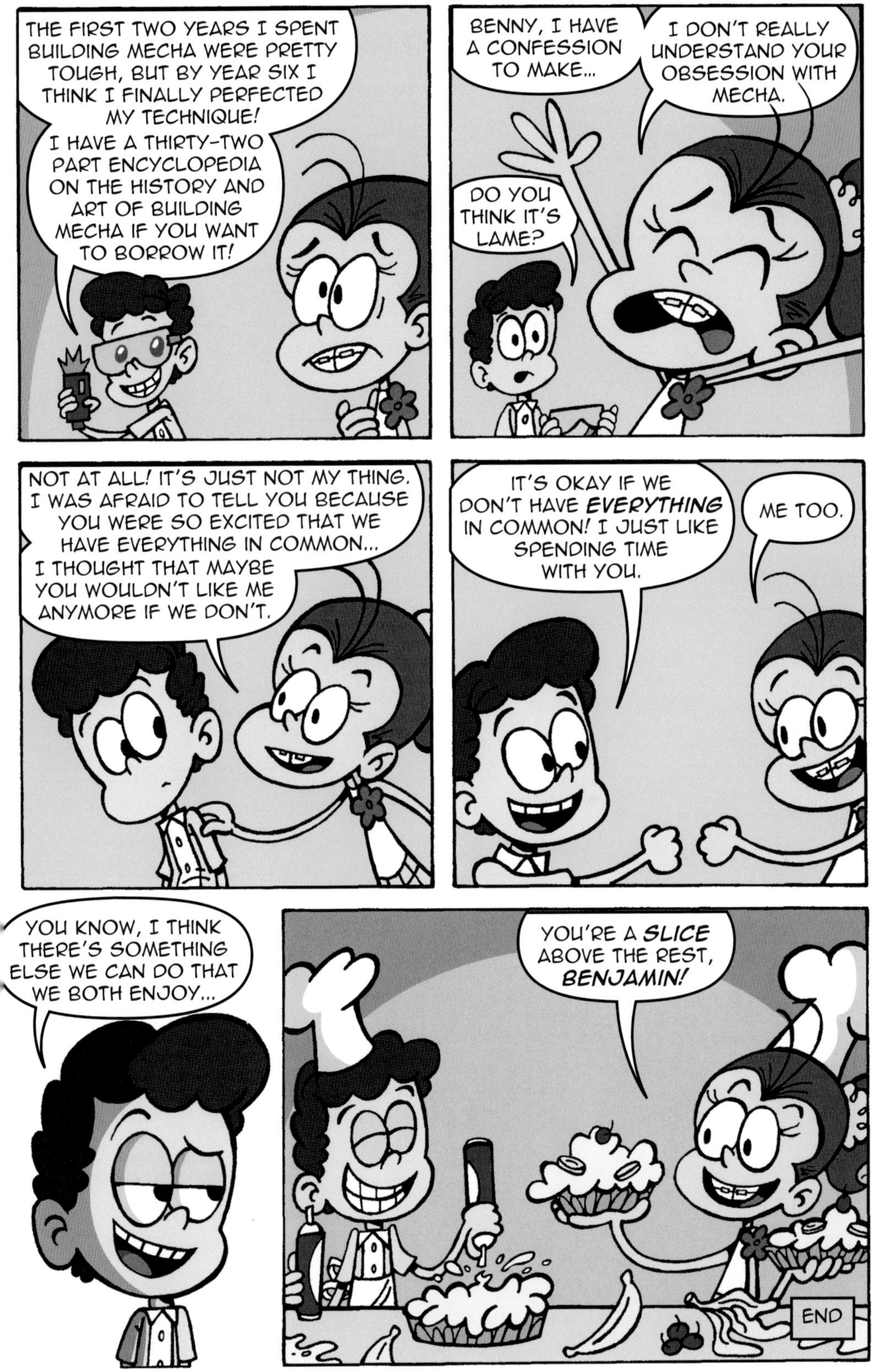
THE FIRST TWO YEARS I SPENT BUILDING MECHA WERE PRETTY TOUGH, BUT BY YEAR SIX I THINK I FINALLY PERFECTED MY TECHNIQUE!
I HAVE A THIRTY-TWO PART ENCYCLOPEDIA ON THE HISTORY AND ART OF BUILDING MECHA IF YOU WANT TO BORROW IT!
BENNY, I HAVE A CONFESSION TO MAKE...
I DON'T REALLY UNDERSTAND YOUR OBSESSION WITH MECHA.
DO YOU THINK IT'S LAME?
NOT AT ALL! IT'S JUST NOT MY THING. I WAS AFRAID TO TELL YOU BECAUSE YOU WERE SO EXCITED THAT WE HAVE EVERYTHING IN COMMON...
I THOUGHT THAT MAYBE YOU WOULDN'T LIKE ME ANYMORE IF WE DON'T.
IT'S OKAY IF WE DON'T HAVE EVERYTHING IN COMMON! I JUST LIKE SPENDING TIME WITH YOU.
ME TOO.
YOU KNOW, I THINK THERE'S SOMETHING ELSE WE CAN DO THAT WE BOTH ENJOY...
YOU'RE A SLICE ABOVE THE REST, BENJAMIN!
END

"STUDY BUDDIES"

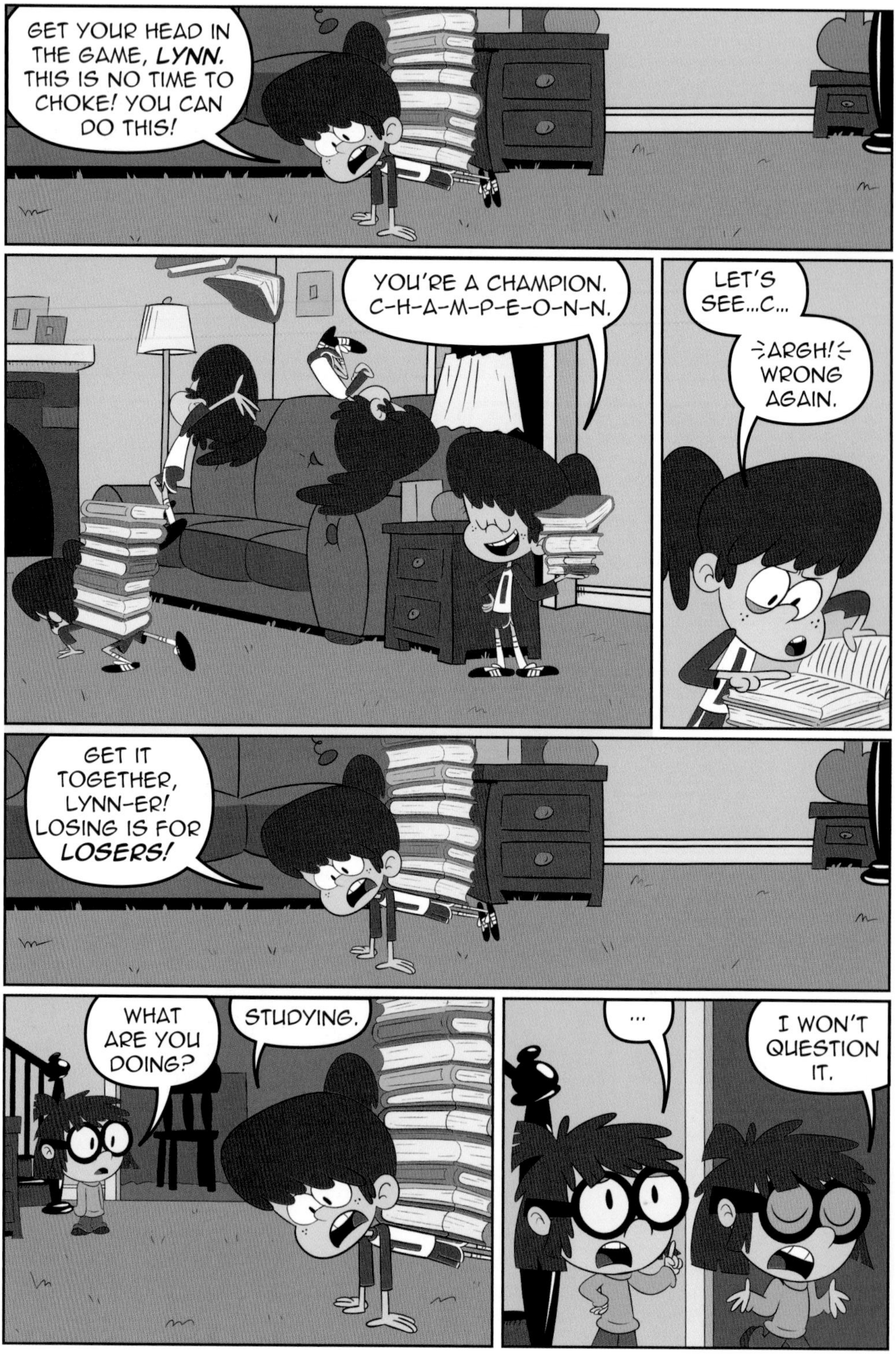
GET YOUR HEAD IN THE GAME, LYNN. THIS IS NO TIME TO CHOKE! YOU CAN DO THIS!
YOU'RE A CHAMPION. C-H-A-M-P-E-O-N-N.
LET'S SEE...C...
ARGH! WRONG AGAIN.
GET IT TOGETHER, LYNN-ER! LOSING IS FOR LOSERS!
WHAT ARE YOU DOING?
STUDYING.
...
I WON'T QUESTION IT.

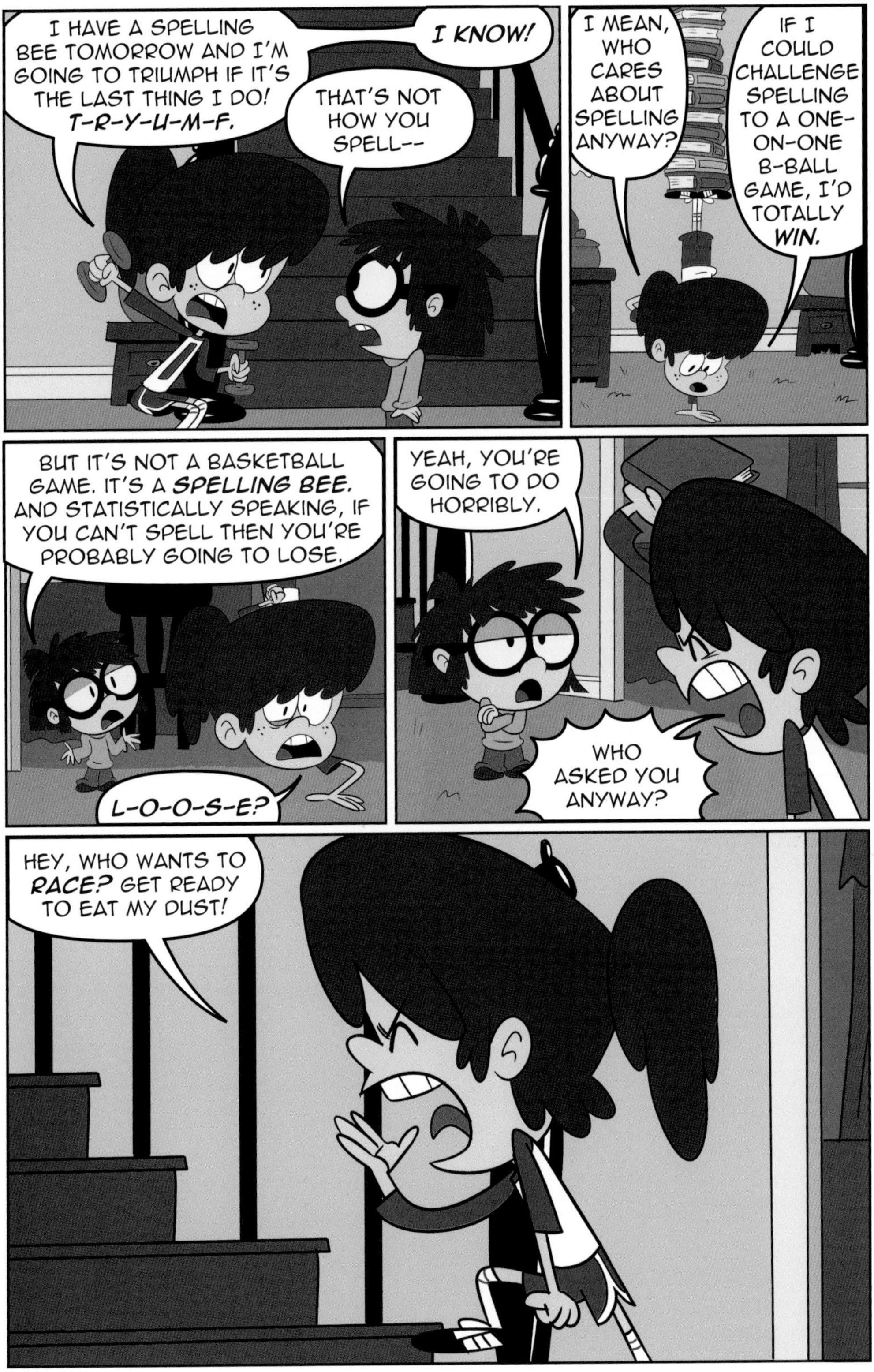
I HAVE A SPELLING BEE TOMORROW AND I'M GOING TO TRIUMPH IF IT'S THE LAST THING I DO! T-R-Y-U-M-F.
THAT'S NOT HOW YOU SPELL--
I KNOW!
I MEAN, WHO CARES ABOUT SPELLING ANYWAY?
IF I COULD CHALLENGE SPELLING TO A ONE-ON-ONE B-BALL GAME, I'D TOTALLY WIN.
BUT IT'S NOT A BASKETBALL GAME. IT'S A SPELLING BEE. AND STATISTICALLY SPEAKING, IF YOU CAN'T SPELL THEN YOU'RE PROBABLY GOING TO LOSE.
L-O-O-S-E?
YEAH, YOU'RE GOING TO DO HORRIBLY.
WHO ASKED YOU ANYWAY?
HEY, WHO WANTS TO RACE? GET READY TO EAT MY DUST!

CURIOUS. WHEN FACED WITH EVIDENCE OF HER POOR SPELLING SKILLS, LYNN HAS A SUBOPTIMAL REACTION.

LYNN + SPELLING = BAD

$$!\Delta, B \vdash ?\Gamma$$
$$\frac{!\Delta, ?B \vdash ?\Gamma}{\Delta \vdash \Gamma} \, ?L$$
$$\frac{\Delta \vdash \Gamma}{\Delta, !B \vdash \Gamma} \, !W$$
$$\frac{\Delta \vdash \Gamma}{\Delta \vdash ?B}$$

SPELLING

$$\frac{\Delta, B[y/x] \vdash}{\Delta, \exists x. B}$$

$$LYNN = y/x$$

BAD = LOSING
LYNN + SPELLING
=
LOSING

LYNN *HATES* LOSING!

76

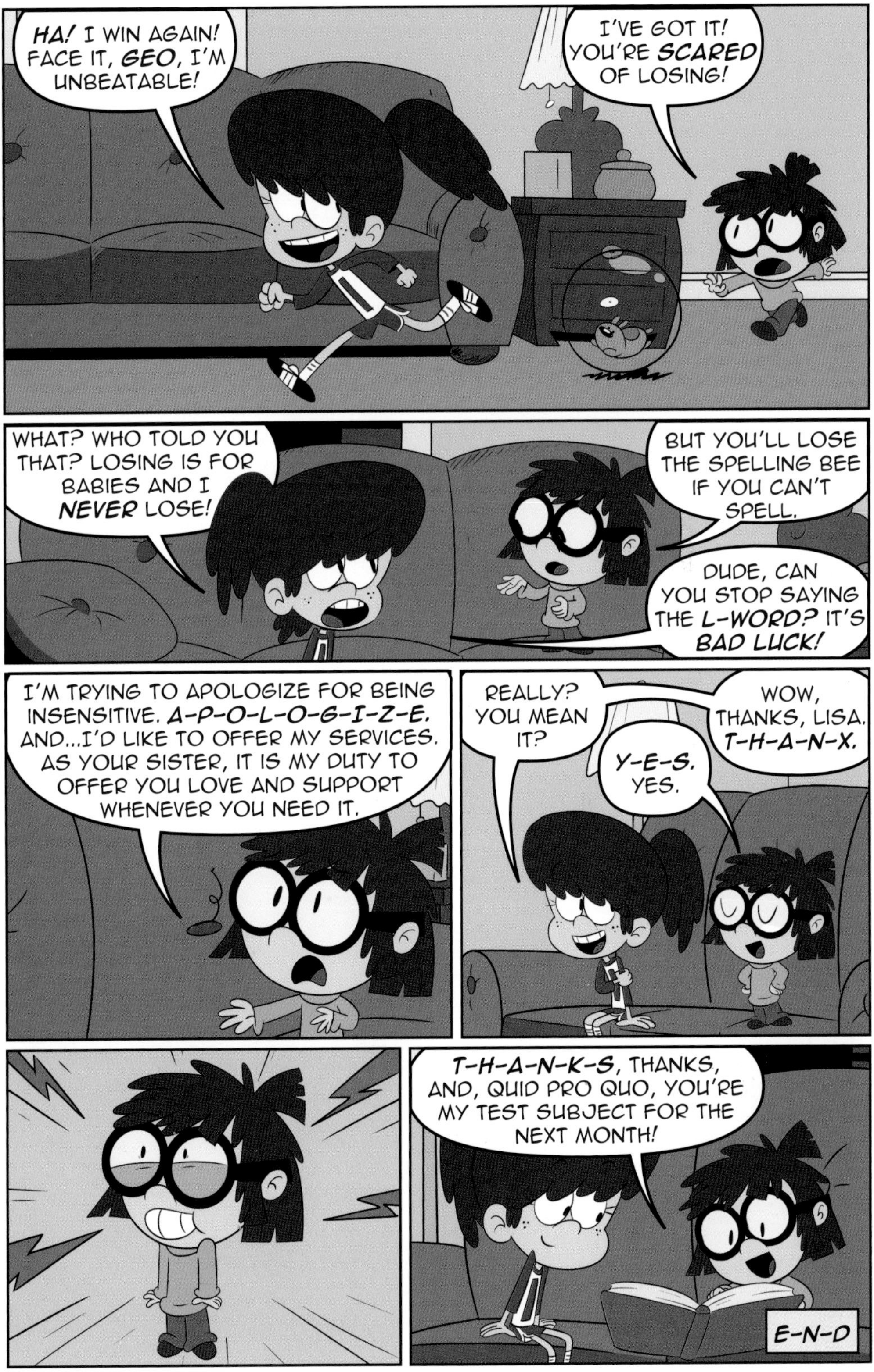
HA! I WIN AGAIN! FACE IT, GEO, I'M UNBEATABLE!
I'VE GOT IT! YOU'RE SCARED OF LOSING!
WHAT? WHO TOLD YOU THAT? LOSING IS FOR BABIES AND I NEVER LOSE!
BUT YOU'LL LOSE THE SPELLING BEE IF YOU CAN'T SPELL.
DUDE, CAN YOU STOP SAYING THE L-WORD? IT'S BAD LUCK!
I'M TRYING TO APOLOGIZE FOR BEING INSENSITIVE. A-P-O-L-O-G-I-Z-E. AND...I'D LIKE TO OFFER MY SERVICES. AS YOUR SISTER, IT IS MY DUTY TO OFFER YOU LOVE AND SUPPORT WHENEVER YOU NEED IT.
REALLY? YOU MEAN IT?
Y-E-S. YES.
WOW, THANKS, LISA. T-H-A-N-X.
T-H-A-N-K-S, THANKS, AND, QUID PRO QUO, YOU'RE MY TEST SUBJECT FOR THE NEXT MONTH!
E-N-D

"RAIN, RAIN, HERE TO STAY"

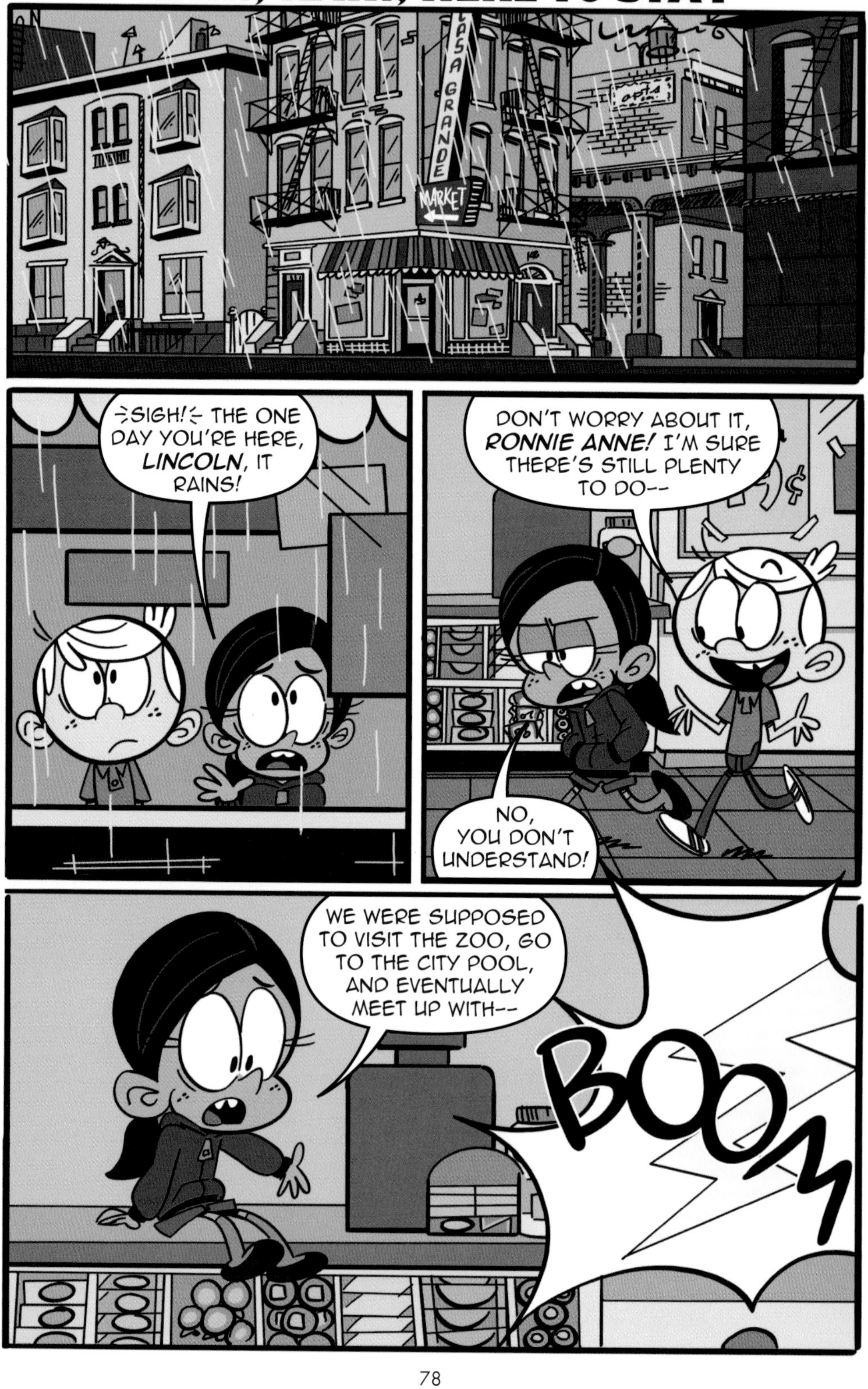

CASA GRANDE
MARKET
⇒SIGH!⇐ THE ONE DAY YOU'RE HERE, **LINCOLN**, IT RAINS!
DON'T WORRY ABOUT IT, **RONNIE ANNE!** I'M SURE THERE'S STILL PLENTY TO DO--
NO, YOU DON'T UNDERSTAND!
WE WERE SUPPOSED TO VISIT THE ZOO, GO TO THE CITY POOL, AND EVENTUALLY MEET UP WITH--
BOOM

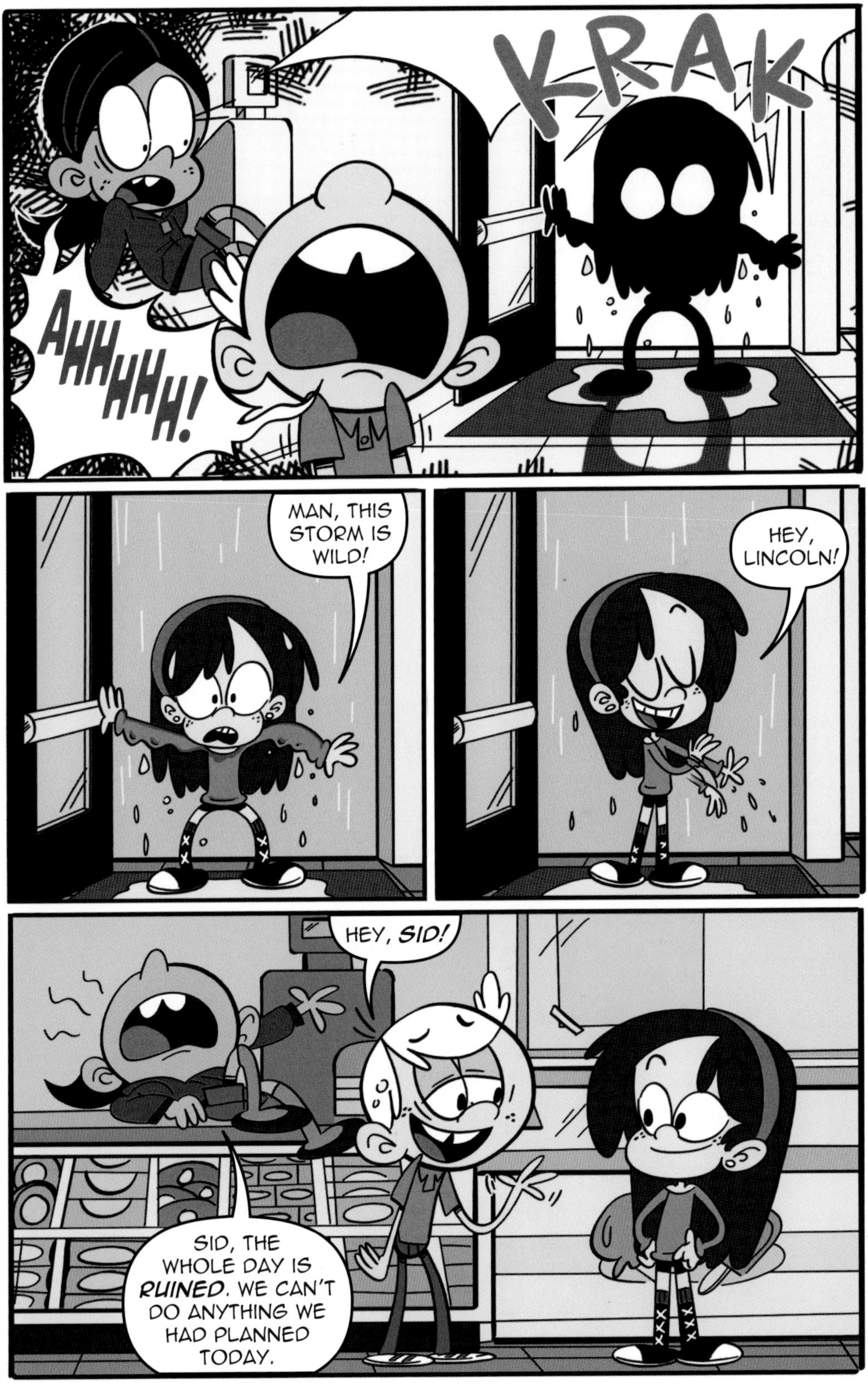
KRAK
AHHHHHH!
MAN, THIS STORM IS WILD!
HEY, LINCOLN!
HEY, SID!
SID, THE WHOLE DAY IS RUINED. WE CAN'T DO ANYTHING WE HAD PLANNED TODAY.

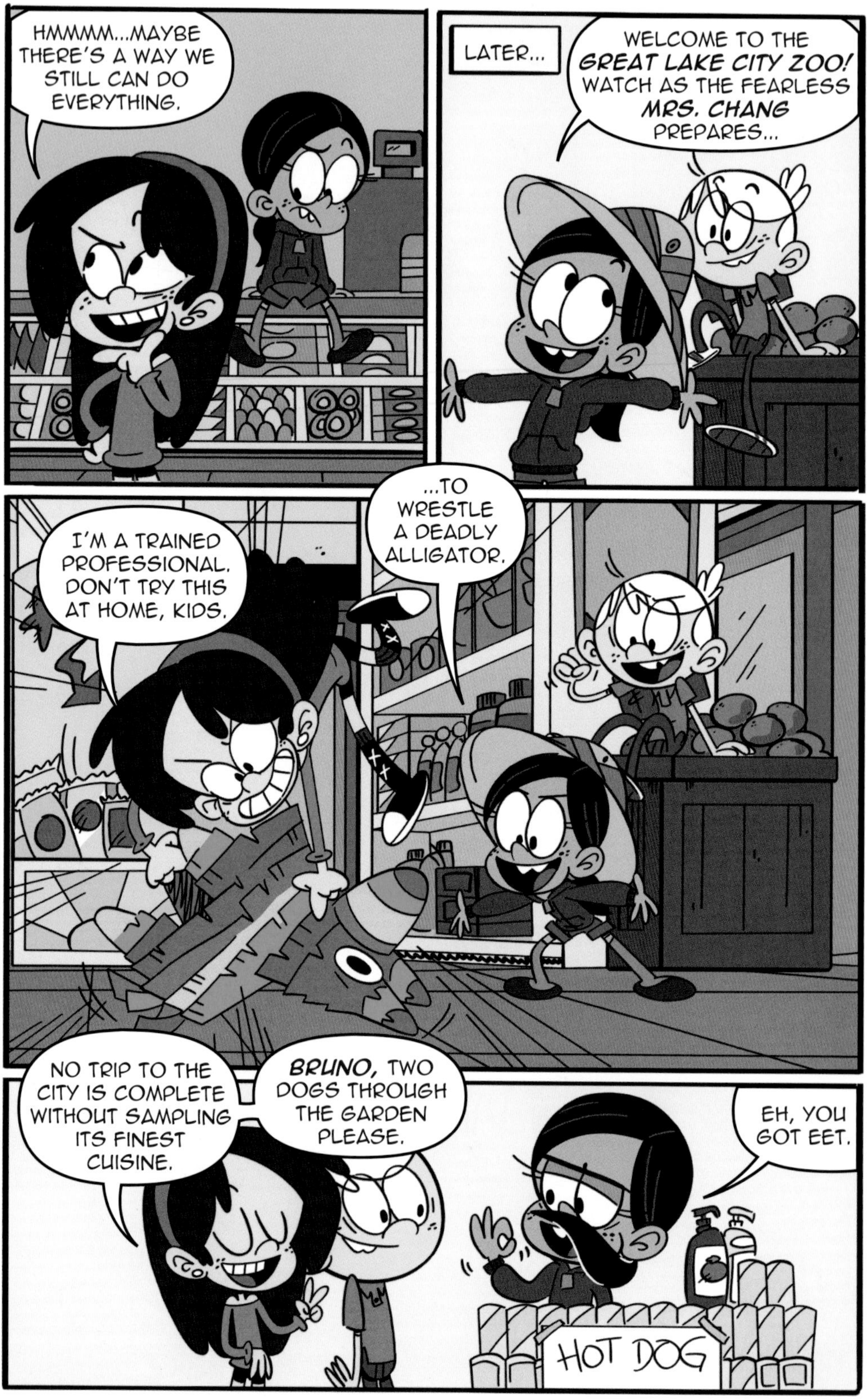
HMMMM...MAYBE THERE'S A WAY WE STILL CAN DO EVERYTHING.
LATER...
WELCOME TO THE **GREAT LAKE CITY ZOO!** WATCH AS THE FEARLESS **MRS. CHANG** PREPARES...
I'M A TRAINED PROFESSIONAL. DON'T TRY THIS AT HOME, KIDS.
...TO WRESTLE A DEADLY ALLIGATOR.
NO TRIP TO THE CITY IS COMPLETE WITHOUT SAMPLING ITS FINEST CUISINE.
BRUNO, TWO DOGS THROUGH THE GARDEN PLEASE.
EH, YOU GOT EET.
HOT DOG

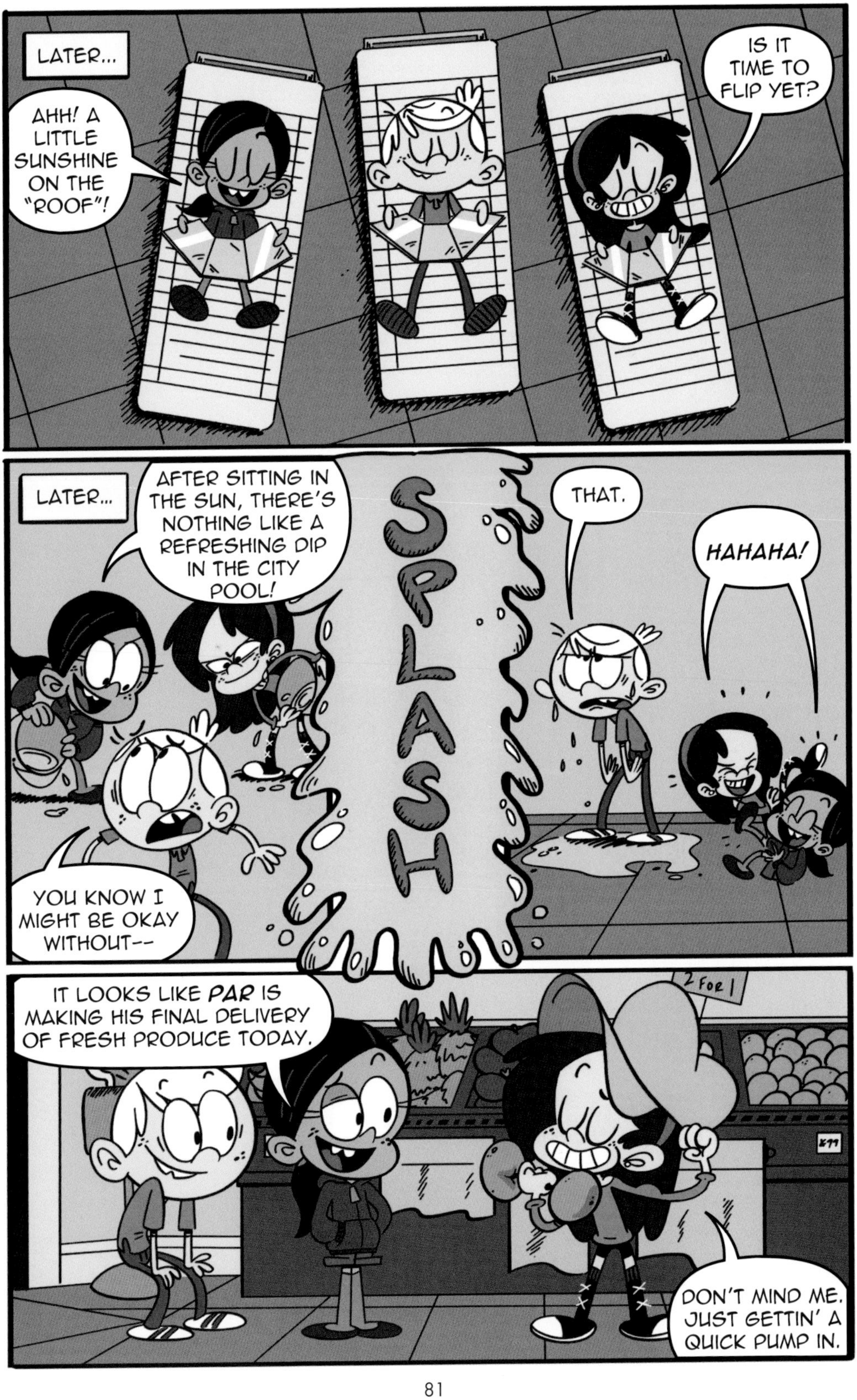
LATER...
AHH! A LITTLE SUNSHINE ON THE "ROOF"!
IS IT TIME TO FLIP YET?
LATER...
AFTER SITTING IN THE SUN, THERE'S NOTHING LIKE A REFRESHING DIP IN THE CITY POOL!
YOU KNOW I MIGHT BE OKAY WITHOUT--
SPLASH
THAT.
HAHAHA!
IT LOOKS LIKE PAR IS MAKING HIS FINAL DELIVERY OF FRESH PRODUCE TODAY.
2 FOR 1
DON'T MIND ME. JUST GETTIN' A QUICK PUMP IN.

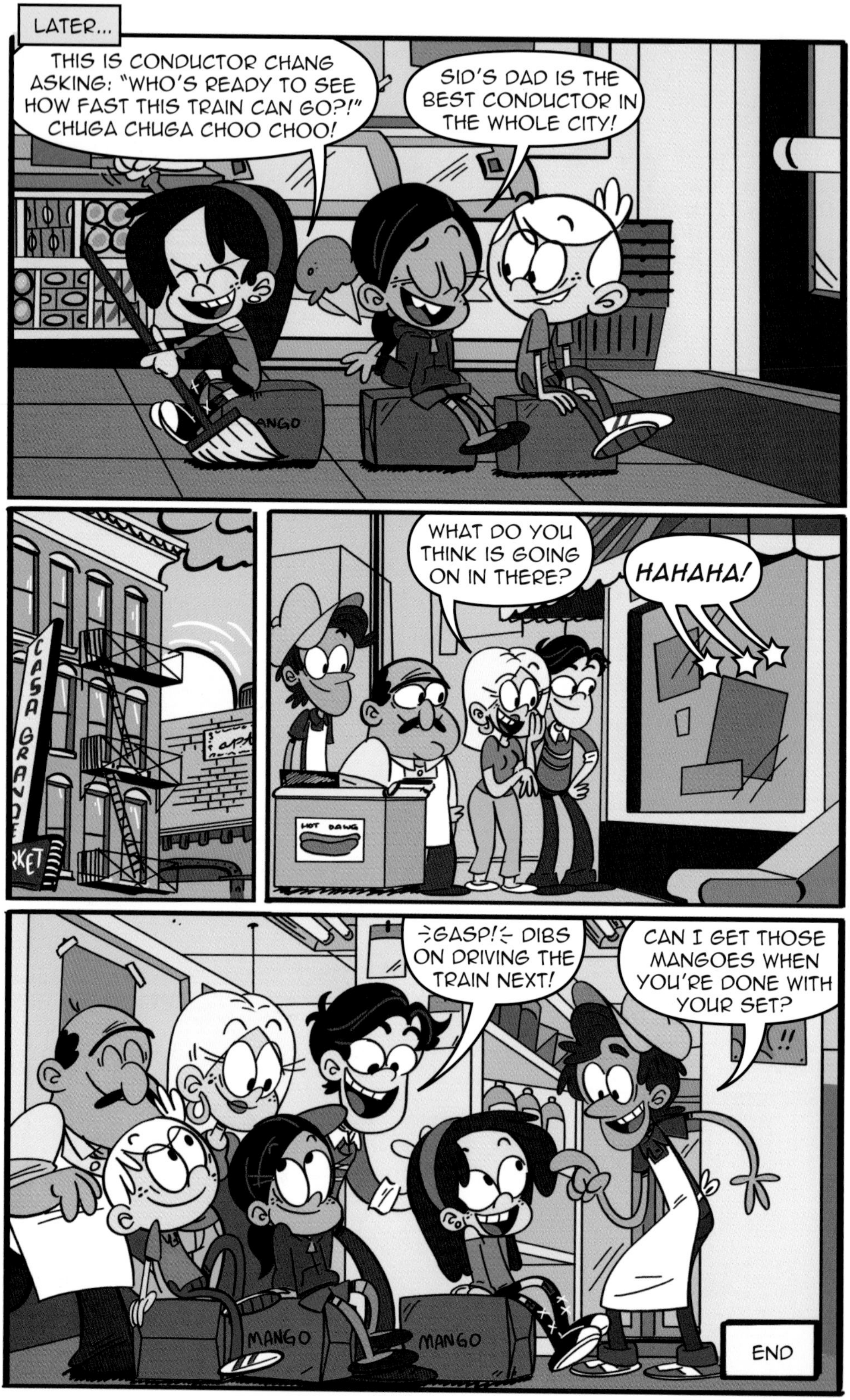
LATER...
THIS IS CONDUCTOR CHANG ASKING: "WHO'S READY TO SEE HOW FAST THIS TRAIN CAN GO?!" CHUGA CHUGA CHOO CHOO!
SID'S DAD IS THE BEST CONDUCTOR IN THE WHOLE CITY!
MANGO
CASA GRANDE
RKET
WHAT DO YOU THINK IS GOING ON IN THERE?
HAHAHA!
HOT DAWG
GASP! DIBS ON DRIVING THE TRAIN NEXT!
CAN I GET THOSE MANGOES WHEN YOU'RE DONE WITH YOUR SET?
MANGO
MANGO
END

"CITY TRICKERS"

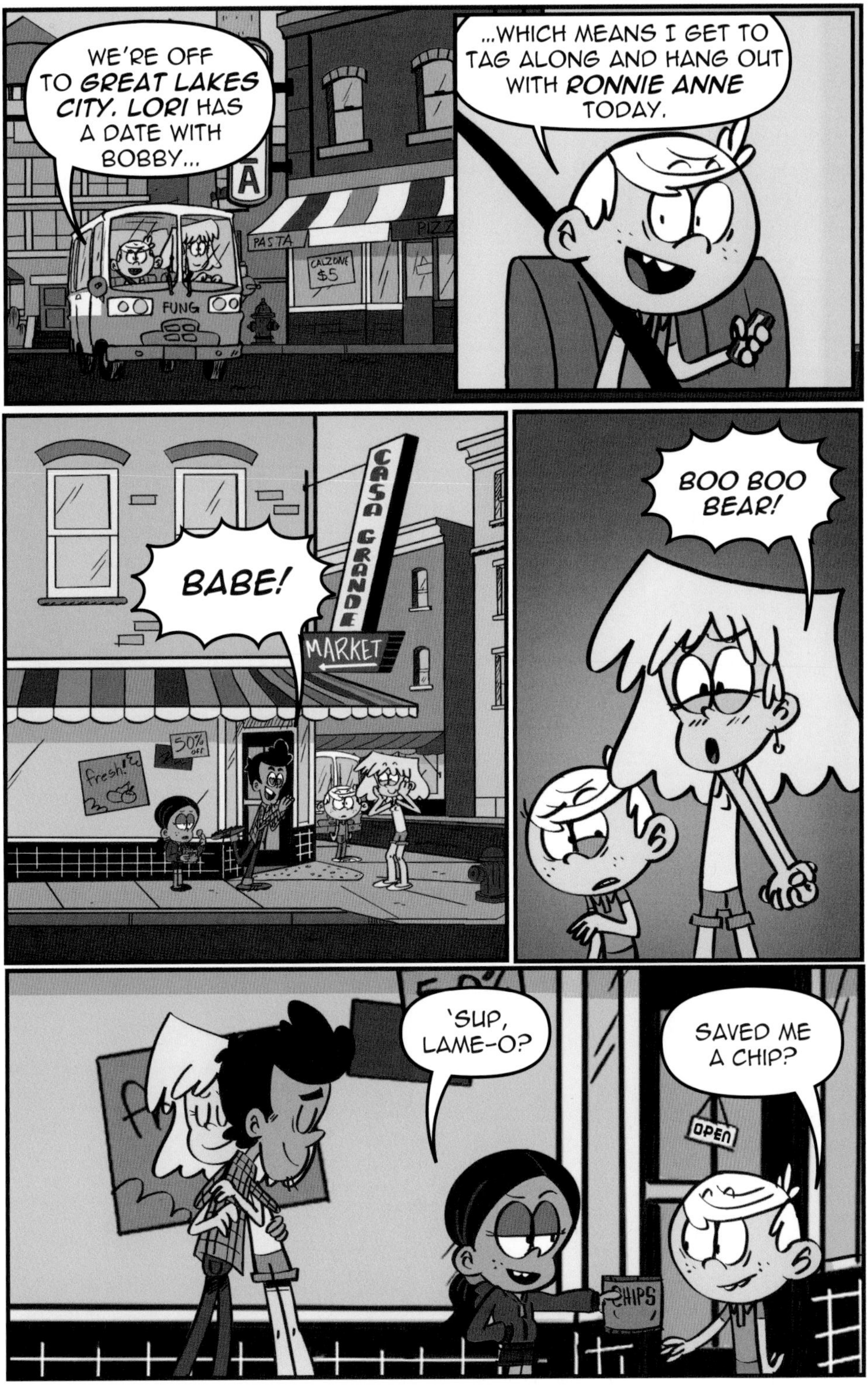
WE'RE OFF TO GREAT LAKES CITY. LORI HAS A DATE WITH BOBBY...
A
PASTA
PIZZ
CALZONE $5
FUNG
...WHICH MEANS I GET TO TAG ALONG AND HANG OUT WITH RONNIE ANNE TODAY.
CASA GRANDE
MARKET
BABE!
50% off
fresh!
BOO BOO BEAR!
'SUP, LAME-O?
SAVED ME A CHIP?
OPEN
CHIPS

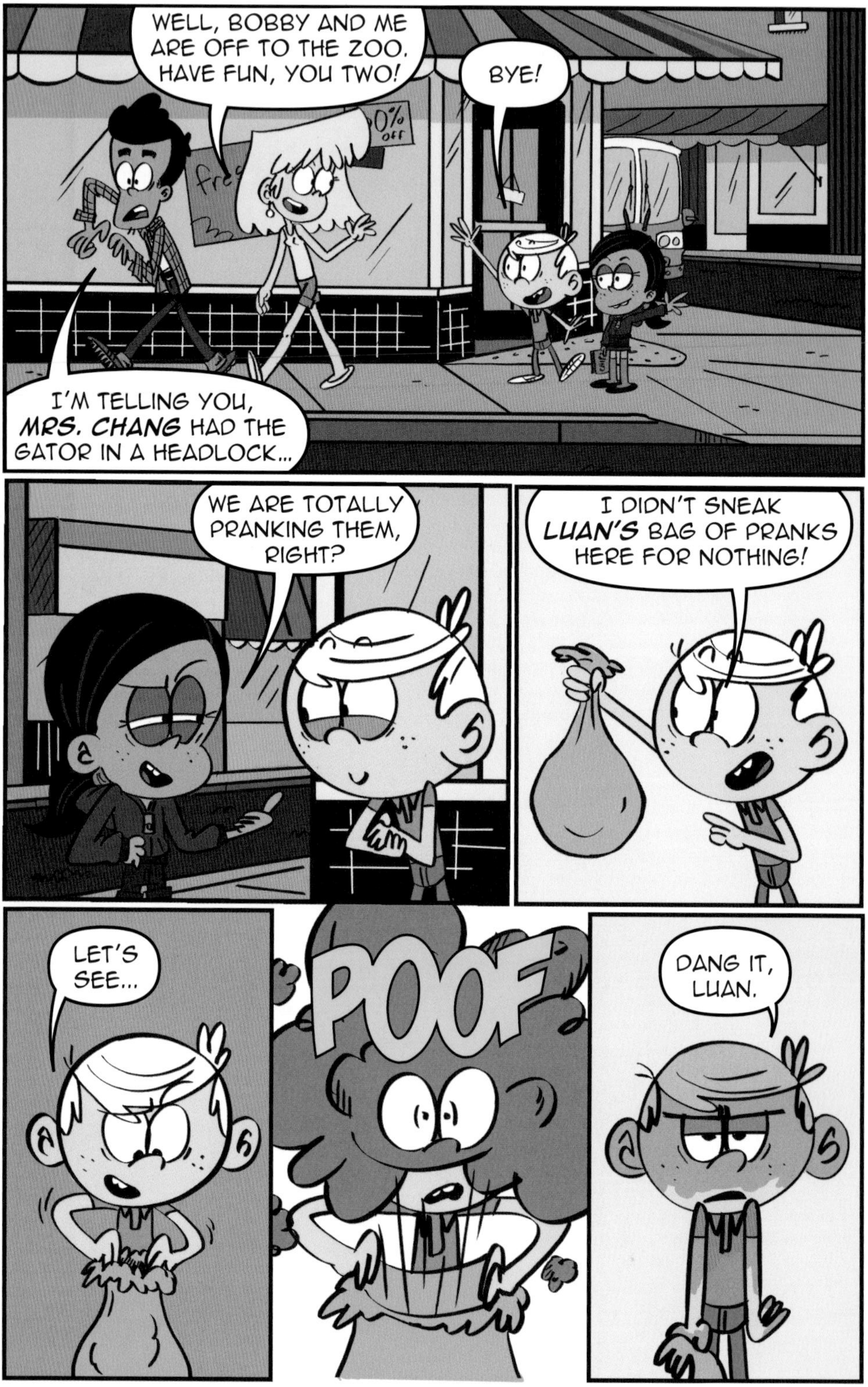

WELL, BOBBY AND ME ARE OFF TO THE ZOO. HAVE FUN, YOU TWO!
BYE!
I'M TELLING YOU, MRS. CHANG HAD THE GATOR IN A HEADLOCK...
WE ARE TOTALLY PRANKING THEM, RIGHT?
I DIDN'T SNEAK LUAN'S BAG OF PRANKS HERE FOR NOTHING!
LET'S SEE...
POOF
DANG IT, LUAN.

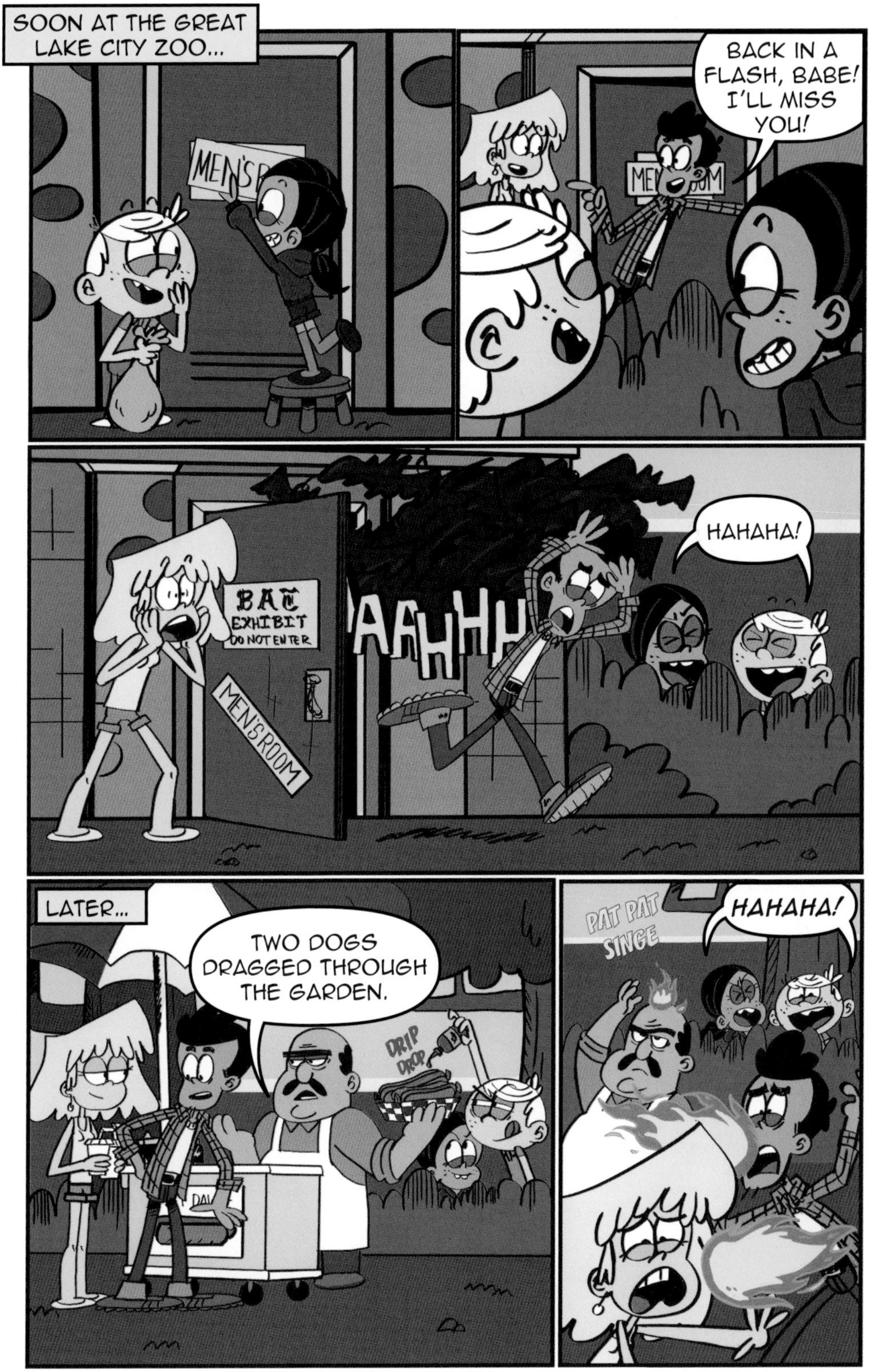
SOON AT THE GREAT LAKE CITY ZOO...
MEN'S R
BACK IN A FLASH, BABE! I'LL MISS YOU!
BAT EXHIBIT DO NOT ENTER
MEN'S ROOM
AAHHH
HAHAHA!
LATER...
TWO DOGS DRAGGED THROUGH THE GARDEN.
DRIP DROP
PAT PAT SINGE
HAHAHA!

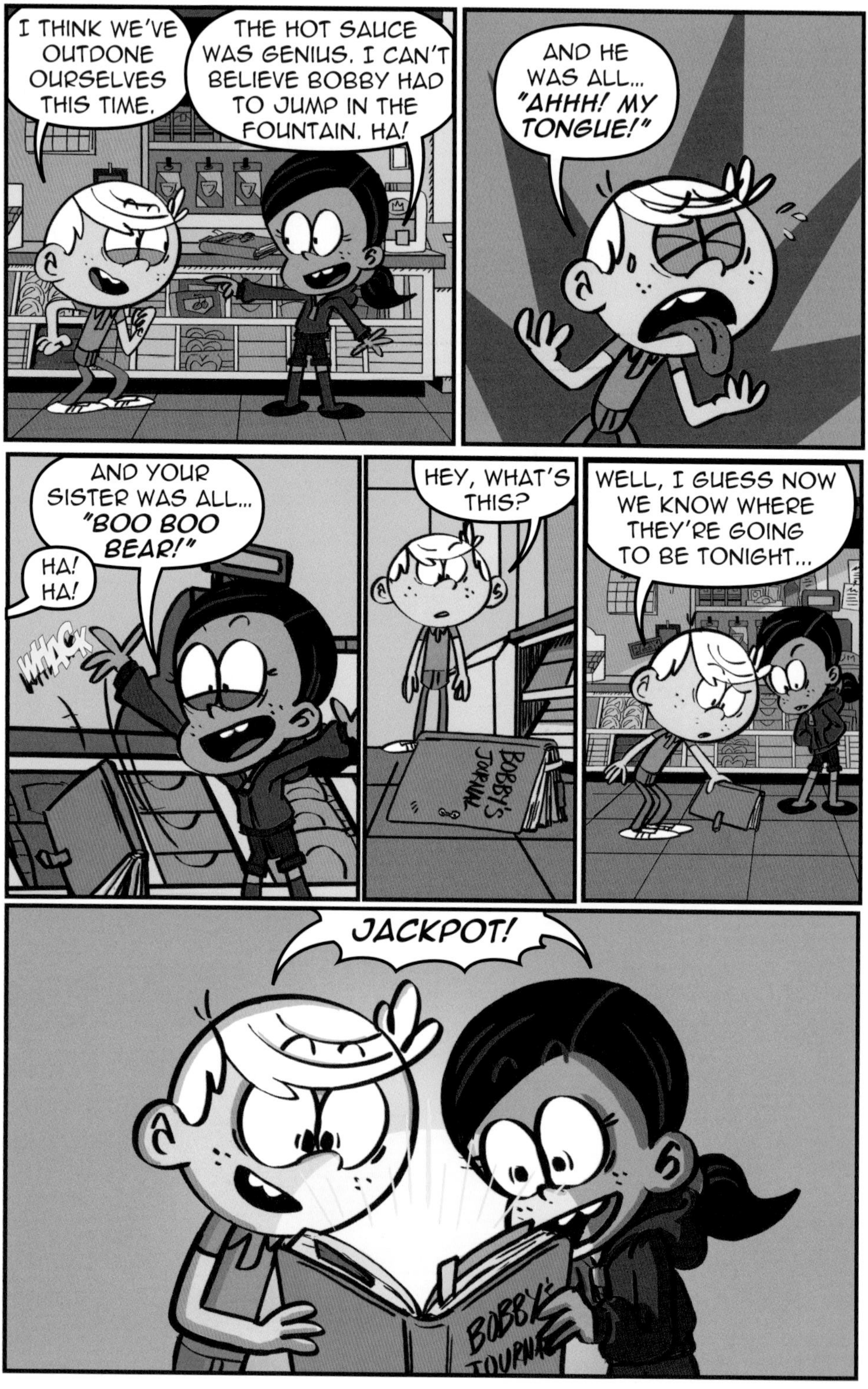
I THINK WE'VE OUTDONE OURSELVES THIS TIME.
THE HOT SAUCE WAS GENIUS. I CAN'T BELIEVE BOBBY HAD TO JUMP IN THE FOUNTAIN. HA!
AND HE WAS ALL... "AHHH! MY TONGUE!"
AND YOUR SISTER WAS ALL... "BOO BOO BEAR!"
HA! HA!
WHACK
HEY, WHAT'S THIS?
BOBBY'S JOURNAL
WELL, I GUESS NOW WE KNOW WHERE THEY'RE GOING TO BE TONIGHT...
JACKPOT!

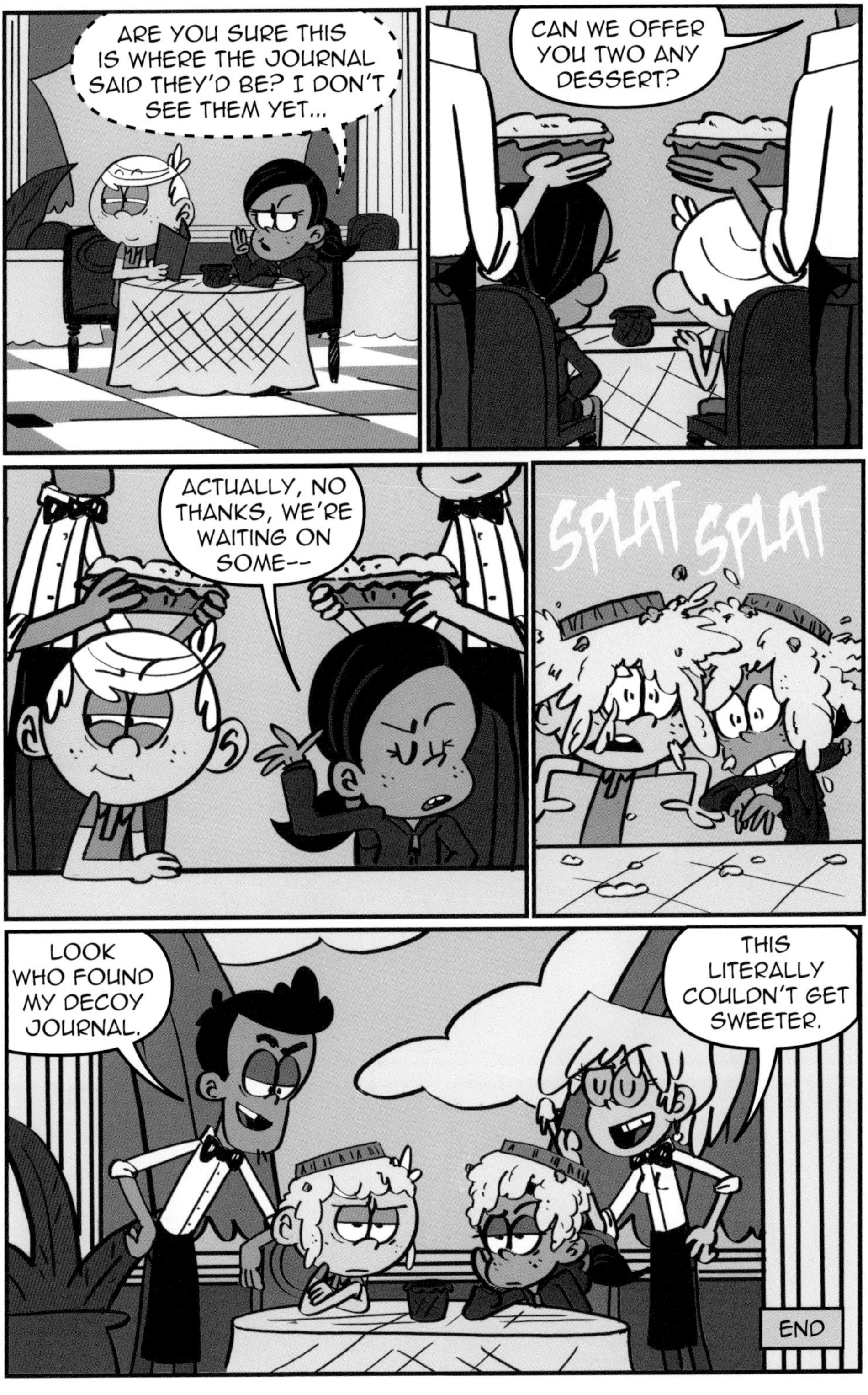
ARE YOU SURE THIS IS WHERE THE JOURNAL SAID THEY'D BE? I DON'T SEE THEM YET...
CAN WE OFFER YOU TWO ANY DESSERT?
ACTUALLY, NO THANKS, WE'RE WAITING ON SOME--
SPLAT SPLAT
LOOK WHO FOUND MY DECOY JOURNAL.
THIS LITERALLY COULDN'T GET SWEETER.
END

"PARTY ANIMALS"

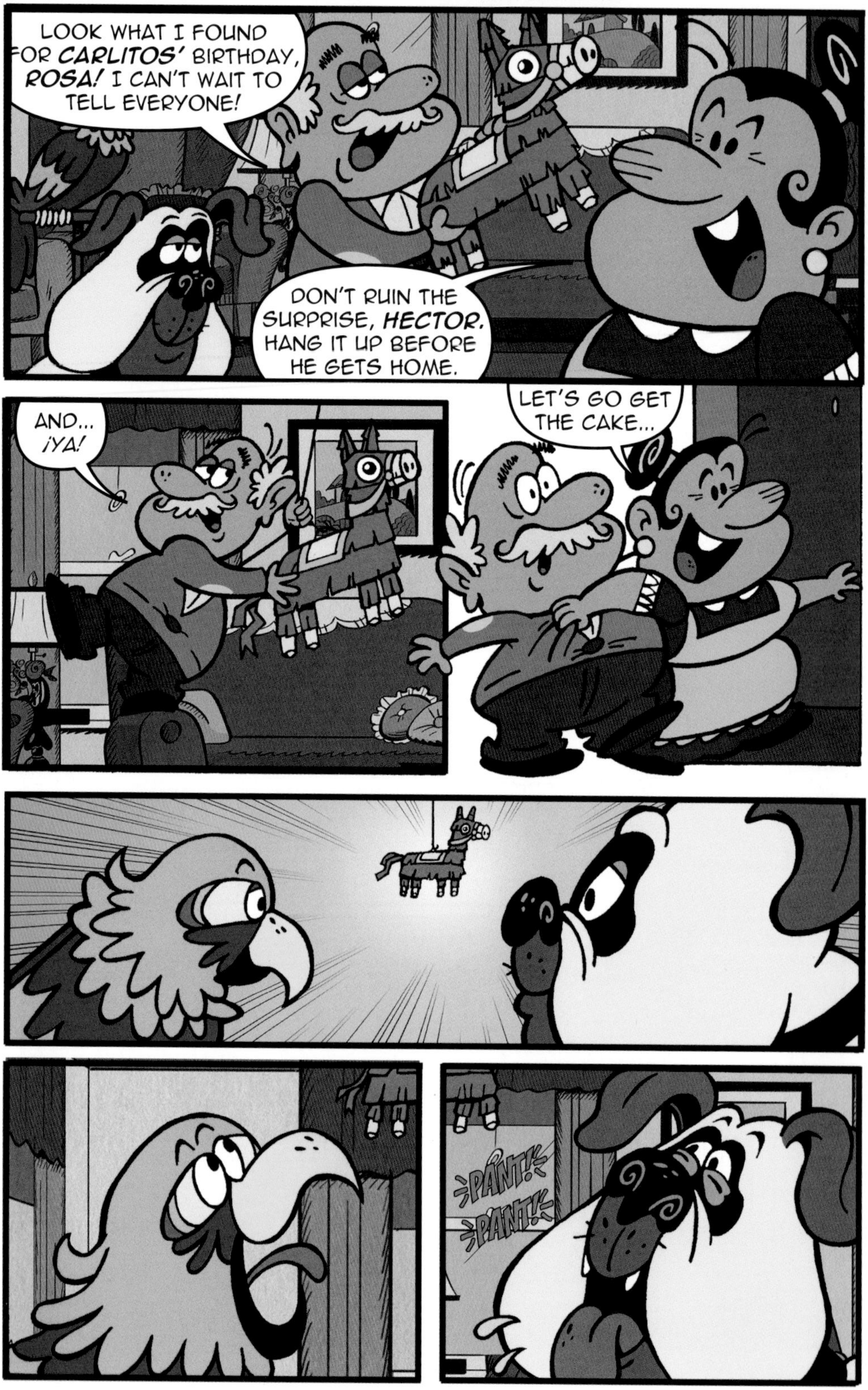
LOOK WHAT I FOUND FOR *CARLITOS'* BIRTHDAY, *ROSA!* I CAN'T WAIT TO TELL EVERYONE!
DON'T RUIN THE SURPRISE, *HECTOR.* HANG IT UP BEFORE HE GETS HOME.
AND... *¡YA!*
LET'S GO GET THE CAKE...
PANT! PANT!

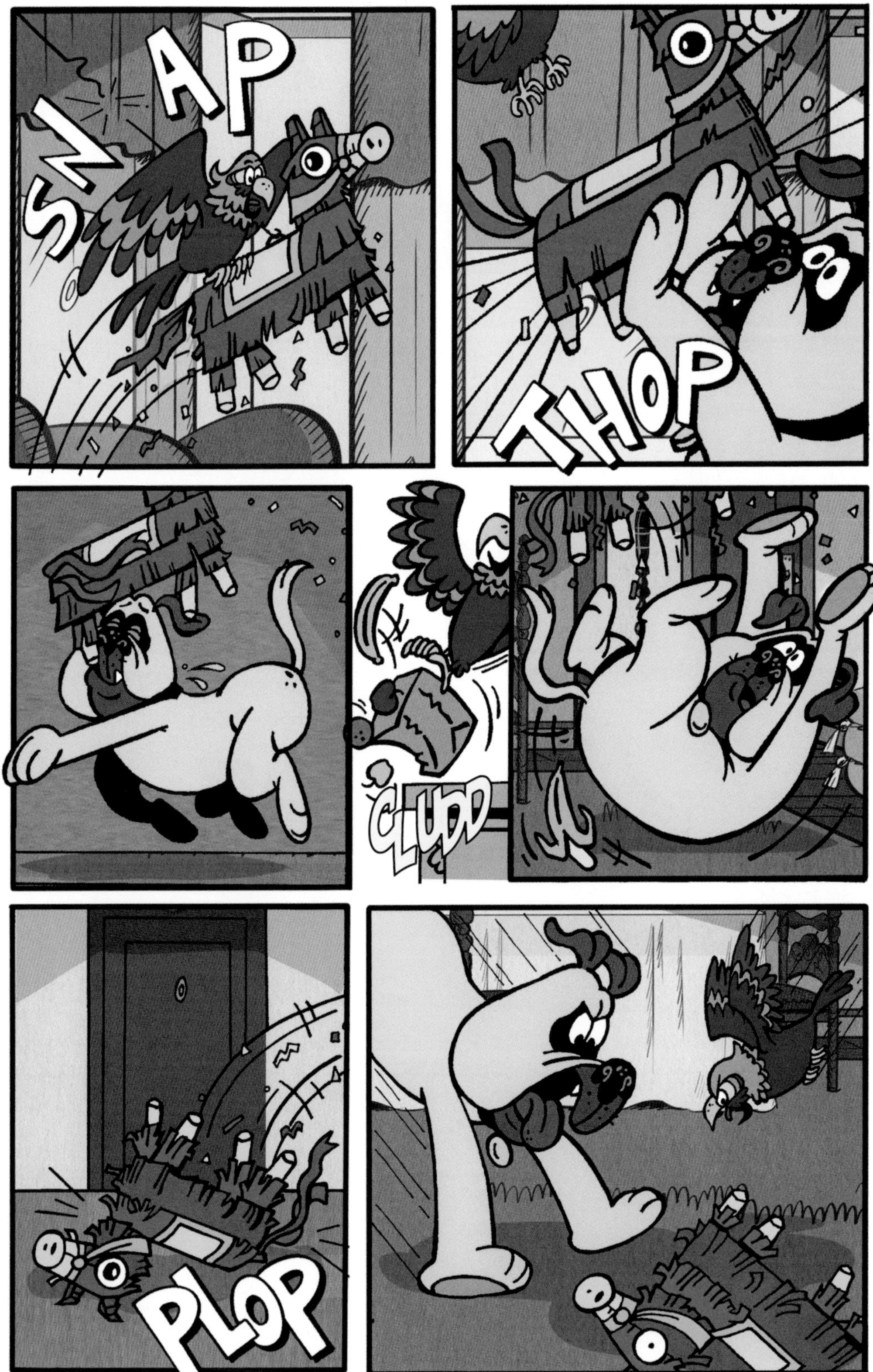
SNAP
THOP
GLUDD
PLOP

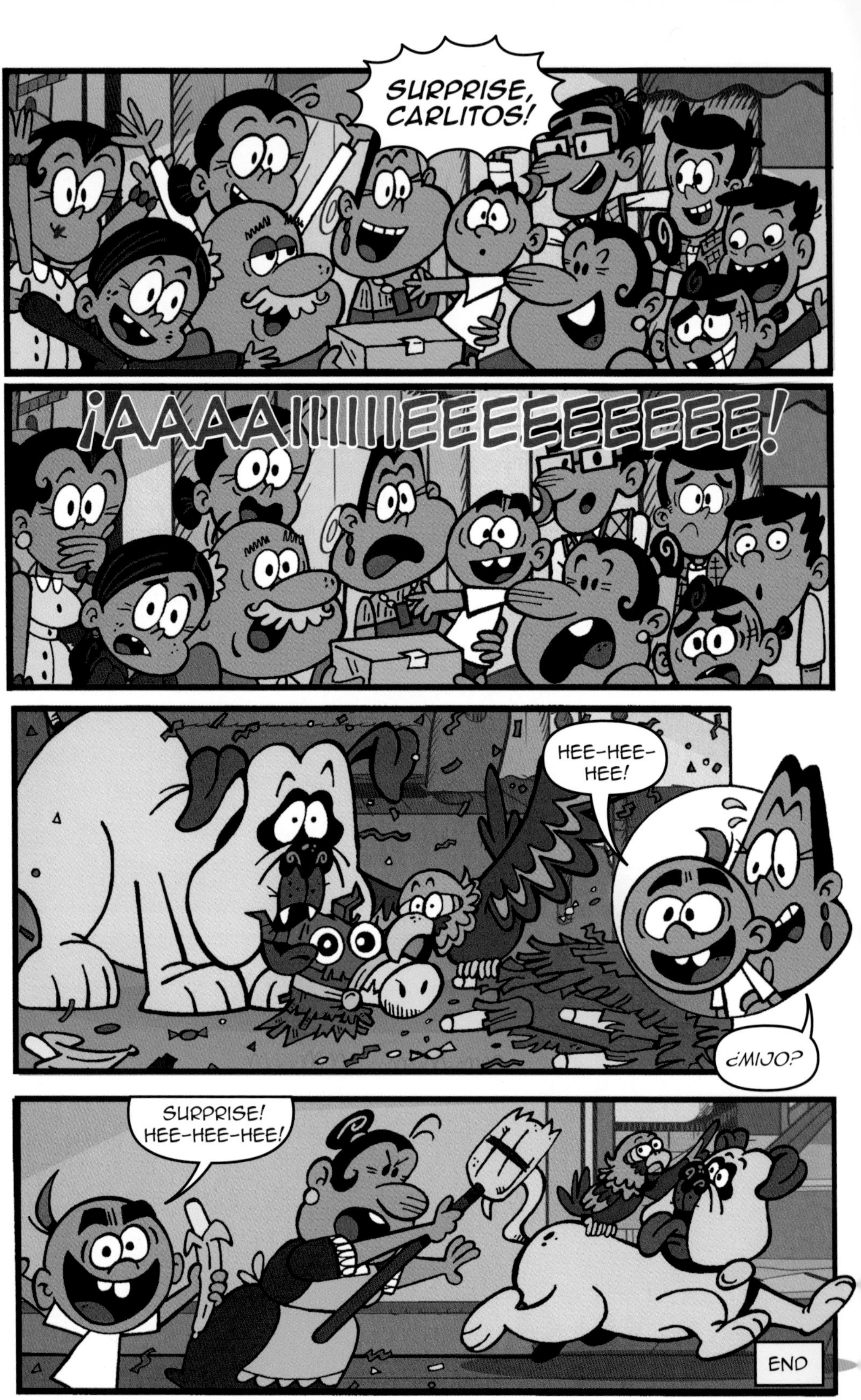
SURPRISE, CARLITOS!
¡AAAAIIIIIIEEEEEEEEEE!
HEE-HEE-HEE!
¿MIJO?
SURPRISE! HEE-HEE-HEE!
END

"GOSSIP GUY"

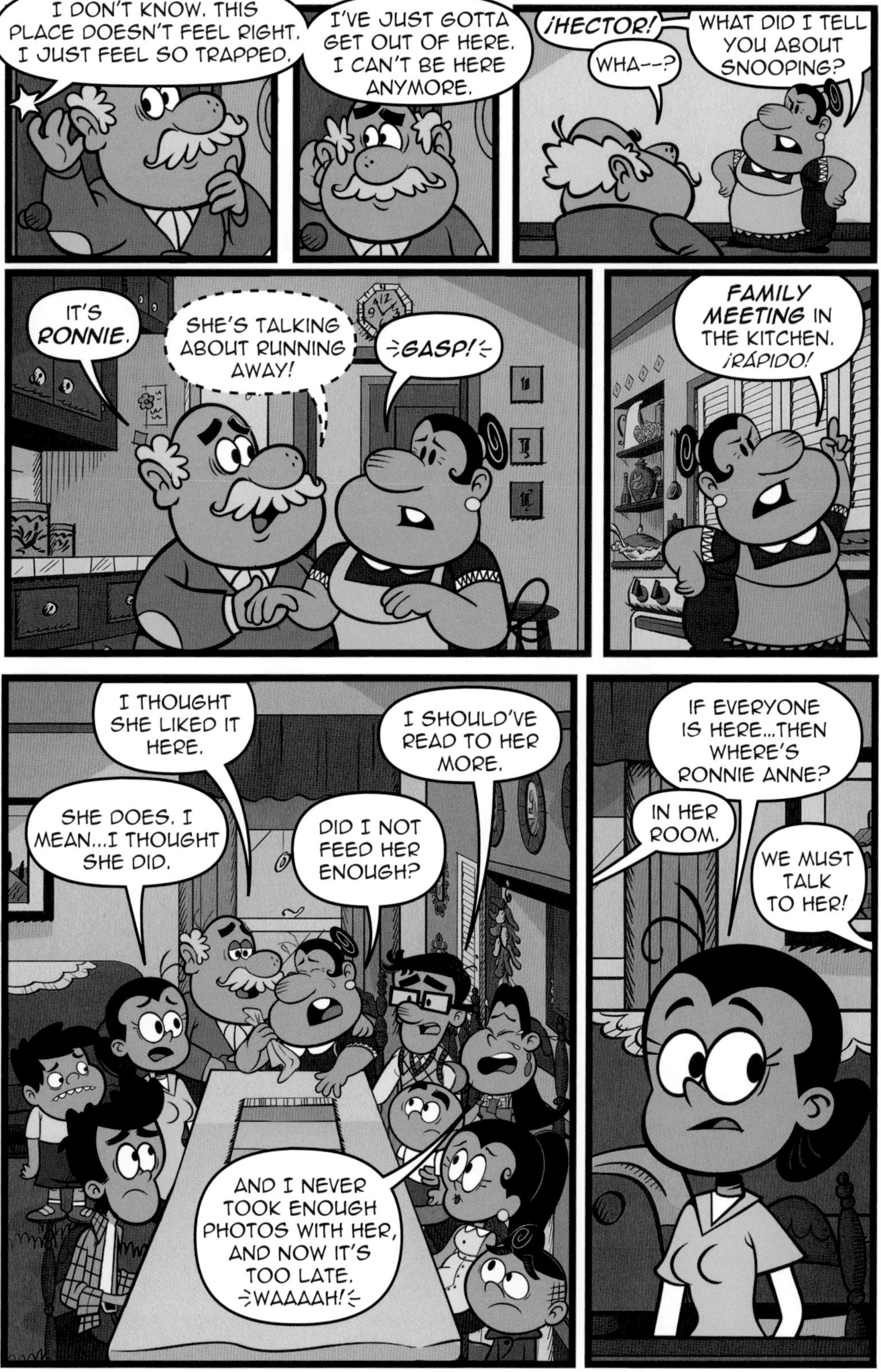
I DON'T KNOW. THIS PLACE DOESN'T FEEL RIGHT. I JUST FEEL SO TRAPPED.
I'VE JUST GOTTA GET OUT OF HERE. I CAN'T BE HERE ANYMORE.
¡HECTOR!
WHA--?
WHAT DID I TELL YOU ABOUT SNOOPING?
IT'S RONNIE.
SHE'S TALKING ABOUT RUNNING AWAY!
GASP!
FAMILY MEETING IN THE KITCHEN. ¡RÁPIDO!
I THOUGHT SHE LIKED IT HERE.
SHE DOES. I MEAN...I THOUGHT SHE DID.
DID I NOT FEED HER ENOUGH?
I SHOULD'VE READ TO HER MORE.
AND I NEVER TOOK ENOUGH PHOTOS WITH HER, AND NOW IT'S TOO LATE. WAAAAH!
IF EVERYONE IS HERE...THEN WHERE'S RONNIE ANNE?
IN HER ROOM.
WE MUST TALK TO HER!

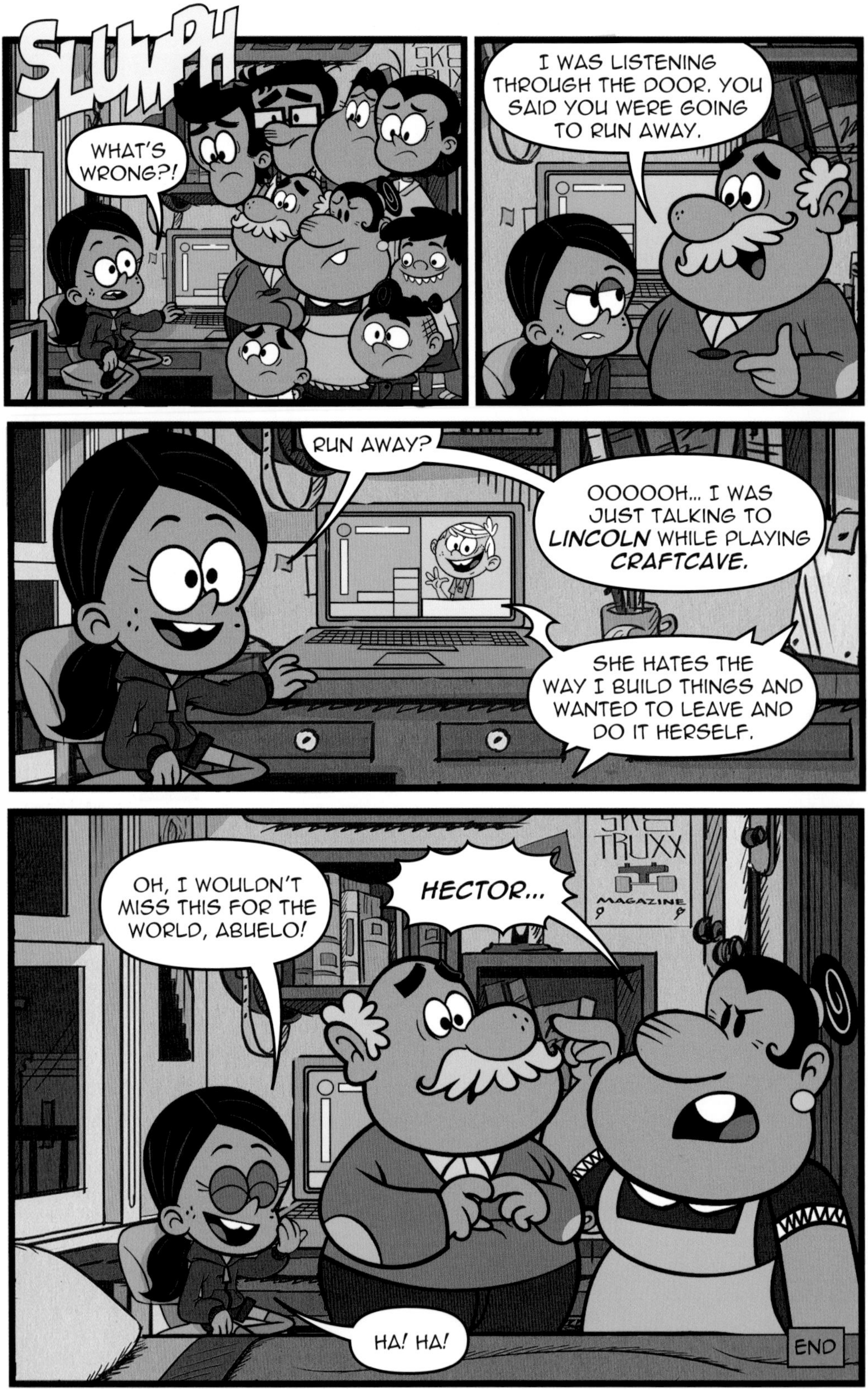

SLUMPH
WHAT'S WRONG?!
I WAS LISTENING THROUGH THE DOOR. YOU SAID YOU WERE GOING TO RUN AWAY.
RUN AWAY?
OOOOOH... I WAS JUST TALKING TO LINCOLN WHILE PLAYING CRAFTCAVE.
SHE HATES THE WAY I BUILD THINGS AND WANTED TO LEAVE AND DO IT HERSELF.
SK8 TRUXX MAGAZINE
OH, I WOULDN'T MISS THIS FOR THE WORLD, ABUELO!
HECTOR...
HA! HA!
END

"WASHED UP"

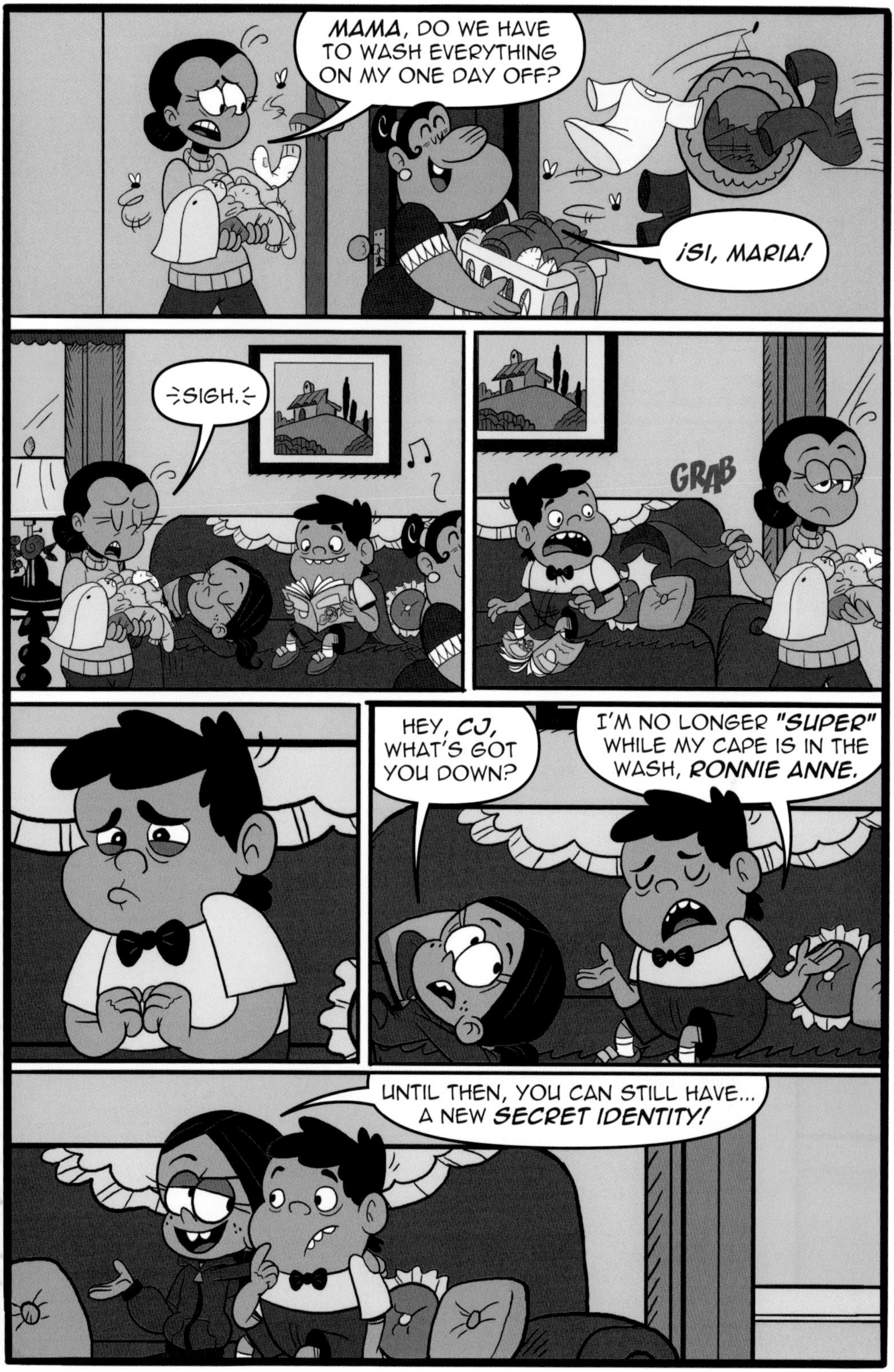
MAMA, DO WE HAVE TO WASH EVERYTHING ON MY ONE DAY OFF?
¡SI, MARIA!
SIGH.
GRAB
HEY, CJ, WHAT'S GOT YOU DOWN?
I'M NO LONGER "SUPER" WHILE MY CAPE IS IN THE WASH, RONNIE ANNE.
UNTIL THEN, YOU CAN STILL HAVE... A NEW SECRET IDENTITY!

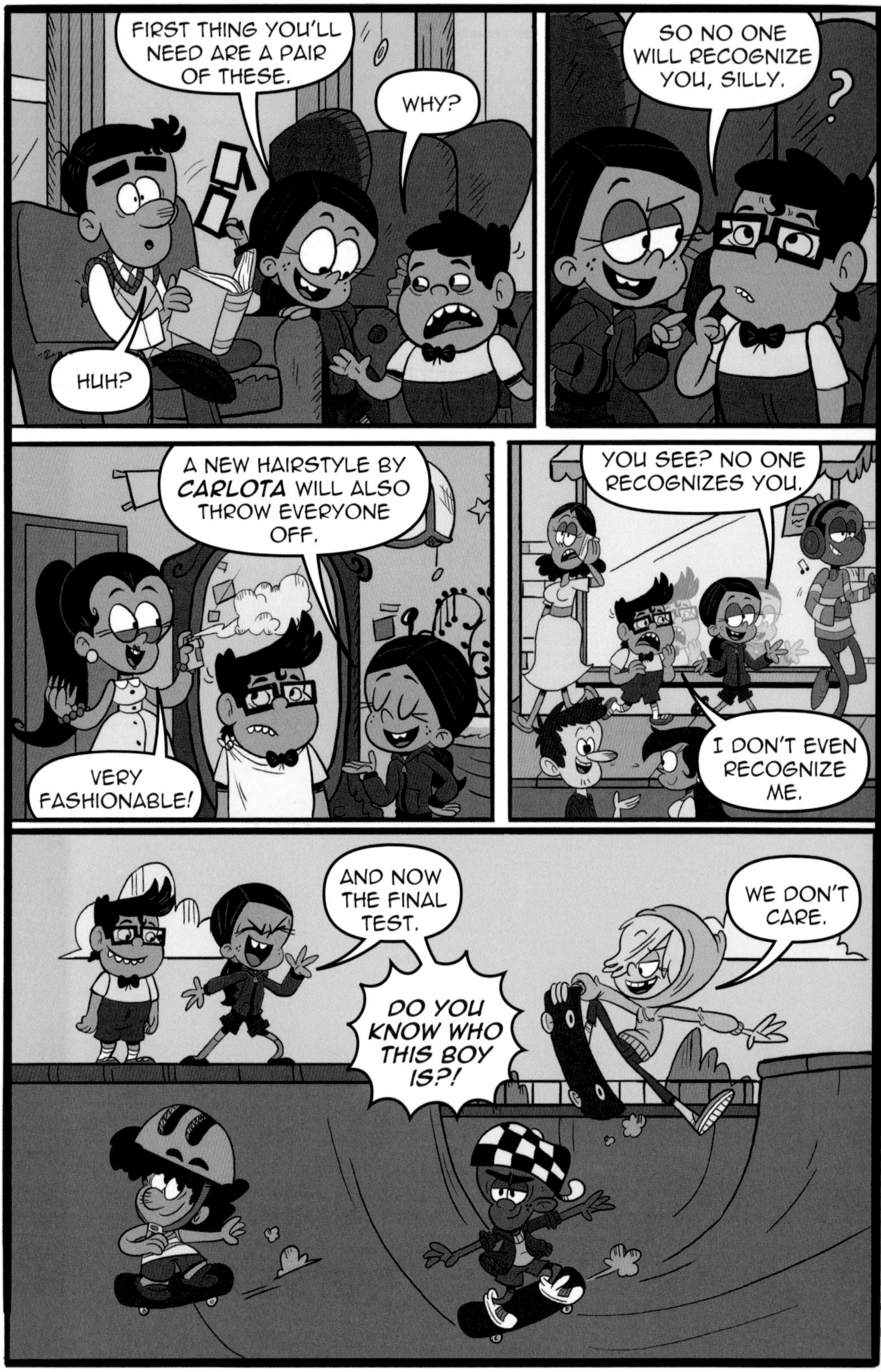
FIRST THING YOU'LL NEED ARE A PAIR OF THESE.
WHY?
HUH?
SO NO ONE WILL RECOGNIZE YOU, SILLY.
?
A NEW HAIRSTYLE BY CARLOTA WILL ALSO THROW EVERYONE OFF.
VERY FASHIONABLE!
YOU SEE? NO ONE RECOGNIZES YOU.
I DON'T EVEN RECOGNIZE ME.
AND NOW THE FINAL TEST.
DO YOU KNOW WHO THIS BOY IS?!
WE DON'T CARE.

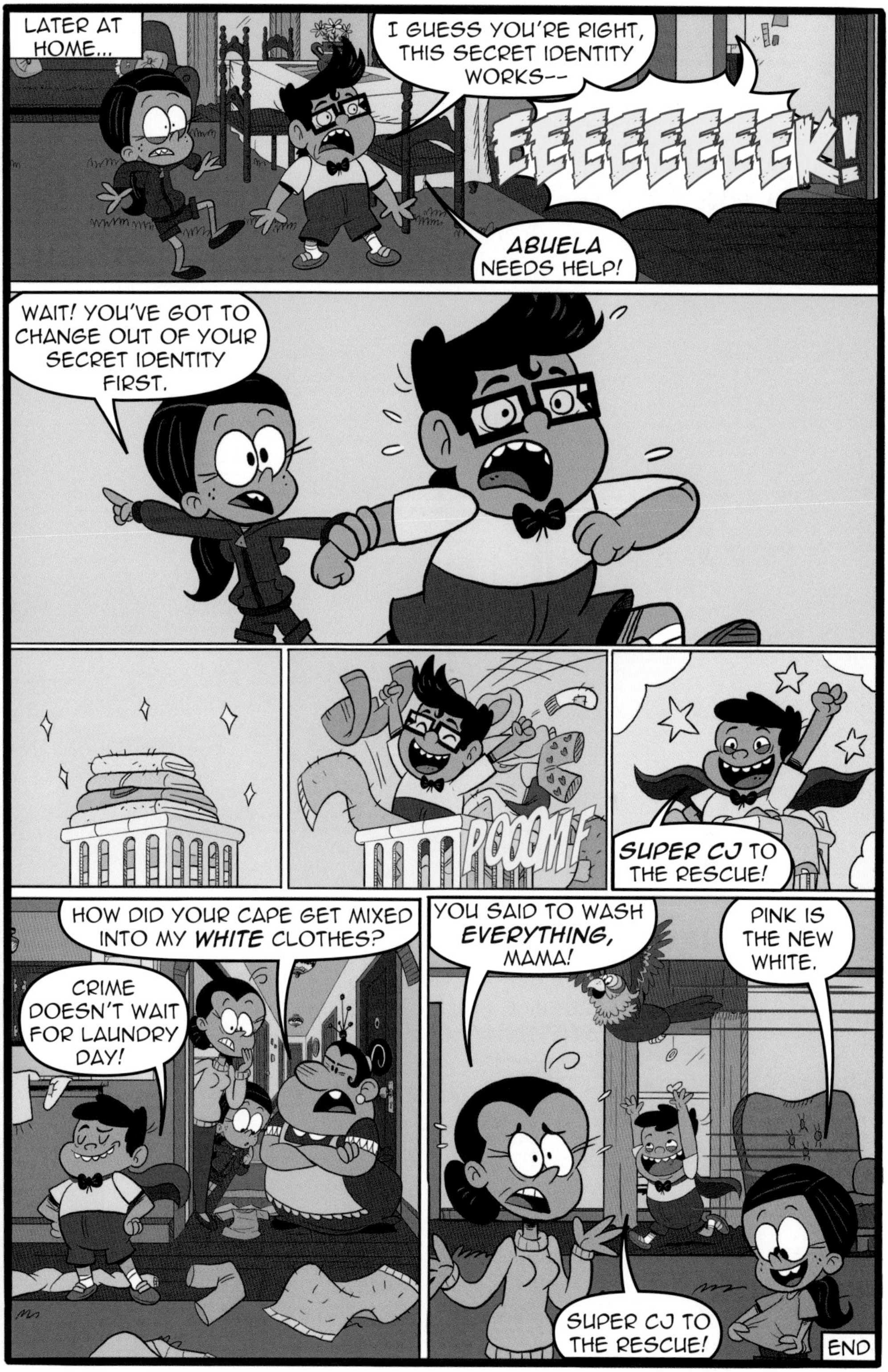
LATER AT HOME...
I GUESS YOU'RE RIGHT, THIS SECRET IDENTITY WORKS--
EEEEEEEEK!
ABUELA NEEDS HELP!
WAIT! YOU'VE GOT TO CHANGE OUT OF YOUR SECRET IDENTITY FIRST.
POOOMF
SUPER CJ TO THE RESCUE!
HOW DID YOUR CAPE GET MIXED INTO MY WHITE CLOTHES?
CRIME DOESN'T WAIT FOR LAUNDRY DAY!
YOU SAID TO WASH EVERYTHING, MAMA!
PINK IS THE NEW WHITE.
SUPER CJ TO THE RESCUE!
END

"LIFE IMITATES ART"

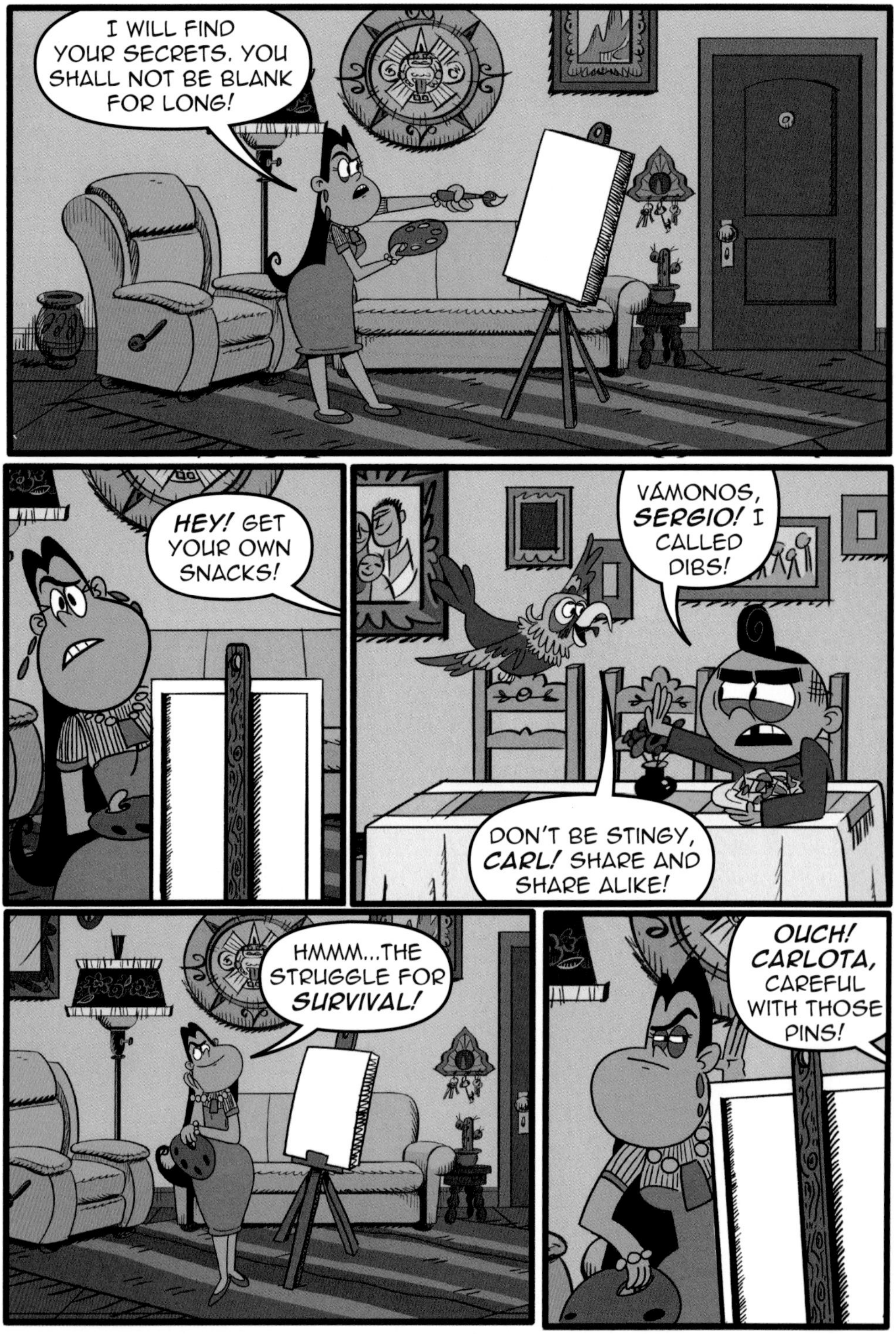

I WILL FIND YOUR SECRETS. YOU SHALL NOT BE BLANK FOR LONG!
HEY! GET YOUR OWN SNACKS!
VÁMONOS, SERGIO! I CALLED DIBS!
DON'T BE STINGY, CARL! SHARE AND SHARE ALIKE!
HMMM...THE STRUGGLE FOR SURVIVAL!
OUCH! CARLOTA, CAREFUL WITH THOSE PINS!

C.J.! RONNIE ANNE! HOLD STILL WHILE I CRAFT MY *MASTERPIECE*!

WHY ARE YOUR MASTERPIECES ALWAYS SO ITCHY?

AH-HA!...THE CHALLENGE OF CREATION!

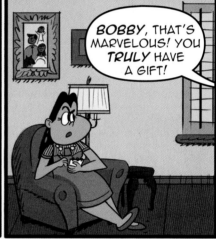

BOBBY, THAT'S MARVELOUS! YOU *TRULY* HAVE A GIFT!

THANKS, *ABUELO*! IT TOOK A LOT OF TIME, BUT IT WAS WORTH IT!

WONDERFUL! THE JOY OF *VICTORY*!

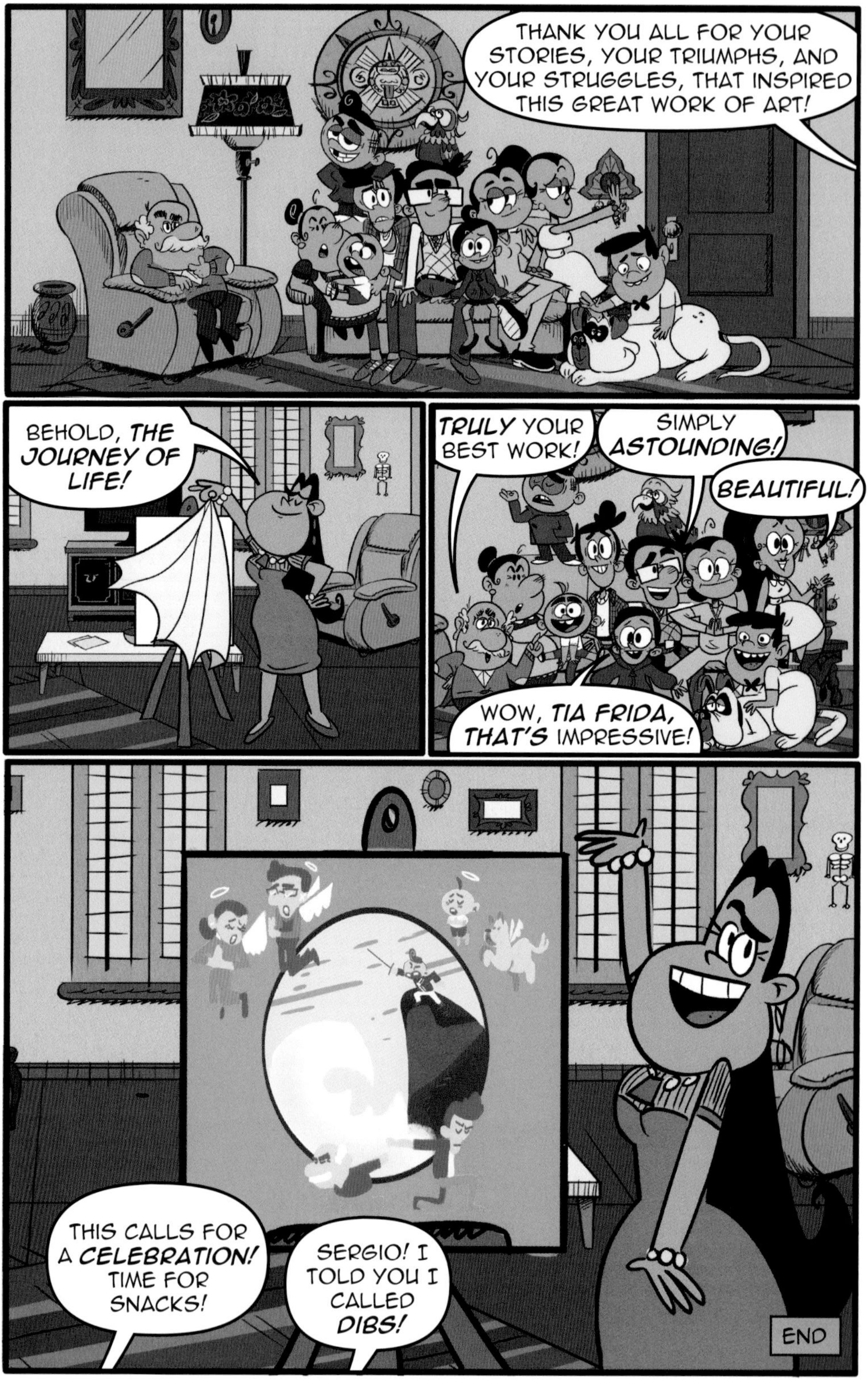
THANK YOU ALL FOR YOUR STORIES, YOUR TRIUMPHS, AND YOUR STRUGGLES, THAT INSPIRED THIS GREAT WORK OF ART!
BEHOLD, THE JOURNEY OF LIFE!
TRULY YOUR BEST WORK!
SIMPLY ASTOUNDING!
BEAUTIFUL!
WOW, TIA FRIDA, THAT'S IMPRESSIVE!
THIS CALLS FOR A CELEBRATION! TIME FOR SNACKS!
SERGIO! I TOLD YOU I CALLED DIBS!
END

"THE GREAT ESCAPE"

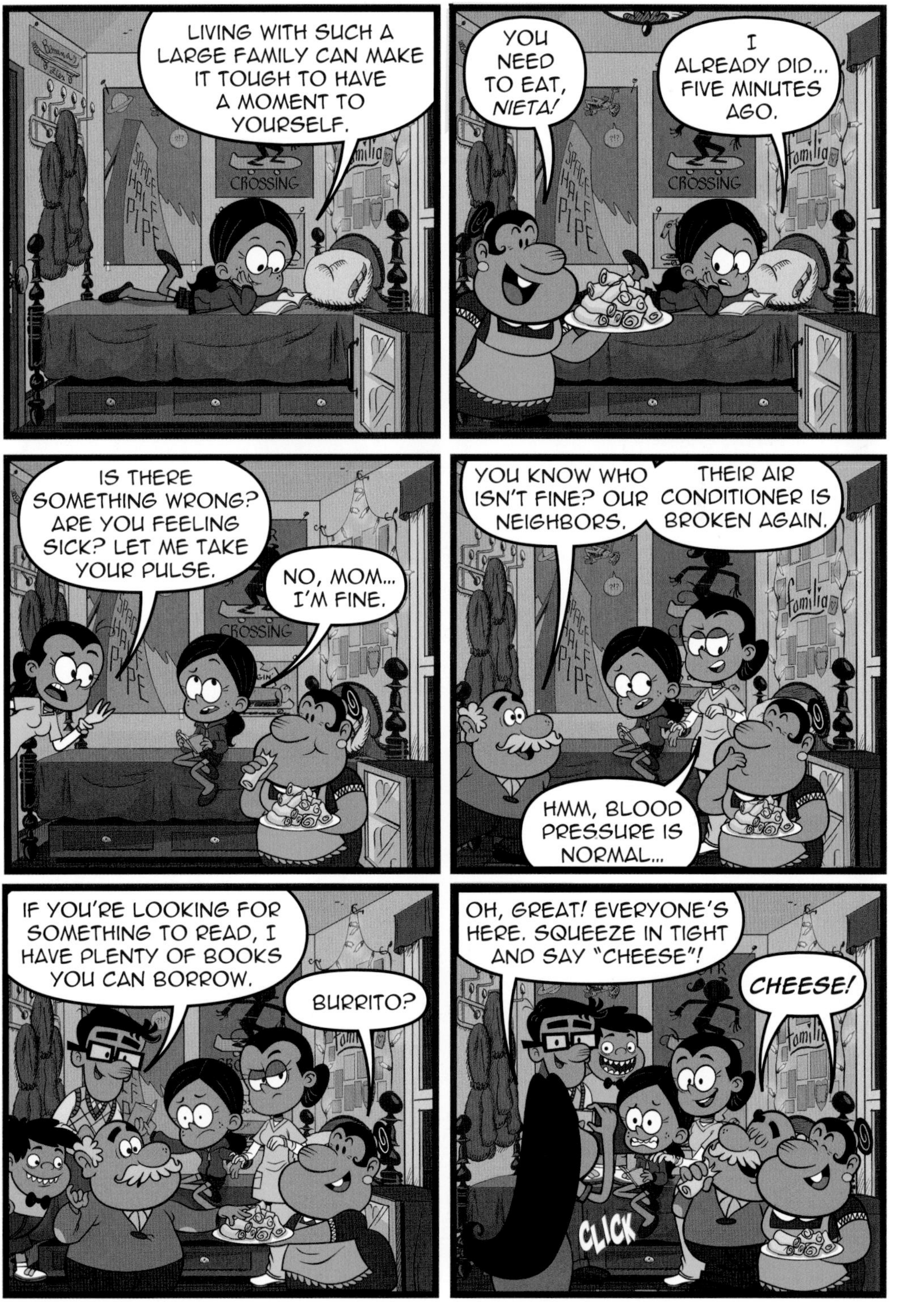
LIVING WITH SUCH A LARGE FAMILY CAN MAKE IT TOUGH TO HAVE A MOMENT TO YOURSELF.
YOU NEED TO EAT, *NIETA!*
I ALREADY DID... FIVE MINUTES AGO.
IS THERE SOMETHING WRONG? ARE YOU FEELING SICK? LET ME TAKE YOUR PULSE.
NO, MOM... I'M FINE.
YOU KNOW WHO ISN'T FINE? OUR NEIGHBORS.
THEIR AIR CONDITIONER IS BROKEN AGAIN.
HMM, BLOOD PRESSURE IS NORMAL...
IF YOU'RE LOOKING FOR SOMETHING TO READ, I HAVE PLENTY OF BOOKS YOU CAN BORROW.
BURRITO?
OH, GREAT! EVERYONE'S HERE. SQUEEZE IN TIGHT AND SAY "CHEESE"!
CHEESE!
CLICK

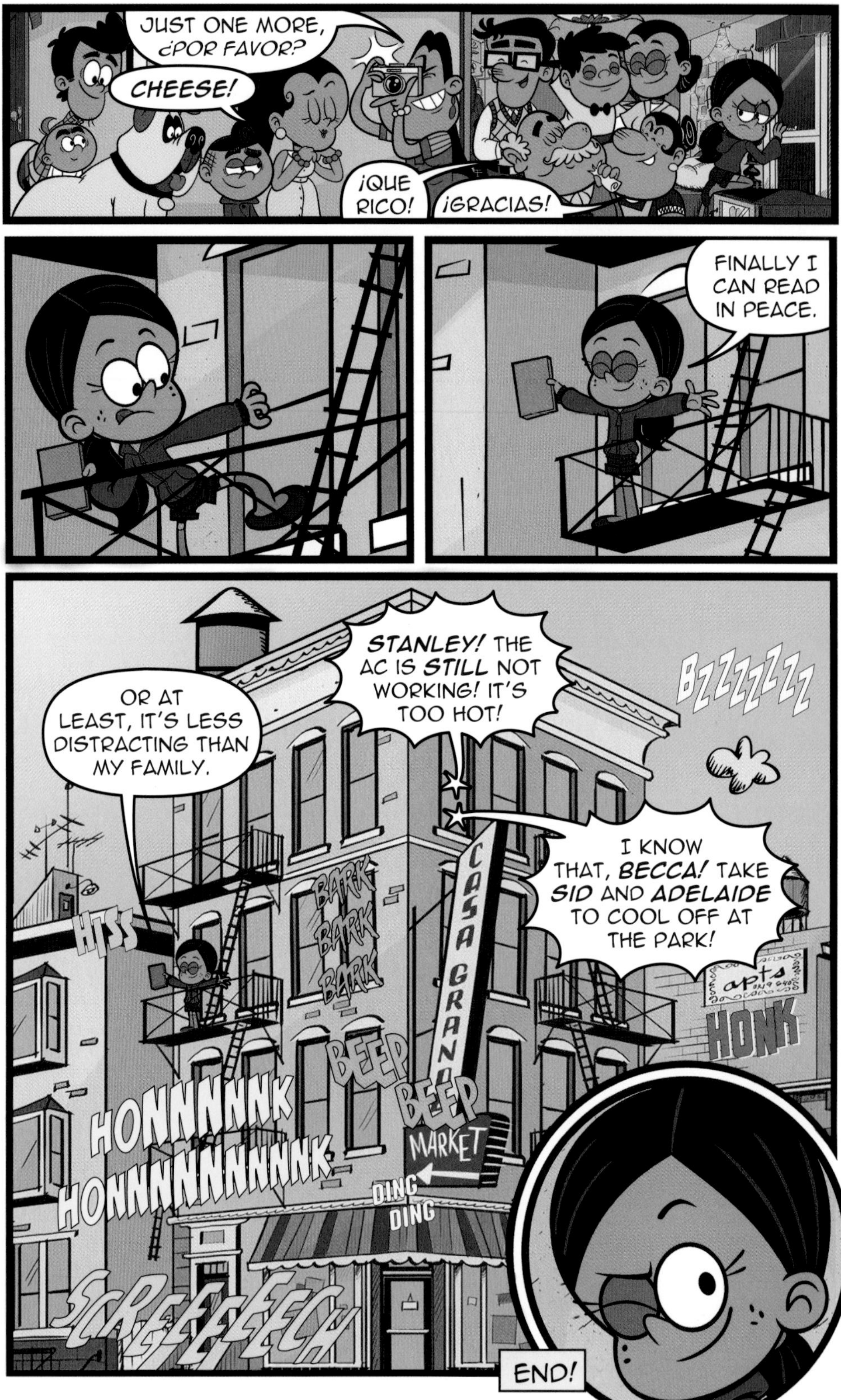
JUST ONE MORE, ¿POR FAVOR?
CHEESE!
¡QUE RICO!
¡GRACIAS!
FINALLY I CAN READ IN PEACE.
OR AT LEAST, IT'S LESS DISTRACTING THAN MY FAMILY.
STANLEY! THE AC IS STILL NOT WORKING! IT'S TOO HOT!
BZZZZZZ
I KNOW THAT, BECCA! TAKE SID AND ADELAIDE TO COOL OFF AT THE PARK!
HISS
BARK BARK BARK
CASA GRAN
apts
HONK
BEEP BEEP
MARKET
HONNNNNK
HONNNNNNNNNK
DING DING
SCREEEEECH
END!

"THE MASKED MAN"

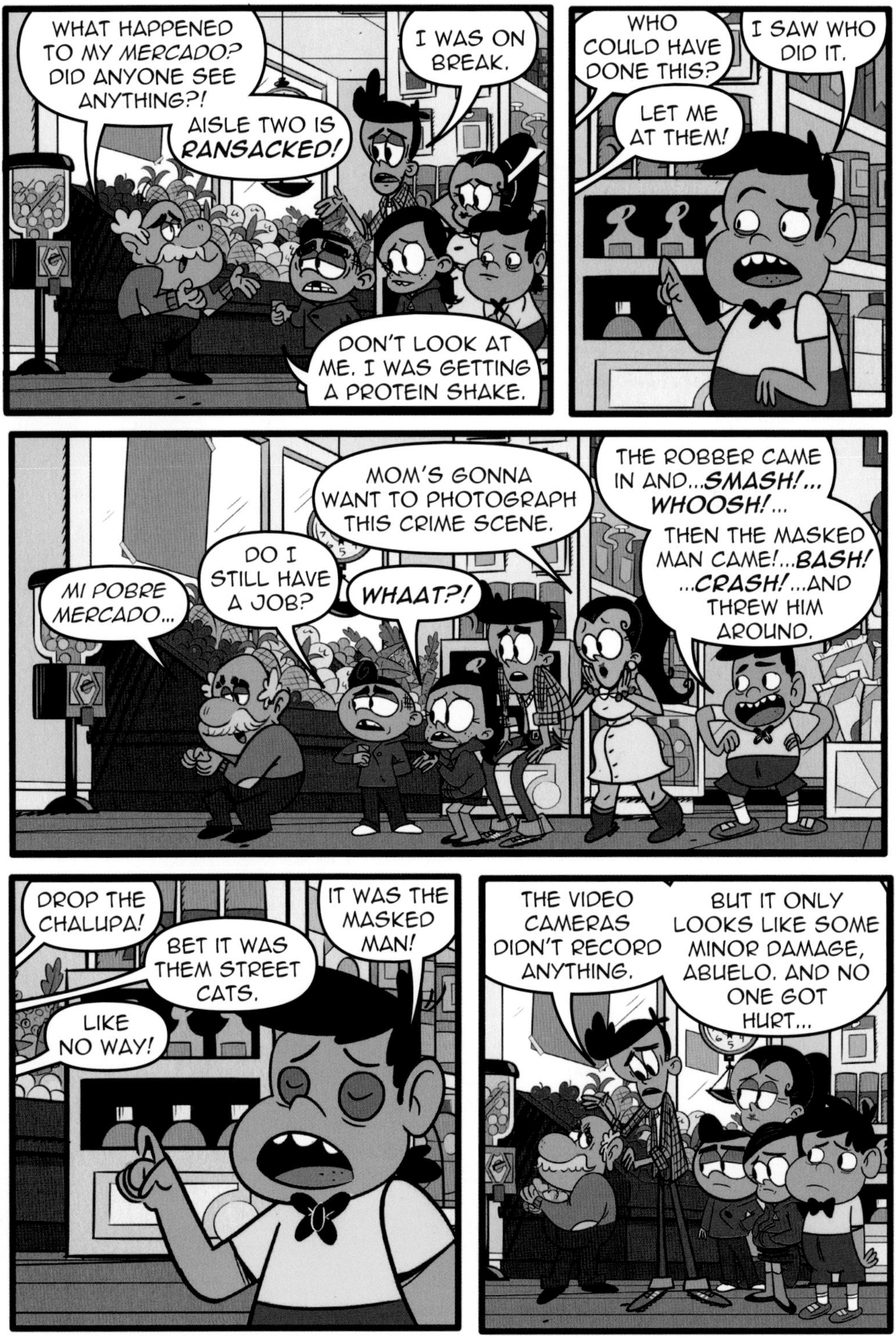
WHAT HAPPENED TO MY *MERCADO*? DID ANYONE SEE ANYTHING?!
AISLE TWO IS *RANSACKED!*
I WAS ON BREAK.
DON'T LOOK AT ME. I WAS GETTING A PROTEIN SHAKE.
WHO COULD HAVE DONE THIS?
LET ME AT THEM!
I SAW WHO DID IT.
MI POBRE MERCADO...
DO I STILL HAVE A JOB?
WHAAT?!
MOM'S GONNA WANT TO PHOTOGRAPH THIS CRIME SCENE.
THE ROBBER CAME IN AND...*SMASH!*... *WHOOSH!*...
THEN THE MASKED MAN CAME!...*BASH!* ...*CRASH!*...AND THREW HIM AROUND.
DROP THE CHALUPA!
BET IT WAS THEM STREET CATS.
LIKE NO WAY!
IT WAS THE MASKED MAN!
THE VIDEO CAMERAS DIDN'T RECORD ANYTHING.
BUT IT ONLY LOOKS LIKE SOME MINOR DAMAGE, ABUELO. AND NO ONE GOT HURT...

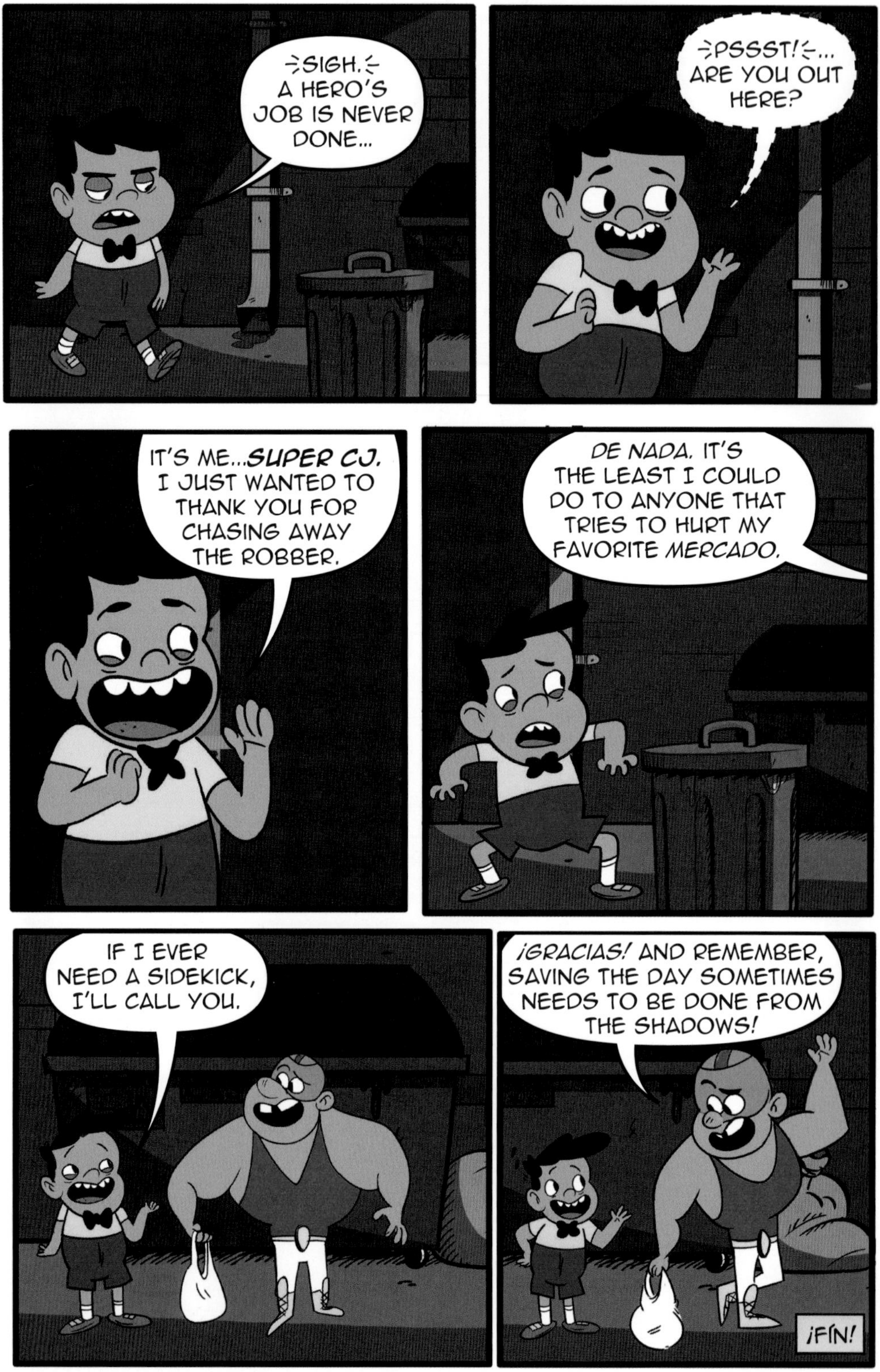

-SIGH.- A HERO'S JOB IS NEVER DONE...
-PSSST!-... ARE YOU OUT HERE?
IT'S ME...**SUPER CJ.** I JUST WANTED TO THANK YOU FOR CHASING AWAY THE ROBBER.
DE NADA. IT'S THE LEAST I COULD DO TO ANYONE THAT TRIES TO HURT MY FAVORITE *MERCADO.*
IF I EVER NEED A SIDEKICK, I'LL CALL YOU.
¡GRACIAS! AND REMEMBER, SAVING THE DAY SOMETIMES NEEDS TO BE DONE FROM THE SHADOWS!
¡FÍN!

"MY BOBBY AND ME"

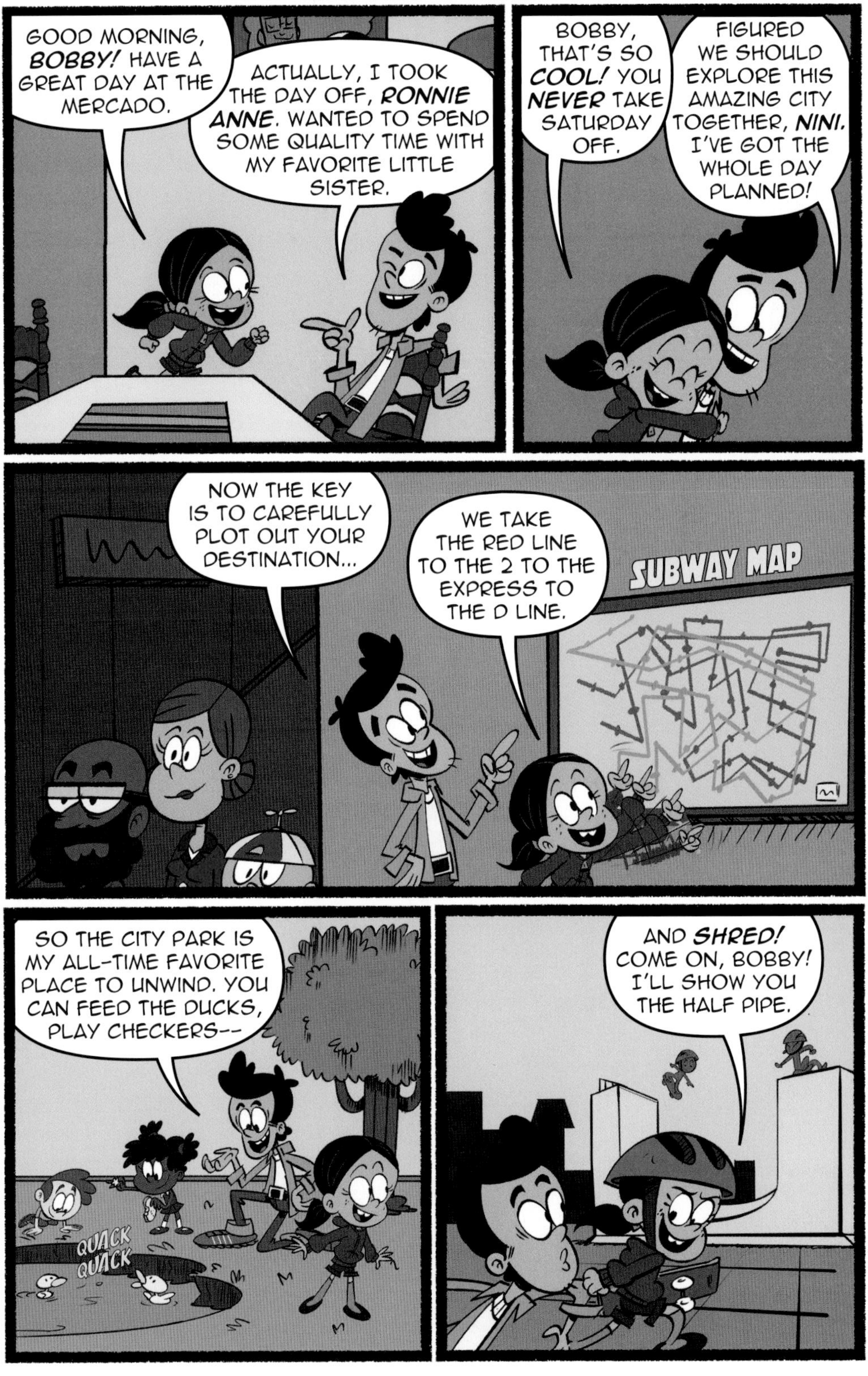
GOOD MORNING, BOBBY! HAVE A GREAT DAY AT THE MERCADO.
ACTUALLY, I TOOK THE DAY OFF, RONNIE ANNE. WANTED TO SPEND SOME QUALITY TIME WITH MY FAVORITE LITTLE SISTER.
BOBBY, THAT'S SO COOL! YOU NEVER TAKE SATURDAY OFF.
FIGURED WE SHOULD EXPLORE THIS AMAZING CITY TOGETHER, NINI. I'VE GOT THE WHOLE DAY PLANNED!
NOW THE KEY IS TO CAREFULLY PLOT OUT YOUR DESTINATION...
WE TAKE THE RED LINE TO THE 2 TO THE EXPRESS TO THE D LINE.
SUBWAY MAP
SO THE CITY PARK IS MY ALL-TIME FAVORITE PLACE TO UNWIND. YOU CAN FEED THE DUCKS, PLAY CHECKERS--
QUACK QUACK
AND SHRED! COME ON, BOBBY! I'LL SHOW YOU THE HALF PIPE.

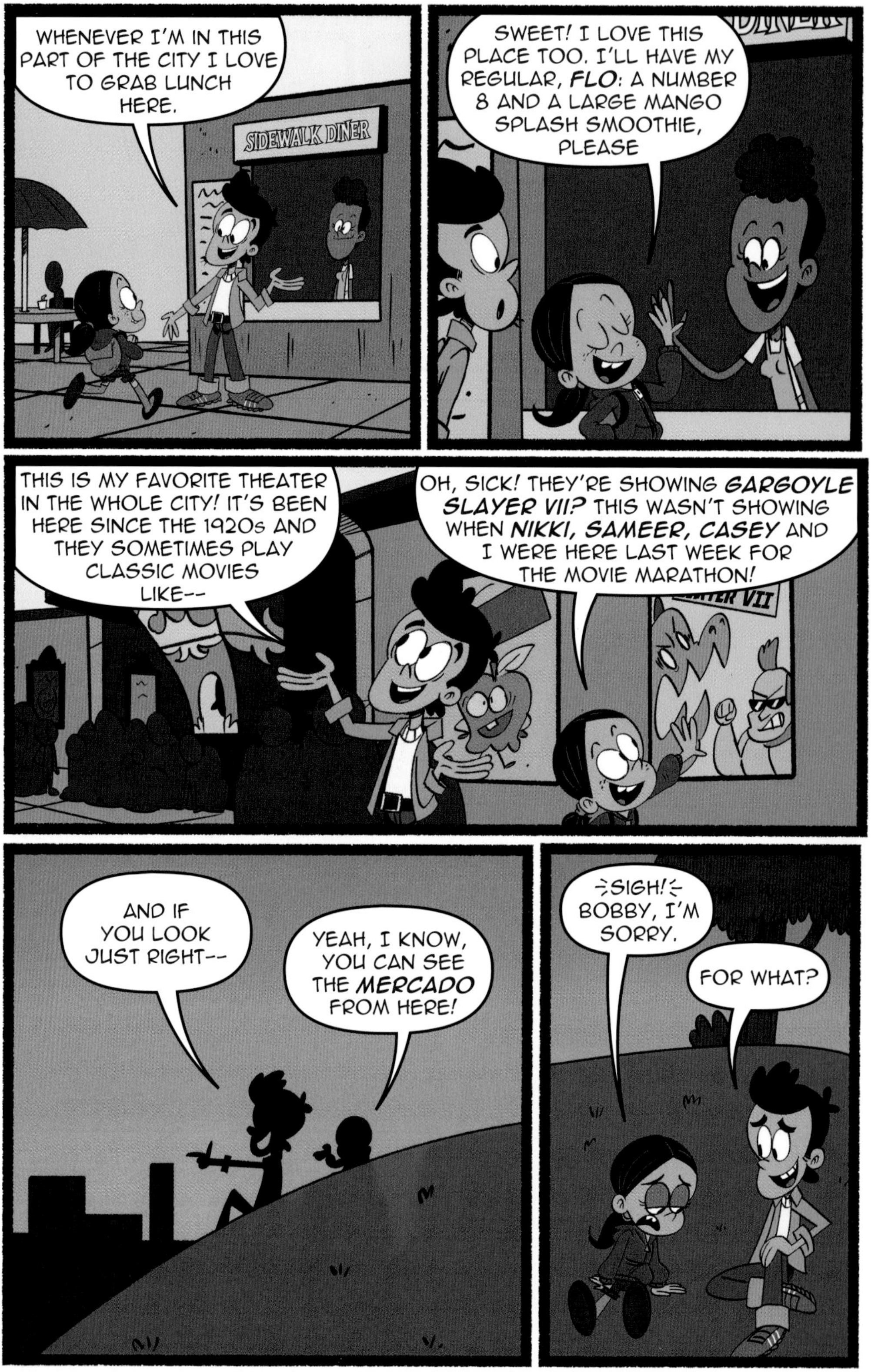
WHENEVER I'M IN THIS PART OF THE CITY I LOVE TO GRAB LUNCH HERE.
SIDEWALK DINER
SWEET! I LOVE THIS PLACE TOO. I'LL HAVE MY REGULAR, **FLO**: A NUMBER 8 AND A LARGE MANGO SPLASH SMOOTHIE, PLEASE
THIS IS MY FAVORITE THEATER IN THE WHOLE CITY! IT'S BEEN HERE SINCE THE 1920s AND THEY SOMETIMES PLAY CLASSIC MOVIES LIKE--
OH, SICK! THEY'RE SHOWING ***GARGOYLE SLAYER VII?*** THIS WASN'T SHOWING WHEN ***NIKKI, SAMEER, CASEY*** AND I WERE HERE LAST WEEK FOR THE MOVIE MARATHON!
AND IF YOU LOOK JUST RIGHT--
YEAH, I KNOW, YOU CAN SEE THE ***MERCADO*** FROM HERE!
SIGH! BOBBY, I'M SORRY.
FOR WHAT?

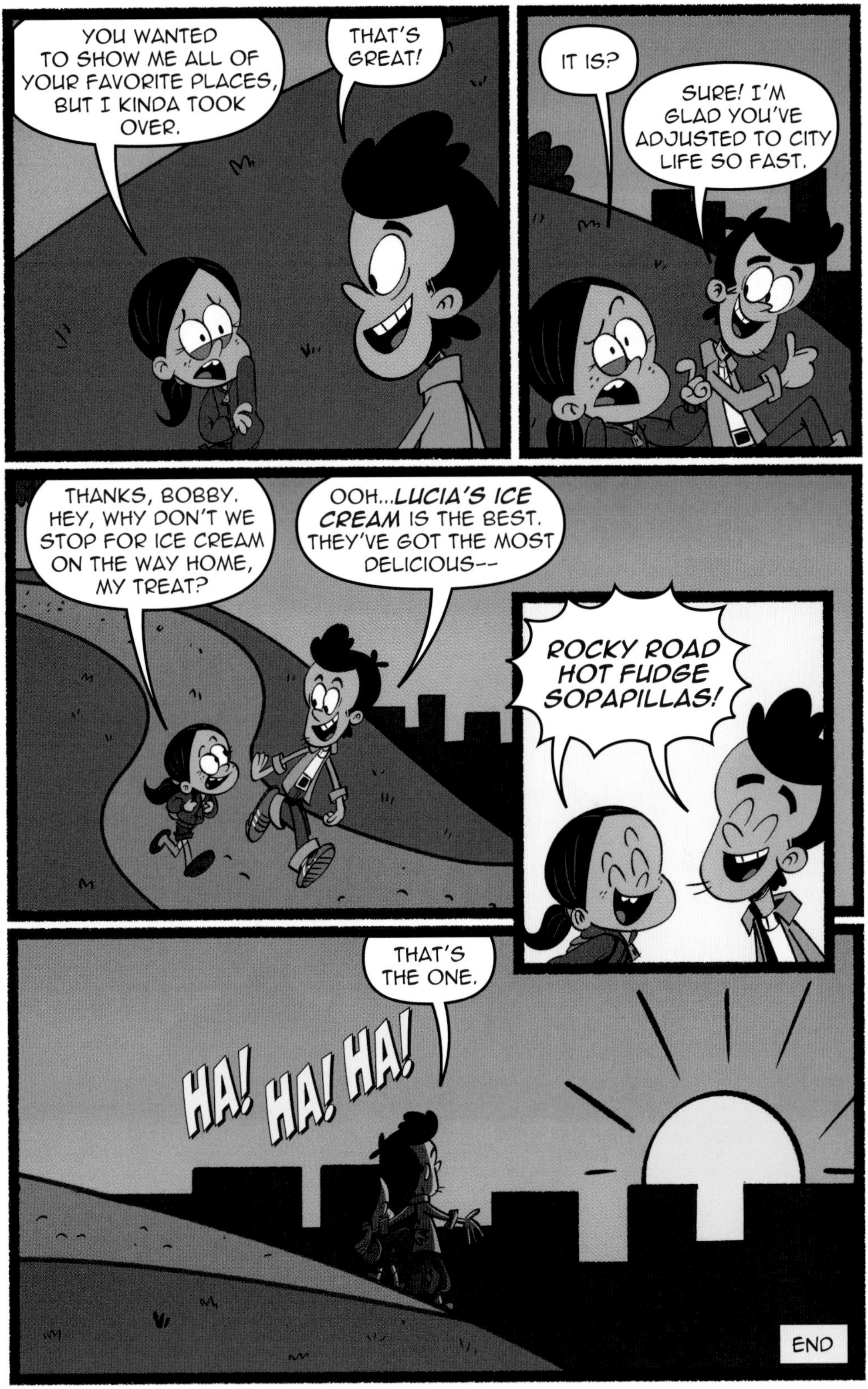
YOU WANTED TO SHOW ME ALL OF YOUR FAVORITE PLACES, BUT I KINDA TOOK OVER.
THAT'S GREAT!
IT IS?
SURE! I'M GLAD YOU'VE ADJUSTED TO CITY LIFE SO FAST.
THANKS, BOBBY. HEY, WHY DON'T WE STOP FOR ICE CREAM ON THE WAY HOME, MY TREAT?
OOH...*LUCIA'S ICE CREAM* IS THE BEST. THEY'VE GOT THE MOST DELICIOUS--
ROCKY ROAD HOT FUDGE SOPAPILLAS!
THAT'S THE ONE.
HA! HA! HA!
END

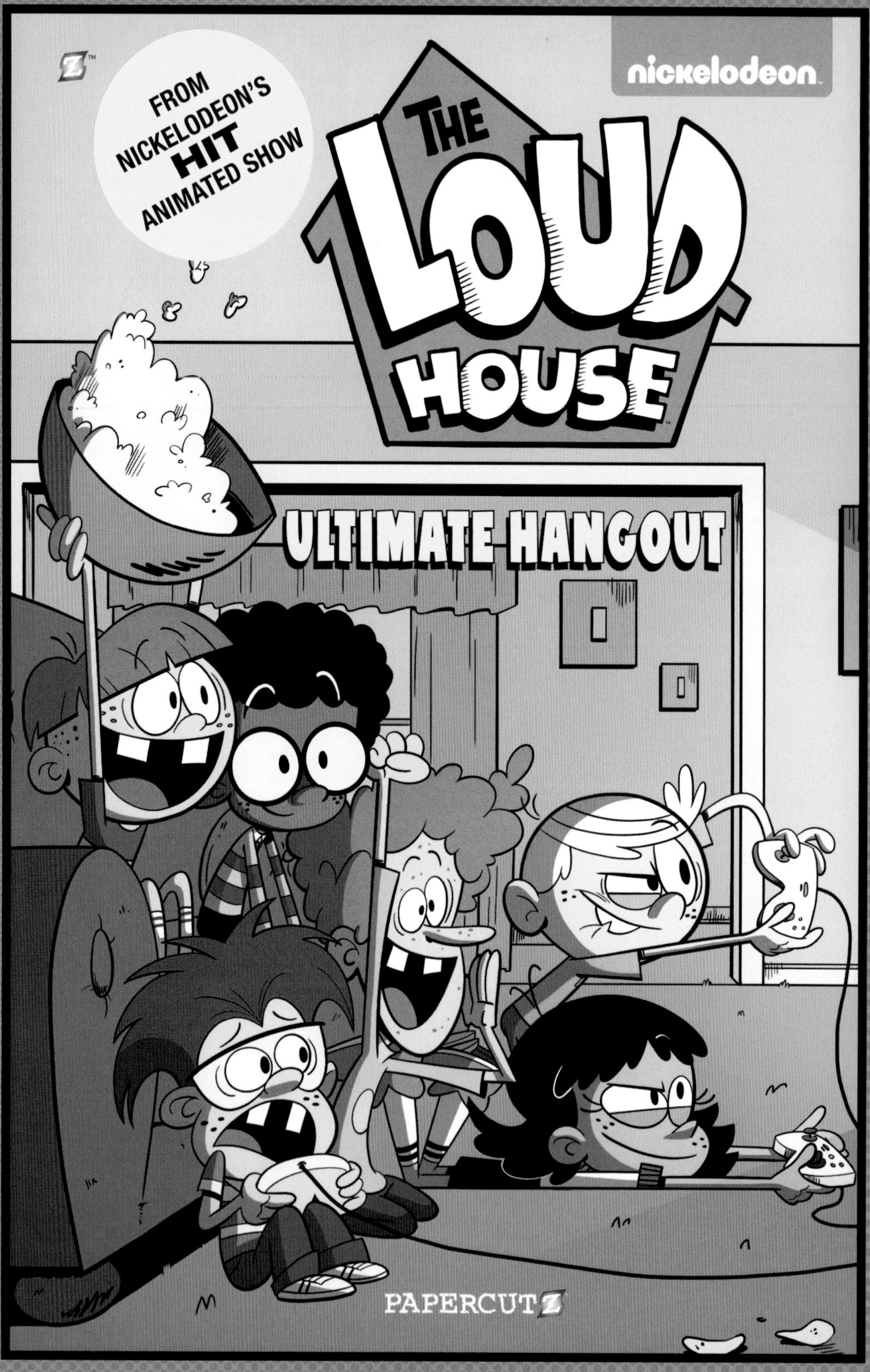
nickelodeon
FROM NICKELODEON'S HIT ANIMATED SHOW
THE LOUD HOUSE
ULTIMATE HANGOUT
PAPERCUTZ

THE LOUD HOUSE #9 Cover Art by Ida Hem, Coloring by Hallie Lal

"THE EMPTY LOUD HOUSE"

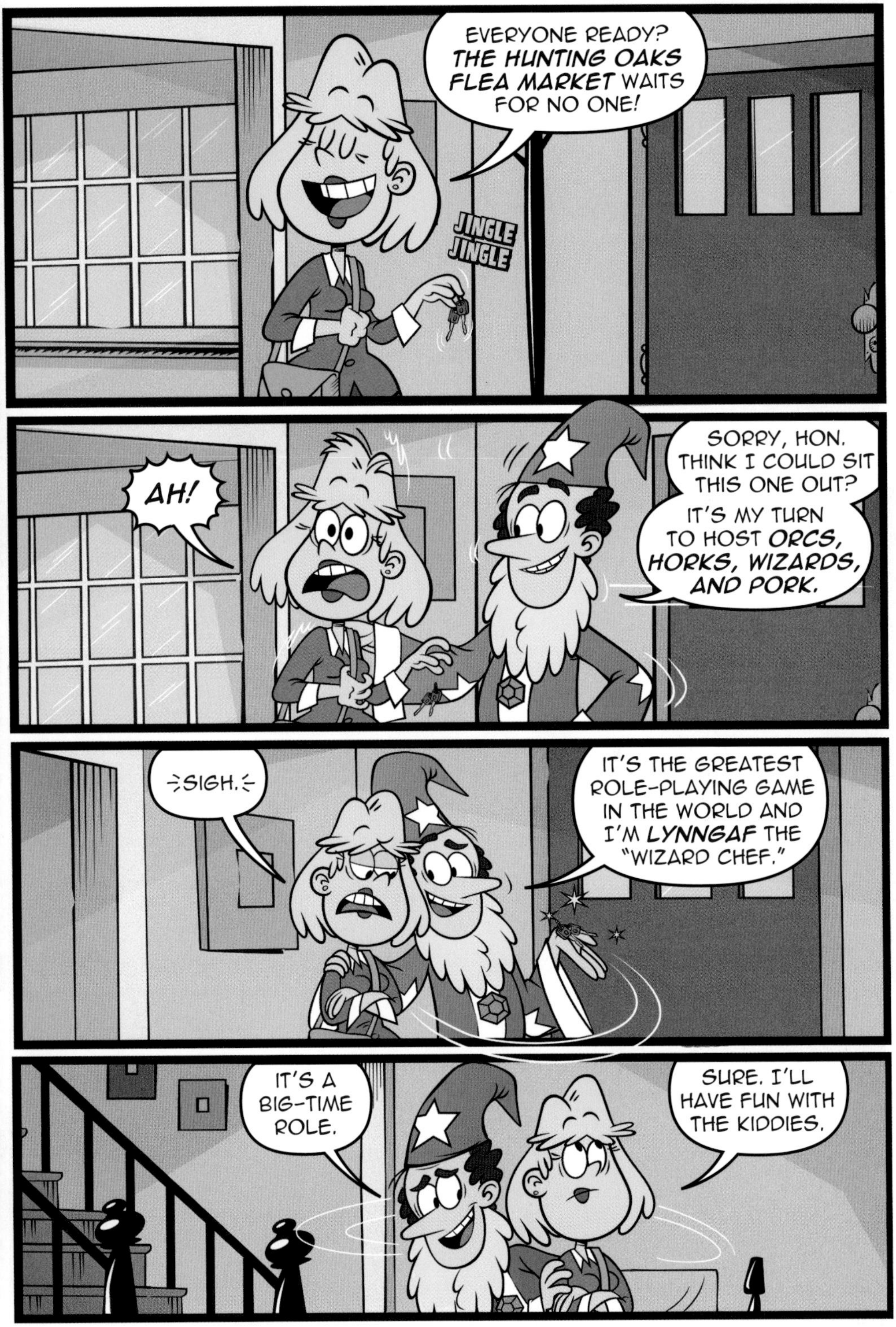
EVERYONE READY? THE HUNTING OAKS FLEA MARKET WAITS FOR NO ONE!
JINGLE JINGLE
AH!
SORRY, HON. THINK I COULD SIT THIS ONE OUT?
IT'S MY TURN TO HOST ORCS, HORKS, WIZARDS, AND PORK.
SIGH.
IT'S THE GREATEST ROLE-PLAYING GAME IN THE WORLD AND I'M LYNNGAF THE "WIZARD CHEF."
IT'S A BIG-TIME ROLE.
SURE. I'LL HAVE FUN WITH THE KIDDIES.

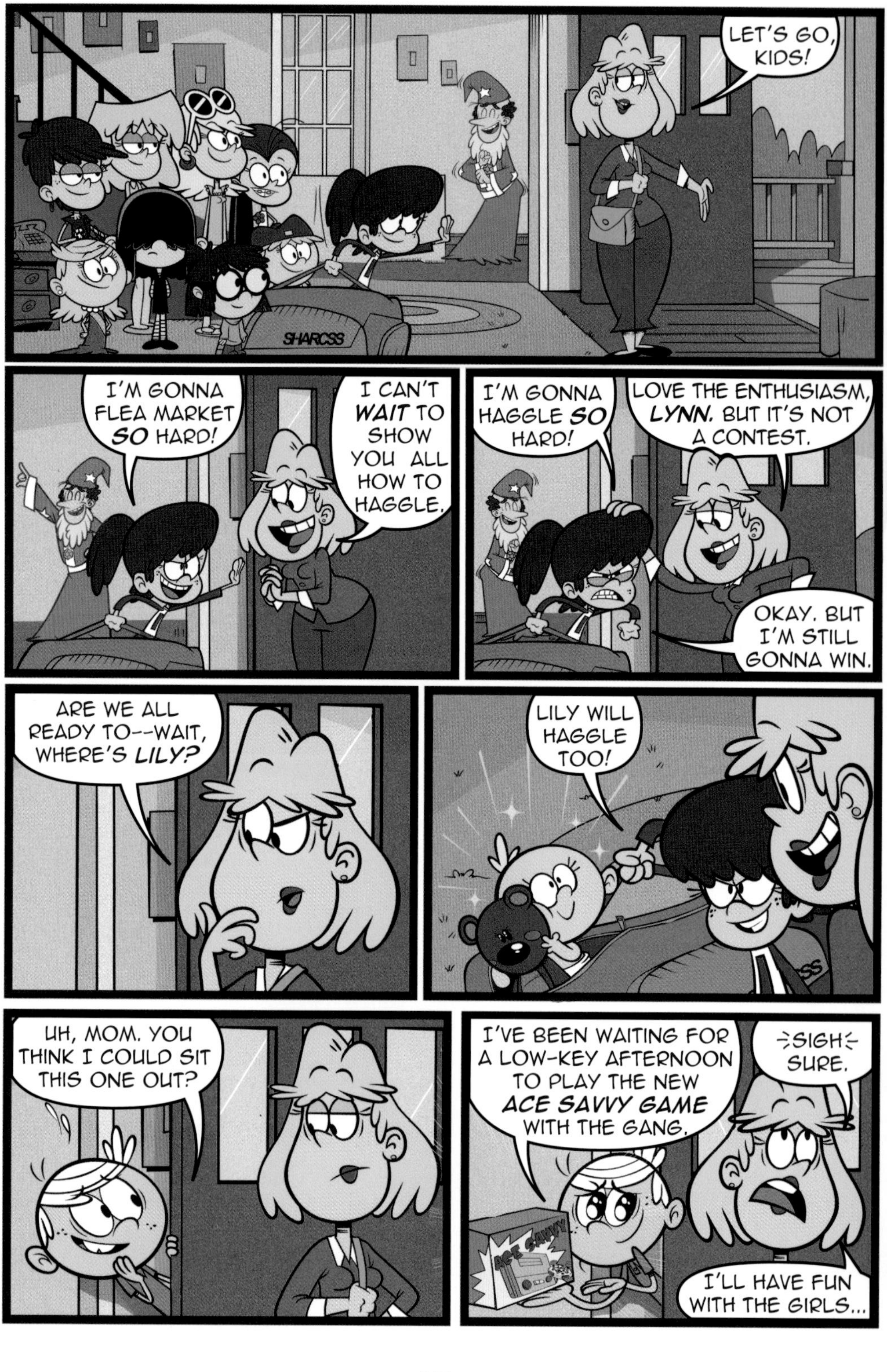
LET'S GO, KIDS!
SHARCSS
I'M GONNA FLEA MARKET SO HARD!
I CAN'T WAIT TO SHOW YOU ALL HOW TO HAGGLE.
I'M GONNA HAGGLE SO HARD!
LOVE THE ENTHUSIASM, LYNN. BUT IT'S NOT A CONTEST.
OKAY. BUT I'M STILL GONNA WIN.
ARE WE ALL READY TO--WAIT, WHERE'S LILY?
LILY WILL HAGGLE TOO!
UH, MOM. YOU THINK I COULD SIT THIS ONE OUT?
I'VE BEEN WAITING FOR A LOW-KEY AFTERNOON TO PLAY THE NEW ACE SAVVY GAME WITH THE GANG.
SIGH SURE.
I'LL HAVE FUN WITH THE GIRLS...

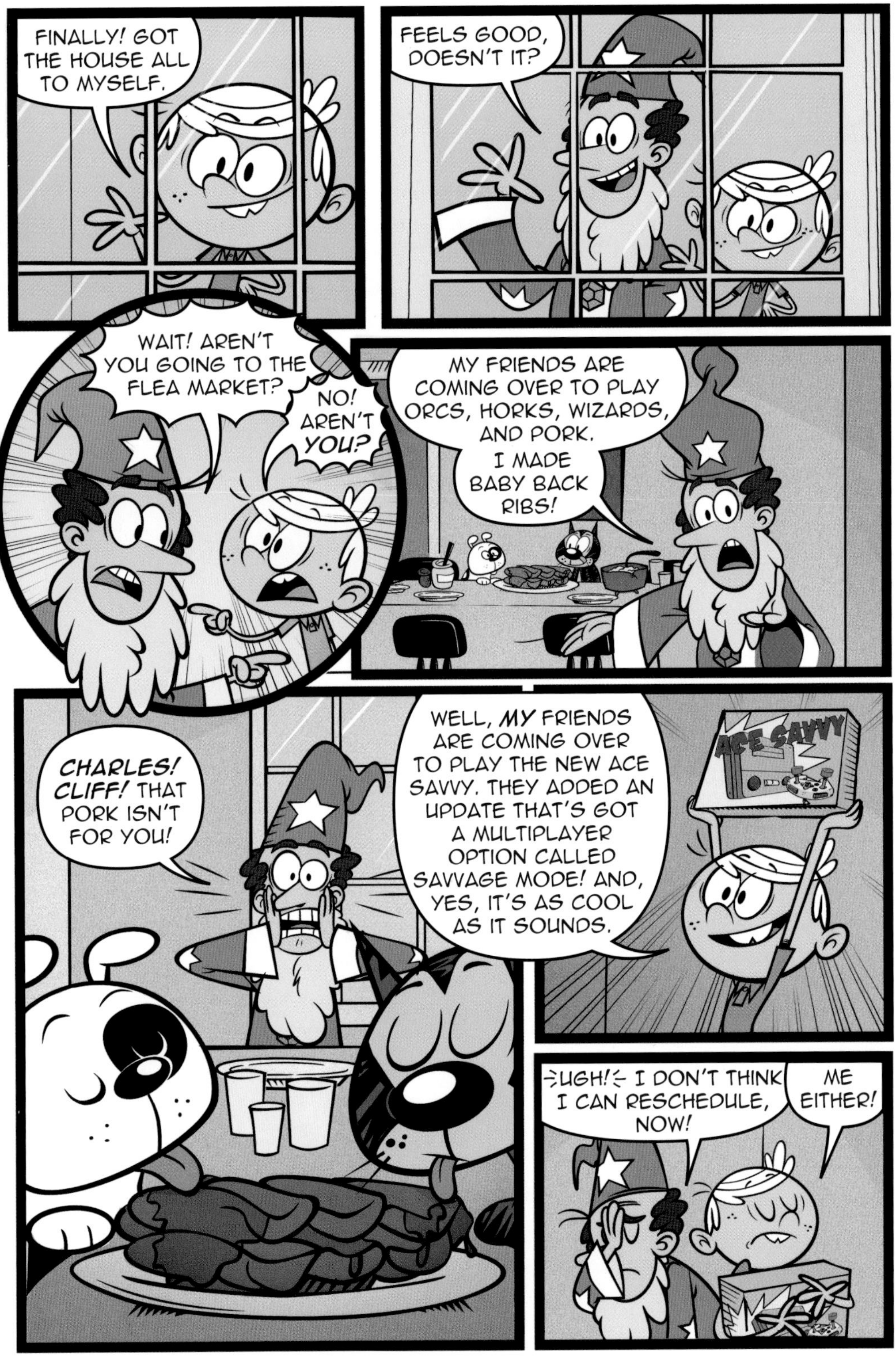
FINALLY! GOT THE HOUSE ALL TO MYSELF.
FEELS GOOD, DOESN'T IT?
WAIT! AREN'T YOU GOING TO THE FLEA MARKET?
NO! AREN'T *YOU?*
MY FRIENDS ARE COMING OVER TO PLAY ORCS, HORKS, WIZARDS, AND PORK.
I MADE BABY BACK RIBS!
WELL, *MY* FRIENDS ARE COMING OVER TO PLAY THE NEW ACE SAVVY. THEY ADDED AN UPDATE THAT'S GOT A MULTIPLAYER OPTION CALLED SAVVAGE MODE! AND, YES, IT'S AS COOL AS IT SOUNDS.
ACE SAVVY
CHARLES! CLIFF! THAT PORK ISN'T FOR YOU!
UGH! I DON'T THINK I CAN RESCHEDULE, NOW!
ME EITHER!

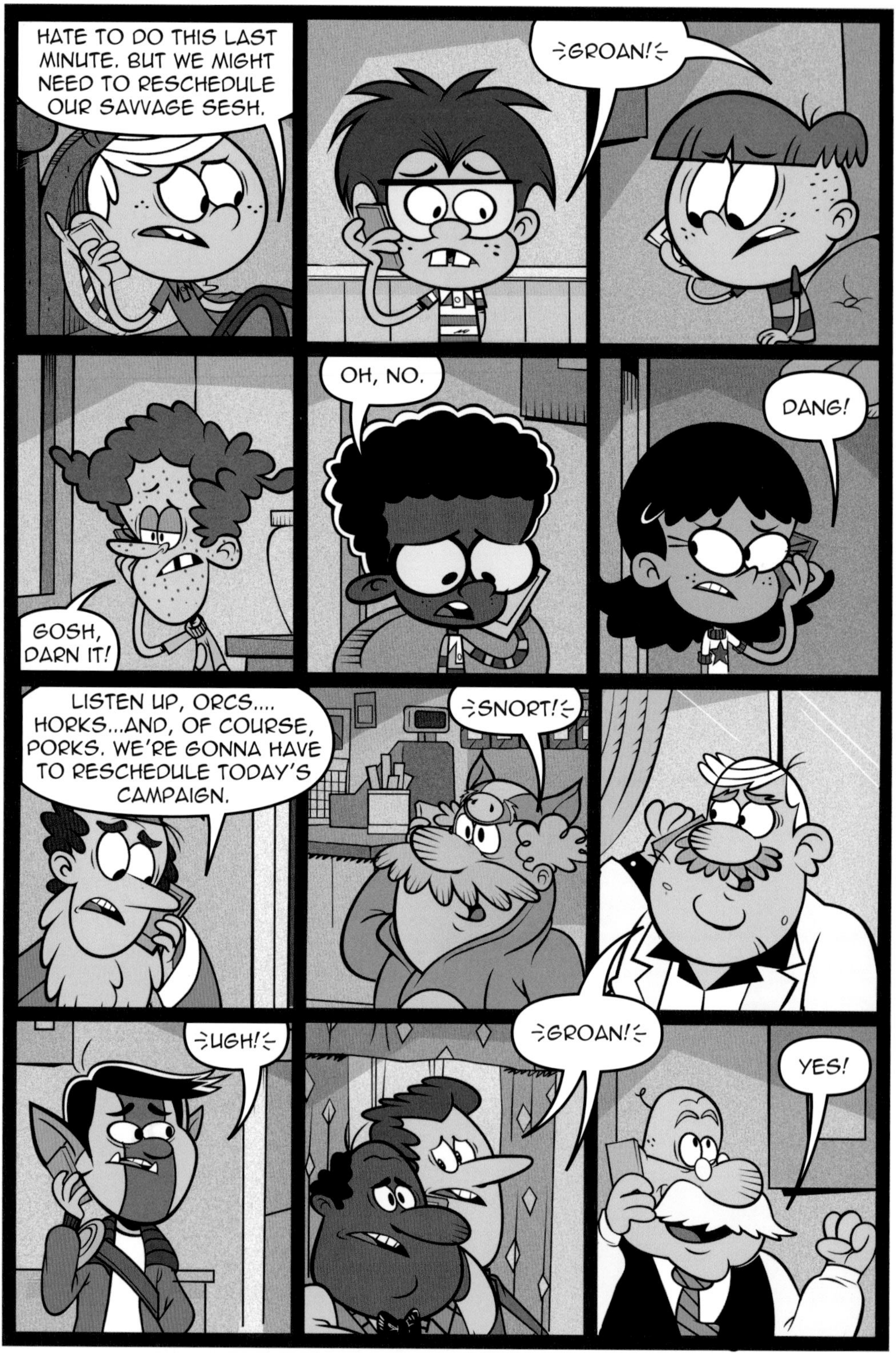
HATE TO DO THIS LAST MINUTE. BUT WE MIGHT NEED TO RESCHEDULE OUR SAVVAGE SESH.
GROAN!
GOSH, DARN IT!
OH, NO.
DANG!
LISTEN UP, ORCS.... HORKS...AND, OF COURSE, PORKS. WE'RE GONNA HAVE TO RESCHEDULE TODAY'S CAMPAIGN.
SNORT!
UGH!
GROAN!
YES!

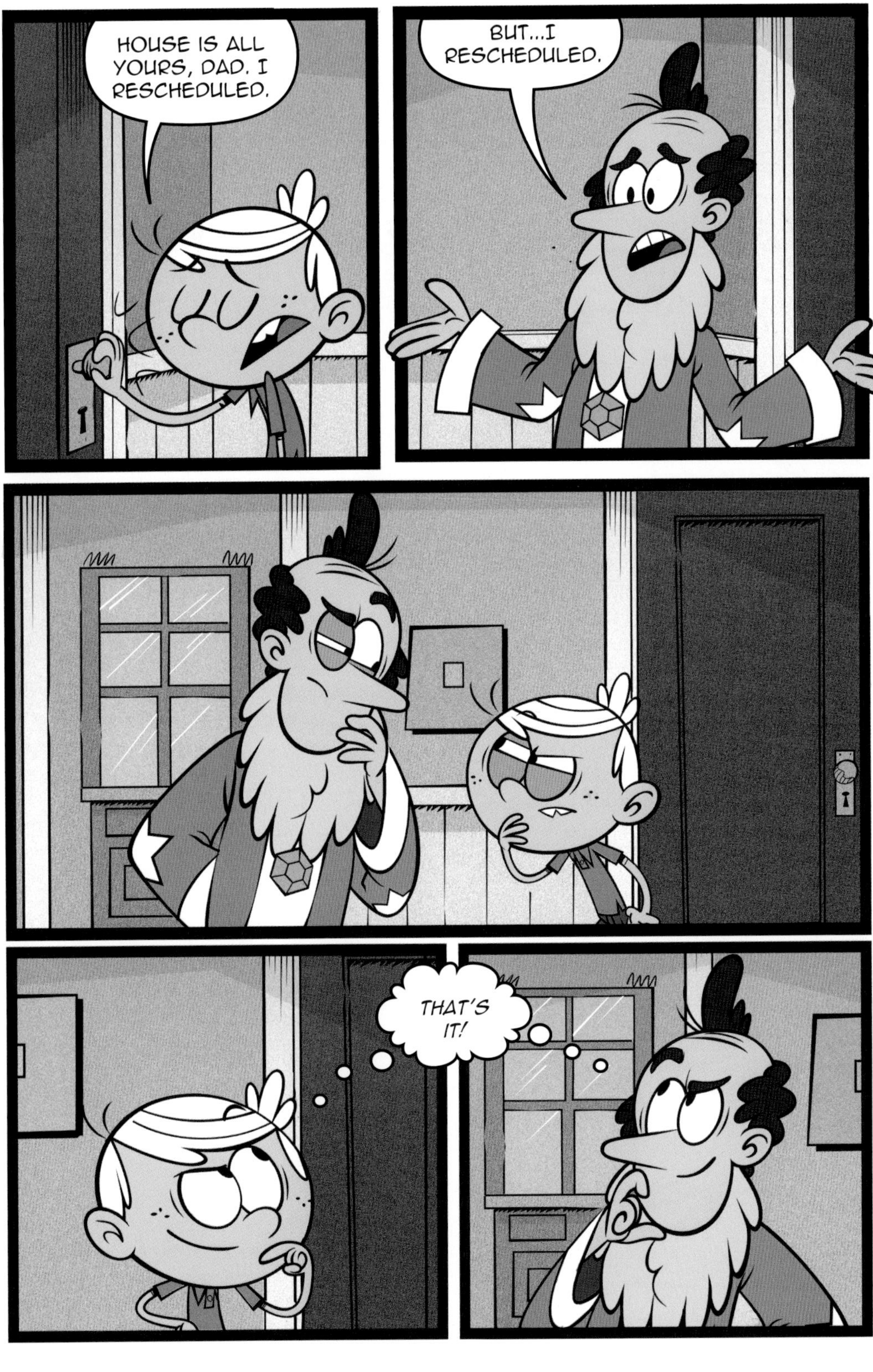
HOUSE IS ALL YOURS, DAD. I RESCHEDULED.
BUT...I RESCHEDULED.
THAT'S IT!

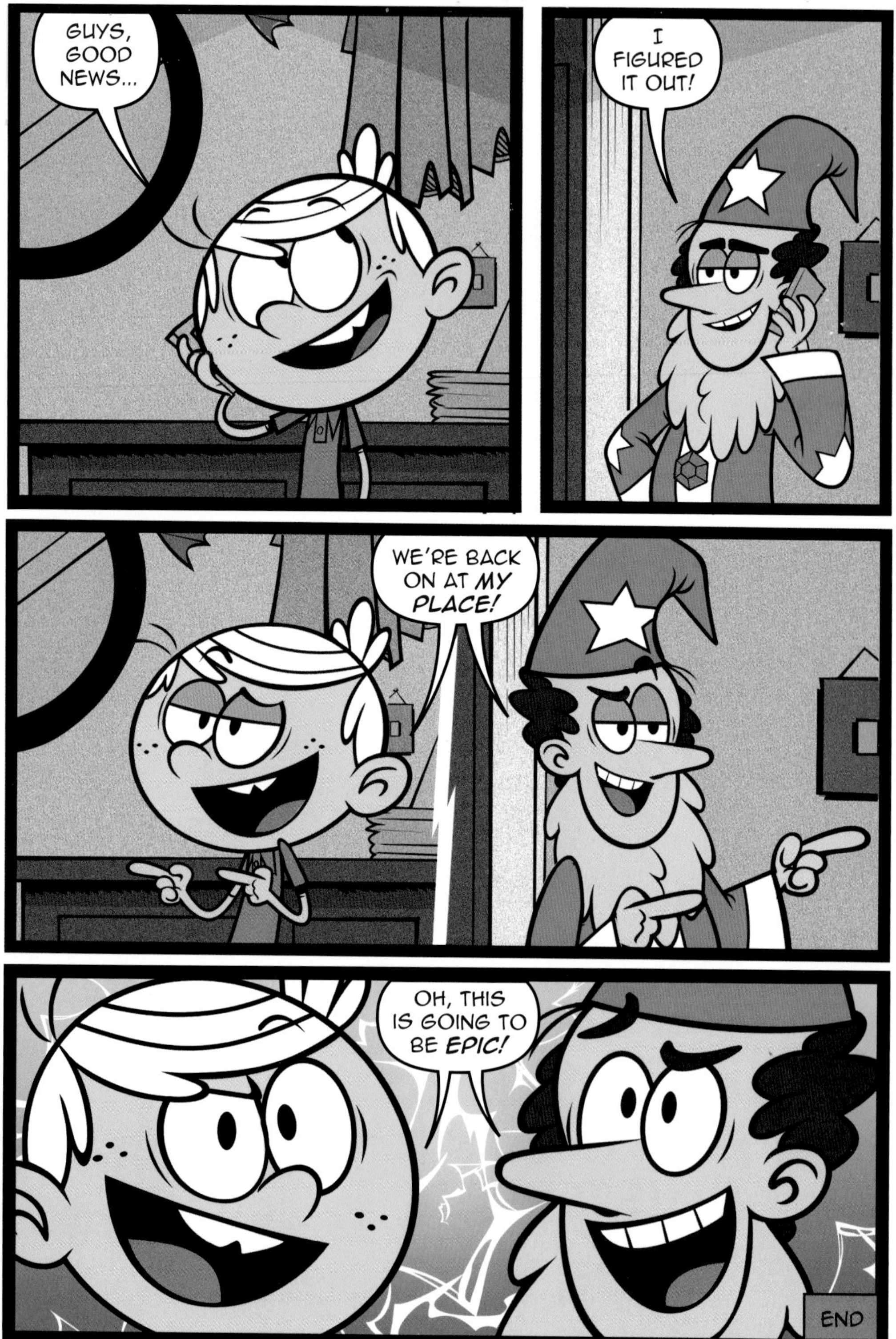
GUYS, GOOD NEWS...
I FIGURED IT OUT!
WE'RE BACK ON AT *MY PLACE!*
OH, THIS IS GOING TO BE *EPIC!*
END

"SPACE RACE"

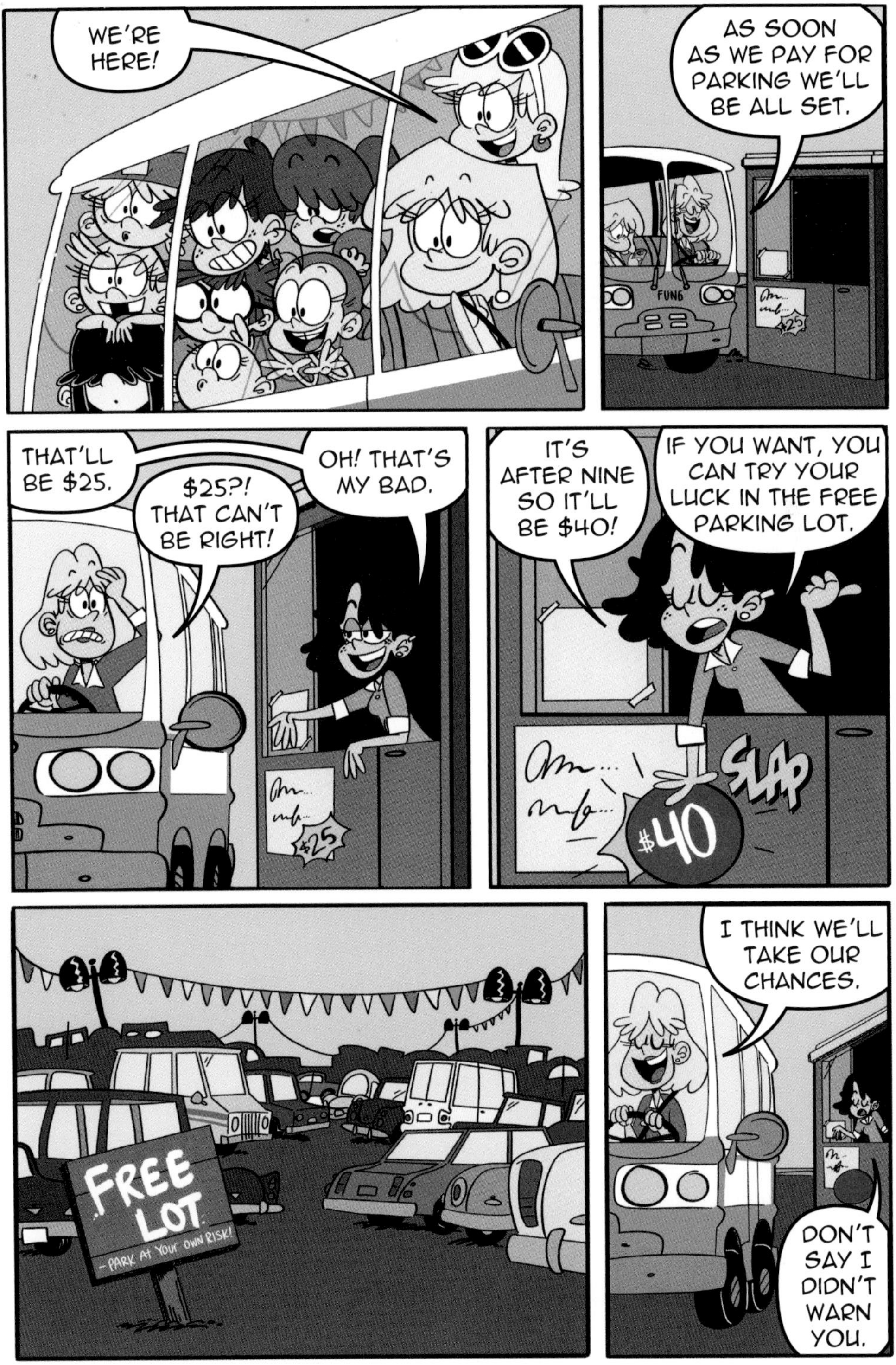

WE'RE HERE!
AS SOON AS WE PAY FOR PARKING WE'LL BE ALL SET.
FUNG
$25
THAT'LL BE $25.
$25?! THAT CAN'T BE RIGHT!
OH! THAT'S MY BAD.
$25
IT'S AFTER NINE SO IT'LL BE $40!
IF YOU WANT, YOU CAN TRY YOUR LUCK IN THE FREE PARKING LOT.
SLAP
$40
FREE LOT
-PARK AT YOUR OWN RISK!
I THINK WE'LL TAKE OUR CHANCES.
DON'T SAY I DIDN'T WARN YOU.

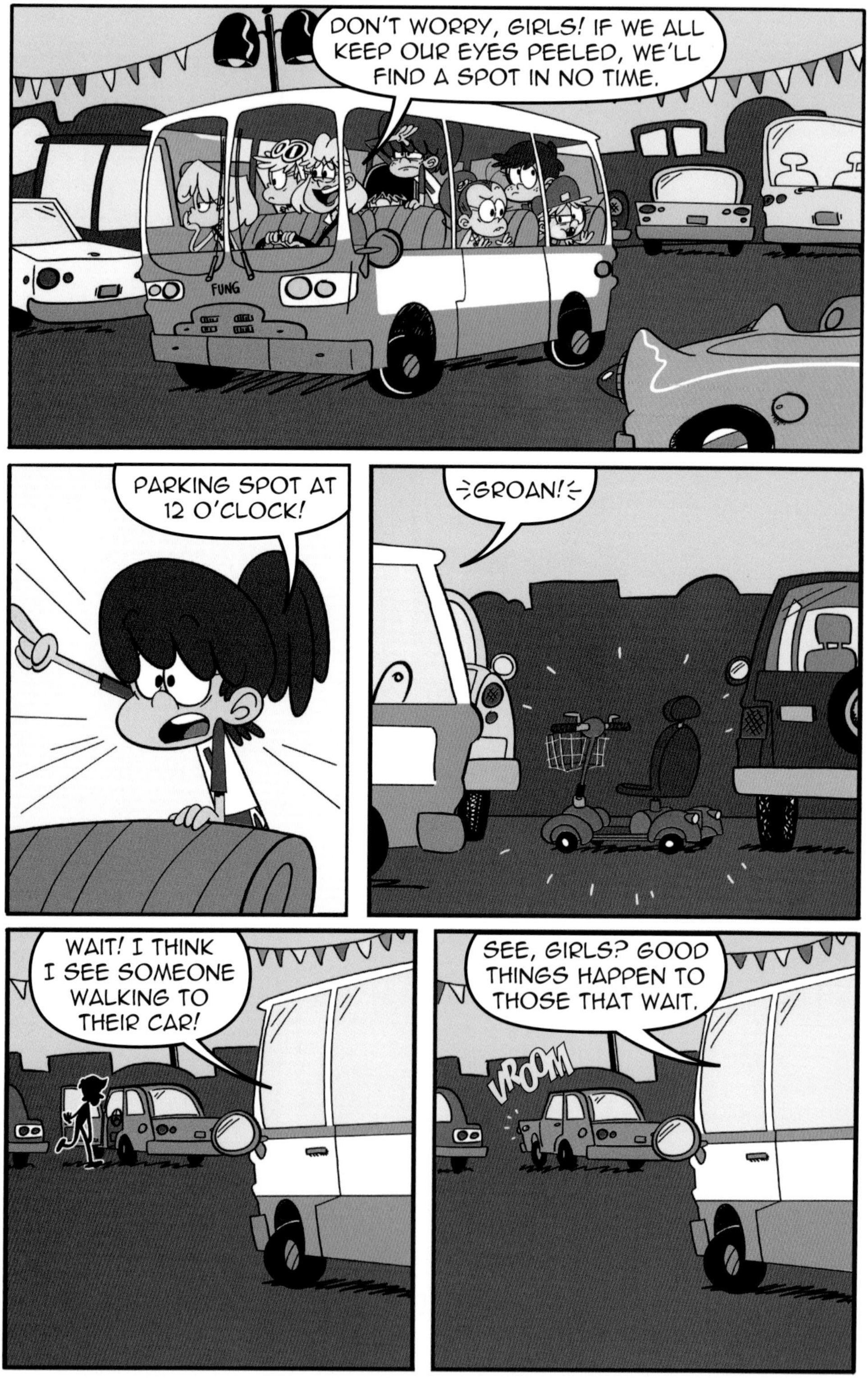
DON'T WORRY, GIRLS! IF WE ALL KEEP OUR EYES PEELED, WE'LL FIND A SPOT IN NO TIME.
FUNG
PARKING SPOT AT 12 O'CLOCK!
GROAN!
WAIT! I THINK I SEE SOMEONE WALKING TO THEIR CAR!
SEE, GIRLS? GOOD THINGS HAPPEN TO THOSE THAT WAIT.
VROOM

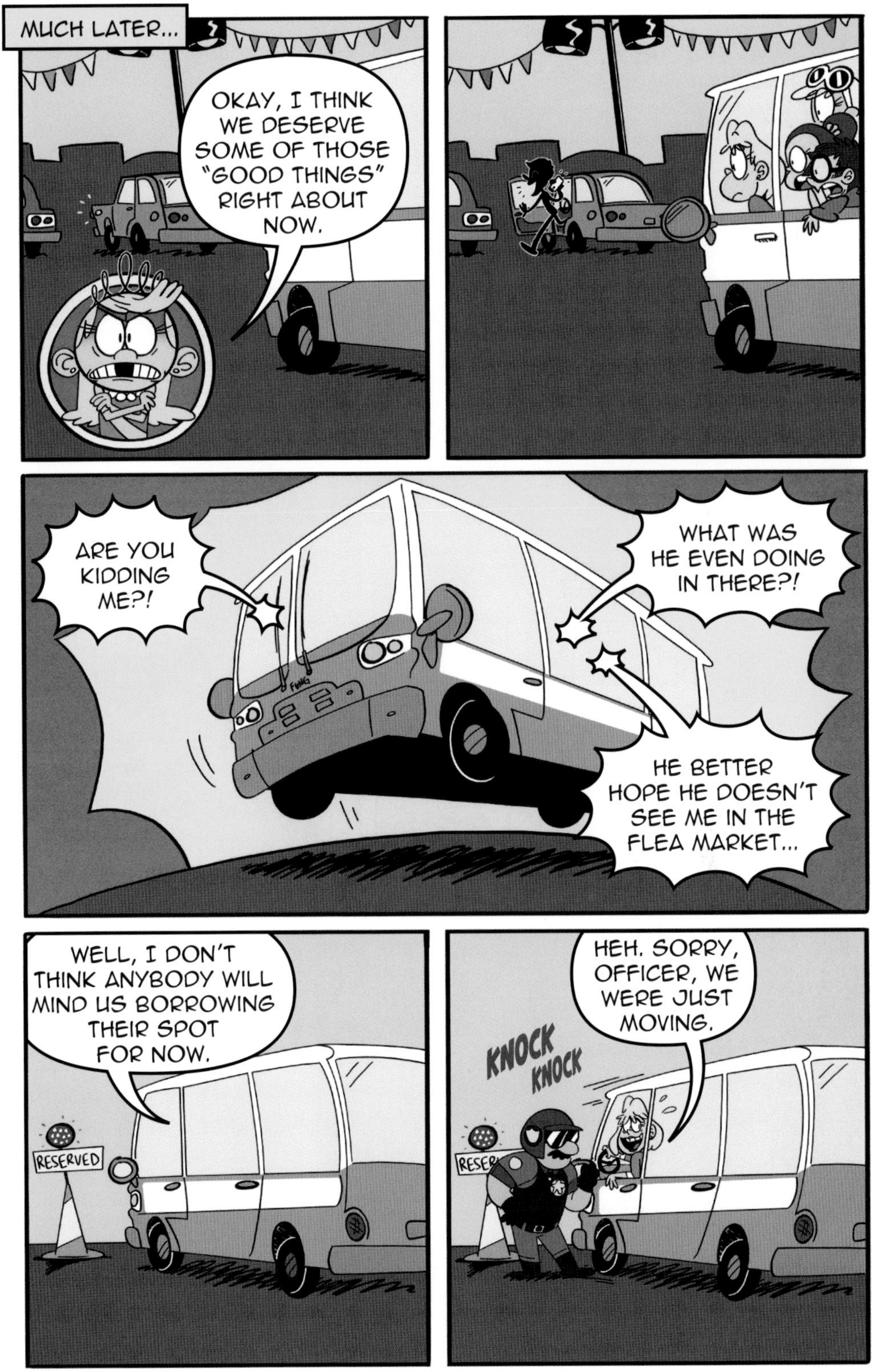
MUCH LATER...
OKAY, I THINK WE DESERVE SOME OF THOSE "GOOD THINGS" RIGHT ABOUT NOW.
ARE YOU KIDDING ME?!
WHAT WAS HE EVEN DOING IN THERE?!
HE BETTER HOPE HE DOESN'T SEE ME IN THE FLEA MARKET...
WELL, I DON'T THINK ANYBODY WILL MIND US BORROWING THEIR SPOT FOR NOW.
RESERVED
KNOCK KNOCK
HEH. SORRY, OFFICER, WE WERE JUST MOVING.

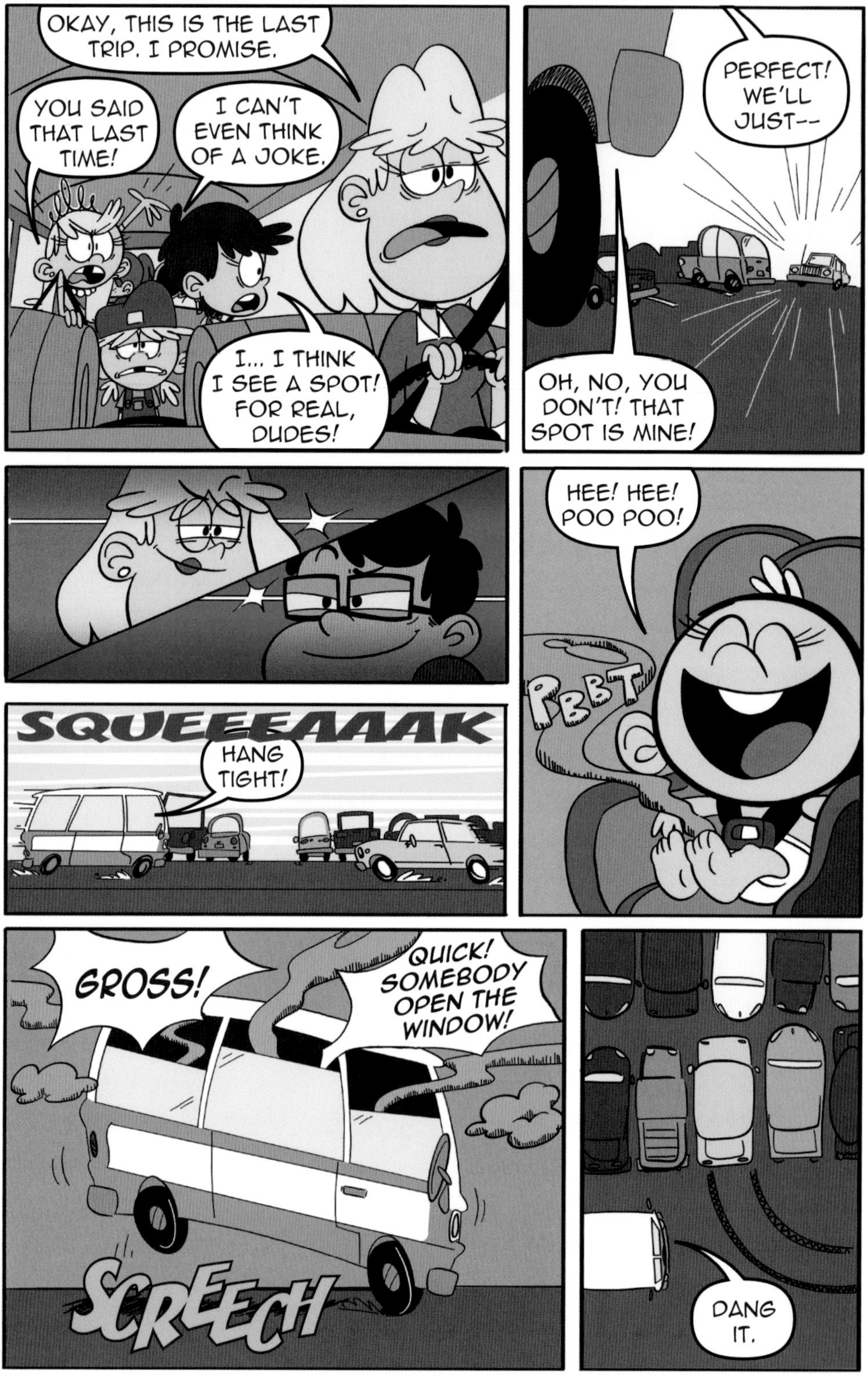
OKAY, THIS IS THE LAST TRIP. I PROMISE.
YOU SAID THAT LAST TIME!
I CAN'T EVEN THINK OF A JOKE.
I... I THINK I SEE A SPOT! FOR REAL, DUDES!
PERFECT! WE'LL JUST--
OH, NO, YOU DON'T! THAT SPOT IS MINE!
HEE! HEE! POO POO!
PBBT
SQUEEEAAAK
HANG TIGHT!
GROSS!
QUICK! SOMEBODY OPEN THE WINDOW!
SCREECH
DANG IT.

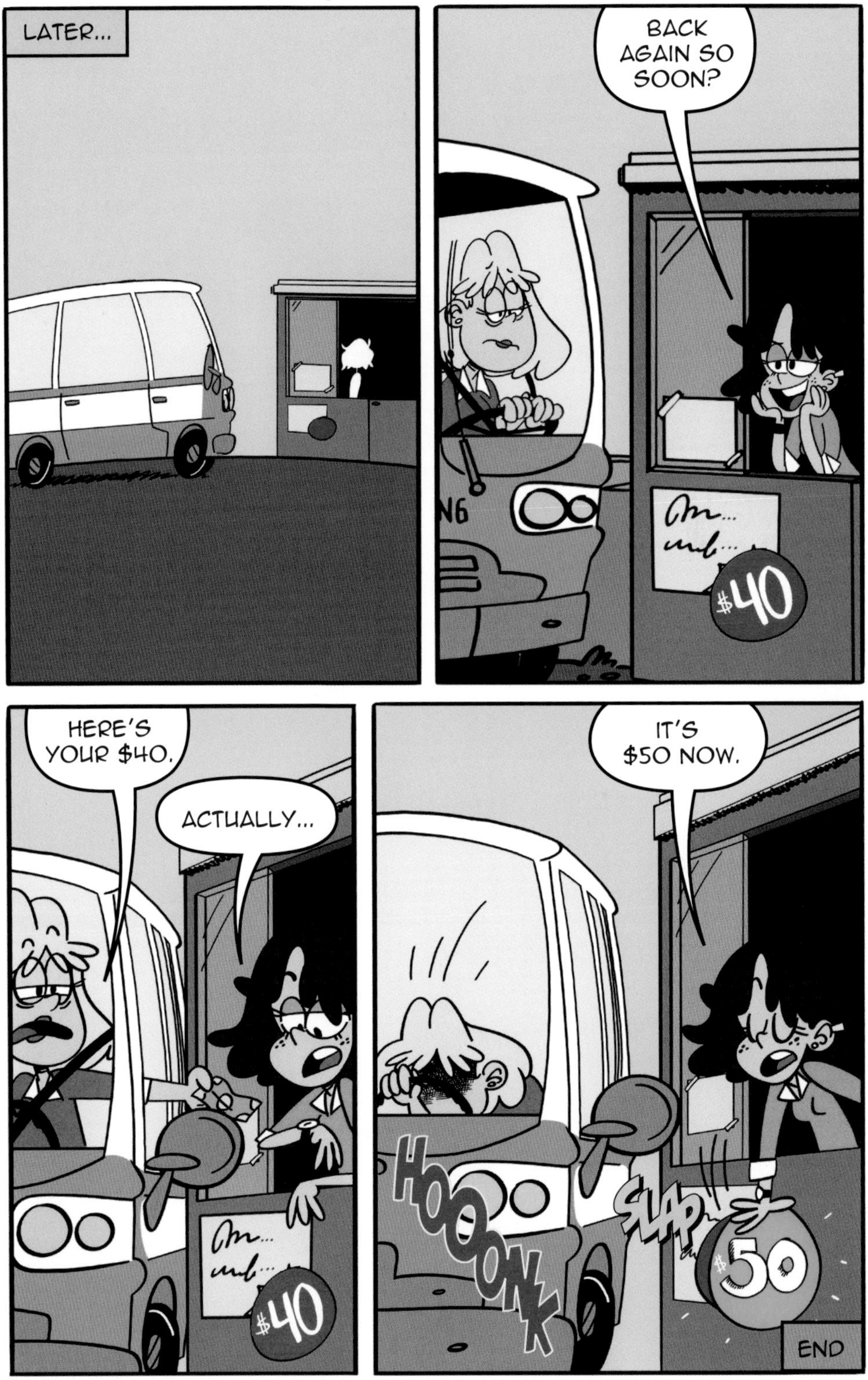
LATER...
BACK AGAIN SO SOON?
$40
HERE'S YOUR $40.
ACTUALLY...
$40
IT'S $50 NOW.
HOOOONK
SLAP
$50
END

"DIVIDE AND CONQUER"

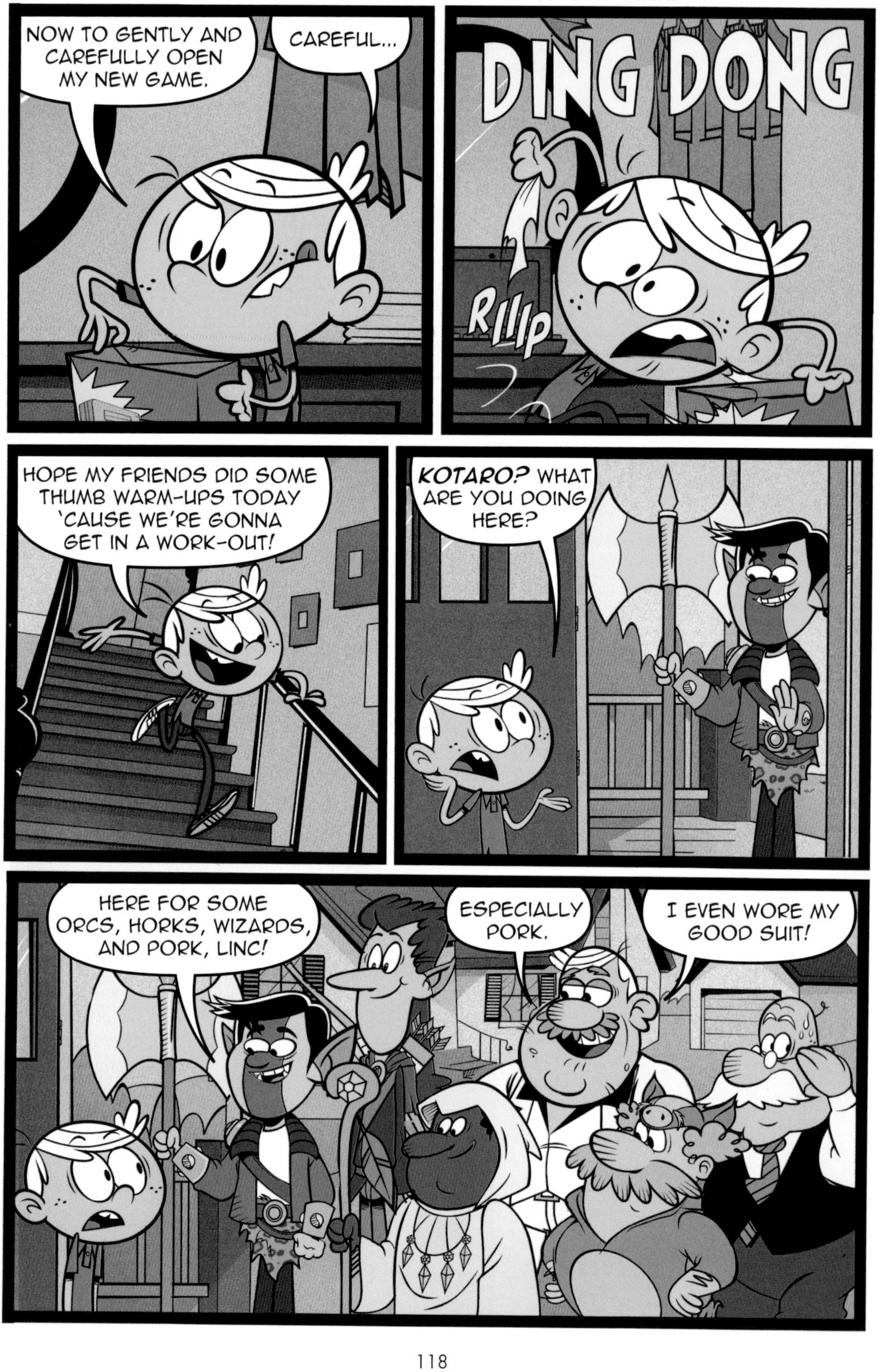
NOW TO GENTLY AND CAREFULLY OPEN MY NEW GAME.
CAREFUL...
DING DONG
RIIIP
HOPE MY FRIENDS DID SOME THUMB WARM-UPS TODAY 'CAUSE WE'RE GONNA GET IN A WORK-OUT!
KOTARO? WHAT ARE YOU DOING HERE?
HERE FOR SOME ORCS, HORKS, WIZARDS, AND PORK, LINC!
ESPECIALLY PORK.
I EVEN WORE MY GOOD SUIT!

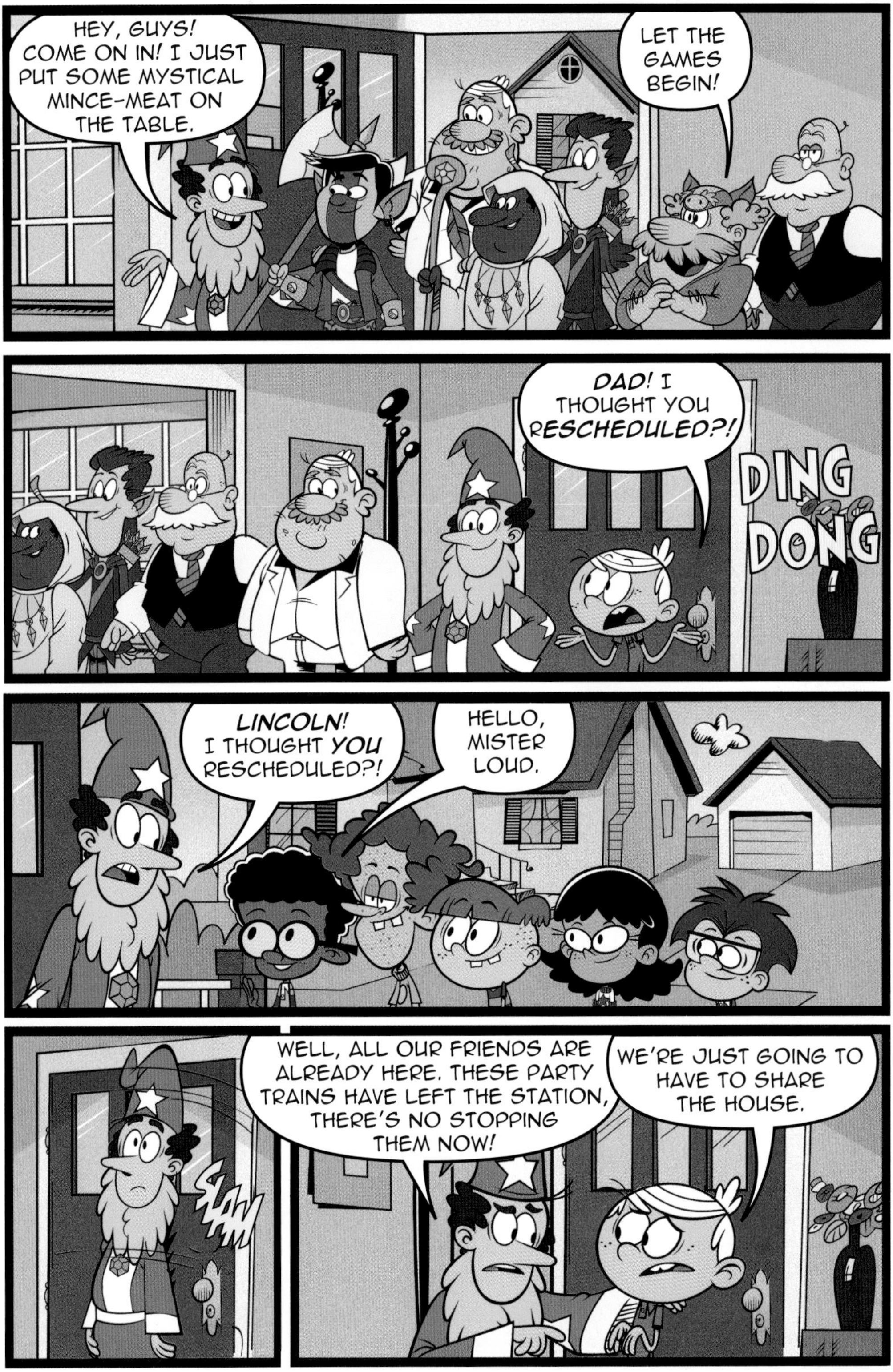
HEY, GUYS! COME ON IN! I JUST PUT SOME MYSTICAL MINCE-MEAT ON THE TABLE.
LET THE GAMES BEGIN!
DAD! I THOUGHT YOU RESCHEDULED?!
DING DONG
LINCOLN! I THOUGHT YOU RESCHEDULED?!
HELLO, MISTER LOUD.
SLAM
WELL, ALL OUR FRIENDS ARE ALREADY HERE. THESE PARTY TRAINS HAVE LEFT THE STATION, THERE'S NO STOPPING THEM NOW!
WE'RE JUST GOING TO HAVE TO SHARE THE HOUSE.

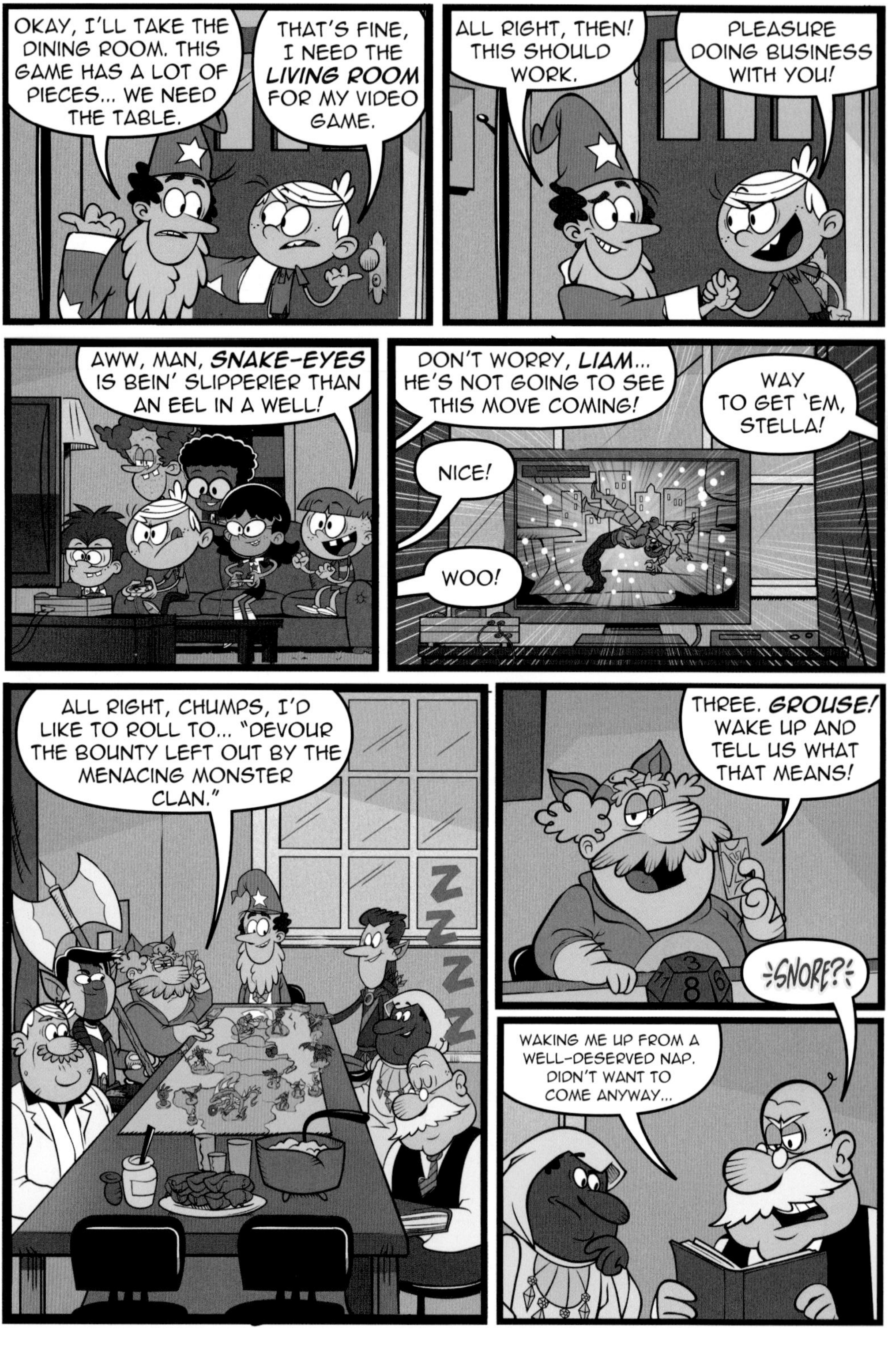
OKAY, I'LL TAKE THE DINING ROOM. THIS GAME HAS A LOT OF PIECES... WE NEED THE TABLE.
THAT'S FINE, I NEED THE LIVING ROOM FOR MY VIDEO GAME.
ALL RIGHT, THEN! THIS SHOULD WORK.
PLEASURE DOING BUSINESS WITH YOU!
AWW, MAN, SNAKE-EYES IS BEIN' SLIPPERIER THAN AN EEL IN A WELL!
DON'T WORRY, LIAM... HE'S NOT GOING TO SEE THIS MOVE COMING!
WAY TO GET 'EM, STELLA!
NICE!
WOO!
ALL RIGHT, CHUMPS, I'D LIKE TO ROLL TO... "DEVOUR THE BOUNTY LEFT OUT BY THE MENACING MONSTER CLAN."
Z Z Z
THREE. GROUSE! WAKE UP AND TELL US WHAT THAT MEANS!
SNORE?
WAKING ME UP FROM A WELL-DESERVED NAP. DIDN'T WANT TO COME ANYWAY...

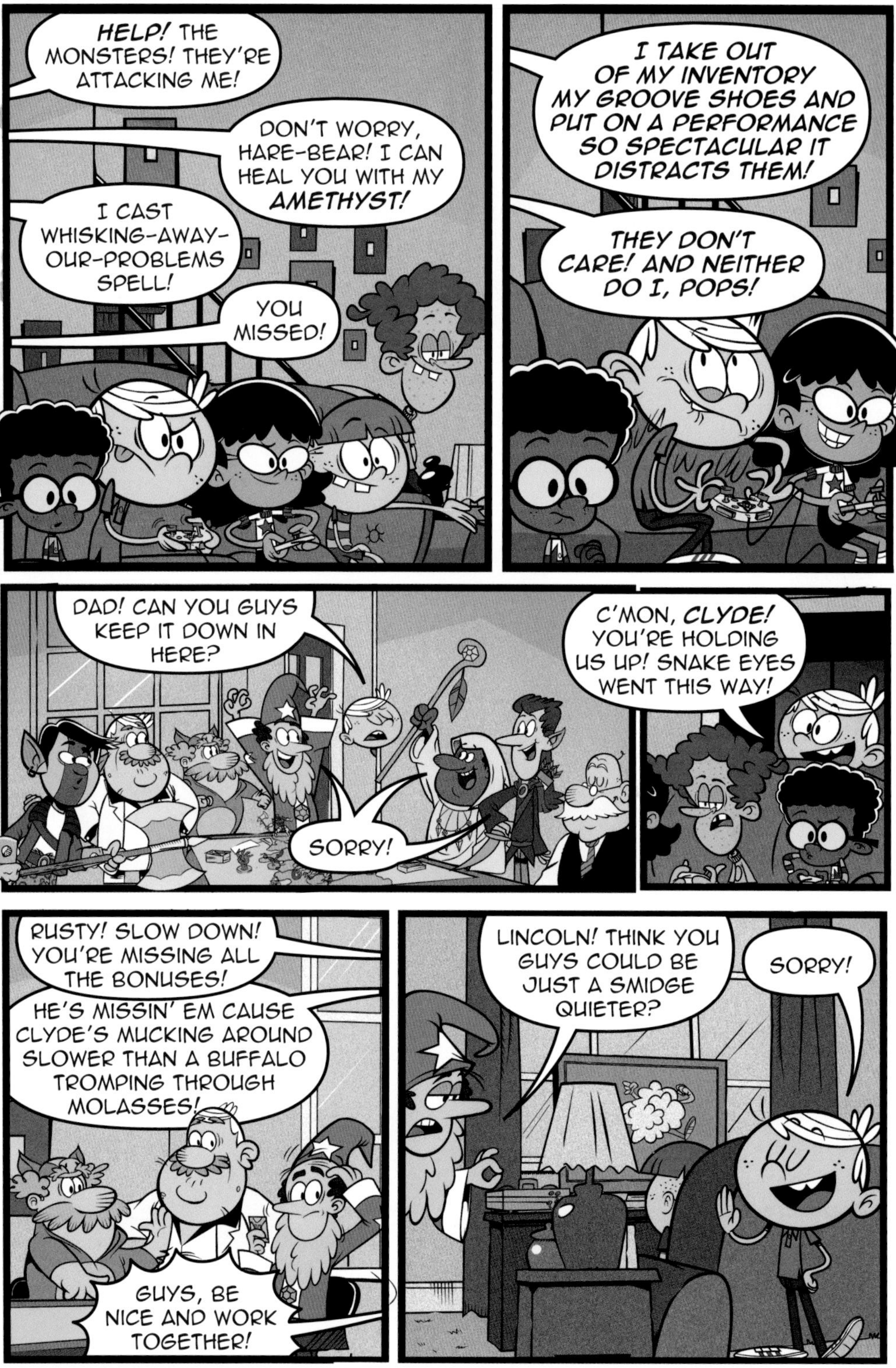
HELP! THE MONSTERS! THEY'RE ATTACKING ME!
DON'T WORRY, HARE-BEAR! I CAN HEAL YOU WITH MY AMETHYST!
I CAST WHISKING-AWAY-OUR-PROBLEMS SPELL!
YOU MISSED!
I TAKE OUT OF MY INVENTORY MY GROOVE SHOES AND PUT ON A PERFORMANCE SO SPECTACULAR IT DISTRACTS THEM!
THEY DON'T CARE! AND NEITHER DO I, POPS!
DAD! CAN YOU GUYS KEEP IT DOWN IN HERE?
SORRY!
C'MON, CLYDE! YOU'RE HOLDING US UP! SNAKE EYES WENT THIS WAY!
RUSTY! SLOW DOWN! YOU'RE MISSING ALL THE BONUSES!
HE'S MISSIN' EM CAUSE CLYDE'S MUCKING AROUND SLOWER THAN A BUFFALO TROMPING THROUGH MOLASSES!
GUYS, BE NICE AND WORK TOGETHER!
LINCOLN! THINK YOU GUYS COULD BE JUST A SMIDGE QUIETER?
SORRY!

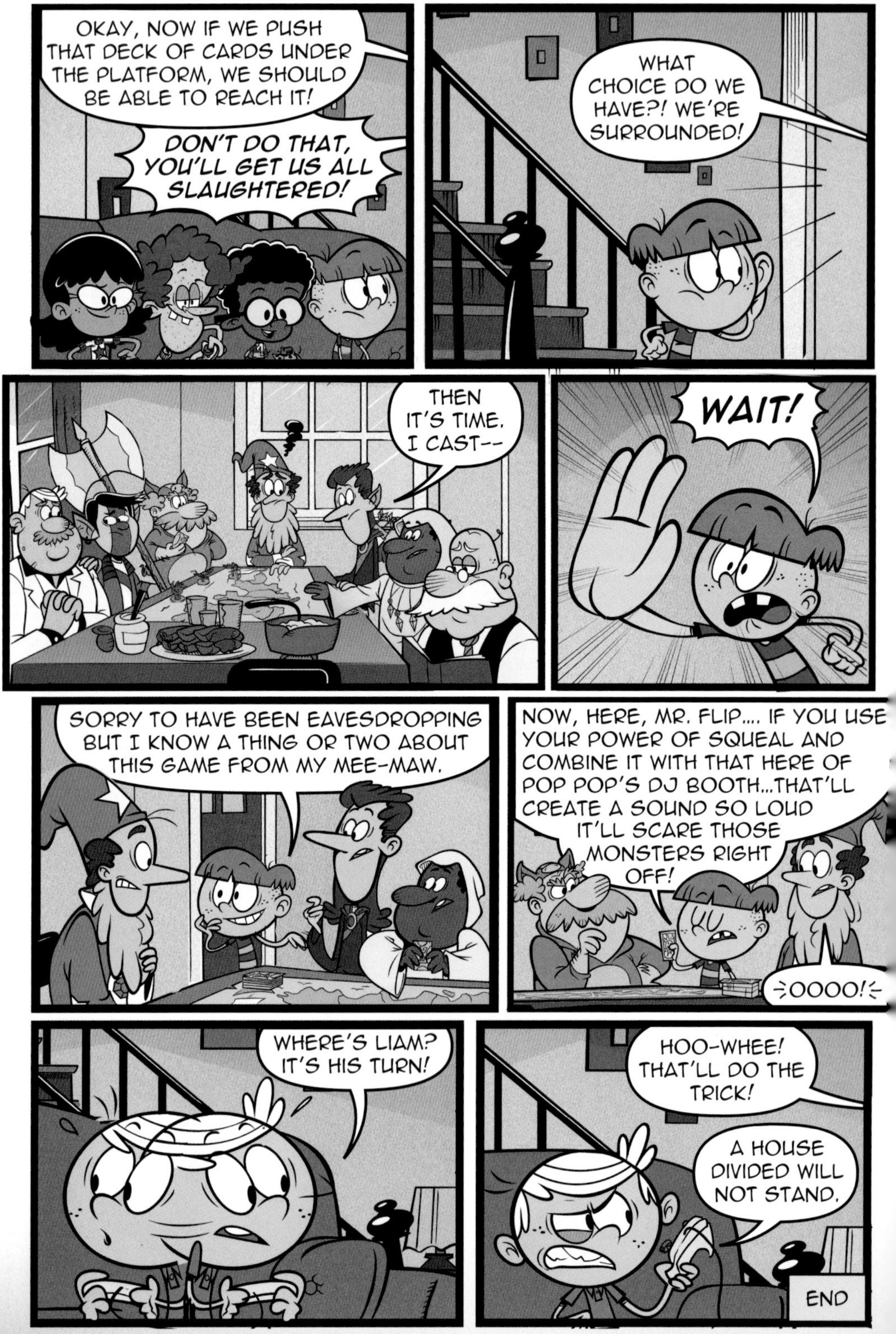
OKAY, NOW IF WE PUSH THAT DECK OF CARDS UNDER THE PLATFORM, WE SHOULD BE ABLE TO REACH IT!
DON'T DO THAT, YOU'LL GET US ALL SLAUGHTERED!
WHAT CHOICE DO WE HAVE?! WE'RE SURROUNDED!
THEN IT'S TIME. I CAST--
WAIT!
SORRY TO HAVE BEEN EAVESDROPPING BUT I KNOW A THING OR TWO ABOUT THIS GAME FROM MY MEE-MAW.
NOW, HERE, MR. FLIP.... IF YOU USE YOUR POWER OF SQUEAL AND COMBINE IT WITH THAT HERE OF POP POP'S DJ BOOTH...THAT'LL CREATE A SOUND SO LOUD IT'LL SCARE THOSE MONSTERS RIGHT OFF!
OOOO!
WHERE'S LIAM? IT'S HIS TURN!
HOO-WHEE! THAT'LL DO THE TRICK!
A HOUSE DIVIDED WILL NOT STAND.
END

"HAGGLE TALE"

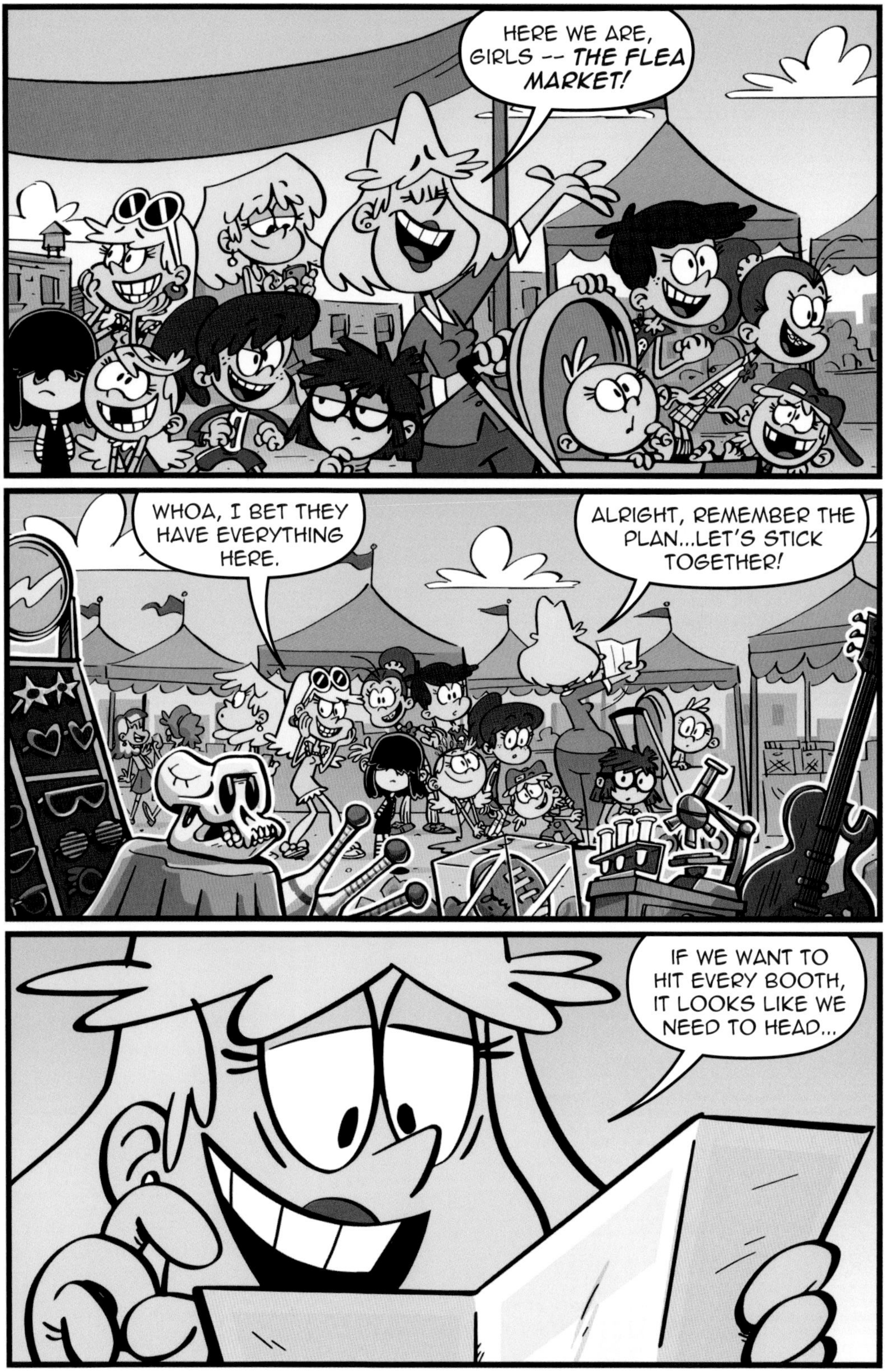
HERE WE ARE, GIRLS -- *THE FLEA MARKET!*
WHOA, I BET THEY HAVE EVERYTHING HERE.
ALRIGHT, REMEMBER THE PLAN...LET'S STICK TOGETHER!
IF WE WANT TO HIT EVERY BOOTH, IT LOOKS LIKE WE NEED TO HEAD...

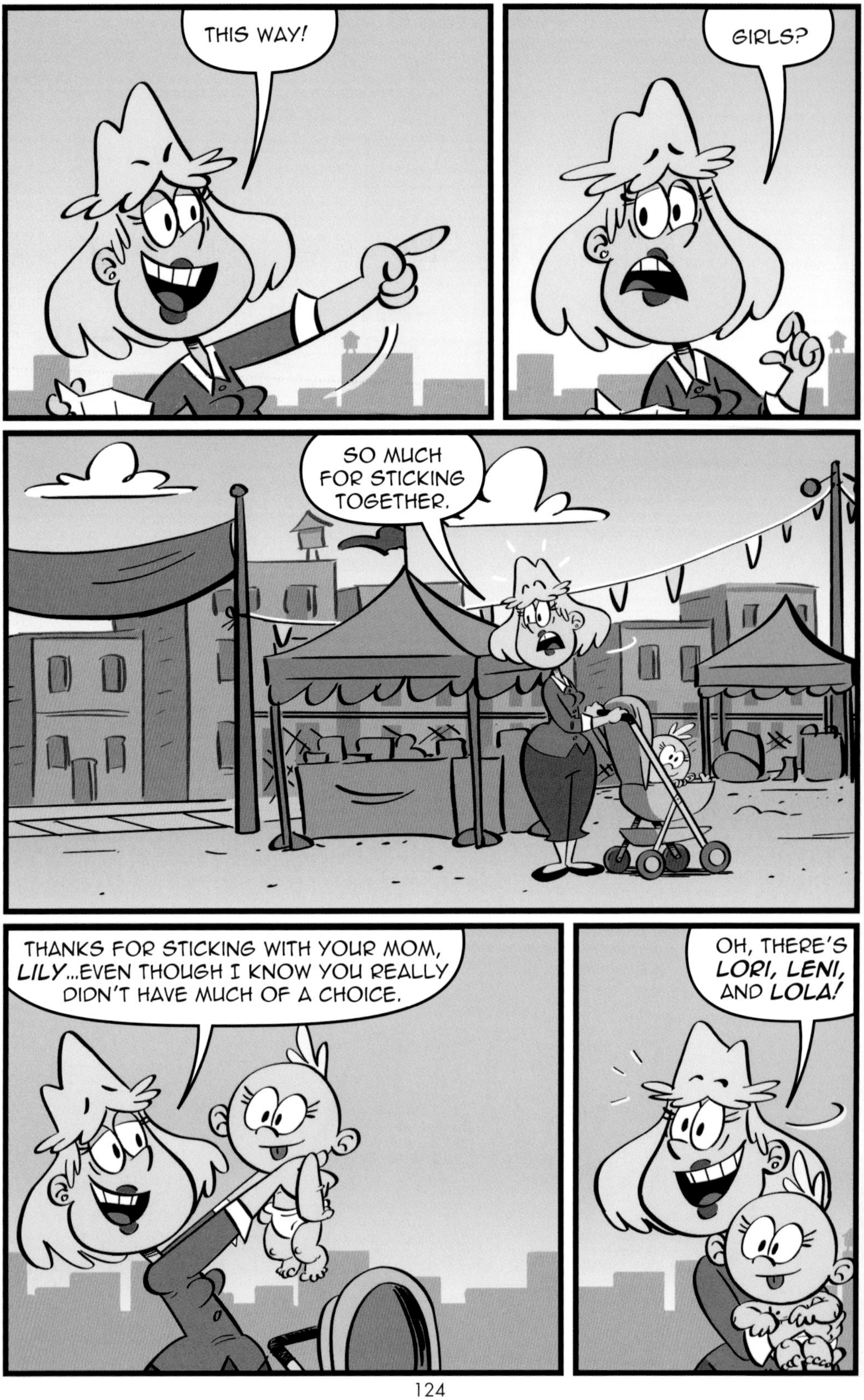
THIS WAY!
GIRLS?
SO MUCH FOR STICKING TOGETHER.
THANKS FOR STICKING WITH YOUR MOM, *LILY*...EVEN THOUGH I KNOW YOU REALLY DIDN'T HAVE MUCH OF A CHOICE.
OH, THERE'S *LORI, LENI,* AND *LOLA!*

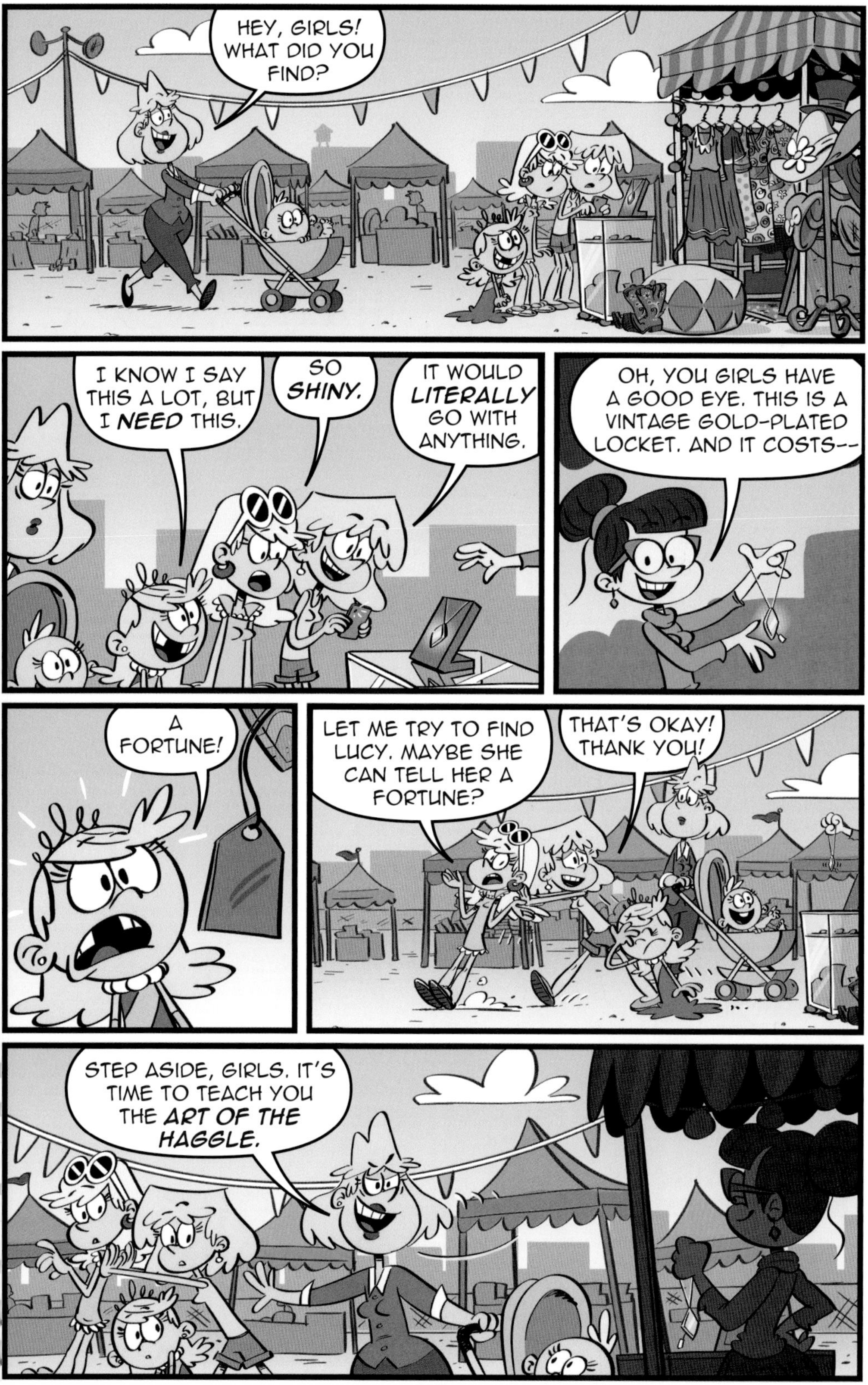
HEY, GIRLS! WHAT DID YOU FIND?
I KNOW I SAY THIS A LOT, BUT I NEED THIS.
SO SHINY.
IT WOULD LITERALLY GO WITH ANYTHING.
OH, YOU GIRLS HAVE A GOOD EYE. THIS IS A VINTAGE GOLD-PLATED LOCKET. AND IT COSTS--
A FORTUNE!
LET ME TRY TO FIND LUCY. MAYBE SHE CAN TELL HER A FORTUNE?
THAT'S OKAY! THANK YOU!
STEP ASIDE, GIRLS. IT'S TIME TO TEACH YOU THE ART OF THE HAGGLE.

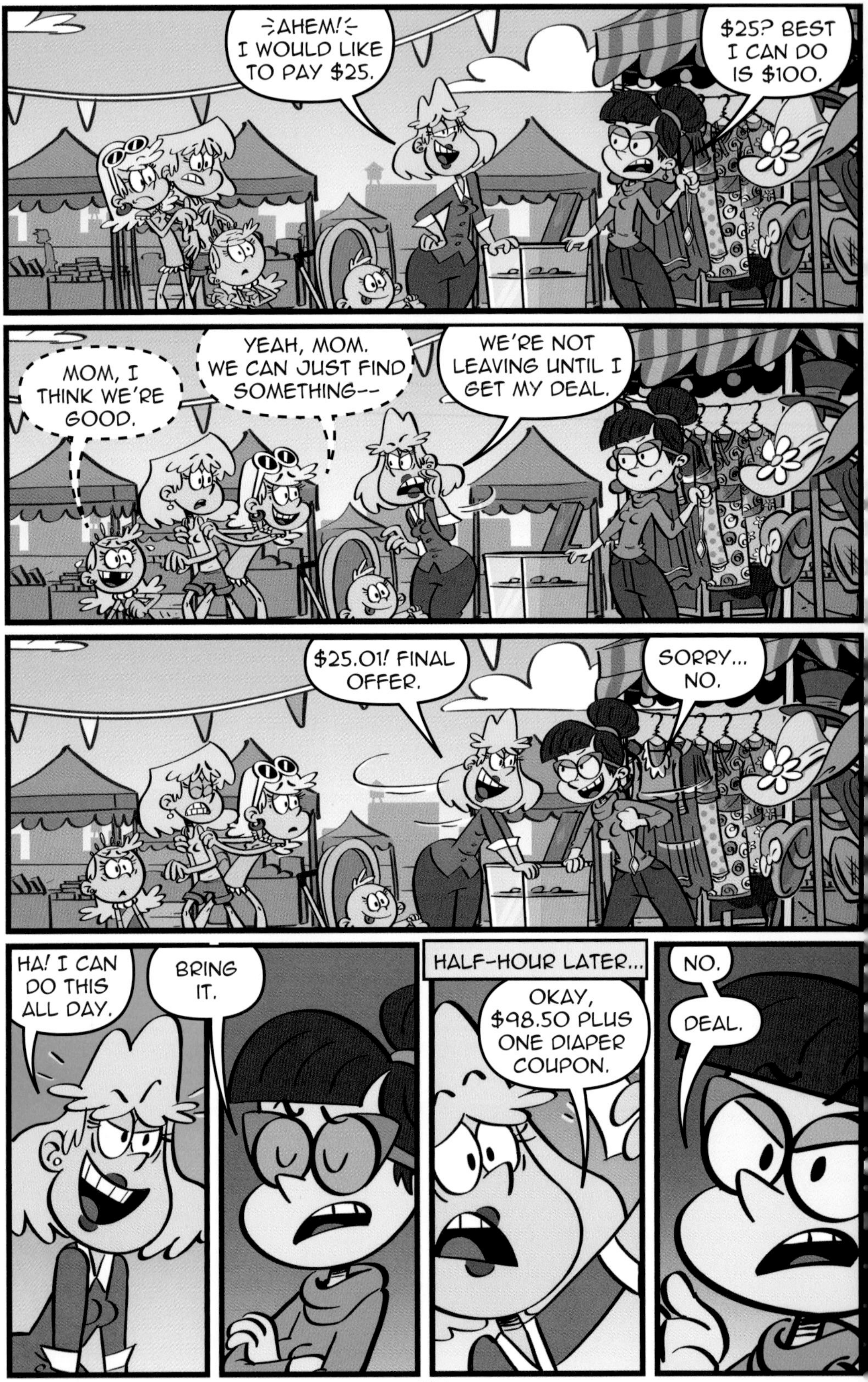

AHEM! I WOULD LIKE TO PAY $25.
$25? BEST I CAN DO IS $100.
MOM, I THINK WE'RE GOOD.
YEAH, MOM. WE CAN JUST FIND SOMETHING--
WE'RE NOT LEAVING UNTIL I GET MY DEAL.
$25.01! FINAL OFFER.
SORRY... NO.
HA! I CAN DO THIS ALL DAY.
BRING IT.
HALF-HOUR LATER...
OKAY, $98.50 PLUS ONE DIAPER COUPON.
NO.
DEAL.

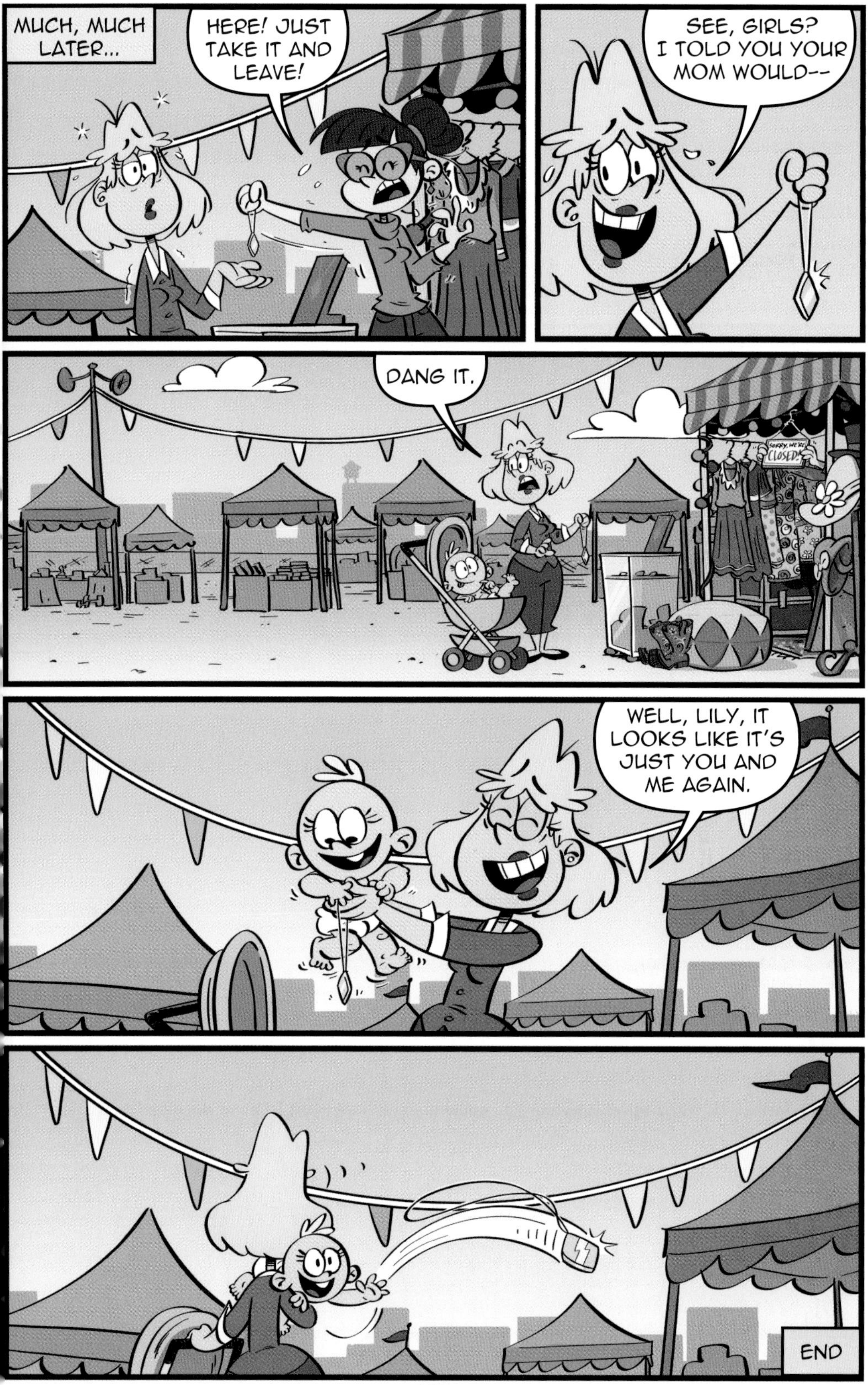
MUCH, MUCH LATER...
HERE! JUST TAKE IT AND LEAVE!
SEE, GIRLS? I TOLD YOU YOUR MOM WOULD--
DANG IT.
SORRY, WE'RE CLOSED!
WELL, LILY, IT LOOKS LIKE IT'S JUST YOU AND ME AGAIN.
END

"PARTY HOPPERS"

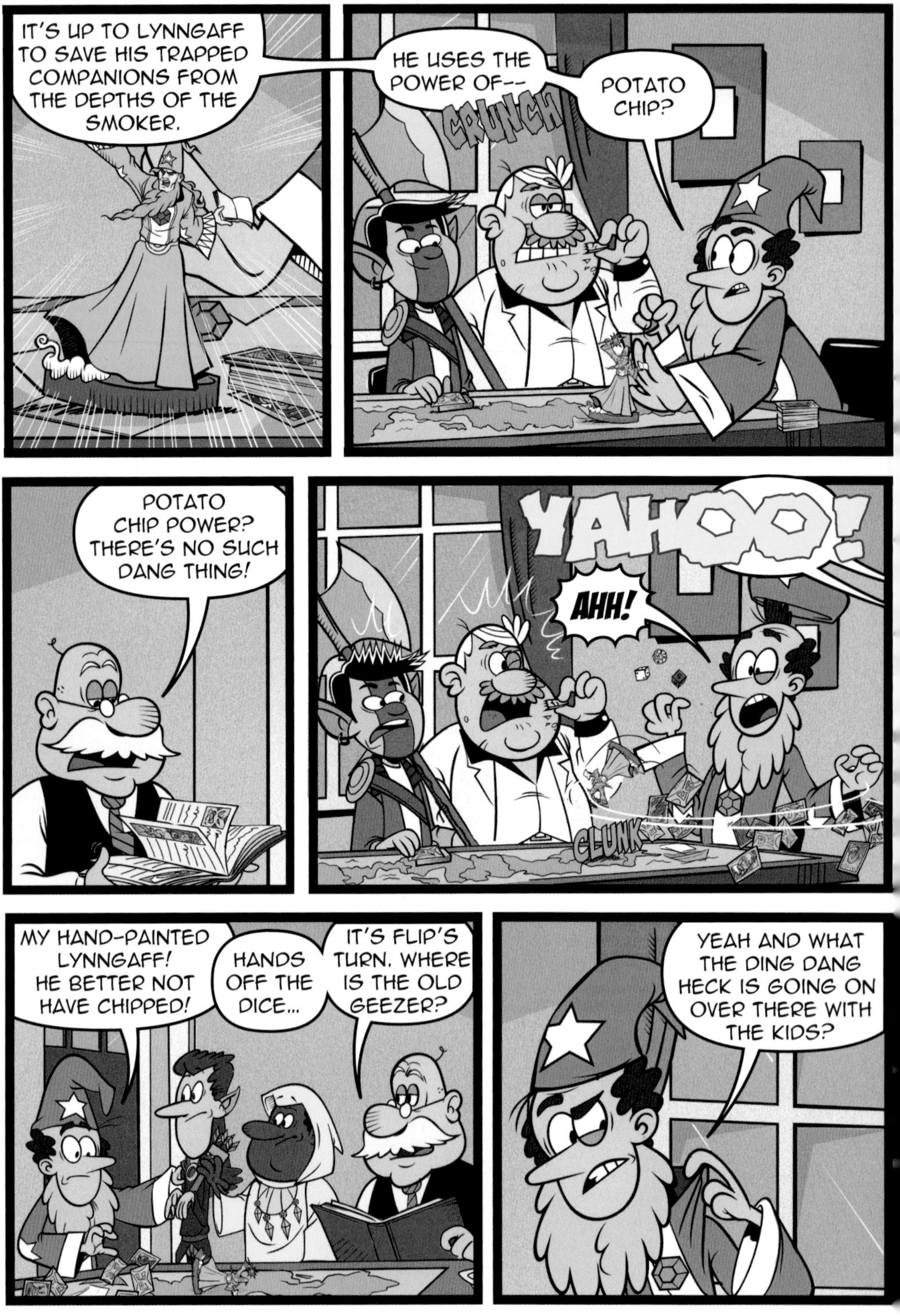

IT'S UP TO LYNNGAFF TO SAVE HIS TRAPPED COMPANIONS FROM THE DEPTHS OF THE SMOKER.
HE USES THE POWER OF--
CRUNCH
POTATO CHIP?
POTATO CHIP POWER? THERE'S NO SUCH DANG THING!
YAHOO!
AHH!
CLUNK
MY HAND-PAINTED LYNNGAFF! HE BETTER NOT HAVE CHIPPED!
HANDS OFF THE DICE...
IT'S FLIP'S TURN. WHERE IS THE OLD GEEZER?
YEAH AND WHAT THE DING DANG HECK IS GOING ON OVER THERE WITH THE KIDS?

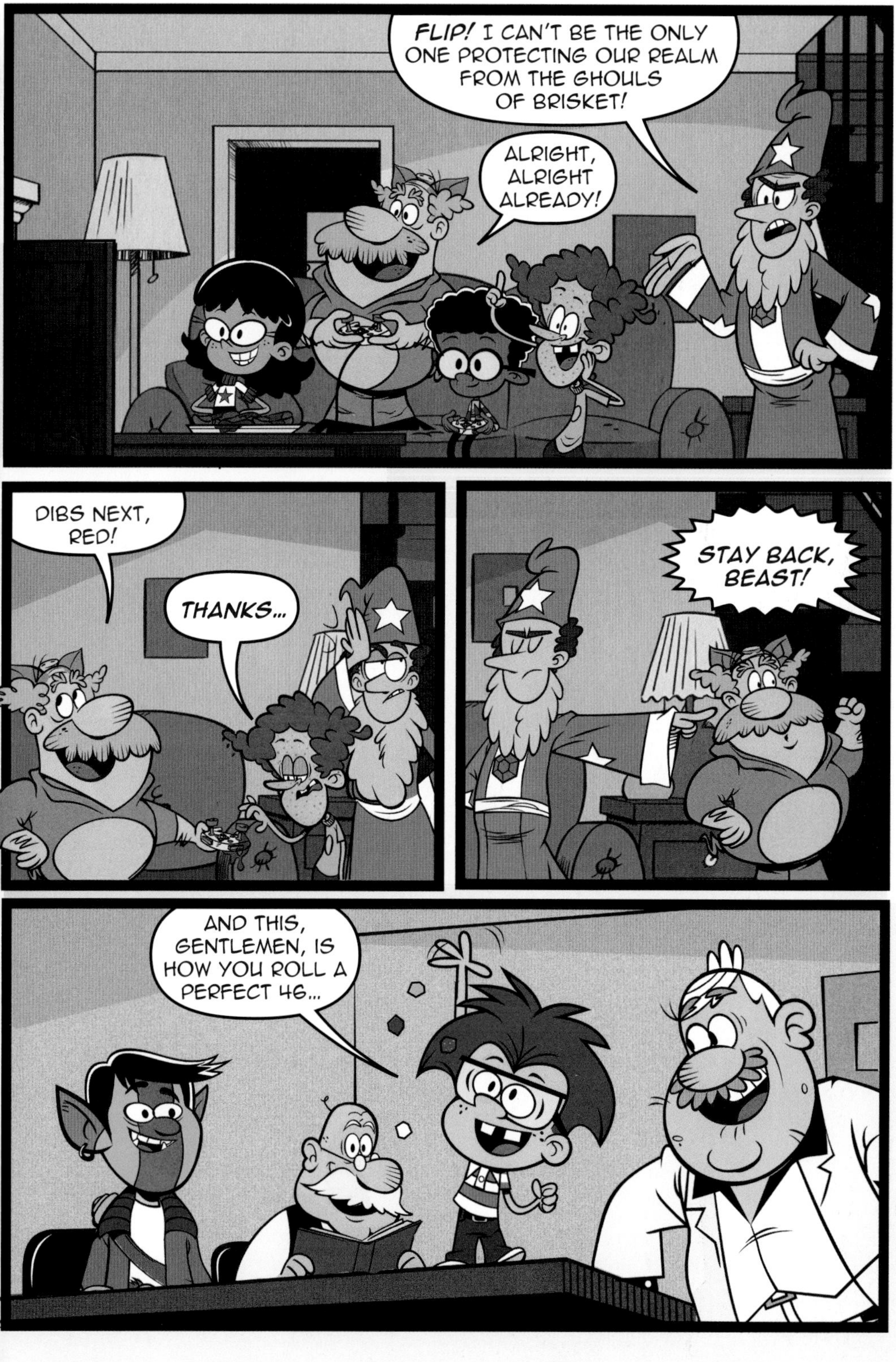
FLIP! I CAN'T BE THE ONLY ONE PROTECTING OUR REALM FROM THE GHOULS OF BRISKET!
ALRIGHT, ALRIGHT ALREADY!
DIBS NEXT, RED!
THANKS...
STAY BACK, BEAST!
AND THIS, GENTLEMEN, IS HOW YOU ROLL A PERFECT 46...

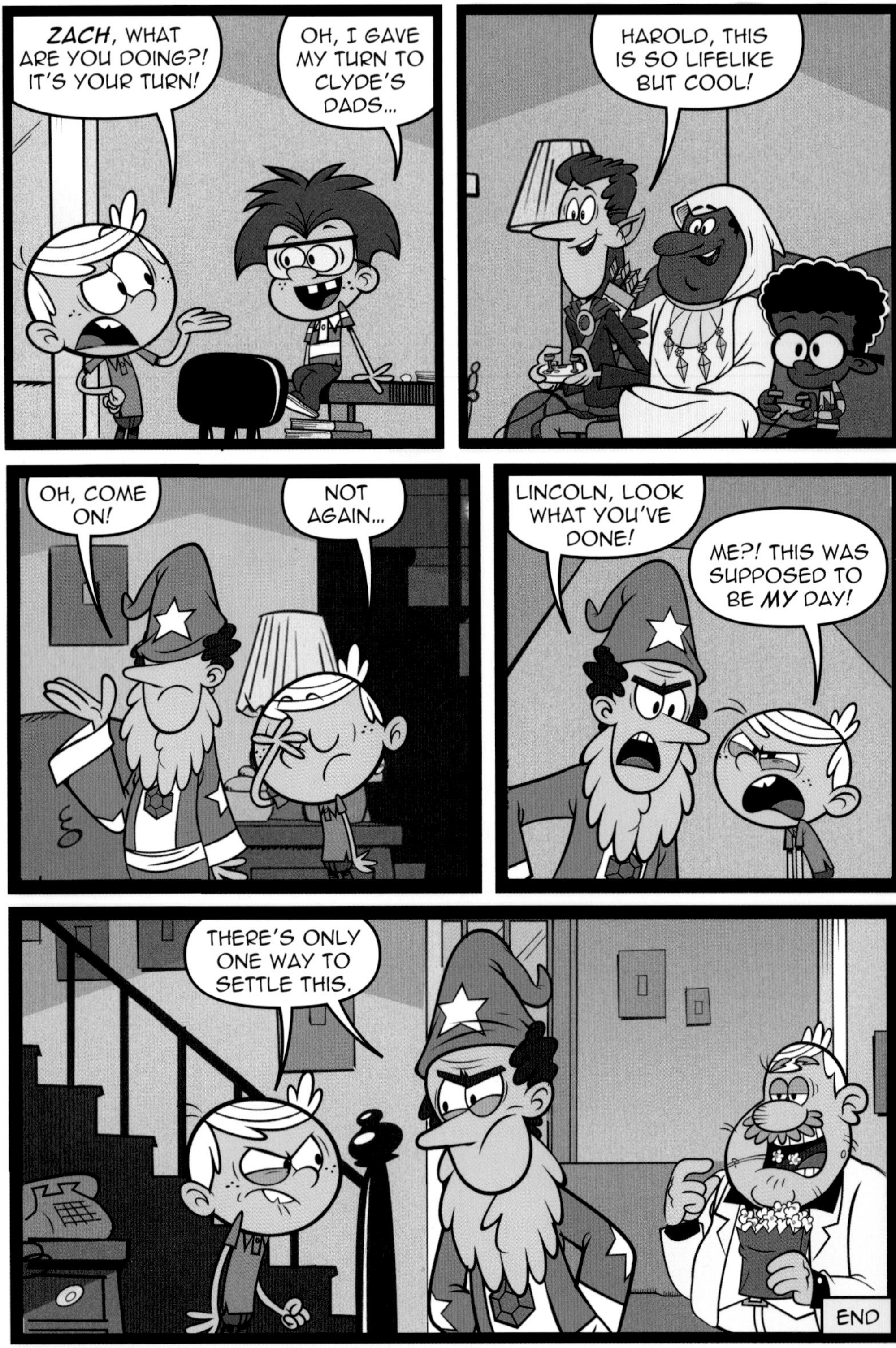

ZACH, WHAT ARE YOU DOING?! IT'S YOUR TURN!
OH, I GAVE MY TURN TO CLYDE'S DADS...
HAROLD, THIS IS SO LIFELIKE BUT COOL!
OH, COME ON!
NOT AGAIN...
LINCOLN, LOOK WHAT YOU'VE DONE!
ME?! THIS WAS SUPPOSED TO BE MY DAY!
THERE'S ONLY ONE WAY TO SETTLE THIS.
END

"THE FLEA MARKET"

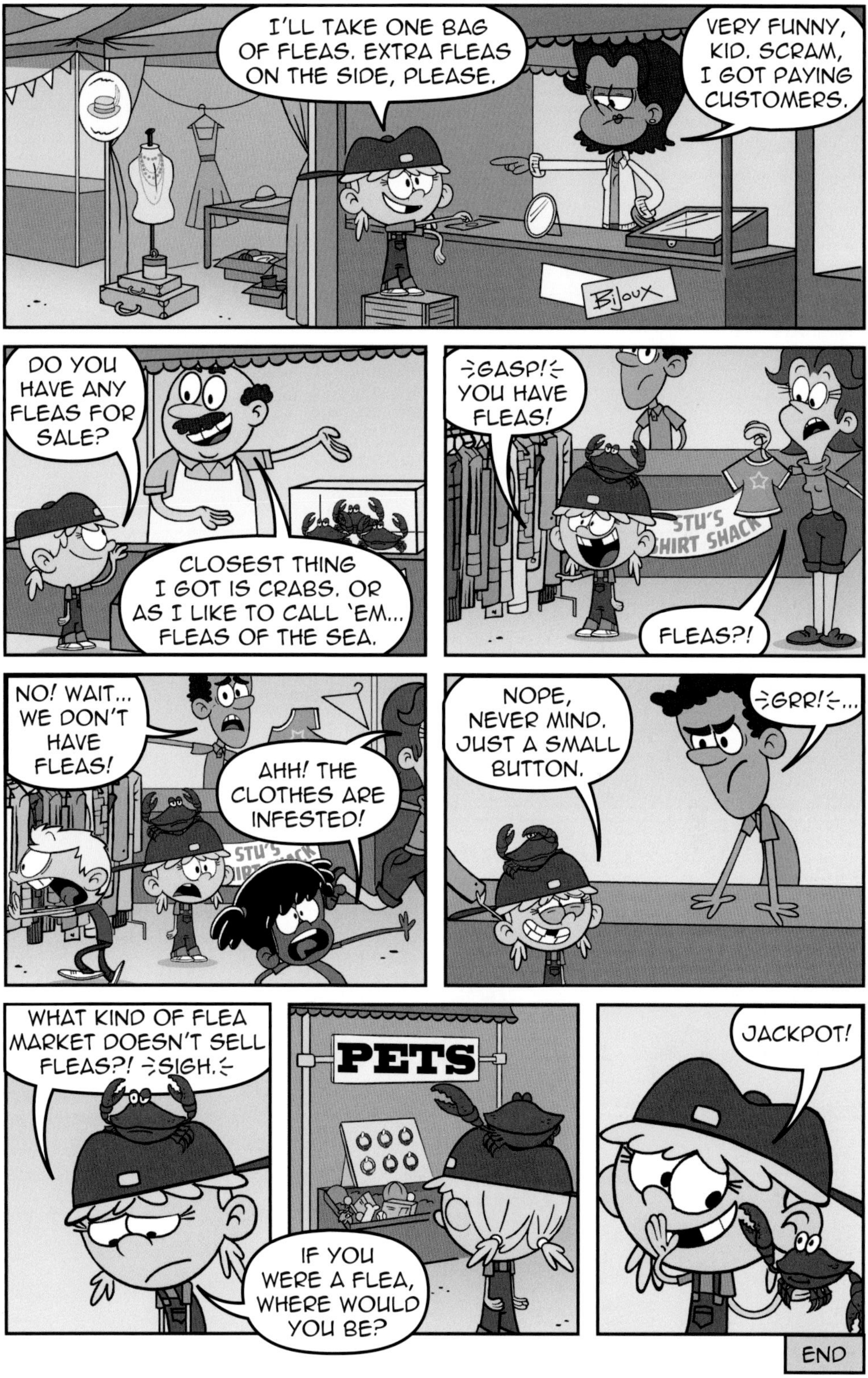

I'LL TAKE ONE BAG OF FLEAS. EXTRA FLEAS ON THE SIDE, PLEASE.
VERY FUNNY, KID. SCRAM, I GOT PAYING CUSTOMERS.
Bijoux
DO YOU HAVE ANY FLEAS FOR SALE?
CLOSEST THING I GOT IS CRABS. OR AS I LIKE TO CALL 'EM... FLEAS OF THE SEA.
GASP! YOU HAVE FLEAS!
STU'S SHIRT SHACK
FLEAS?!
NO! WAIT... WE DON'T HAVE FLEAS!
AHH! THE CLOTHES ARE INFESTED!
NOPE, NEVER MIND. JUST A SMALL BUTTON.
GRR!...
WHAT KIND OF FLEA MARKET DOESN'T SELL FLEAS?! SIGH.
IF YOU WERE A FLEA, WHERE WOULD YOU BE?
PETS
JACKPOT!
END

"RACE TO THE THRONE"

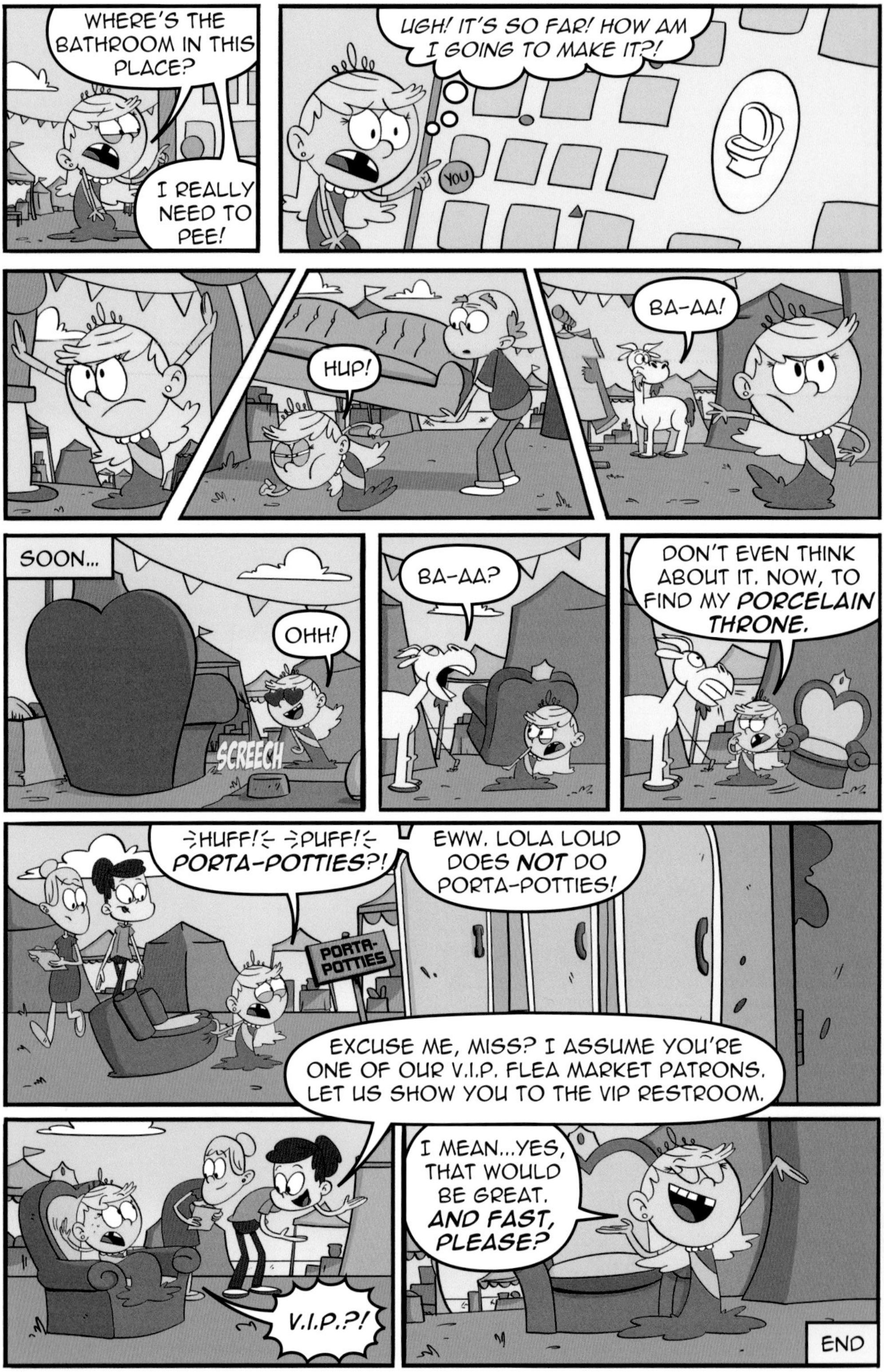

WHERE'S THE BATHROOM IN THIS PLACE?
I REALLY NEED TO PEE!
UGH! IT'S SO FAR! HOW AM I GOING TO MAKE IT?!
YOU
HUP!
BA-AA!
SOON...
OHH!
SCREECH
BA-AA?
DON'T EVEN THINK ABOUT IT. NOW, TO FIND MY PORCELAIN THRONE.
HUFF! PUFF! PORTA-POTTIES?!
PORTA-POTTIES
EWW. LOLA LOUD DOES NOT DO PORTA-POTTIES!
EXCUSE ME, MISS? I ASSUME YOU'RE ONE OF OUR V.I.P. FLEA MARKET PATRONS. LET US SHOW YOU TO THE VIP RESTROOM.
V.I.P.?!
I MEAN...YES, THAT WOULD BE GREAT. AND FAST, PLEASE?
END

"RECORD TIME"

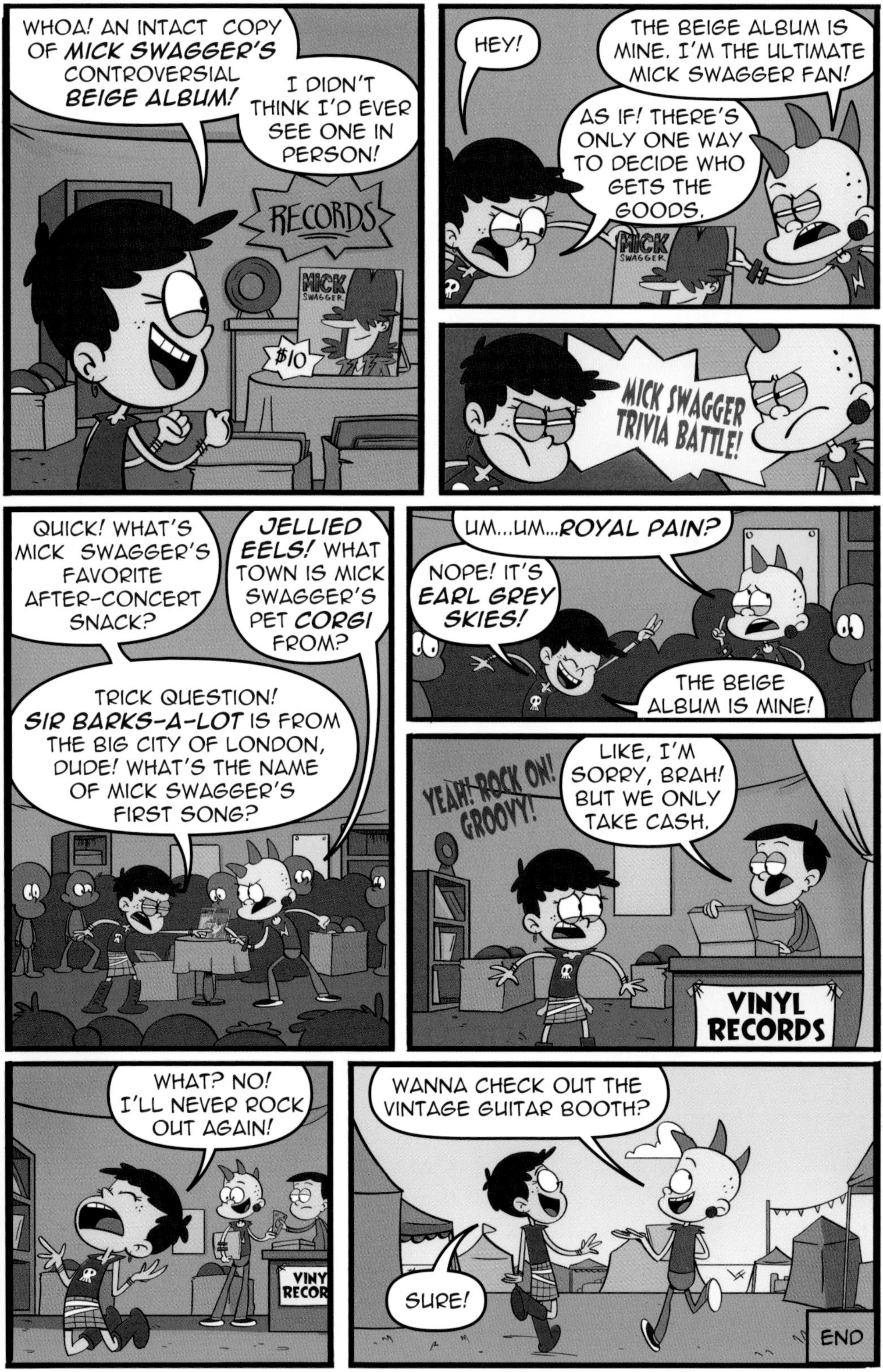
WHOA! AN INTACT COPY OF MICK SWAGGER'S CONTROVERSIAL BEIGE ALBUM!
I DIDN'T THINK I'D EVER SEE ONE IN PERSON!
RECORDS
MICK SWAGGER
$10
HEY!
THE BEIGE ALBUM IS MINE. I'M THE ULTIMATE MICK SWAGGER FAN!
AS IF! THERE'S ONLY ONE WAY TO DECIDE WHO GETS THE GOODS.
MICK SWAGGER
MICK SWAGGER TRIVIA BATTLE!
QUICK! WHAT'S MICK SWAGGER'S FAVORITE AFTER-CONCERT SNACK?
JELLIED EELS! WHAT TOWN IS MICK SWAGGER'S PET CORGI FROM?
TRICK QUESTION! SIR BARKS-A-LOT IS FROM THE BIG CITY OF LONDON, DUDE! WHAT'S THE NAME OF MICK SWAGGER'S FIRST SONG?
UM...UM...ROYAL PAIN?
NOPE! IT'S EARL GREY SKIES!
THE BEIGE ALBUM IS MINE!
YEAH! ROCK ON! GROOVY!
LIKE, I'M SORRY, BRAH! BUT WE ONLY TAKE CASH.
VINYL RECORDS
WHAT? NO! I'LL NEVER ROCK OUT AGAIN!
WANNA CHECK OUT THE VINTAGE GUITAR BOOTH?
SURE!
END

"THE SAUCY LINE"

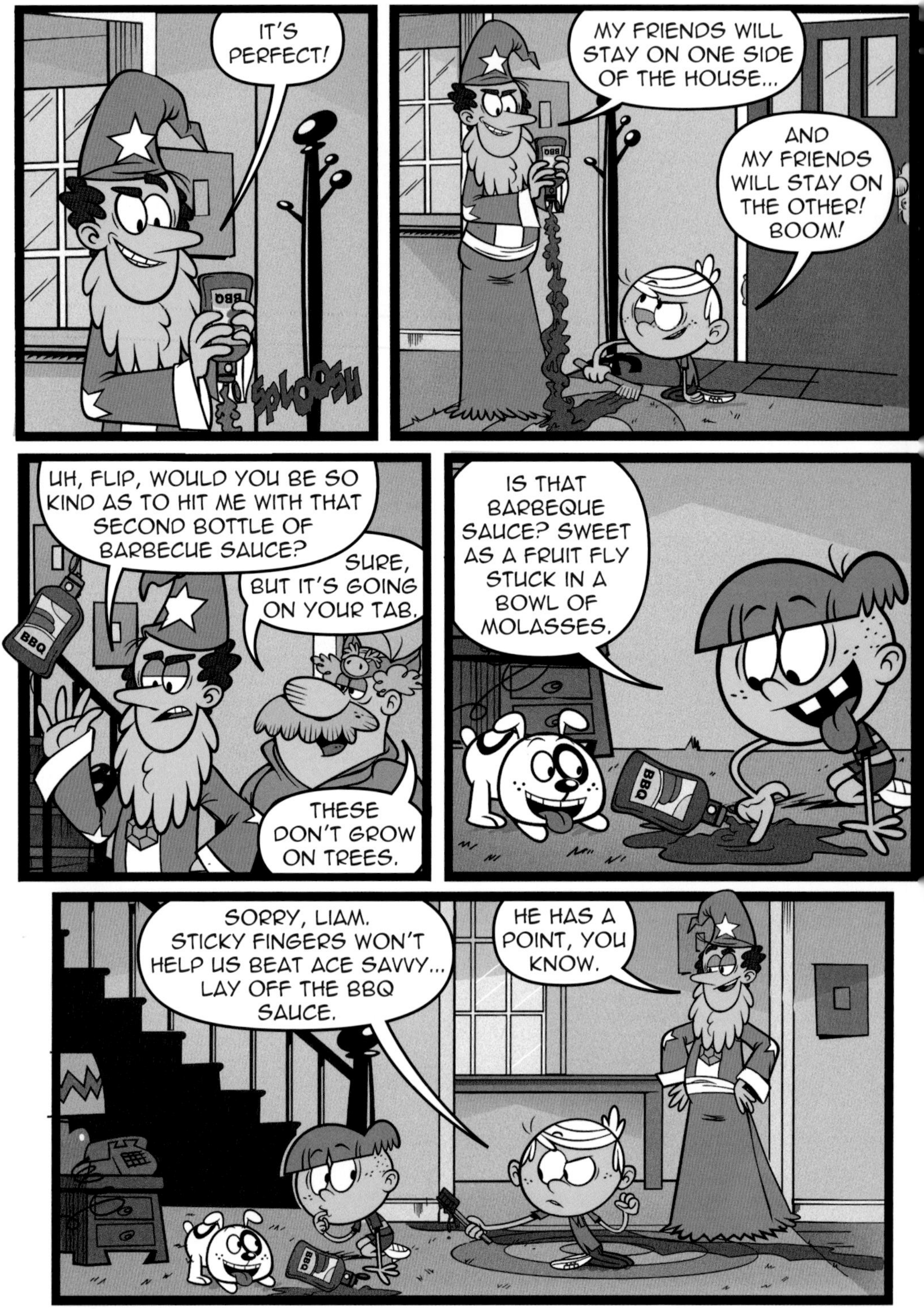

IT'S PERFECT!
SPLOOSH
MY FRIENDS WILL STAY ON ONE SIDE OF THE HOUSE...
AND MY FRIENDS WILL STAY ON THE OTHER! BOOM!
UH, FLIP, WOULD YOU BE SO KIND AS TO HIT ME WITH THAT SECOND BOTTLE OF BARBECUE SAUCE?
SURE, BUT IT'S GOING ON YOUR TAB.
THESE DON'T GROW ON TREES.
IS THAT BARBEQUE SAUCE? SWEET AS A FRUIT FLY STUCK IN A BOWL OF MOLASSES.
SORRY, LIAM. STICKY FINGERS WON'T HELP US BEAT ACE SAVVY... LAY OFF THE BBQ SAUCE.
HE HAS A POINT, YOU KNOW.

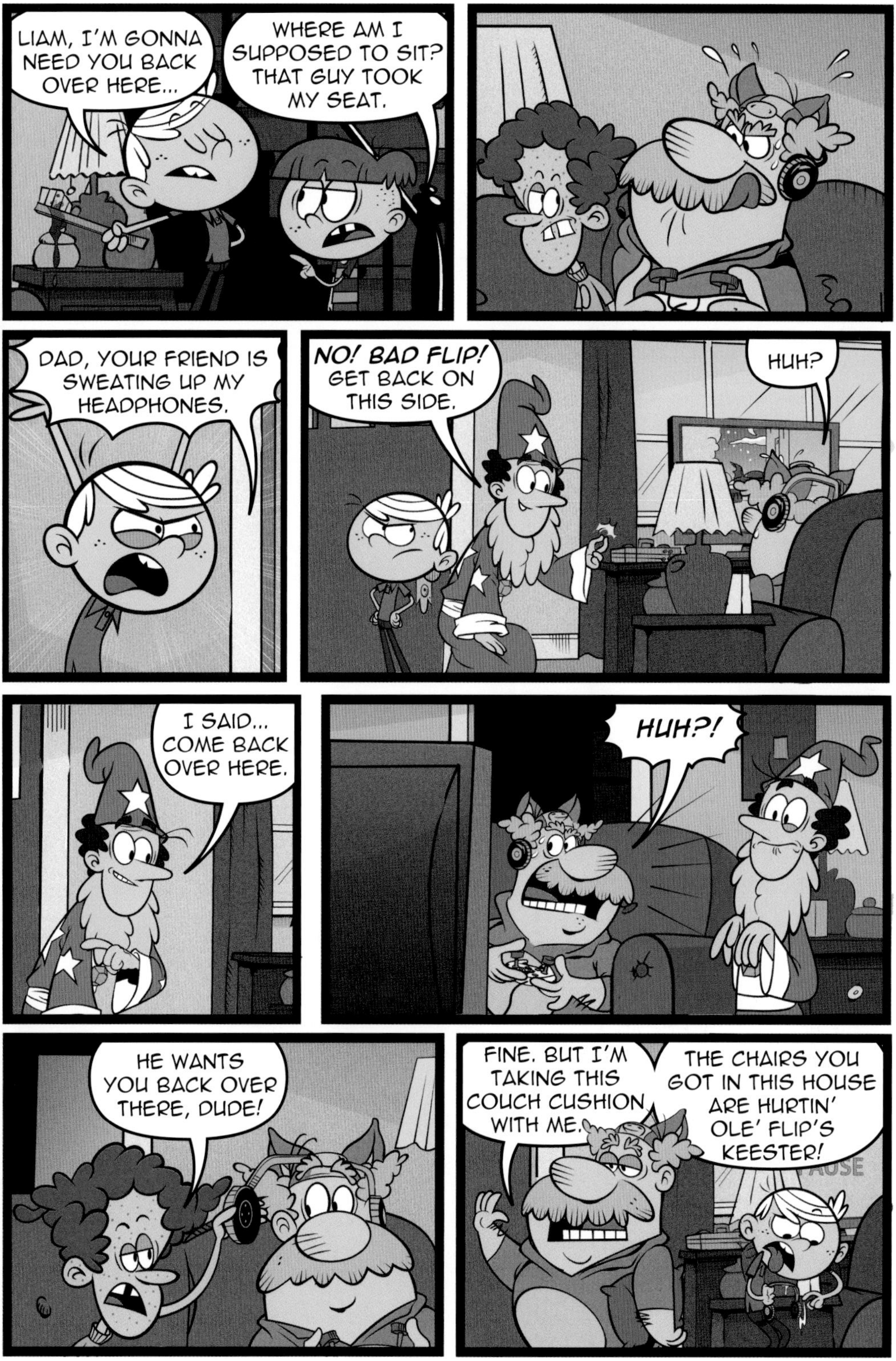
LIAM, I'M GONNA NEED YOU BACK OVER HERE...
WHERE AM I SUPPOSED TO SIT? THAT GUY TOOK MY SEAT.
DAD, YOUR FRIEND IS SWEATING UP MY HEADPHONES.
NO! BAD FLIP! GET BACK ON THIS SIDE.
HUH?
I SAID... COME BACK OVER HERE.
HUH?!
HE WANTS YOU BACK OVER THERE, DUDE!
FINE. BUT I'M TAKING THIS COUCH CUSHION WITH ME.
THE CHAIRS YOU GOT IN THIS HOUSE ARE HURTIN' OLE' FLIP'S KEESTER!
PAUSE

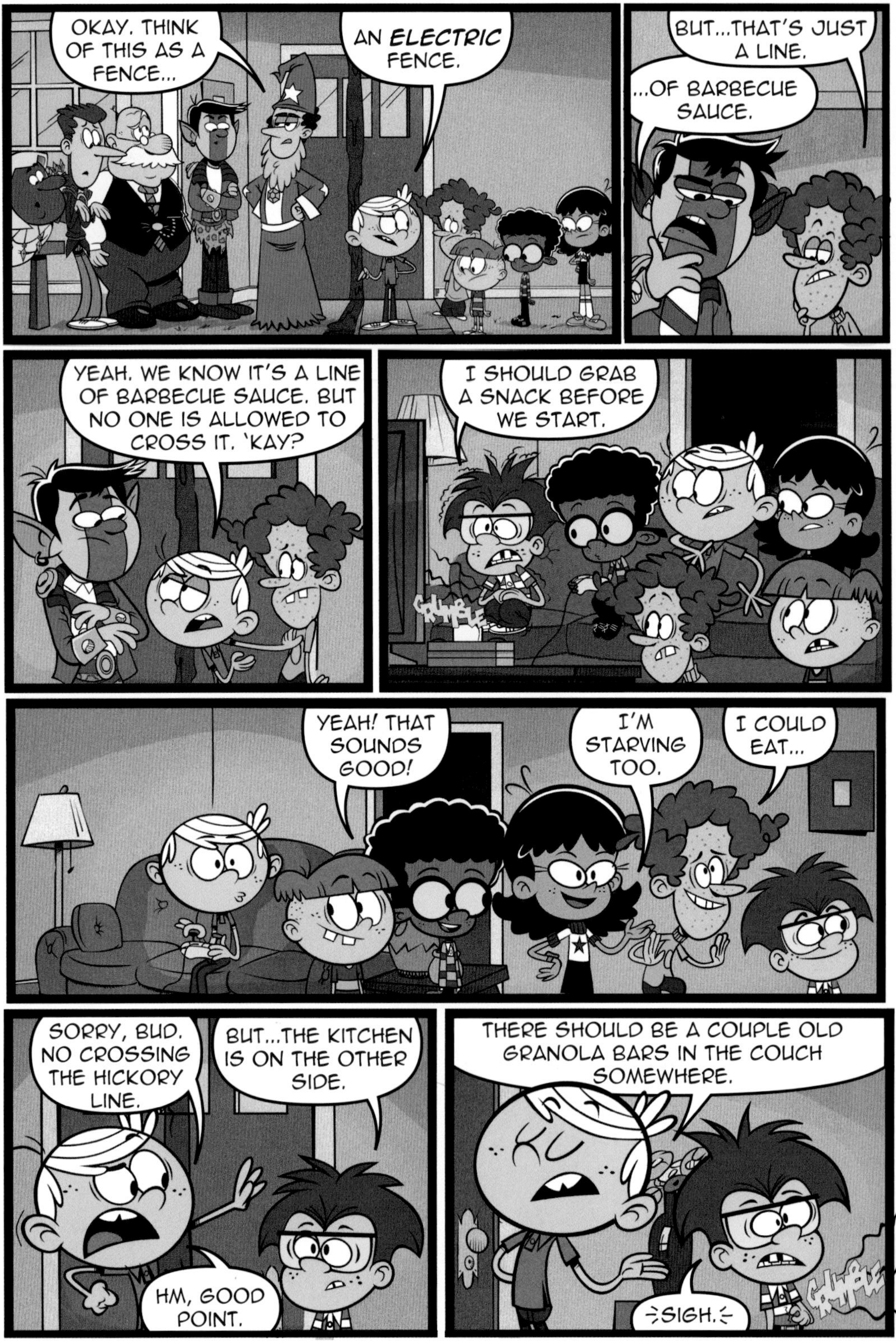
OKAY. THINK OF THIS AS A FENCE...
AN ELECTRIC FENCE.
BUT...THAT'S JUST A LINE.
...OF BARBECUE SAUCE.
YEAH. WE KNOW IT'S A LINE OF BARBECUE SAUCE. BUT NO ONE IS ALLOWED TO CROSS IT. 'KAY?
I SHOULD GRAB A SNACK BEFORE WE START.
GRUMBLE
YEAH! THAT SOUNDS GOOD!
I'M STARVING TOO.
I COULD EAT...
SORRY, BUD. NO CROSSING THE HICKORY LINE.
BUT...THE KITCHEN IS ON THE OTHER SIDE.
HM, GOOD POINT.
THERE SHOULD BE A COUPLE OLD GRANOLA BARS IN THE COUCH SOMEWHERE.
SIGH.
GRUMBLE

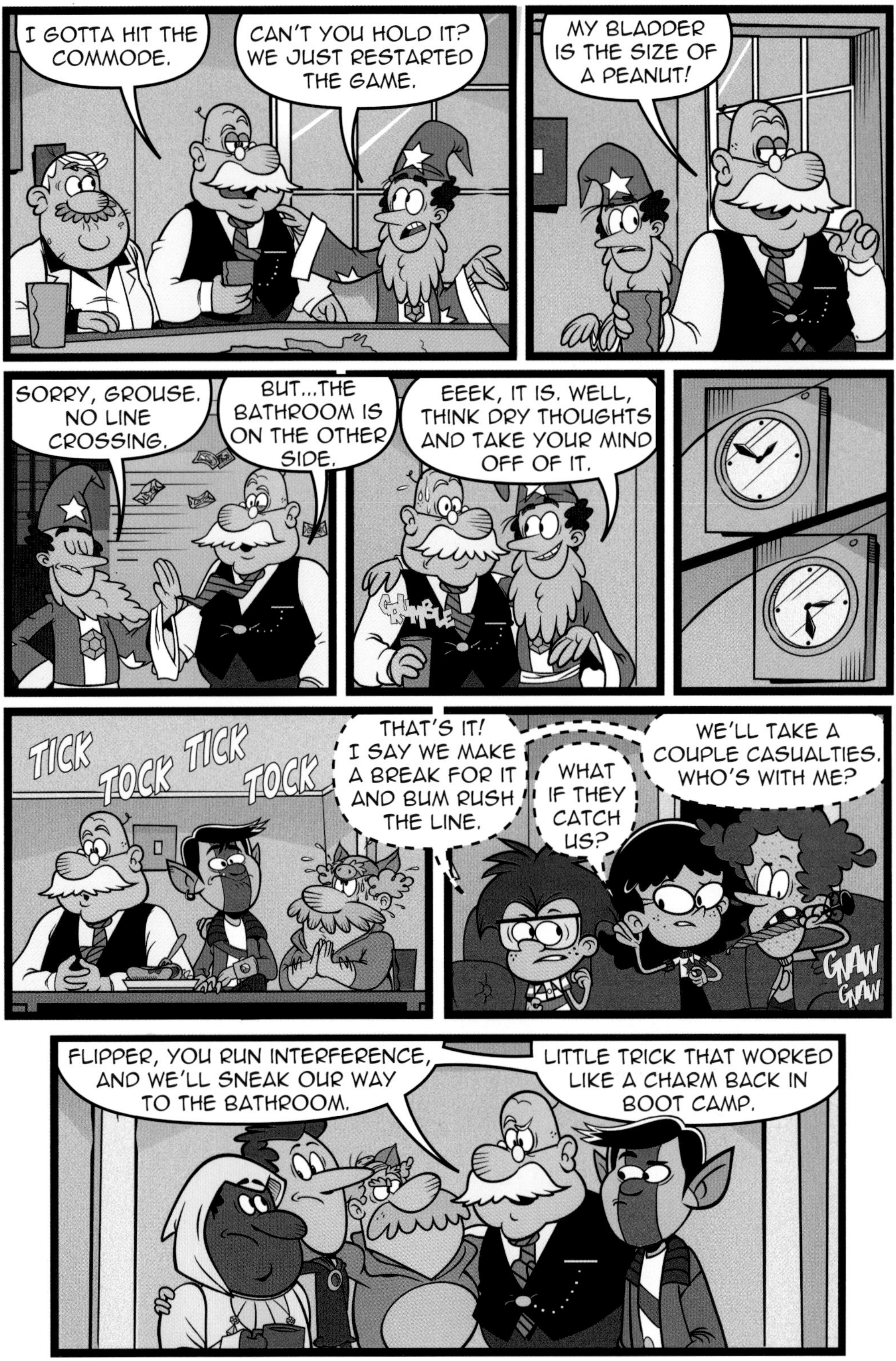
I GOTTA HIT THE COMMODE.
CAN'T YOU HOLD IT? WE JUST RESTARTED THE GAME.
MY BLADDER IS THE SIZE OF A PEANUT!
SORRY, GROUSE. NO LINE CROSSING.
BUT...THE BATHROOM IS ON THE OTHER SIDE.
EEEK, IT IS. WELL, THINK DRY THOUGHTS AND TAKE YOUR MIND OFF OF IT.
GRUMBLE
TICK TOCK TICK TOCK
THAT'S IT! I SAY WE MAKE A BREAK FOR IT AND BUM RUSH THE LINE.
WHAT IF THEY CATCH US?
WE'LL TAKE A COUPLE CASUALTIES. WHO'S WITH ME?
GNAW GNAW
FLIPPER, YOU RUN INTERFERENCE, AND WE'LL SNEAK OUR WAY TO THE BATHROOM.
LITTLE TRICK THAT WORKED LIKE A CHARM BACK IN BOOT CAMP.

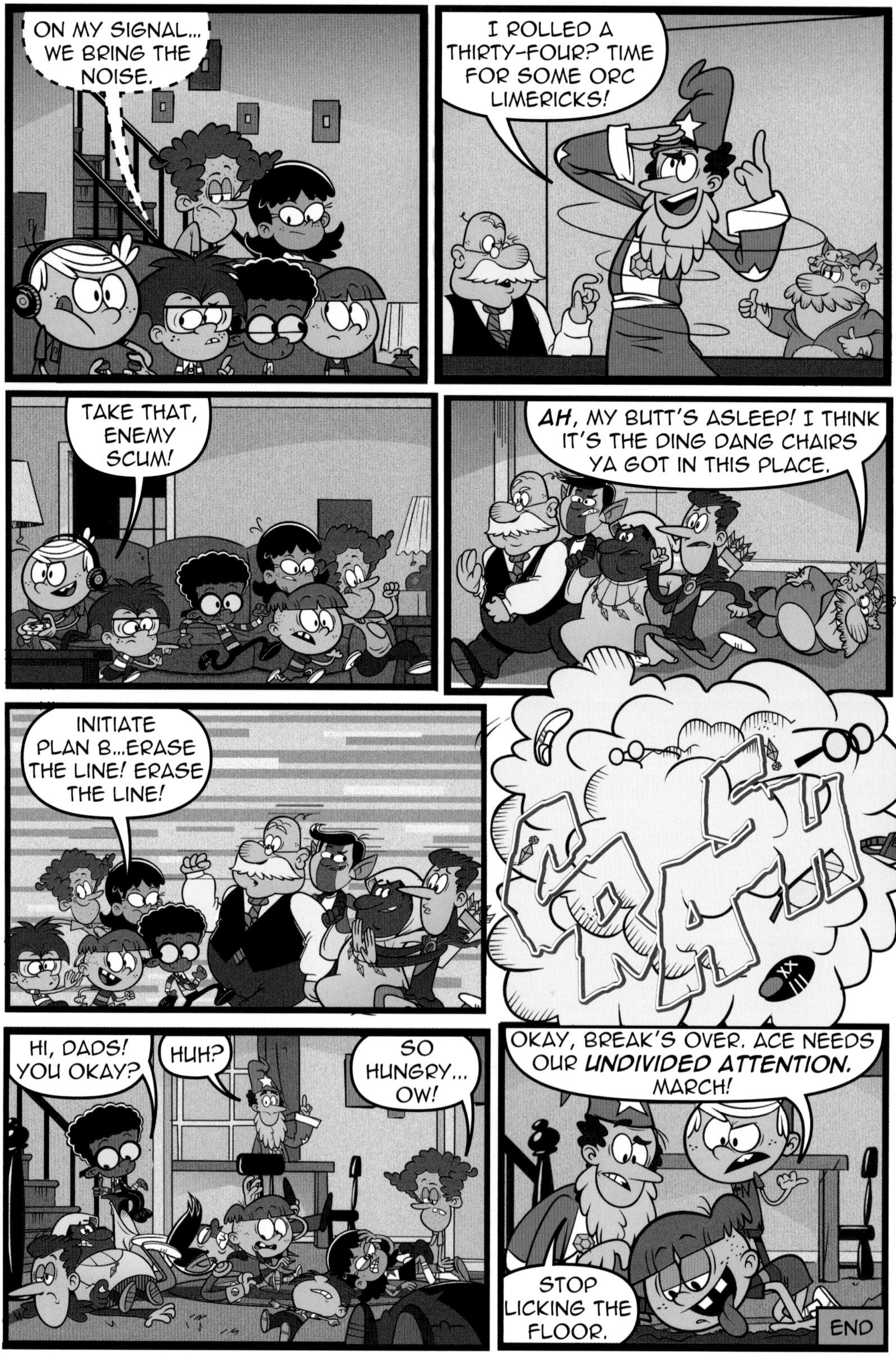
ON MY SIGNAL... WE BRING THE NOISE.
I ROLLED A THIRTY-FOUR? TIME FOR SOME ORC LIMERICKS!
TAKE THAT, ENEMY SCUM!
AH, MY BUTT'S ASLEEP! I THINK IT'S THE DING DANG CHAIRS YA GOT IN THIS PLACE.
INITIATE PLAN B...ERASE THE LINE! ERASE THE LINE!
HI, DADS! YOU OKAY?
HUH?
SO HUNGRY... OW!
OKAY, BREAK'S OVER. ACE NEEDS OUR UNDIVIDED ATTENTION. MARCH!
STOP LICKING THE FLOOR.
END

"NO STRINGS"

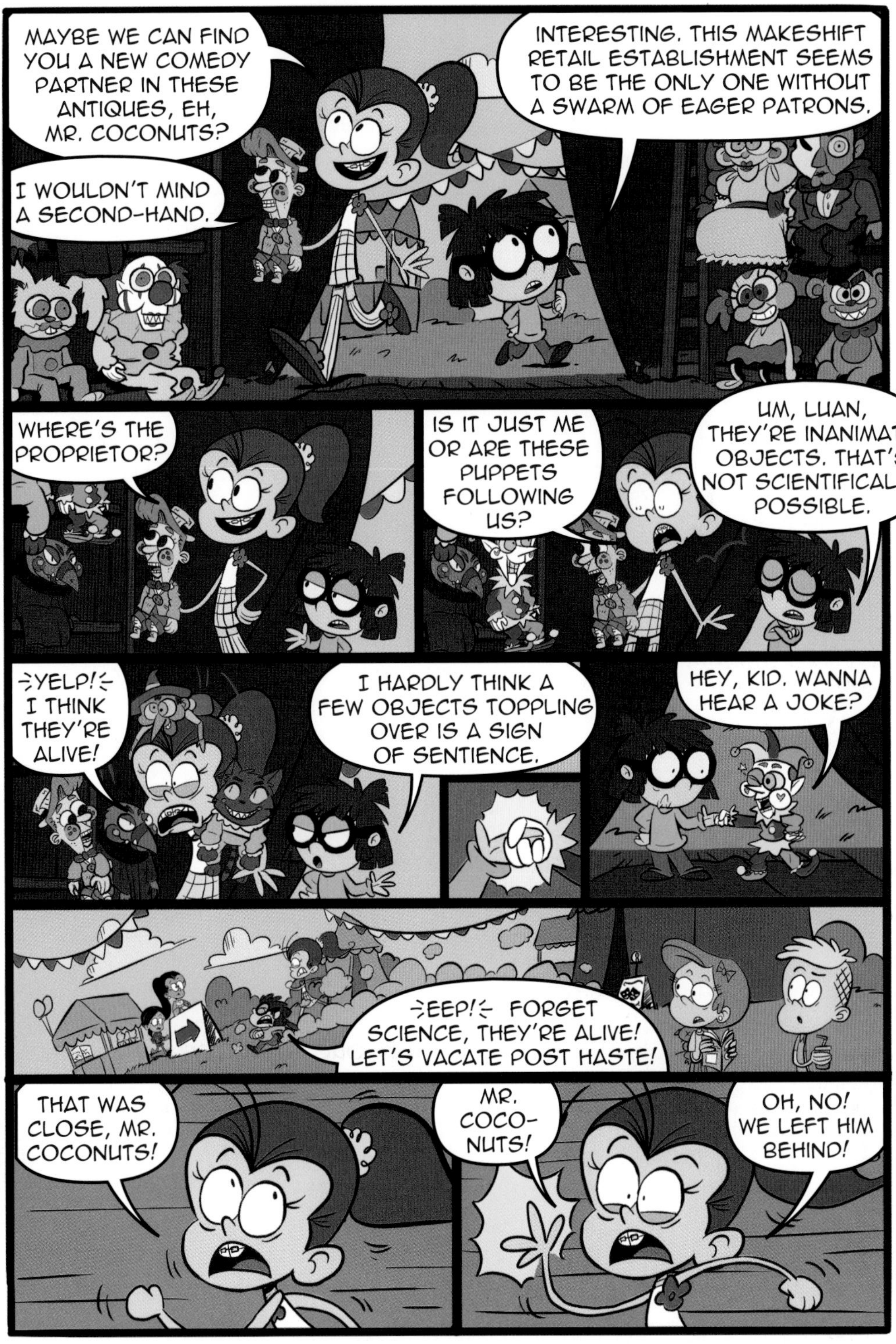
MAYBE WE CAN FIND YOU A NEW COMEDY PARTNER IN THESE ANTIQUES, EH, MR. COCONUTS?
I WOULDN'T MIND A SECOND-HAND.
INTERESTING. THIS MAKESHIFT RETAIL ESTABLISHMENT SEEMS TO BE THE ONLY ONE WITHOUT A SWARM OF EAGER PATRONS.
WHERE'S THE PROPRIETOR?
IS IT JUST ME OR ARE THESE PUPPETS FOLLOWING US?
UM, LUAN, THEY'RE INANIMATE OBJECTS. THAT'S NOT SCIENTIFICALLY POSSIBLE.
YELP! I THINK THEY'RE ALIVE!
I HARDLY THINK A FEW OBJECTS TOPPLING OVER IS A SIGN OF SENTIENCE.
HEY, KID. WANNA HEAR A JOKE?
EEP! FORGET SCIENCE, THEY'RE ALIVE! LET'S VACATE POST HASTE!
THAT WAS CLOSE, MR. COCONUTS!
MR. COCO-NUTS!
OH, NO! WE LEFT HIM BEHIND!

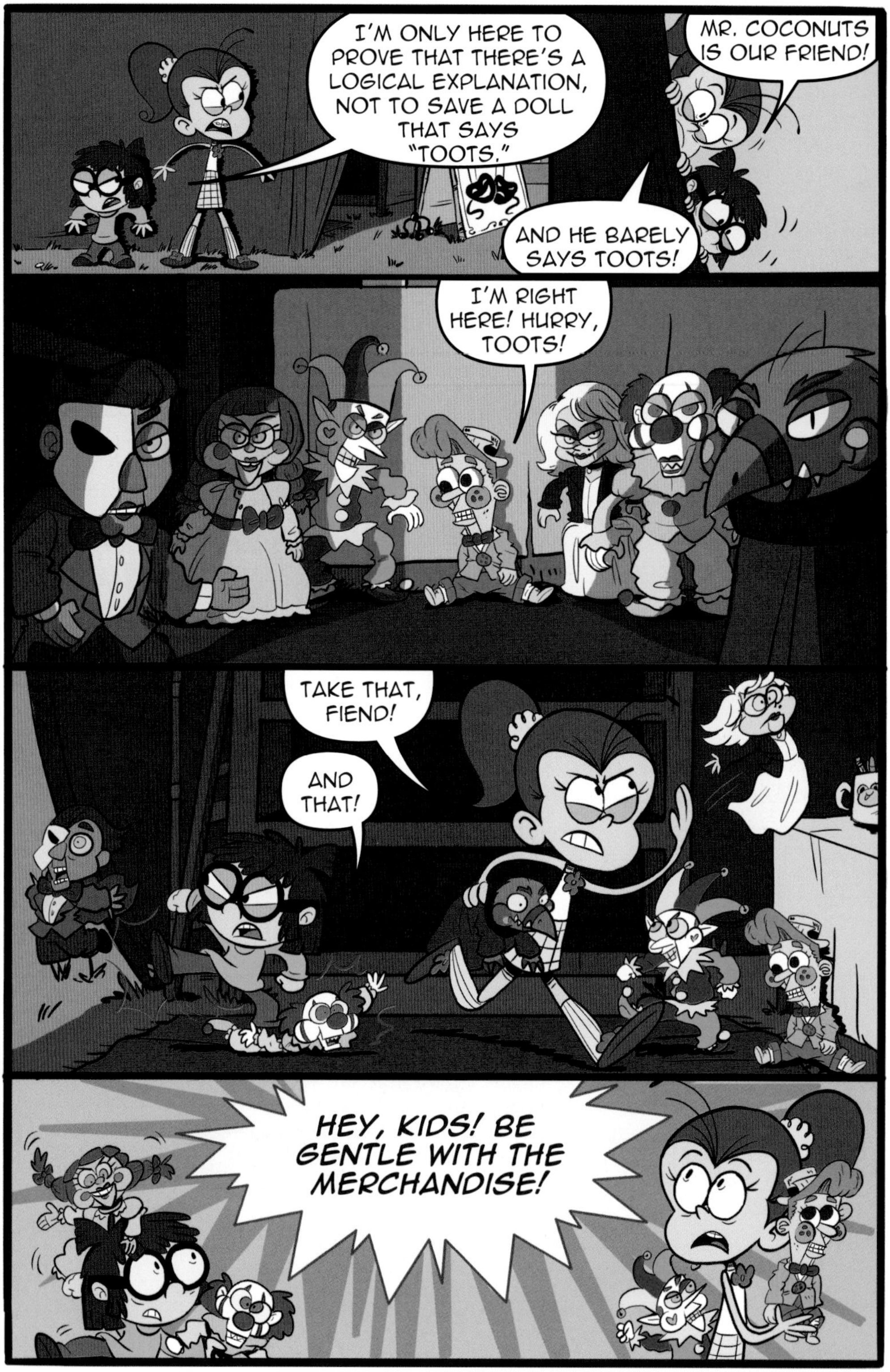
I'M ONLY HERE TO PROVE THAT THERE'S A LOGICAL EXPLANATION, NOT TO SAVE A DOLL THAT SAYS "TOOTS."
MR. COCONUTS IS OUR FRIEND!
AND HE BARELY SAYS TOOTS!
I'M RIGHT HERE! HURRY, TOOTS!
TAKE THAT, FIEND!
AND THAT!
HEY, KIDS! BE GENTLE WITH THE MERCHANDISE!

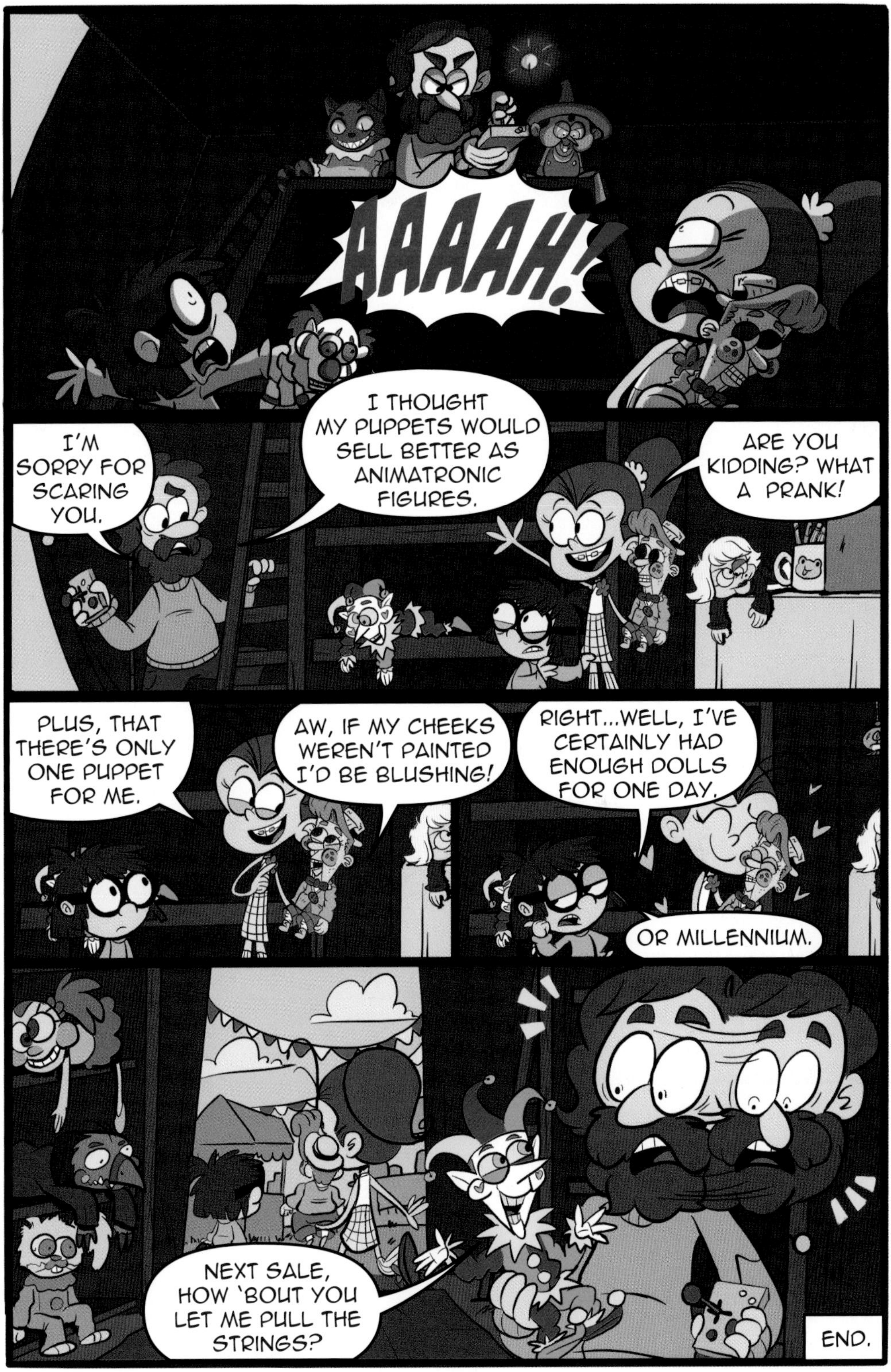
AAAAH!
I'M SORRY FOR SCARING YOU.
I THOUGHT MY PUPPETS WOULD SELL BETTER AS ANIMATRONIC FIGURES.
ARE YOU KIDDING? WHAT A PRANK!
PLUS, THAT THERE'S ONLY ONE PUPPET FOR ME.
AW, IF MY CHEEKS WEREN'T PAINTED I'D BE BLUSHING!
RIGHT...WELL, I'VE CERTAINLY HAD ENOUGH DOLLS FOR ONE DAY.
OR MILLENNIUM.
NEXT SALE, HOW 'BOUT YOU LET ME PULL THE STRINGS?
END.

"SLAM JUNK"

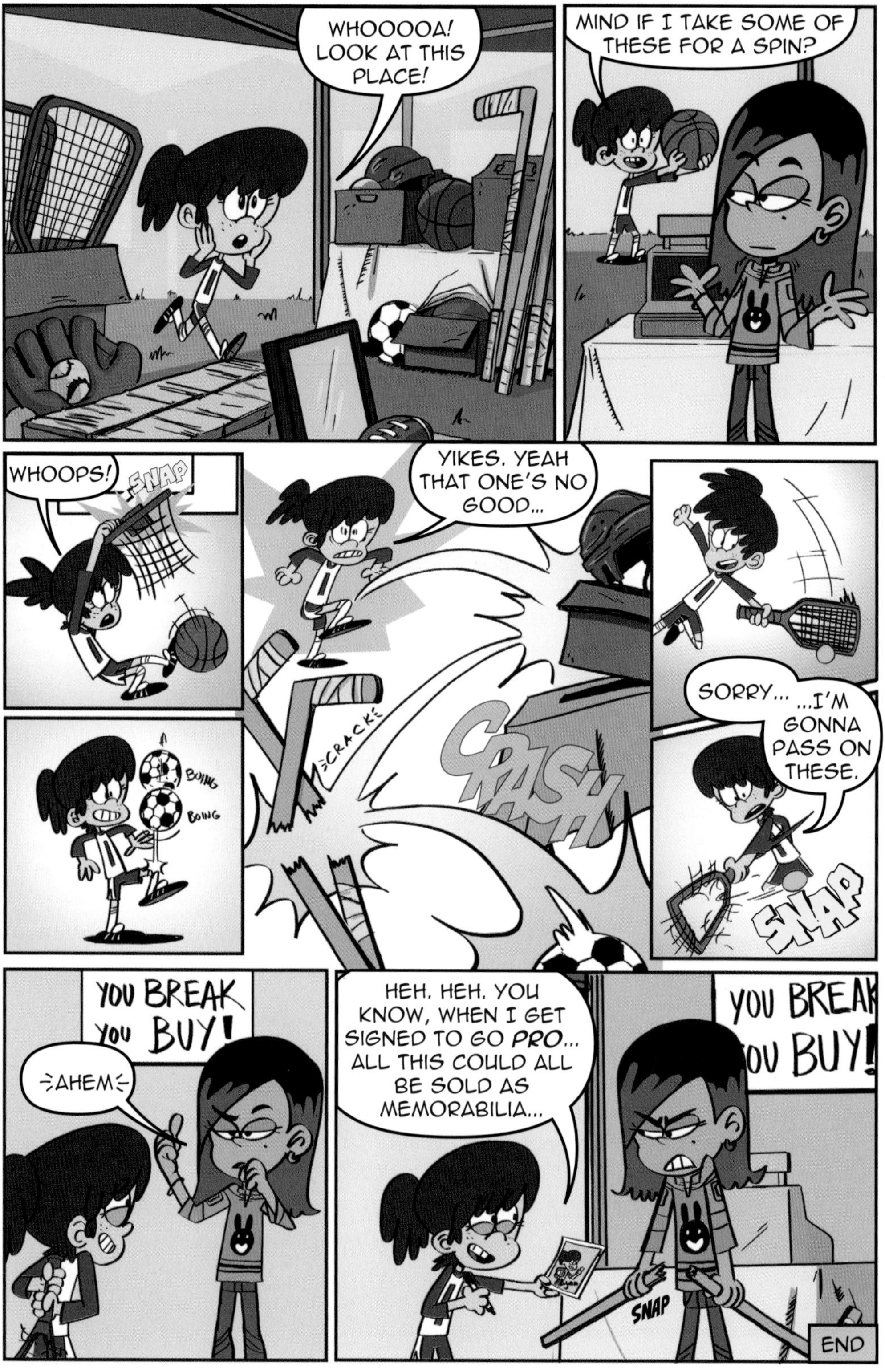

WHOOOOA! LOOK AT THIS PLACE!
MIND IF I TAKE SOME OF THESE FOR A SPIN?
WHOOPS!
SNAP
YIKES. YEAH THAT ONE'S NO GOOD...
BOING
BOING
CRACK
CRASH
SORRY... ...I'M GONNA PASS ON THESE.
SNAP
YOU BREAK YOU BUY!
AHEM
HEH. HEH. YOU KNOW, WHEN I GET SIGNED TO GO *PRO*... ALL THIS COULD ALL BE SOLD AS MEMORABILIA...
YOU BREAK YOU BUY!
SNAP
END

"IT'S MY PARTY"

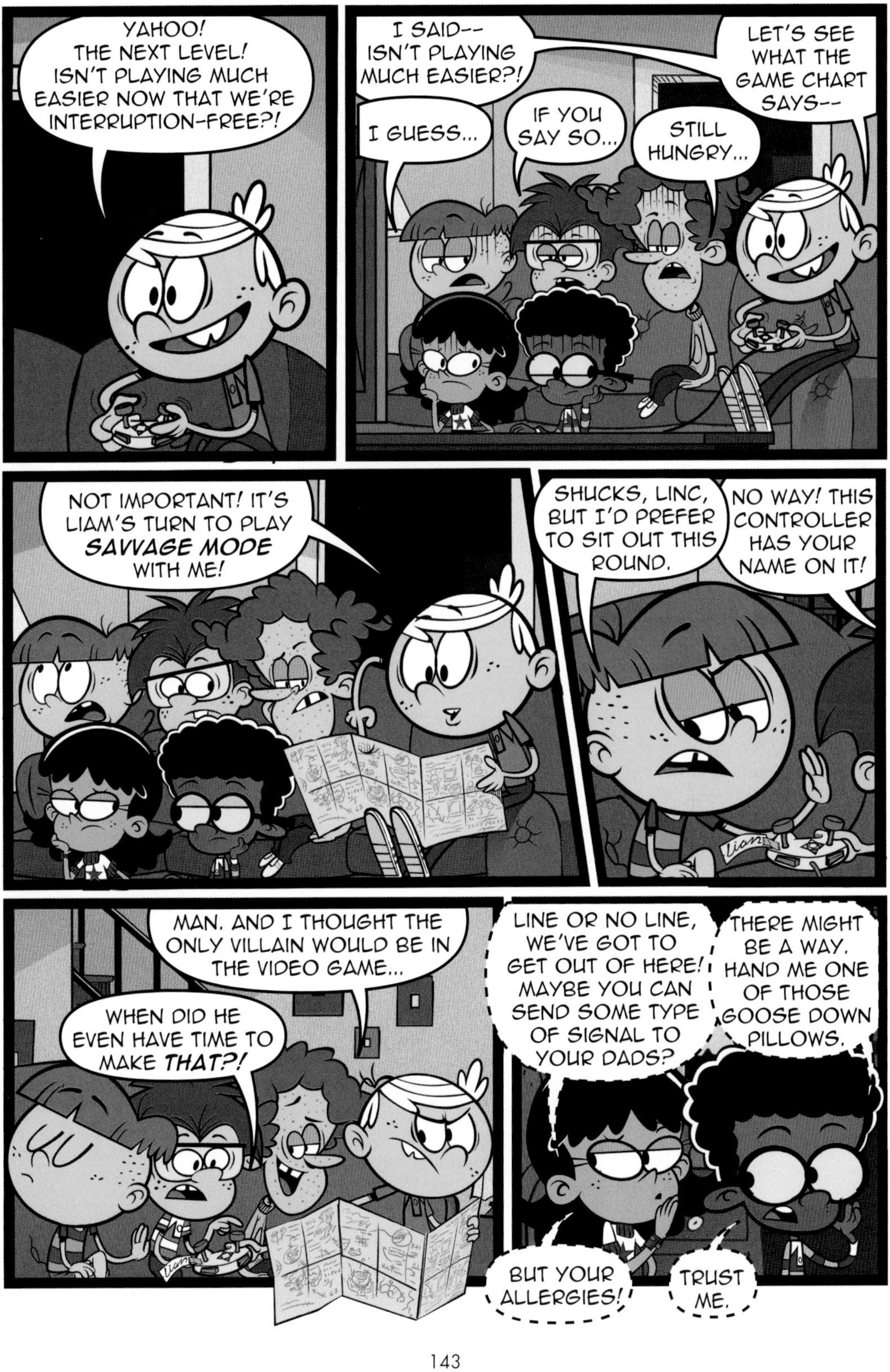

YAHOO! THE NEXT LEVEL! ISN'T PLAYING MUCH EASIER NOW THAT WE'RE INTERRUPTION-FREE?!
I SAID-- ISN'T PLAYING MUCH EASIER?!
I GUESS...
IF YOU SAY SO...
STILL HUNGRY...
LET'S SEE WHAT THE GAME CHART SAYS--
NOT IMPORTANT! IT'S LIAM'S TURN TO PLAY *SAVAGE MODE* WITH ME!
SHUCKS, LINC, BUT I'D PREFER TO SIT OUT THIS ROUND.
NO WAY! THIS CONTROLLER HAS YOUR NAME ON IT!
LIAM
MAN. AND I THOUGHT THE ONLY VILLAIN WOULD BE IN THE VIDEO GAME...
WHEN DID HE EVEN HAVE TIME TO MAKE *THAT*?!
LINE OR NO LINE, WE'VE GOT TO GET OUT OF HERE! MAYBE YOU CAN SEND SOME TYPE OF SIGNAL TO YOUR DADS?
THERE MIGHT BE A WAY. HAND ME ONE OF THOSE GOOSE DOWN PILLOWS.
BUT YOUR ALLERGIES!
TRUST ME.

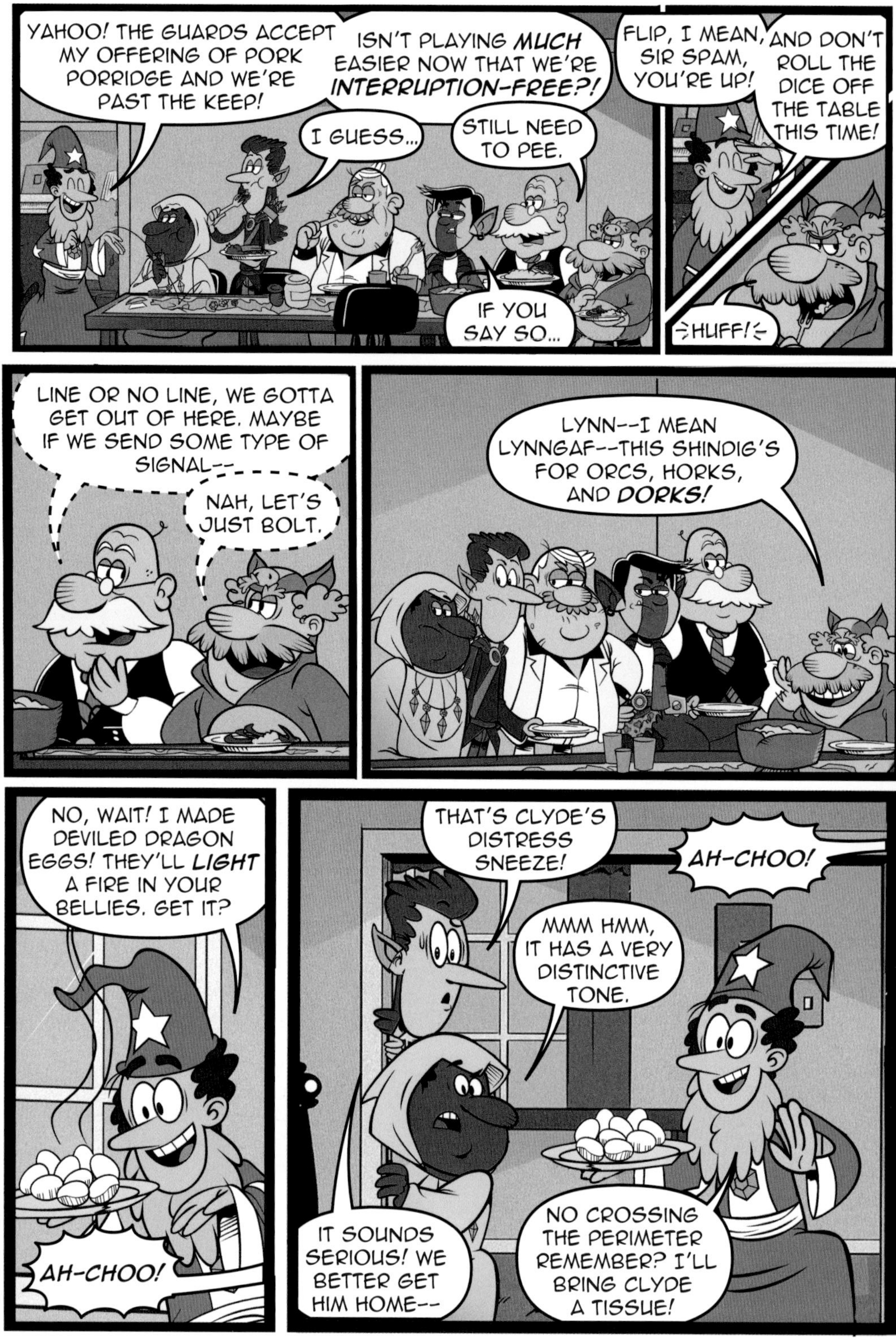

YAHOO! THE GUARDS ACCEPT MY OFFERING OF PORK PORRIDGE AND WE'RE PAST THE KEEP!
ISN'T PLAYING MUCH EASIER NOW THAT WE'RE INTERRUPTION-FREE?!
I GUESS...
STILL NEED TO PEE.
IF YOU SAY SO...
FLIP, I MEAN, SIR SPAM, YOU'RE UP!
AND DON'T ROLL THE DICE OFF THE TABLE THIS TIME!
HUFF!
LINE OR NO LINE, WE GOTTA GET OUT OF HERE. MAYBE IF WE SEND SOME TYPE OF SIGNAL--
NAH, LET'S JUST BOLT.
LYNN--I MEAN LYNNGAF--THIS SHINDIG'S FOR ORCS, HORKS, AND DORKS!
NO, WAIT! I MADE DEVILED DRAGON EGGS! THEY'LL LIGHT A FIRE IN YOUR BELLIES. GET IT?
AH-CHOO!
THAT'S CLYDE'S DISTRESS SNEEZE!
AH-CHOO!
MMM HMM, IT HAS A VERY DISTINCTIVE TONE.
IT SOUNDS SERIOUS! WE BETTER GET HIM HOME--
NO CROSSING THE PERIMETER REMEMBER? I'LL BRING CLYDE A TISSUE!

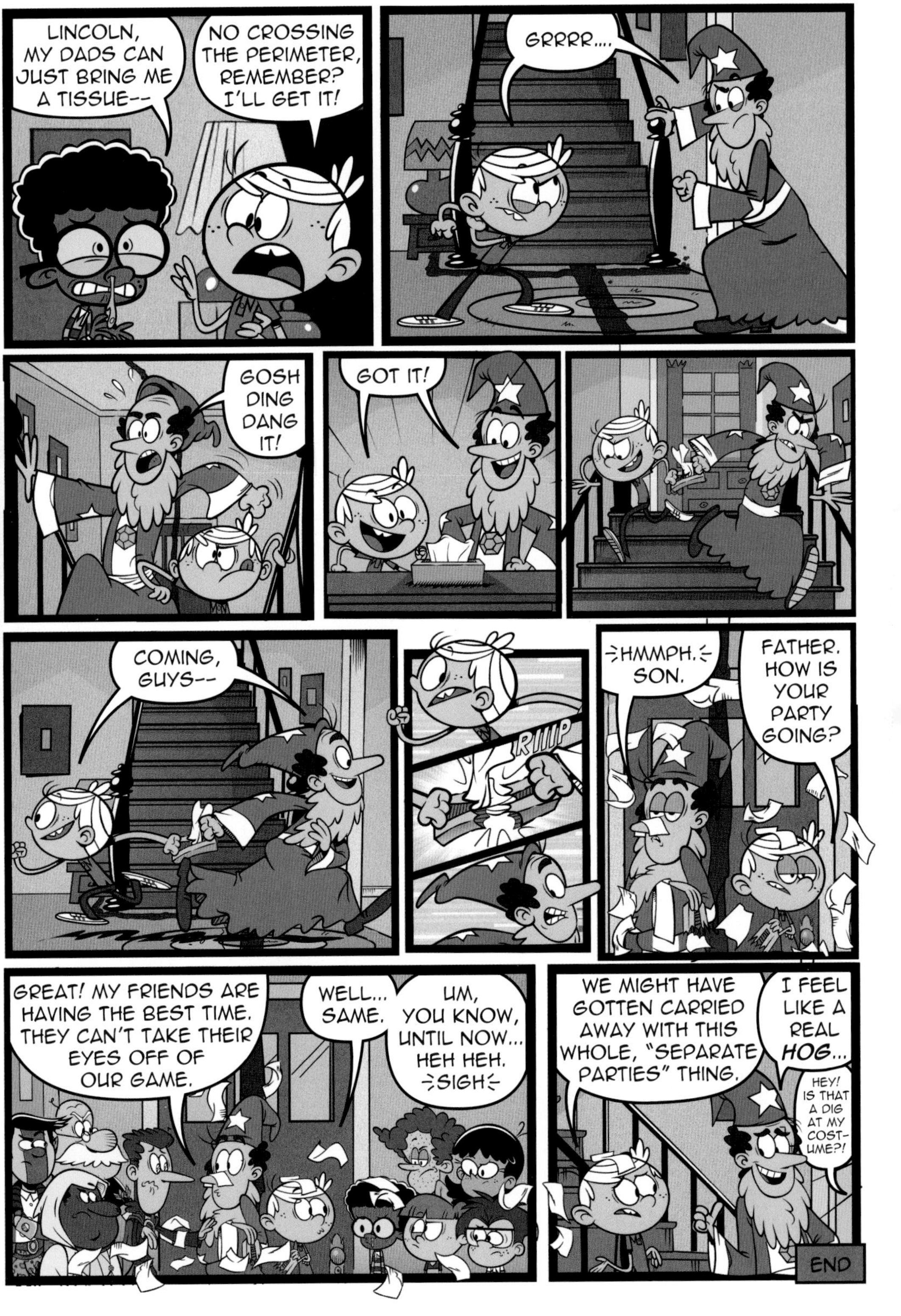
LINCOLN, MY DADS CAN JUST BRING ME A TISSUE--
NO CROSSING THE PERIMETER, REMEMBER? I'LL GET IT!
GRRRR....
GOSH DING DANG IT!
GOT IT!
COMING, GUYS--
RIIIP
HMMPH. SON.
FATHER. HOW IS YOUR PARTY GOING?
GREAT! MY FRIENDS ARE HAVING THE BEST TIME. THEY CAN'T TAKE THEIR EYES OFF OF OUR GAME.
WELL... SAME.
UM, YOU KNOW, UNTIL NOW... HEH HEH. SIGH
WE MIGHT HAVE GOTTEN CARRIED AWAY WITH THIS WHOLE, "SEPARATE PARTIES" THING.
I FEEL LIKE A REAL HOG...
HEY! IS THAT A DIG AT MY COSTUME?!
END

"EYE ON THE BALL"

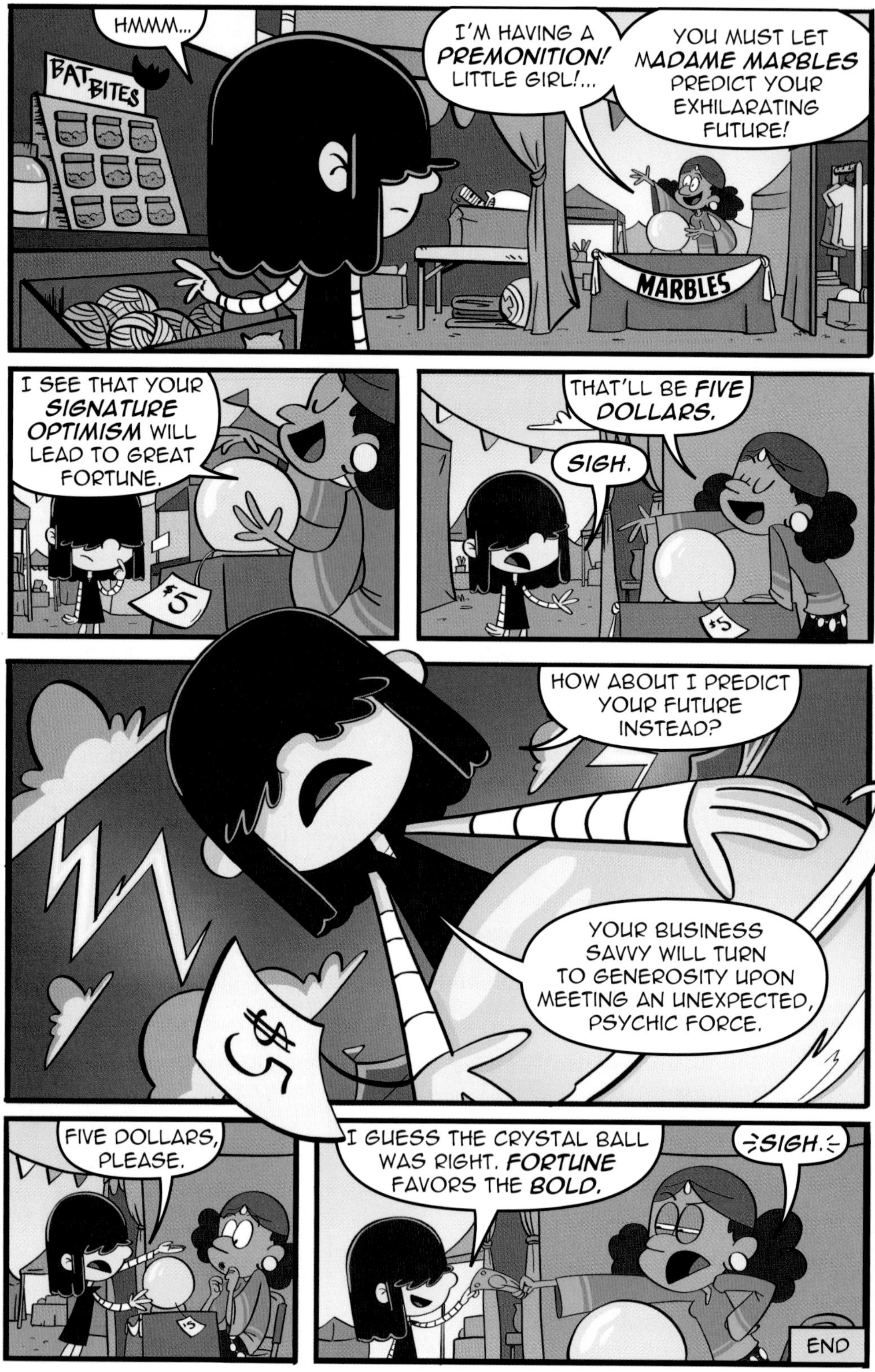
BAT BITES
HMMM...
I'M HAVING A PREMONITION! LITTLE GIRL!...
YOU MUST LET MADAME MARBLES PREDICT YOUR EXHILARATING FUTURE!
MARBLES
I SEE THAT YOUR SIGNATURE OPTIMISM WILL LEAD TO GREAT FORTUNE.
$5
THAT'LL BE FIVE DOLLARS.
SIGH.
$5
HOW ABOUT I PREDICT YOUR FUTURE INSTEAD?
YOUR BUSINESS SAVVY WILL TURN TO GENEROSITY UPON MEETING AN UNEXPECTED, PSYCHIC FORCE.
$5
FIVE DOLLARS, PLEASE.
$5
I GUESS THE CRYSTAL BALL WAS RIGHT. FORTUNE FAVORS THE BOLD.
SIGH.
END

"THE PERFECT GIFT"

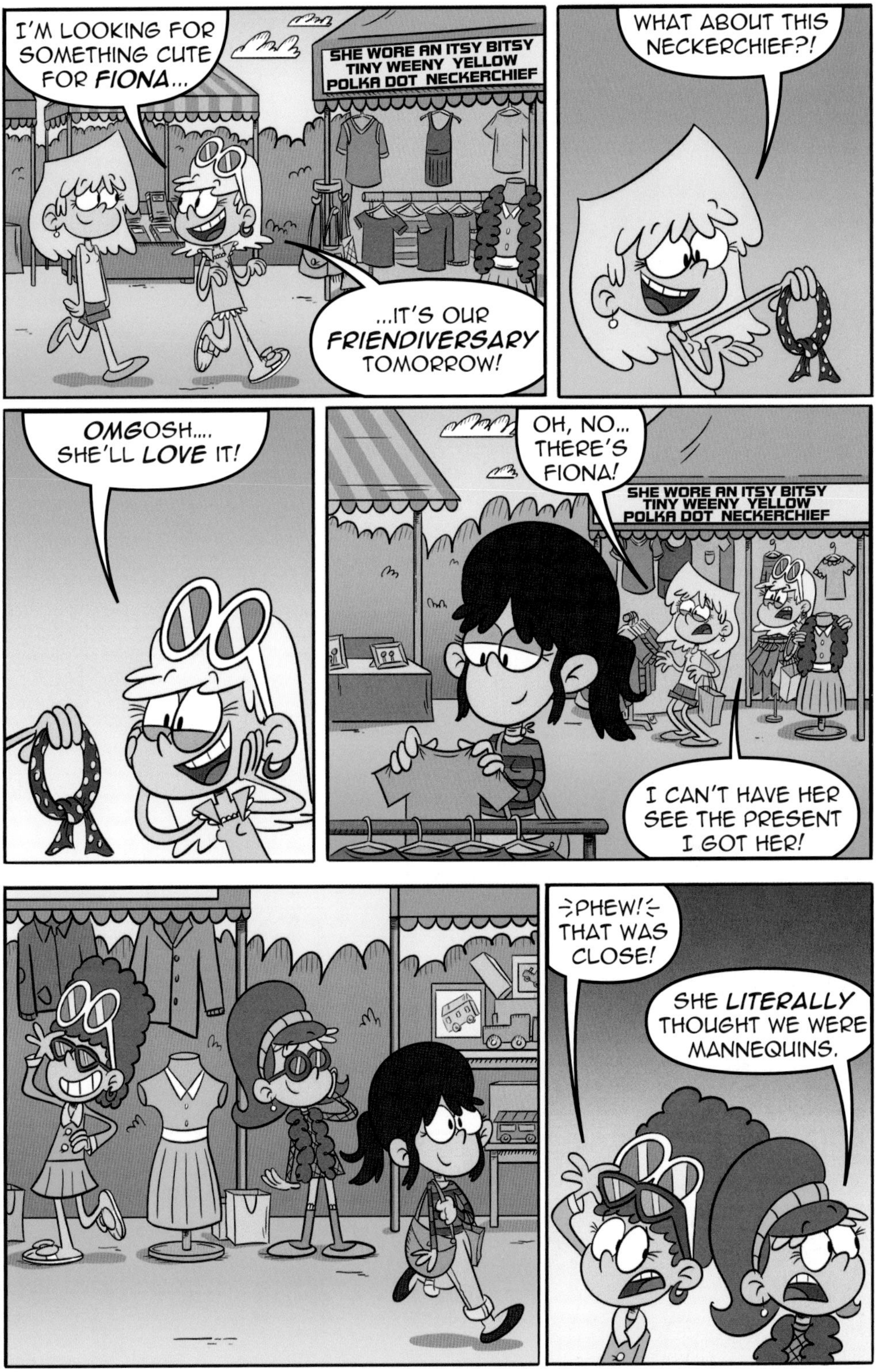
I'M LOOKING FOR SOMETHING CUTE FOR *FIONA*...
SHE WORE AN ITSY BITSY TINY WEENY YELLOW POLKA DOT NECKERCHIEF
...IT'S OUR *FRIENDIVERSARY* TOMORROW!
WHAT ABOUT THIS NECKERCHIEF?!
*OMG*OSH.... SHE'LL *LOVE* IT!
OH, NO... THERE'S FIONA!
SHE WORE AN ITSY BITSY TINY WEENY YELLOW POLKA DOT NECKERCHIEF
I CAN'T HAVE HER SEE THE PRESENT I GOT HER!
PHEW! THAT WAS CLOSE!
SHE *LITERALLY* THOUGHT WE WERE MANNEQUINS.

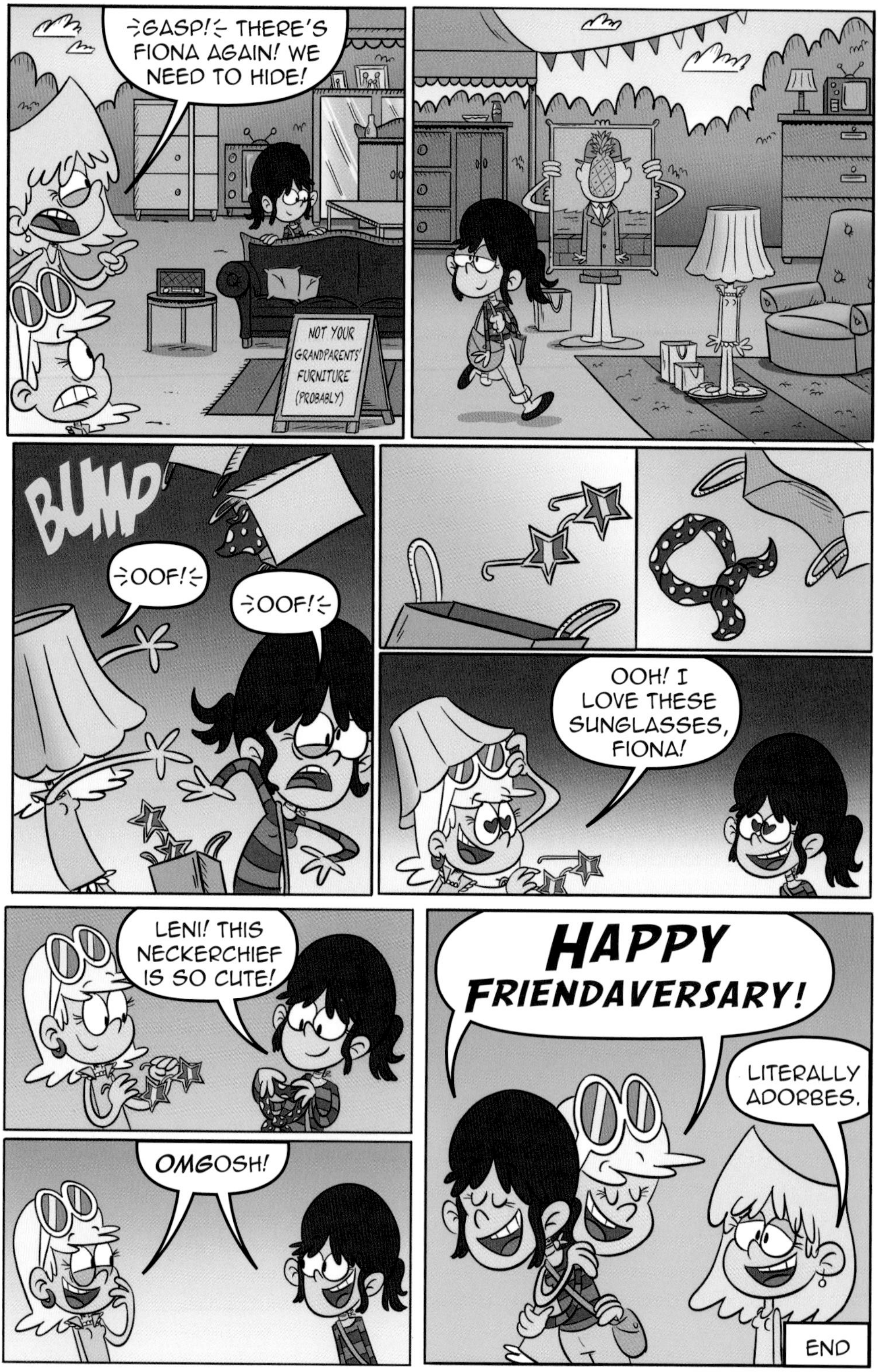
GASP! THERE'S FIONA AGAIN! WE NEED TO HIDE!
NOT YOUR GRANDPARENTS' FURNITURE (PROBABLY)
BUMP
OOF!
OOF!
OOH! I LOVE THESE SUNGLASSES, FIONA!
LENI! THIS NECKERCHIEF IS SO CUTE!
OMGOSH!
HAPPY FRIENDAVERSARY!
LITERALLY ADORBES.
END

"FLEA RIDDLE"

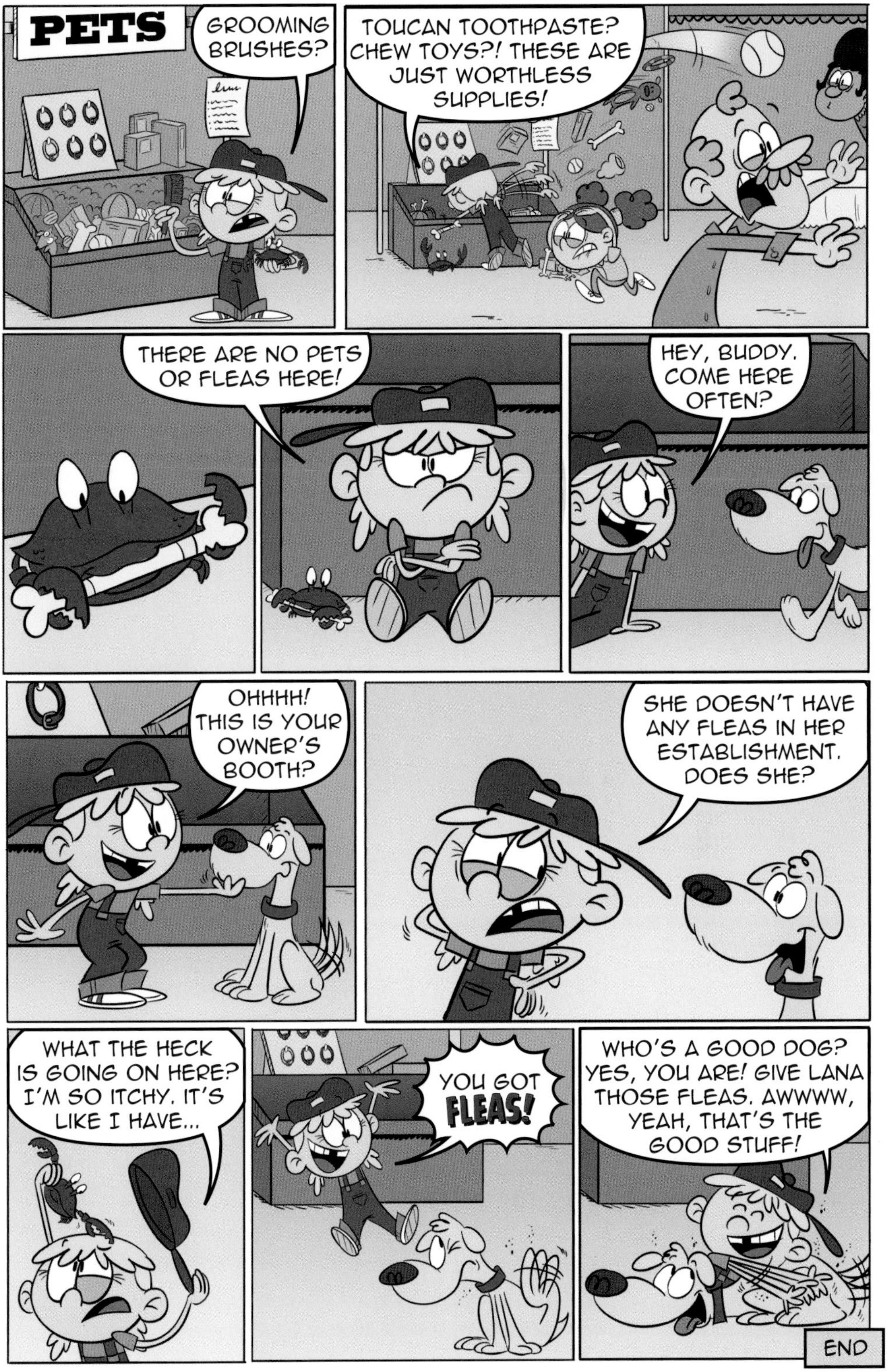
PETS
GROOMING BRUSHES?
TOUCAN TOOTHPASTE? CHEW TOYS?! THESE ARE JUST WORTHLESS SUPPLIES!
THERE ARE NO PETS OR FLEAS HERE!
HEY, BUDDY. COME HERE OFTEN?
OHHHH! THIS IS YOUR OWNER'S BOOTH?
SHE DOESN'T HAVE ANY FLEAS IN HER ESTABLISHMENT. DOES SHE?
WHAT THE HECK IS GOING ON HERE? I'M SO ITCHY. IT'S LIKE I HAVE...
YOU GOT FLEAS!
WHO'S A GOOD DOG? YES, YOU ARE! GIVE LANA THOSE FLEAS. AWWWW, YEAH, THAT'S THE GOOD STUFF!
END

"PARTY MIXER"

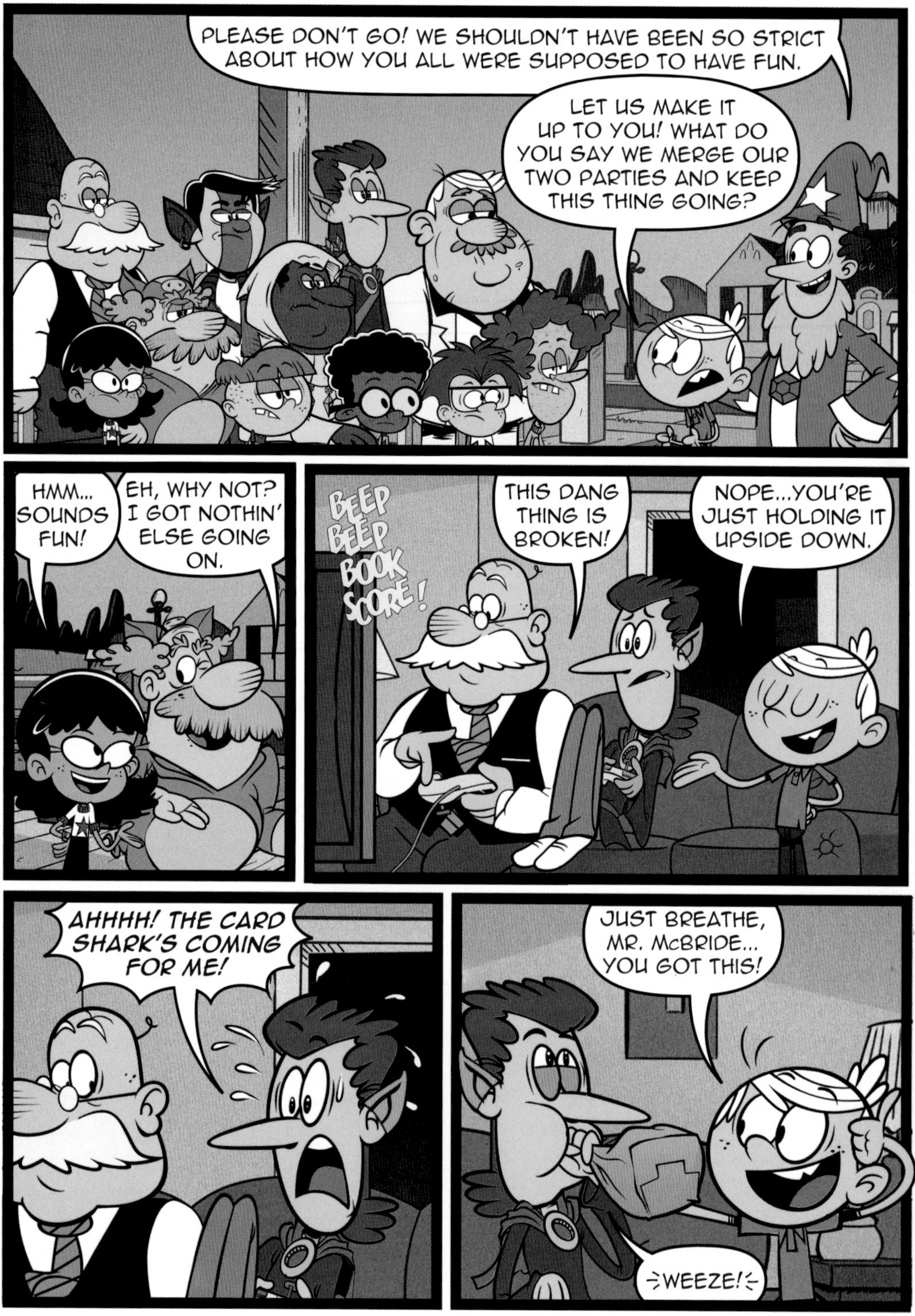
PLEASE DON'T GO! WE SHOULDN'T HAVE BEEN SO STRICT ABOUT HOW YOU ALL WERE SUPPOSED TO HAVE FUN.
LET US MAKE IT UP TO YOU! WHAT DO YOU SAY WE MERGE OUR TWO PARTIES AND KEEP THIS THING GOING?
HMM... SOUNDS FUN!
EH, WHY NOT? I GOT NOTHIN' ELSE GOING ON.
BEEP BEEP BOOK SCORE!
THIS DANG THING IS BROKEN!
NOPE...YOU'RE JUST HOLDING IT UPSIDE DOWN.
AHHHH! THE CARD SHARK'S COMING FOR ME!
JUST BREATHE, MR. McBRIDE... YOU GOT THIS!
WEEZE!

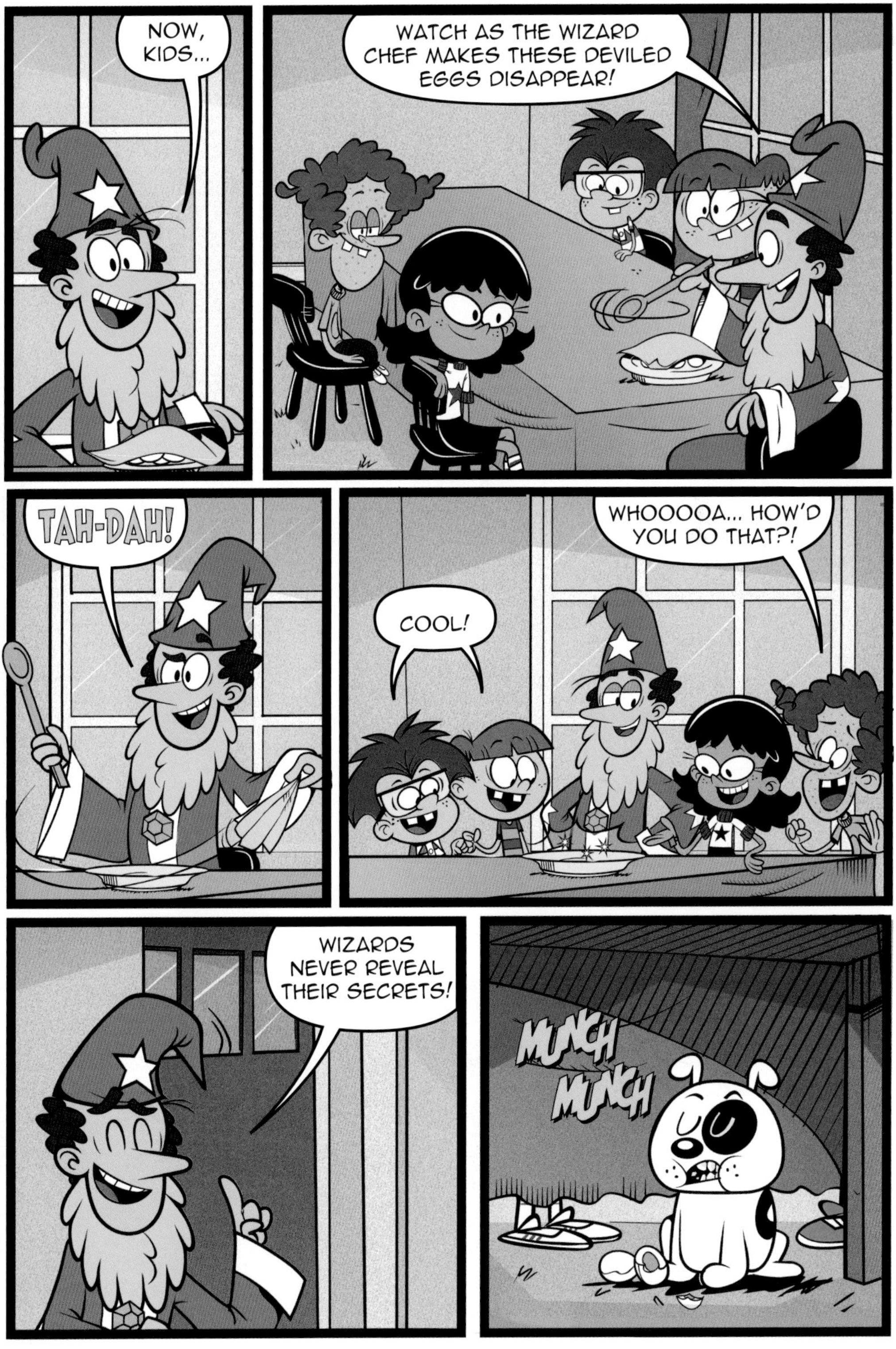
NOW, KIDS...
WATCH AS THE WIZARD CHEF MAKES THESE DEVILED EGGS DISAPPEAR!
TAH-DAH!
COOL!
WHOOOOA... HOW'D YOU DO THAT?!
WIZARDS NEVER REVEAL THEIR SECRETS!
MUNCH
MUNCH

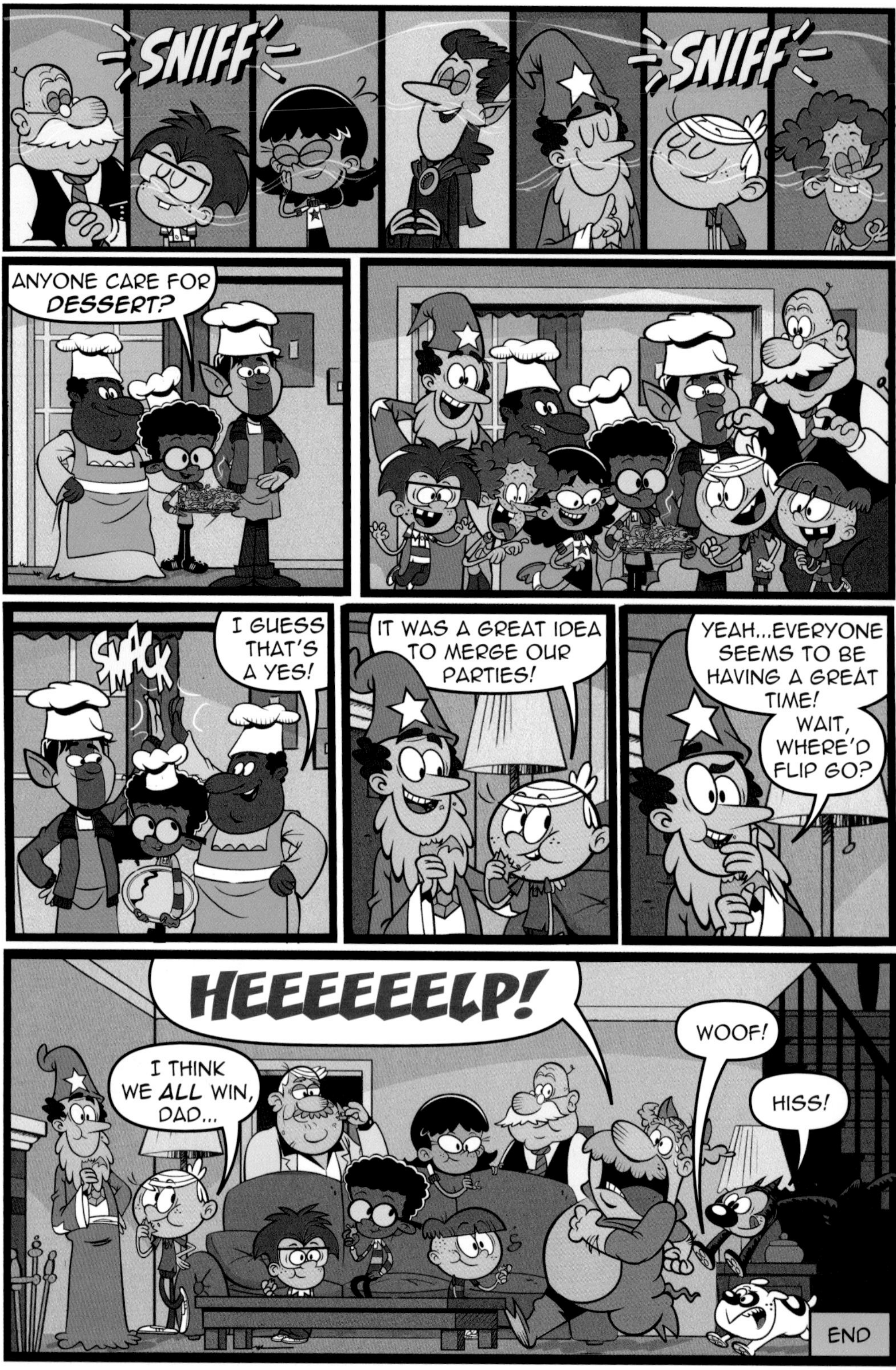
SNIFF
SNIFF
ANYONE CARE FOR DESSERT?
SMACK
I GUESS THAT'S A YES!
IT WAS A GREAT IDEA TO MERGE OUR PARTIES!
YEAH...EVERYONE SEEMS TO BE HAVING A GREAT TIME!
WAIT, WHERE'D FLIP GO?
HEEEEEELP!
I THINK WE ALL WIN, DAD...
WOOF!
HISS!
END

"THE LONG ROAD HOME"

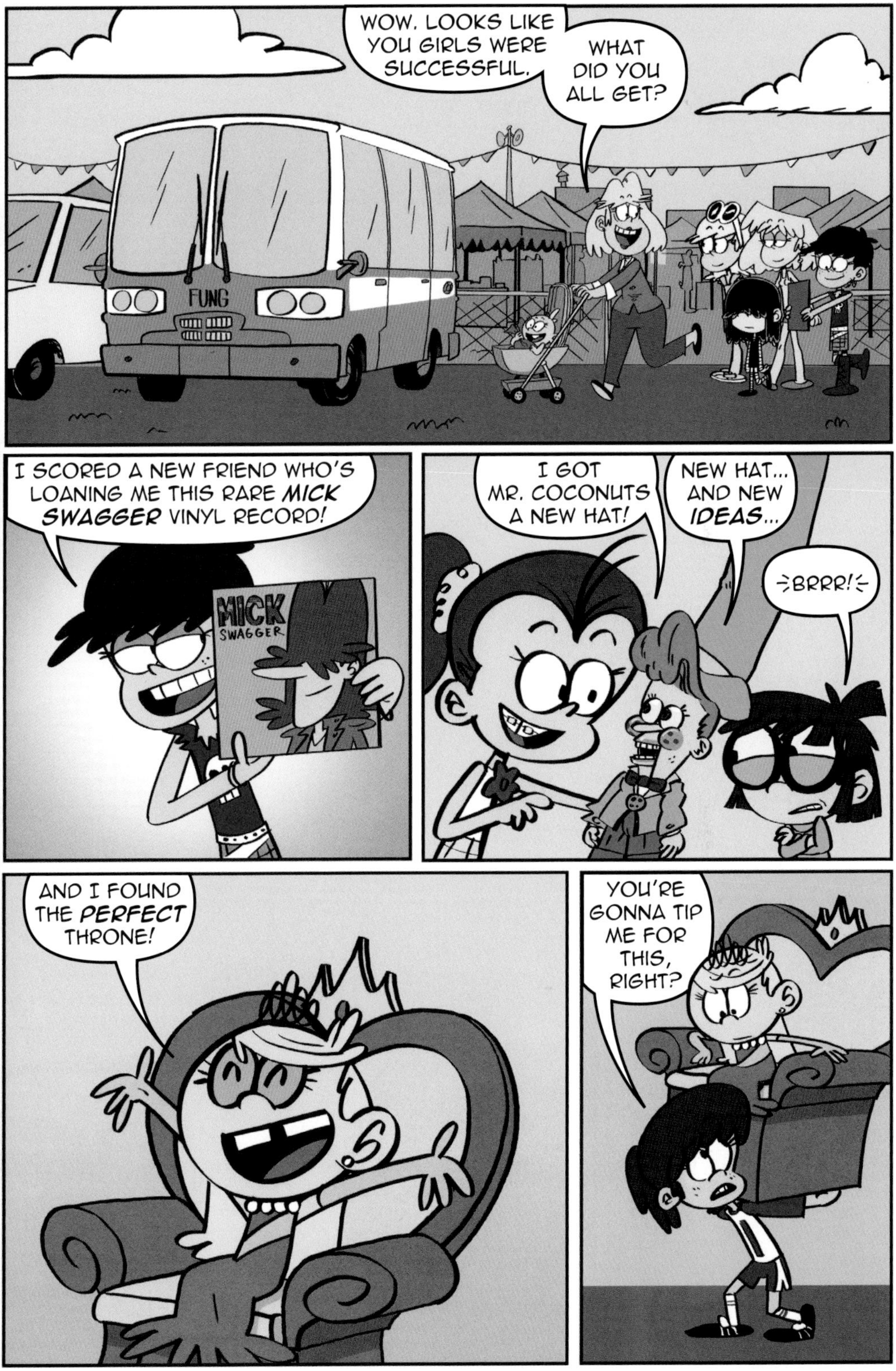

WOW. LOOKS LIKE YOU GIRLS WERE SUCCESSFUL.
WHAT DID YOU ALL GET?
FUNG
I SCORED A NEW FRIEND WHO'S LOANING ME THIS RARE MICK SWAGGER VINYL RECORD!
MICK SWAGGER
I GOT MR. COCONUTS A NEW HAT!
NEW HAT... AND NEW IDEAS...
BRRR!
AND I FOUND THE PERFECT THRONE!
YOU'RE GONNA TIP ME FOR THIS, RIGHT?

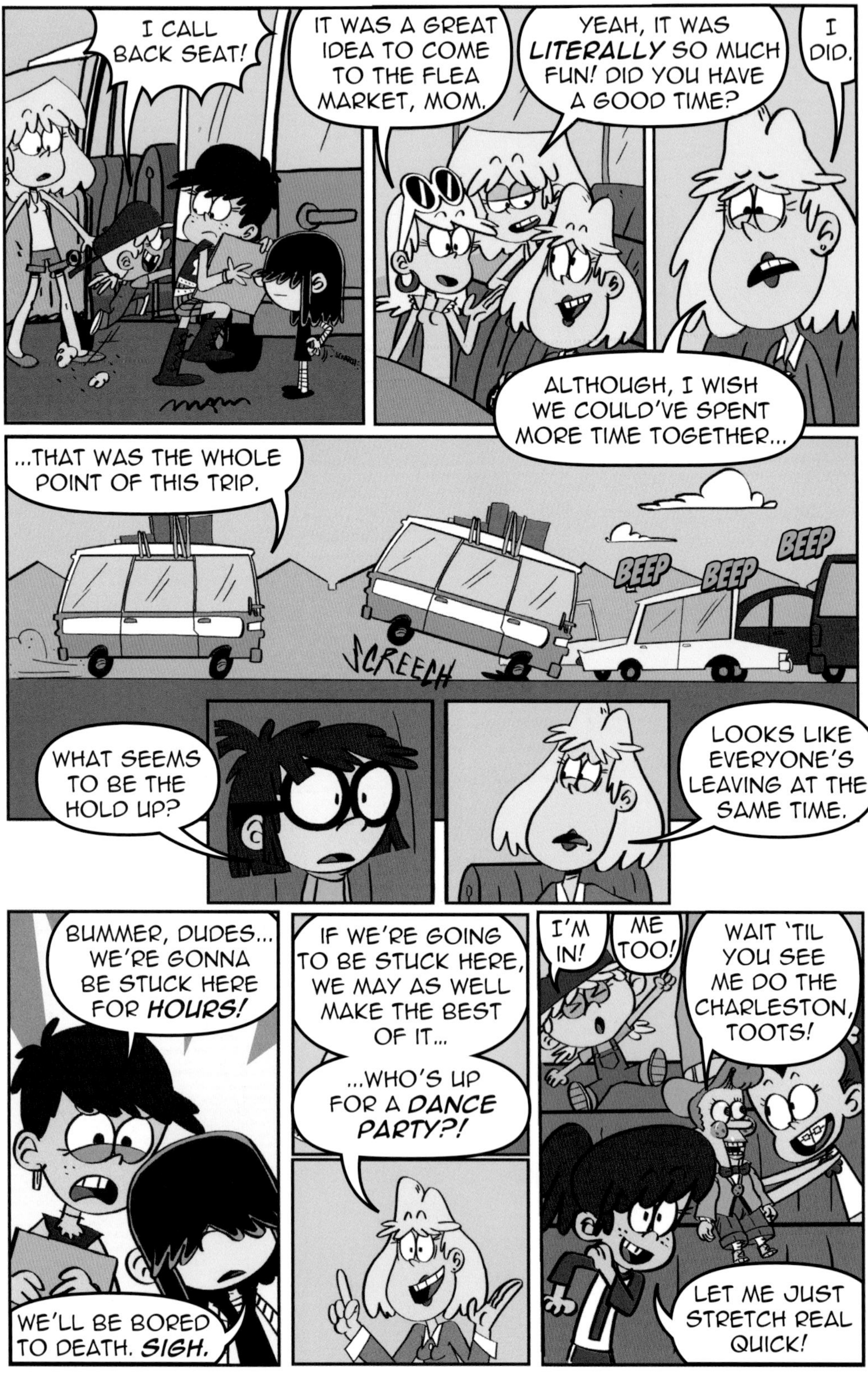
I CALL BACK SEAT!
IT WAS A GREAT IDEA TO COME TO THE FLEA MARKET, MOM.
YEAH, IT WAS LITERALLY SO MUCH FUN! DID YOU HAVE A GOOD TIME?
I DID.
ALTHOUGH, I WISH WE COULD'VE SPENT MORE TIME TOGETHER...
...THAT WAS THE WHOLE POINT OF THIS TRIP.
SCREECH
BEEP
BEEP
BEEP
WHAT SEEMS TO BE THE HOLD UP?
LOOKS LIKE EVERYONE'S LEAVING AT THE SAME TIME.
BUMMER, DUDES... WE'RE GONNA BE STUCK HERE FOR HOURS!
WE'LL BE BORED TO DEATH. SIGH.
IF WE'RE GOING TO BE STUCK HERE, WE MAY AS WELL MAKE THE BEST OF IT...
...WHO'S UP FOR A DANCE PARTY?!
I'M IN!
ME TOO!
WAIT 'TIL YOU SEE ME DO THE CHARLESTON, TOOTS!
LET ME JUST STRETCH REAL QUICK!

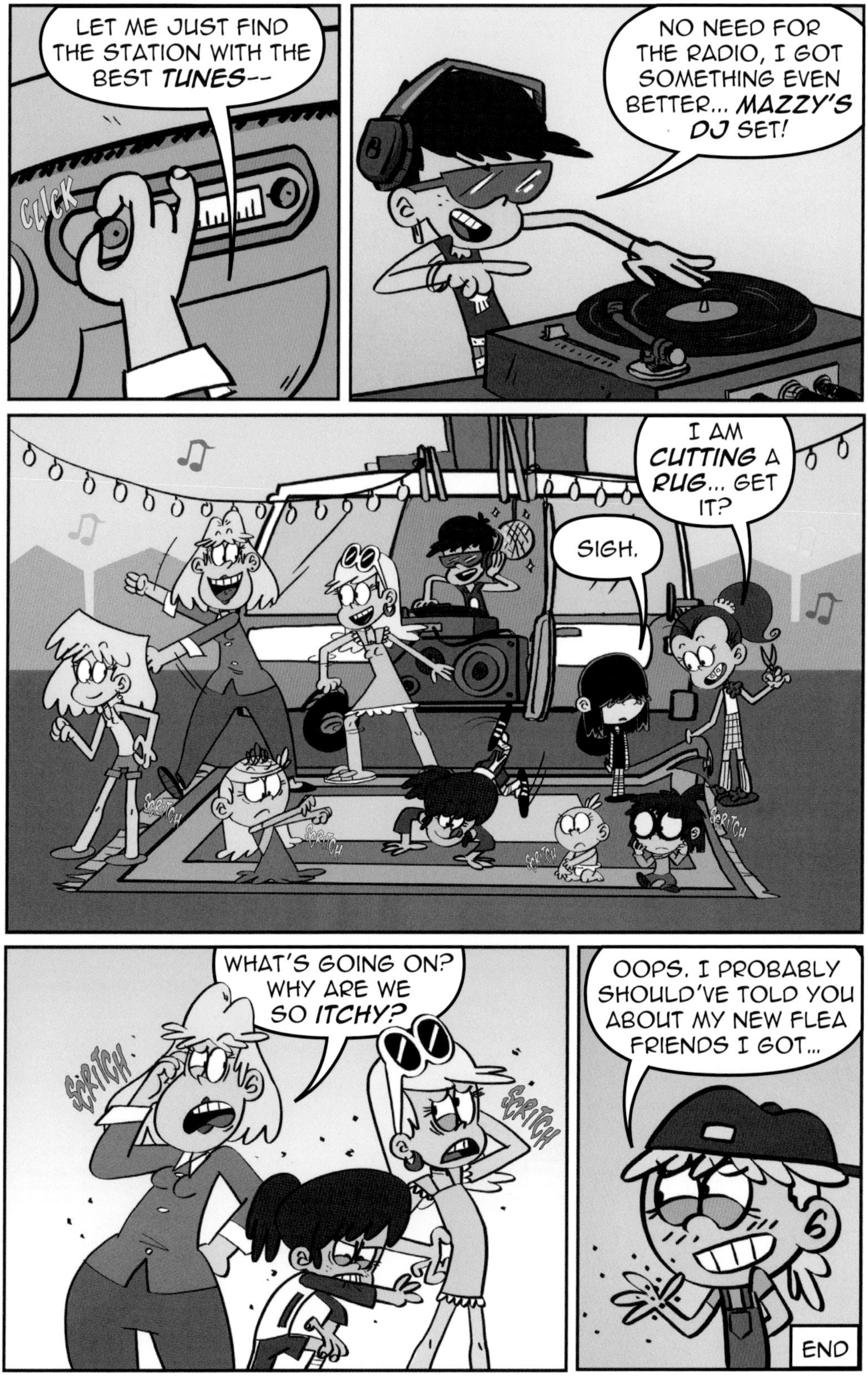
LET ME JUST FIND THE STATION WITH THE BEST TUNES--
CLICK
NO NEED FOR THE RADIO, I GOT SOMETHING EVEN BETTER... MAZZY'S DJ SET!
I AM CUTTING A RUG... GET IT?
SIGH.
SCRITCH
SCRITCH
SCRITCH
SCRITCH
WHAT'S GOING ON? WHY ARE WE SO ITCHY?
SCRITCH
SCRITCH
OOPS. I PROBABLY SHOULD'VE TOLD YOU ABOUT MY NEW FLEA FRIENDS I GOT...
END

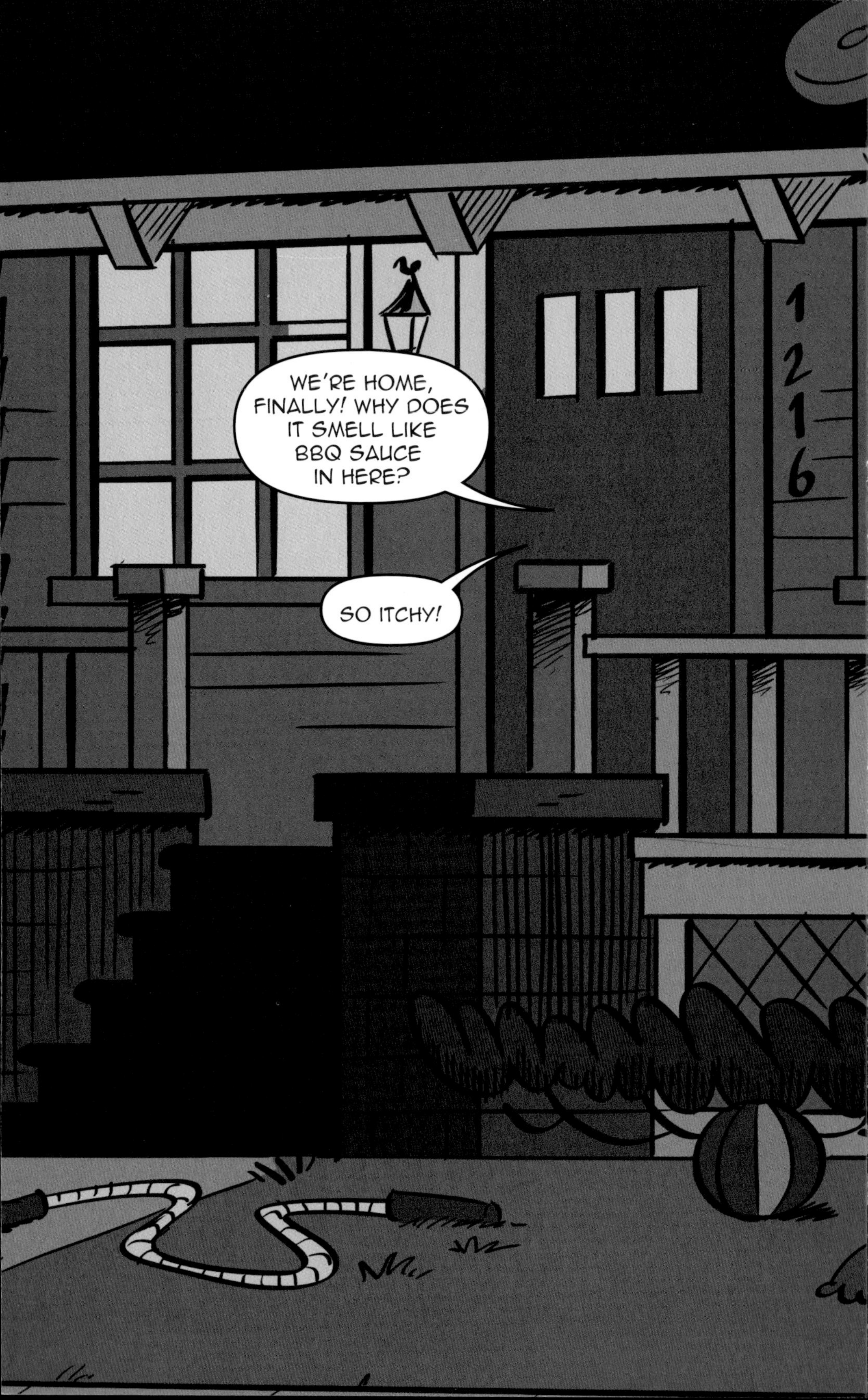
1216
WE'RE HOME, FINALLY! WHY DOES IT SMELL LIKE BBQ SAUCE IN HERE?
SO ITCHY!

Here's a special preview of THE LOUD HOUSE #10 "The Many Faces of Lincoln Loud"!

"LUCY OF MELANCHOLIA"

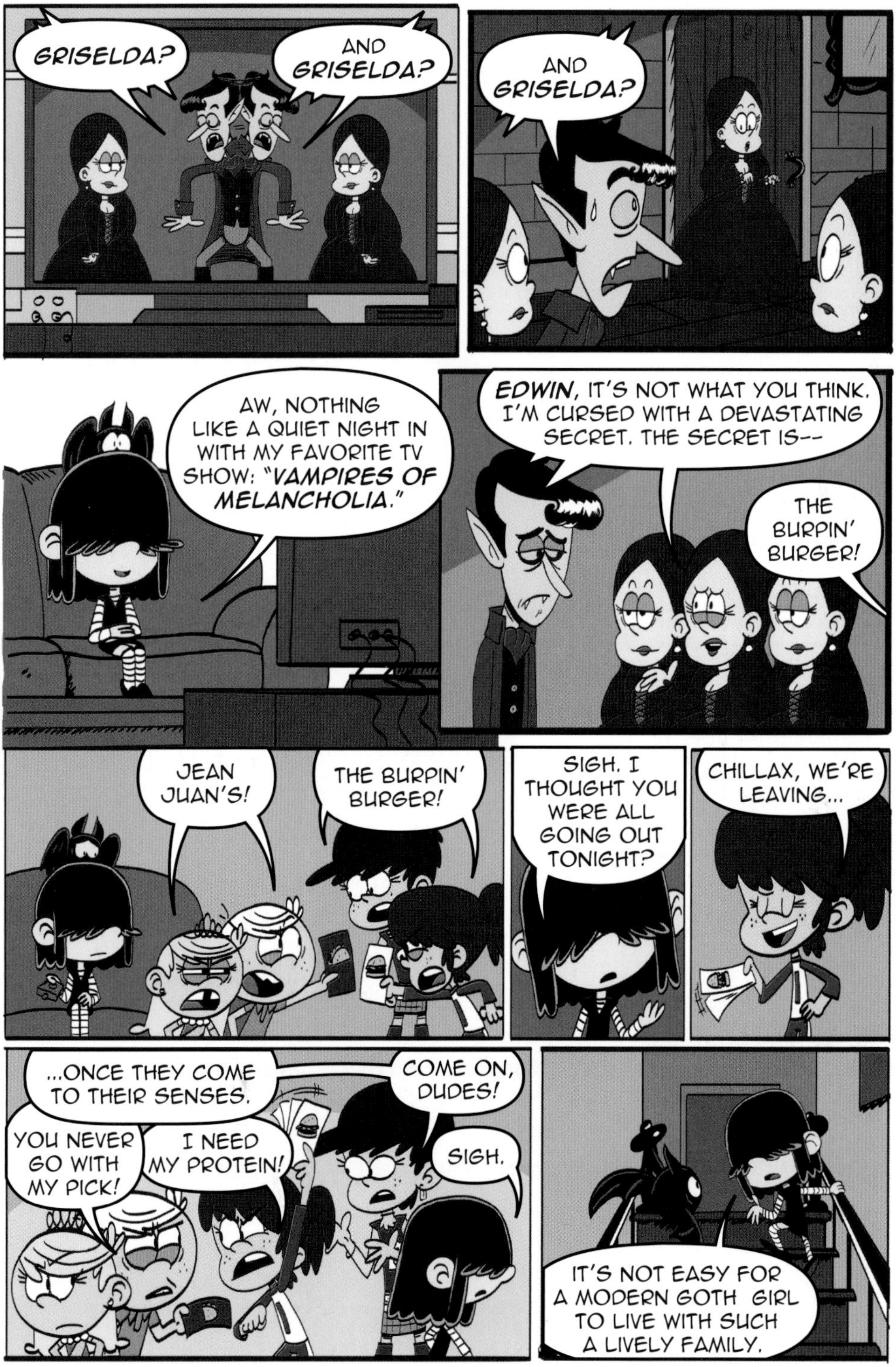
GRISELDA?
AND GRISELDA?
AND GRISELDA?
AW, NOTHING LIKE A QUIET NIGHT IN WITH MY FAVORITE TV SHOW: "VAMPIRES OF MELANCHOLIA."
EDWIN, IT'S NOT WHAT YOU THINK. I'M CURSED WITH A DEVASTATING SECRET. THE SECRET IS--
THE BURPIN' BURGER!
JEAN JUAN'S!
THE BURPIN' BURGER!
SIGH. I THOUGHT YOU WERE ALL GOING OUT TONIGHT?
CHILLAX, WE'RE LEAVING...
...ONCE THEY COME TO THEIR SENSES.
COME ON, DUDES!
YOU NEVER GO WITH MY PICK!
I NEED MY PROTEIN!
SIGH.
IT'S NOT EASY FOR A MODERN GOTH GIRL TO LIVE WITH SUCH A LIVELY FAMILY.

Caitlin Fein—Writer, Gizelle Orbino—Artist, Colorist, Wilson Ramos Jr.—Letterer

⇒YAWN!⇐ I WISH I LIVED SOMEWHERE DARK AND QUIET. SOMEWHERE LIKE.... LIKE...

ZZZZ.

LUCINDA! THE SUN SETS. IT'S TIME TO RISE.

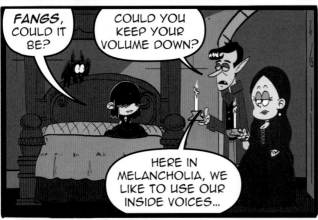

FANGS, COULD IT BE?

COULD YOU KEEP YOUR VOLUME DOWN?

HERE IN MELANCHOLIA, WE LIKE TO USE OUR INSIDE VOICES...

I'M HOME.

THIS BOOK IS EVERYTHING.

SSSSH.

SHHHHH.

Modern Embalming Practices

UM, SORRY...

SHHHHH.

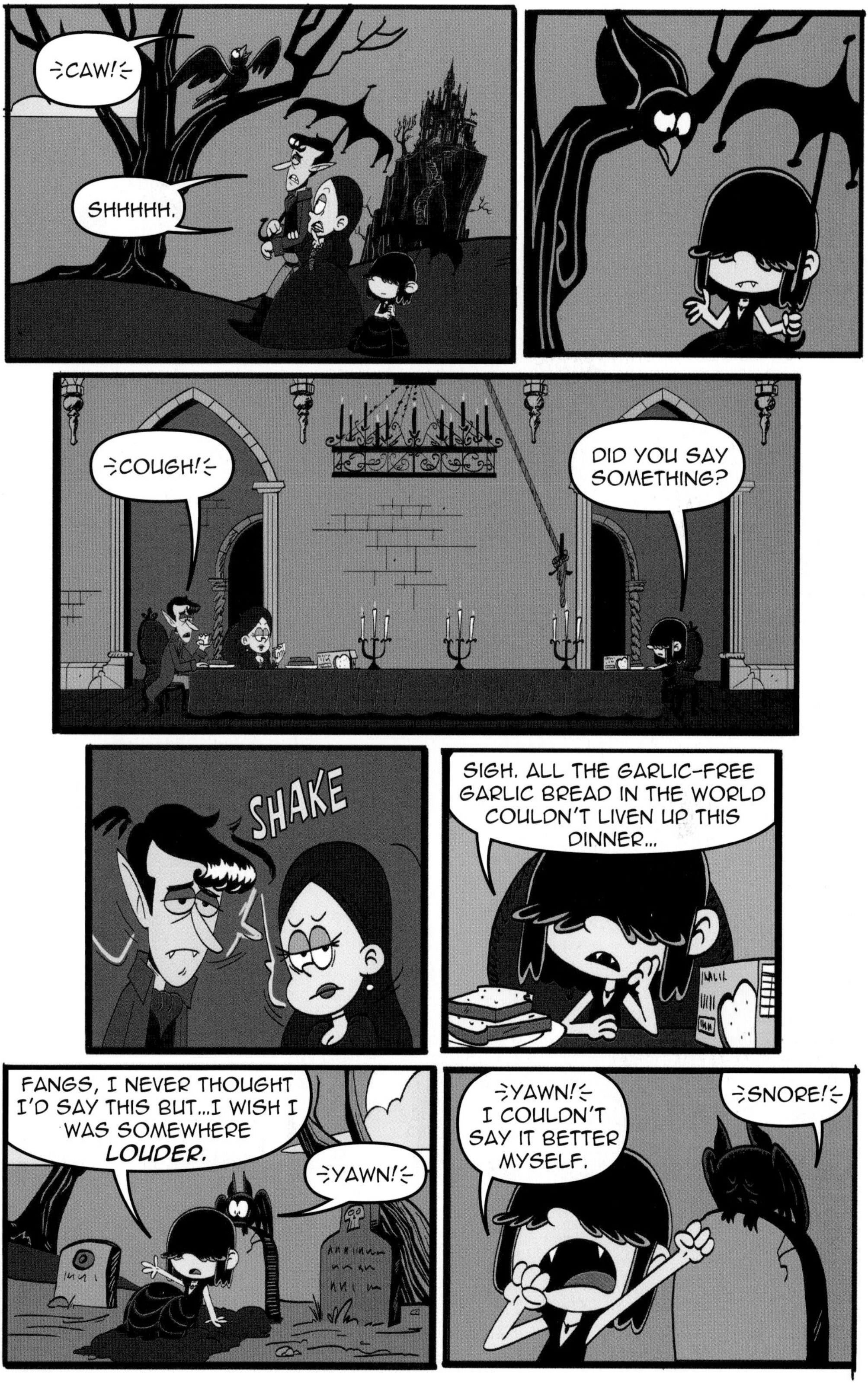
CAW!
SHHHHH.
COUGH!
DID YOU SAY SOMETHING?
SHAKE
SIGH. ALL THE GARLIC-FREE GARLIC BREAD IN THE WORLD COULDN'T LIVEN UP THIS DINNER...
FANGS, I NEVER THOUGHT I'D SAY THIS BUT...I WISH I WAS SOMEWHERE LOUDER.
YAWN!
YAWN! I COULDN'T SAY IT BETTER MYSELF.
SNORE!

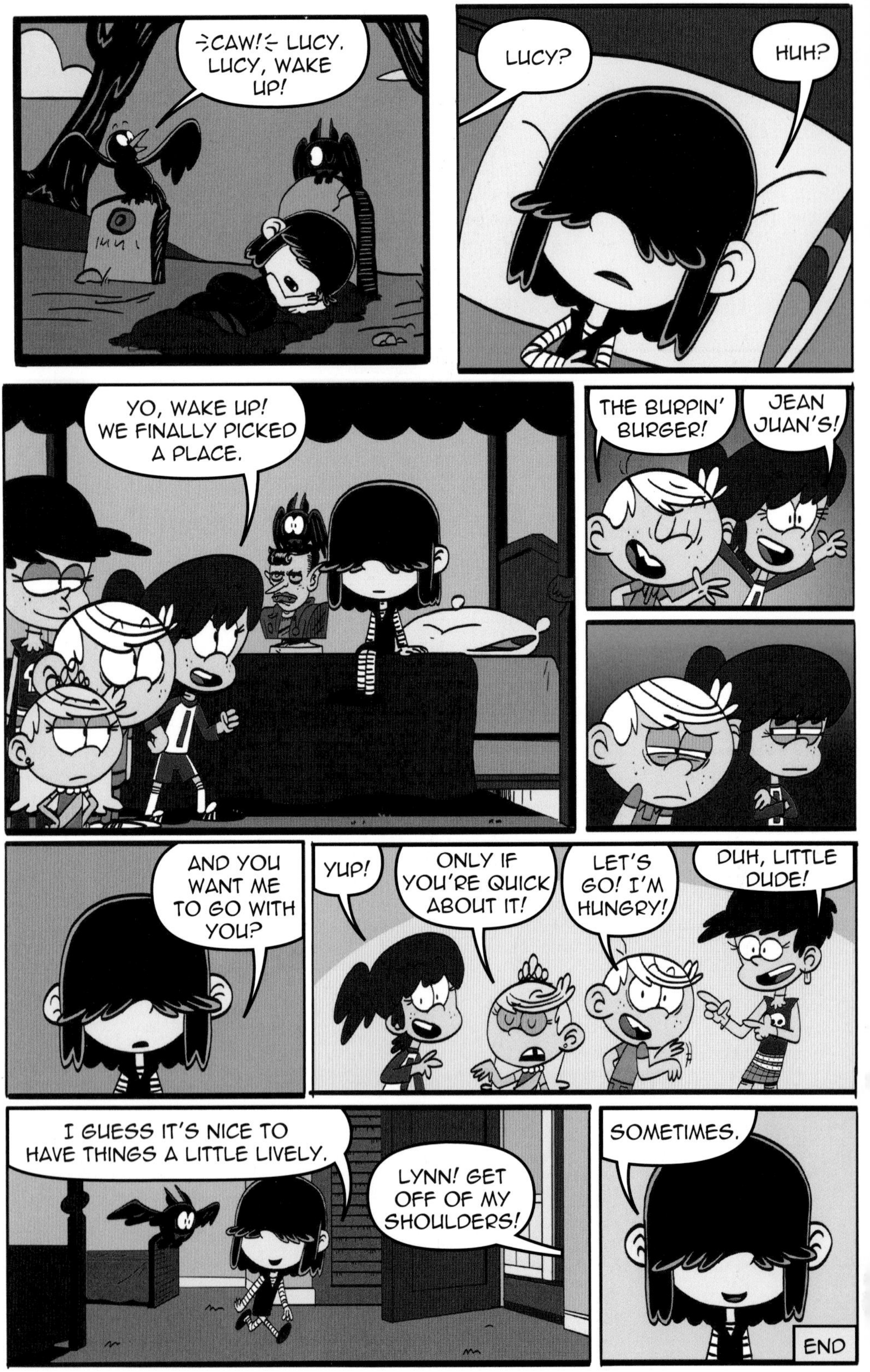
CAW! LUCY. LUCY, WAKE UP!
LUCY?
HUH?
YO, WAKE UP! WE FINALLY PICKED A PLACE.
THE BURPIN' BURGER!
JEAN JUAN'S!
AND YOU WANT ME TO GO WITH YOU?
YUP!
ONLY IF YOU'RE QUICK ABOUT IT!
LET'S GO! I'M HUNGRY!
DUH, LITTLE DUDE!
I GUESS IT'S NICE TO HAVE THINGS A LITTLE LIVELY.
LYNN! GET OFF OF MY SHOULDERS!
SOMETIMES.
END

THE LOUD HOUSE #10 "The Many Faces of Lincoln Loud" is available now wherever books are sold!